SHAVING WITH OCCAM

SHAVING WITH OCCAM

by

Jacob M. Appel

Hollywood Books International
the fiction imprint of Press Americana

Published by
Hollywood Books International
the fiction imprint of Press Americana
americanpopularculture.com

Library of Congress Cataloging-in-Publication Data

Names: Appel, Jacob M., 1973- author.
Title: Shaving with Occam / Jacob M. Appel.
Description: Hollywood : Press Americana, [2022] | Summary: "The first
   nineteen years of Henrietta Brigander's life were distinguished by
   matchless luxury: summers at Newport and Saratoga, outings on her
   father's yacht, cotillions on the dance cards of Kennedys and
   Vanderbilts. Then a schizophrenic break followed by a series of
   devastating financial setbacks left her destitute on the streets of New
   York City. Yet Henrietta never looks back, carving out a niche for
   herself as "Granny Flamingo, aka The Mad Bird Lady of East 14th Street."
   But when she suspects one of her fellow psychiatric patients has been
   murdered, Henrietta is forced into yet another role-that of relentless
   detective"-- Provided by publisher.
Identifiers: LCCN 2021040333 | ISBN 9781735360133 (paperback)
Subjects: LCGFT: Novels.
Classification: LCC PS3601.P662 S53 2022 | DDC 813/.6--dc23
LC record available at https://lccn.loc.gov/2021040333

In everyone there sleeps
A sense of life lived according to love.
To some it means the difference they could make
By loving others, but across most it sweeps
As all they might have done had they been loved.
That nothing cures.

—Philip Larkin

For Rosie and Kaely

CONTENTS

SECTION ONE

CHAPTER ONE

My name's Henrietta Brigander, aka Granny Flamingo, aka The Mad Bird Lady of East 14th Street, and here's my secret: just because I'm crazy does not mean I'm stupid. You'd be surprised how many people lose sight of this—people who should know better, like the head shrinkers at Mount Hebron, and my case worker, Ms. Celery Stalk, who seems out to prove that just because you're sane doesn't mean you're intelligent, and pretty much everyone else, at least some of the time, except other crazy folks, and, of course, P.J., who recognizes the wisdom of madness, and whom I'd have married ages ago, except he's a nurse and I'm a patient, which means he could get fired. Also, he's already married, and only twenty-six, so that's not going to happen. Like I said, I may be a lunatic—by DSM standards, at least—but I'm no fool. That doesn't stop people from speaking to me the way Mama used to address the Portuguese gardener at the summer cottage, loud and slow as though he were short a few feathers of a whole duck, rather than merely a foreigner, or others from adopting a singsong cheer, almost cooing, as though trying to soothe a dumb beast—the voice our housekeeper assumed to coax my brother's pet ferrets from the pantry. And no, that's not a delusion. We Briganders did own a summer cottage in Newport. And a seat on the Stock Exchange. Hard to imagine Henrietta B. once dined on Tiffany silver. Even for me. Or that Governor Rockefeller read me bedtime stories. Before the Briganders got their deserts: daily cognac in one generation and schizophrenic twins in the next can do that to a family.

    Which leads me in a roundabout way to murder. I'd come in off the street about a month ago—on my own two feet and of my own free will—unlike the last several times, when I had the pleasure of an escort from the 13th Precinct. No, this time I *wanted* a few days in the bin, because the weather had turned, and besides, I don't like being on the outside for Halloween. Too much trouble lurking about. I can hear my Uncle Dewey, wherever the old cigar-chomper is now, complaining about how the taxpayers would be shelling out $4000 a night for my stay on the unit, when a suite in the Waldorf-Astoria Hotel costs a quarter of that, but nobody was offering me any suites at the Waldorf, and Uncle Dewey never tried to get a sound night's sleep in the Hamilton Arms Women's Shelter. Anyway.

If you know the right things to say, it's hard for the hospital to throw you out. Especially when you've got two bona fide suicide attempts under your belt like yours truly—once, after my brother Rusky's so-called accident, when I overdosed on Trilafon, and a second time, for no good reason I can think of, when I jumped off the Staten Island Ferry and had to be hauled in by Harbor Patrol. The ferry was moored at the dock, but I'm still considered high risk, so nobody's taking any chances. All I have to do is tell the physician-on-call the voices are urging me to stroll down to the waterfront again, and I've got "three hots and a cot" for at least the better part of a week. Not that my *real* voices would ever say anything like that. Not these days. They're rather friendly, most of the time—except when they get angry, or afraid, just like everybody else. Which is why I don't see the point of medication.

So I walked into the Psych ER—they call it the CPEP now, for Comprehensive Psychiatric Emergency Program, but all that means is they can hold you for seventy-two hours, rather than twenty-four, before they decide whether to admit you. Mount Hebron Hospital has officially been rebranded St. Dymphna's–South, thanks to one of those healthcare mega-mergers, but the only way this affects me is the food's not as good, because at Mount Hebron every meal was certified kosher, by default, swathed in cling wrap and blessed by an Orthodox rabbi, while under its new management, the hospital basically serves the same cardboard you get at Bellevue or Metropolitan or in the holding pen at Rikers. But Mount Hebron is *my* hospital—I was born there fifty-seven years ago, back when it was a *real* Jewish hospital, and I've been getting cared for there ever since—even though these days most of the junior doctors come from places I couldn't find on a map of the world. Progress, I suppose. I try not to be judgmental. But there's something about a Jewish doctor that puts the soul at ease. When I was a girl, we'd go to Doc Weingarten on Park Avenue for checkups (a dead ringer for that old-time comedian, Morey Amsterdam), who spoke with a German accent and peppered his physicals with Bosch Belt humor. And later, after I left Bryn Mawr, I spent two years in treatment with Dr. Kavarsky, a Ukrainian refugee with thin-rimmed spectacles and a salt-and-pepper beard. Jews have been taking care of Briganders and

Van Duyns since the Mayflower Compact, Mama claimed, though the Briganders were actually French Huguenots and the Van Duyns came from Rotterdam via Curacao, but sometimes sentiment is truer than history, especially when it comes to one's own heritage. Anyway.

So I triaged into the Psych ER—the CPEP—secretly hoping that P.J. might be doing an extra shift downstairs, even though I knew he preferred the units, but just my luck the swing nurse was Mr. Brauer, who everybody calls Sarge, because he insists he did a tour in Iraq. I know better. I once heard him spelling his name on the phone—he was trying to have a package redelivered—and he said B as in Boy, R as in Roger, A as in Apple, U as in Umbrella...and then—here's the kicker—E as in Elephant. Who in heaven's name says E as in Elephant? Certainly not a combat veteran. It's Bravo-Romeo-Alpha-Uniform-Echo-Romeo. NATO Phonetic Alphabet. You don't need a commission from West Point to know that. So he's no veteran, but he *is* a fool, and the physician-on-call that night, a mousy young Indian woman named Dr. Bhatt, wasn't a particularly gifted creature either—or maybe it was a cultural thing—but listening to the pair of them interviewing an obvious malingerer with their kid-gloves laced to the elbows proved excruciating. I know these interviews are supposed to be confidential—HIPAA regulations and all that—but the Psych ER isn't exactly Fort Knox and you can hear more or less everything through the drywall. And over the years I *have* heard practically everything: voracious canoodling; one of the social workers on the telephone, begging her husband not to leave her *for her sister*; Miss Alpenwasser, the deputy director of nursing, firing a patient care associate for theft. Stealing office paper, allegedly, by the ream and gross. And by far the most savory of overheard conversations: Dr. Mallet, on a moonlighting shift, phoning the benefits office to find out whether he could invest a portion of his 403B in emus. (Next time I saw him, it required all my willpower not to ask him to prescribe emu oil for my arthritis.) But that afternoon all I heard was the malingerer, whom I later learned was called Big George, talking smoke rings around Sarge and Dr. Bhatt. *He* had also claimed he was a decorated combat veteran—Marine Corps, Desert Storm—and that he'd hitchhiked from St. Louis, Missouri, to set himself on fire at the 9-11 Memorial. "That's what the voices want," he reported. "It's half of their secret plan. Only the Chinese know the other half."

I was alone in the waiting area, except for Monty, a tubby Dominican with a chinstrap beard who passed for night shift security. The selfish bastard had an old-fashioned portable box radio on his knee, blaring a soccer match in Spanish. I could hardly hear Big George, but I couldn't exactly complain to Monty that he was screwing with my eavesdropping.

Dr. Bhatt seemed to have no inkling she was being snookered. "So you have a pacemaker and four stents," she echoed. "Any other medical problems? Besides your schizoaffective disorder and PTSD, I mean."

Ask him his pay grade, I wanted to shout. *Ask him his MOS.* Every serviceman knows his Military Occupational Specialty and his E-code. I learned this from Tecumseh Muhammed, who really did serve in the military, repairing jeeps and Humvees in Germany, before he lost an eye and ended up sleeping on a cardboard palette. We looked after each other sometimes, me and Tecumseh Muhammed, when he wasn't on a binge, which was rarely, those days, but he's *not* somebody I'd marry, even if he asked. Not anymore. If Papa were still alive, though, I might have married him, out of sheer contrariness, just to see my old man's face when his daughter showed up for Christmas Eve cocktails at the St. Regis with a disfigured Black Seminole who'd done nine years in Dannemora for carving up the driver of a Greyhound bus. Over an ice cream cone, I might add. Over whether he could bring a goddam vanilla wafer cone aboard the Omaha Express. So I know all about E-codes and occupational specialties, and Dr. Bhatt probably can't distinguish a hand grenade from a hedgehog. *Ask him his unit! For God's sake*, I thought. It's not that I wanted Big George to get ratted out, only that I hate incompetence. How could anyone with a medical degree have ever believed this guy to be mentally ill?

I read someplace that they conducted a study in which they sent fake patients into psychiatric hospitals—graduate students pretending to be actively psychotic—and asked the doctors to spot them. They couldn't. But then they went back and interviewed the other patients, the *real* crackups, and do you know what? Us crazy folks picked out the imposters every time. I'm not sure where the meaning lies in that, if any, but you don't need to be Sigmund Freud to realize something's off. Or maybe the system is screwed up this way *by design*—the dysfunction serves some higher purpose neither the doctors nor the patients are aware of. That wouldn't surprise me either. The bottom line is that Big George, who couldn't have been more than five foot eight in his stocking feet, but broad-shouldered, stepped out of that examination room grinning like he'd just made it with a Rockette. Had his over-shirt untucked too. Not half-bad looking for a fellow pushing sixty, and he knew it. Big George settled onto a bench in the waiting area, folding his arms across his chest and letting his legs splay. "How's the Lou?" I asked—feeling social.

"You got the wrong dude, miss. I'm George."

"The Lou," I repeated. "St. Louis, Missouri. These walls have ears."

"Great town," said Big George, unfazed. "Gotta love it."

I've been to St. Louis, Missouri. As a teenager. For a gymnastics tournament. We rode to the top of the Arch, and I threw up, and Jennie Kimball ducked into a stall inside the men's restroom at the Dred Scot Museum with a Mormon missionary from Wyoming. Now she's a television meteorologist for NBC—I saw her once in a store window, on fifty simultaneous screens—while I'm feigning my way into psychiatric wards. Life works like that. Nothing to do but accept it. Only what I really wanted to know was what happened to that Mormon kid. Probably, I guessed, he'd been promoted to deacon or elder by now. I wrote to Jennie last year to ask if she remembered his name, so I could look him up online, but didn't receive a response. I didn't take it personally. I figured forecasting the weather kept her rather busy.

I was in a mood that night to toy a bit with Big George. "You been to the capitol?" I asked. "In St. Louis. I hear it's really something."

"That it is," agreed George. "You ain't seen nothing like it."

George was beaming now, all dimples and teeth, but also looking me over. Deciding whether it was worth flirting with a woman who'd wear a size thirty-two dress, if she even owned a dress, and not three pairs of fuchsia sweatpants. I know that look too well—ambivalent, fatalistic. So different from the stares you get when you're a seventeen-year-old gymnast at Brearley. I grinned too, but more for myself than for Big George—and he must have sensed this, with his man-tuition, because he wasn't amused. "Something funny?" he asked.

I lowered my voice, so Sarge didn't hear from the nursing station. "Nothing really. It's only the capital of Missouri is in Jefferson City."

That wiped the gloss off his grill pretty quick. An authentic psychotic might have put my crown through the plaster, or clung to his false truth, or just continued smiling with benighted indifference, but Big George wore the grimace of a movie gangster who'd had the tables turned on him by his own henchmen. Can't describe it any other way. His brow knotted and he hooked his thumbs through his empty belt loops. "Maybe I knew that," he said. "Why's it your business?"

"Just saying," I said.

But he had a point. It *wasn't* any of my business. At least, not more than it was anybody else's. In theory, if some dude wants to hop from ER to ER claiming he's from St. Louis, Missouri, making an ass of himself until he gets caught, that's between him and the shrinks and the taxpayers—only, I don't like people not knowing stuff. You might call that my pet peeve. That's really what drove me nuts about Tecumseh Muhammed. Not the binges and the benders. Not even when he sold off my belongings for a fix. But when I read in the free paper that the actress Deanna Durbin has died, or I pointed out that some fellow on the subway looked like Prince Rainier of Monaco, or I told a story about the time my grandmother's sister, Bertie Ida, went on a sleigh date in Green-Wood Cemetery with Grover Whalen—and he answered, "Who the fuck is that?"—not so that I'd explain, not so I'd tell him that Whalen served as master of ceremonies at the 1939 World's Fair in Flushing, but to make a point that he didn't know nor care, it was then I wanted to drag him to the big Barnes & Noble on Fifth Avenue and make him read books on Old New York and Hollywood's Golden Age and 1950s television until he couldn't see straight. I realize that was my problem, obviously, not his. Although it's kind of difficult to understand how a grown man can sleep against the plinth of the General Daniel Butterfield statue for three straight nights and not once wonder which war the guy fought in. "Look, George," I whispered. "I'm on your side."

"I didn't realize there were sides."

"Of course, you didn't. You're new to this, aren't you?"

"I don't know what you're talking about, miss." Big George stuffed his arms into his pockets and shut his eyes, his eyeballs bulging under his lids like the bearded dragons' at the Bronx Zoo. Against my better judgment, I hoped he'd start flirting with me. I glanced toward Monty, ensconced opposite the magnetically-sealed doors, to be sure he remained engrossed in his soccer match.

"You got off lucky this time. But one day soon you're going to come across a real hard-ass, like Dr. Mallet or Dr. Robustelli, and he's going to ask you what the date of the Marine Corps Birthday Ball is—and what are you going to say then?"

Big George shrugged; his eyes remained closed. "I'll figure something out."

"I'm trying to help you, okay. The second you step foot on the unit, the attending psychiatrist is going to figure out you're not schizoaffective, and you're not a veteran, and basically everything you just told the Keystone Kops in there is absolute bullshit."

"Not *everything*," said Big George. A smile seeped across his face and he opened his eyes—first one, then the other, then both. "I do have four stents and a pacemaker."

I found myself liking Big George. *Immensely.* I had a sense he was taking a shine to me as well. "Next time, tell them you're depressed," I said. "It's hard to fake psychosis. Trust me. Although that bit about 'only the Chinese knowing the other half' wasn't half bad. But if you claim you're depressed—boring, run-of-the-mill depressed—and that you're going to jump off the Williamsburg Bridge, how are they supposed to prove otherwise?"

"Jeez. You sound like an expert."

With more than two hundred psychiatric admissions over thirty-seven years, I *am* an expert. Sometimes I think I should print up a book titled *Malingering for Dummies* and sell it at the Port Authority Bus Terminal, but I'm probably better off holding onto my secrets. To be prepared for all contingencies, as they say. "Just trying to be helpful," I replied. "And it's November 10, by the way. The Marine Corps Birthday Ball. In case anybody asks."

"You're something else, lady," said Big George. "Really."

I could sense he meant this as a compliment and I blushed. Honestly, it had been a long time since anybody set my blood rushing—certainly not Tecumseh Muhammed. "I'm Henrietta," I said. "But people call me Granny Flamingo."

Lots of women my age would be ashamed to call themselves Granny anything, but I got over that eons ago. The only part of it I don't like is that it gives the impression that I'm a grandmother, which I'm not. In obstetrics terms, I'm what they call "G4 P0040," which is a highfaluting way of saying I've had three elective abortions and a miscarriage. Sometimes I wish I'd been "G5 P0041," which is OB-GYN lingo for a mother, but it's too late for that; I guess the one solace is that after I'm gone, there won't be any Briganders or Van Duyns for the Fates and the Furies to push around anymore. Granny Flamingo is the last of her line—like Incas the Carolina parakeet and Booming Ben the heath hen and Orange Band the dusky seaside sparrow. Soon enough, the Briganders will be historical detritus. As dead as dodos.

"So what's your deal, Miss Granny Flamingo? Why are *you* here?" Big George sized me up again, but slower, almost savoring. "And what's with the birds?"

A natural question. It's not every day you meet a woman sporting a hat with a two foot tall plush flamingo protruding from it; I've also got ibises on my blouse, cranes on my hoodie, even penguins crocheted along my socks. And I have an entire shopping cart full of stuffed parrots and peacocks and pigeons that I've amassed from dumpsters and rummage sales, and, once in a while, from shoplifting at FAO Schwarz. *Everybody* knows me by my flamingo hat, including the hospital staff, which was probably why they let me keep it, although they're technically supposed to lock up our headwear with our valuables, except for religious garb, like Jewish skullcaps, and that's a hard sell for a fluorescent pink shorebird. It's another pointless rule to protect us crazies from ourselves. I ask you: who on earth ever committed suicide by hat?

So what *is* my deal? And what's with the birds? I reckon a superficial answer is that birds give me a sense of identity. I'm Granny Flamingo, The Mad Bird Lady of East 14th Street, like the disabled guy who plays saxophone and foot tambourine simultaneously opposite Rockefeller Center is the Half Man Jazz Band, and another fellow we used to travel with, whose real name was Stu Sucram, was known as Niagara Falls for stripping down to his underwear on summer afternoons and wandering Central Park wearing a wooden barrel around his loins like a bath towel. Even as a little girl, I was always fascinated by birds—the sandpipers and plover at Hyannisport, the pelicans that stalked our skiff at Key West, the raptors that Uncle Dewey's wife, Genevieve, rehabilitated on her family's ranch in Montana. The most traumatic moment of my childhood occurred at the summer cottage when Papa's Weimaraner fetched home the neighbor's escaped myna bird and deposited it beside his morning *Wall Street Journal*.

Why I loved birds so much specifically—as opposed, let's say, to butterflies or rabbits—that's one of those cosmic mysteries that only the Jungians and their ilk can answer. But ever since I departed Bryn Mawr, what I've wanted more than anything else is a bird of my own. A parakeet or a cockatiel. Or, in my fantasies, a hyacinth macaw. There was a time when I imagined I could work in the aviary at the zoo, which might not seem such an accomplishment when you've had three cousins serve in the United States Senate, but is still apparently too much to hope for when you're schizophrenic and "medication non-compliant," their fancy term for "not doped up." At least, that's what my old case worker, Mr. Lemonade, used to say— and he had a point. Who's going to hire a crazy woman whose last job was teaching lanyard and latch hook at a summer camp in the Berkshires during the Carter Administration?

Sometimes, on particularly gray days, I daydreamed of opening my own pet store. Nothing elaborate, mind you. I'm not exactly up to founding the next PetSmart. Just a small, cozy nook, maybe in an outer borough shopping plaza—the kind of outdoor mall where you'd also find a jovial Italian barber with an old-time pole and a gnarled, doom-saying Swiss cobbler who resoles boots and repairs mechanical watches. And I wouldn't sell anything outlandish; Rusky's ferrets and Mama's anteater, which had been a wedding gift from Salvador Dali, long ago convinced me that simple and sweet is the way to go with animals. Puppies, hamsters. An assortment of parrots and amazons and canaries, maybe a pair of black-hooded conures for the back office and a toucan for the window display. Tecumseh Muhammed laughed at the notion—lovingly, but dismissive. He insisted on highlighting the obvious: a pet shop requires capital, bank loans. Who's going to trust that kind of dough to a woman who can't rustle up enough cash for a new raincoat?

I didn't tell any of this to Big George. Instead, I said, "I'm here because I've got to be *somewhere* and here's as good a place as any." But I feared sounding too walled off, so I added, "I found the hat years ago in a Hefty bag behind an off-Broadway theater. You might say I made it the centerpiece of my style and I've been accessorizing around it ever since."

"What play was it from?" asked Big George.

"Excuse me?"

"I did some acting in my day," he said. "I thought I might know the play."

That flustered me. Because I *didn't* know the name of play— I'd never even tried to find out—but that's exactly the kind of thing I'd *want* to know. And it was the kind of question Tecumseh Muhammed would never have thought to ask. I sensed I might like Big George too much for my own well-being, so I resolved to put the brakes on my feelings until I could think things through, but that's easier said than done. Fortunately, the PCA appeared at that instant to lead Big George across the hall for his required admission EKG and, a moment later, a battalion of transit police dragged in Angry O'Dell, cuffed and masked, shouting about a stolen screwdriver.

Angry O'Dell was a real patient. Floridly paranoid. I'd crossed paths with him in ERs before—at Maimonides Hospital, I think. Maybe Bronx Lebanon. Hard to keep track. Once he rammed a computer-on-wheels through the window of a nursing station—that was at King's County—but the reason everyone called him Angry, when the name on his ID read Arnold, was that the left side of his rawboned face didn't work properly, so he wore a perpetual sneer. Not a guy to mess with. But NYPD was able to calm him down a bit by pledging to investigate the missing screwdriver, and Dr. Bhatt authorized them to remove the cuffs and mask if he promised not to spit. O'Dell scowled. "Nobody's spitting," he said. "All I want is my fucking screwdriver." He sported a beige trench coat and a heavily-battered trilby.

"You'll get your screwdriver," lied Dr. Bhatt. "Just work with us."

The junior doctor scurried off to obtain a history from the EMTs, leaving me alone with the madman and the indifferent security guard. I didn't need any official report to figure out what had transpired: Angry O'Dell, who is as schizophrenic as they come—it takes a wingnut to know a wingnut, as they say—had probably been at his shelter when he started imagining that one of the other residents had pinched a screwdriver that he likely had never possessed in the first place. Or that he had misplaced on his own many years before, maybe on a 4-H outing, or helping his father install a boiler, or holding up a convenience store. At the shelter, it no longer mattered if the screwdriver had existed or how he'd lost it. What mattered was that he wanted it back—and it wasn't there to be returned. Unpleasantness ensued. The only outstanding question was whether anyone had been injured before the authorities arrived to cuff him. Probably not, or they'd have hauled him off to a forensic unit. I genuinely felt bad for O'Dell, and if the likes of me is taking pity on you, you know you're in trouble.

O'Dell lumbered to the edge of the "red line": a strip of crimson electrical tape that marked the floor between the patient waiting area and the security vestibule. He eyed Monty like you might the man who'd stolen your screwdriver—if you were screwed inside a coffin and rapidly running out of air. "What's that you're listening to, man?" asked O'Dell. "Latin baseball?"

"Latin football," I interjected. "Soccer."

"I used to play baseball," said O'Dell—my answer flying past him. "Sandlot. In Queens." As quickly as he'd taken an interest in Monty, he now shifted his focus to me, his pupils fiery and glazed like the cores of exotic marbles. "You don't believe me?"

"Why wouldn't I believe you?"

O'Dell chewed over my reply. "You'd better. I was the best damn shortstop between Whitestone and the Rockaways. Scouts had me pegged as the next Cal Ripken—only with a stronger arm from the hole. You believe me?"

"Of course, I believe you." I even knew what he was talking about. My brother had been Andover's star first basemen when Big Blue advanced to the Central New England championship in 1978. Best left-handed hitter out of Phillips Academy since George H.W. Bush. Only Bush went on to captain Yale into two College World Series, and later got himself elected President, while Rusky dropped out of Dartmouth the spring before I left Bryn Mawr and later fell down an elevator shaft at the Brooklyn County Courthouse, where he'd gone to fight a ticket for turnstile jumping.

The elevator door had opened, but no cab stood on the other side, just sixty feet of empty air. The coroner ruled his plunge an accident—mechanical failure. But behind every mechanical failure is a human failure, as far as I'm concerned, even if the authorities were too lazy to investigate. Or maybe on the take from the company that operated the elevator. The bottom line is that nobody gives a darn when a psychiatric patient gets killed—nobody except his own kin, that is—not even if he's a Brigander. As far as I'm concerned, the elevator inspector should have gone to prison. Nothing like that happened, obviously, although I visited the 84th Precinct each morning for a month to plead for an investigation and wrote letters to every elected official in the city. Since I was homeless, I figured any politician whose neighborhood I'd slept in was my de facto representative, but none of them were interested in pursuing justice for Rusky. The so-called accident was merely fodder for the tabloids. They used my brother's real name in the reports. Reginald Van Duyn Brigander. "Beats Rap, Takes Fall," had been the headline in the *Post*.

I wanted to tell somebody how my brother got his nickname. When he was about seven, maybe even younger, Mama's cousin, Adelaide—a priggish mothball of a spinster—asked him what he wanted to be when he grew up, and he replied, without rhyme or reason, "The Czar of Russia." And he became Rusky from that moment forward. But Angry O'Dell was the wrong person for this story, so all I said was, "Cal Ripken had a damn strong arm."

"Mine was stronger. Like iron," said O'Dell. "Until they stole my fucking screwdriver."

That was when the trouble started. First came shouting from the nursing station—Sarge's distinctive baritone: "The fucking cameras are down again! How the hell am I supposed to do my fucking job without any fucking cameras?!" There are security cameras concealed all over the CPEP—in the patient waiting area, in the interview rooms, in the kitchen—so the staff can snoop on us crazies when we're not looking. It's enough to make you paranoid, especially if you're paranoid already. We're not even supposed to know they're there, of course. That's why the key to malingering is always to remain in character. Sort of like method acting. You never know when somebody is spying on you. But in Sarge's case, the reason he'd gotten so worked up about the cameras was that now he had to drag his sorry ass out of his swivel chair to eyeball us every fifteen minutes. Sure enough, the lazy fool appeared in person seconds later. "You," he barked at Monty. "You search this new guy yet?"

Monty held up his middle finger. "I'll search him when I'm good and ready."

There's a backstory here. Sarge's ex-wife, Mary Lou, is a phlebotomist in pediatrics, and Sarge couldn't handle that she'd been dating Monty. Not that she'd *left him* for Monty. Nothing like that. *He'd* left *her*. More than two years earlier, for one of the techs in the chemistry lab. But the idea of his ex going out with the flabby Dominican blowhard got under his collar. What's that they say? When you sleep with someone, you sleep with everyone they've ever slept with before. Well, maybe the reverse is also true. You sleep with everyone they sleep with *after* you too. And Sarge clearly didn't like the notion of sharing a bed with Monty Castillo, who, in addition to looking rather like the Iberian pigs Grandma Brigander fattened up for Easter, had a vast compendium of false information ready at his fingertips. He could speak with impressive confidence on the ferocity of the South American lion or the logistics of the Soviet moon landing, and once, it pains me to report, on the marriage of Fred Astaire and Ginger Rogers—who, as you probably know, shared as much of a romance as chalk and cheese. It's also worth mentioning that Sarge was a stickler, one of those guys who can't let anything slide. Monty, on the other hand, was the union rep for 1199—his whole purpose in life was to get away with stuff. Oil and water. You knew there'd be warfare, even if Monty didn't have his pecker up Mary Lou's cooch.

You're wondering how I'm aware of all this. Like I said—I like to know stuff. And I'm a keen observer. You might say Mount Hebron is my own personal soap opera. Some gals watch *Days of Our Lives* or *General Hospital*. I follow the spats and flings of the ancillary staff on the psych ward. One of these days I should write a tell-all book. *The Other Side of Crazy: A Behind the Scenes Look at Psychiatric Care in Mount Hebron* by Henrietta Florence Brigander. Sort of like Nellie Bly's *Ten Days in a Madhouse*, only about the caregivers, rather than the patients. Not that I'm really ever going to publish a book. I'm not *that* delusional. But it's nice to have pipe dreams, even if you know they're merely pipe dreams. Otherwise, life's just one long series of blisters and bed bug bites and cracked teeth.

"This is total bullshit, Castillo," shouted Sarge. "Do your goddam job. You've got no business putting everyone else's lives at risk."

Monty rolled his eyes and nudged the volume on the soccer match higher.

"What the fuck wrong with you?" demanded Sarge. "I swear I'm going to write you up for this. How do you know he's not carrying a steak knife under that coat?"

"I'll take my chances," said the guard. But slowly, with all the vigor of a dying mule, he retrieved the security wand from its hook and shuffled toward O'Dell. "All right, Cal Ripken," he said, "Time to find those concealed steak knives. Stand up straight, arms out."

But Angry O'Dell had other ideas. "Get away from me," he barked, pacing the confines of the waiting area with increasing intensity. "You're a thief!"

"It's just a metal detector," said Monty. "Not a big deal."

Fear gleamed in the patient's eyes. I knew that look well. They needed to sedate O'Dell, and rapidly, before someone *did* get hurt. But I kept my own counsel. No good ever came from offering gratuitous clinical advice, not when you're ninety-four credits short of a bachelor's degree. *Call for backup*, I shouted inside my head. *Haldol 5, Ativan 2.*

Yet Dr. Bhatt chose to negotiate with the patient, not to medicate him. "What's wrong, Mr. O'Dell?" she asked. "I thought we were working together."

"He should have been searched and changed already," grumbled Sarge.

"Be a team player," Monty exhorted the patient. "Let's not have trouble." He inched closer, wielding the wand as though approaching a fly with a swatter. "Interesting thing about Cal Ripken," added the guard, as though to enlighten the entire CPEP, "is that he didn't plan on playing pro baseball at all. He wanted to take holy orders. They say Cardinal Shehan of Baltimore had to personally talk him out of the priesthood."

And then O'Dell's trilby was on the floor and his few teeth deep into Dr. Bhatt's bare forearm. Suddenly, Sarge and Monty suspended their feud and joined forces, maneuvering together seamlessly, like appendages of the same organism. Within seconds, the pair had restrained the patient, summoned additional officers and pinned the deranged man to the wainscoting. Poor Dr. Bhatt appeared shell-shocked, the puncture wounds from O'Dell's canines visible above her wrist. (I wanted to reassure her that at least the bite was human; I still recall the distant July 4th when the gardener's toddler, Tiago, required rabies prophylaxis for a raccoon bite—the rococo concave bows of the beast's dental arcade scarring the boy's chest and shoulders, his mad wails rising above the holiday fireworks.) For O'Dell now came the Haldol and Ativan injections with a vengeance—along with four-point leather restraints. Nobody paid me any heed through the commotion, although technically speaking, the protocol was to have me relocated. I sat beneath the Patients' Bill of Rights like a spectator at a bull fight. When four additional guards arrived and carried O'Dell to the seclusion room, each with his hands clasped around one limb as though hauling a sedan chair, they left me alone in the waiting area for nearly five minutes. Clearly, a violation of policy. If I'd wanted to commit "suicide by hat," they'd certainly afforded me enough opportunity. Eventually, the PCA returned with Big George in tow—the pair of them bantering about something frivolous. This PCA was a slender blonde girl named Katrina, a real looker, and I found myself growing jealous.

"Did I miss anything?" asked Big George. Completely oblivious.

"Nothing a B-52 couldn't cure."

Big George shot me a puzzled look.

"You really *are* new to this, aren't you? A B-52 is 5 milligrams of Haldol and 2 milligrams of Ativan. The standard ER cocktail—the madman's Mai Tai. Say, if you're not from St. Louis, where are you from?"

"Here and there. That's too long a story for now."

Which meant, implicitly, that there'd be a *later*. I swear my heart fluttered like a teenager's—like the time Michael Landon sat in the box next to ours at Saratoga.

"And what about you?" asked Big George. "Are you really nuts? Or just faking?"

I answered honestly: "Both."

"You don't seem so crazy," said Big George. "If you don't mind my saying."

"Oh, I am," I assured him—and I told him my tale, or at least a sanitized version of it, careful to keep my voice low so Katrina couldn't hear. Not that she cared. She was far too busy gleaning beauty tips from one of those magazines for adolescent girls. *You're not a teenager*, I wanted to cry, to shake her. *Grow up already, for Christ's sake.* I hated the way she lacquered each of her nails a different color. Most of what I shared with Big George was the voices—how for years I'd refused to accept that I was psychotic, and that then I'd embraced it. "It's all a matter of perspective. Of social context," I added. "Nobody drugged up Joan of Arc."

"You got a point." Big George gnawed his lip. "Never thought of that."

I have a whole *shpiel* prepared on the subject—about St. Francis talking to animals and Martin Luther hearing the voice of God in an outhouse, about Van Gogh and Robert Lowell and Edvard Munch's *Scream*—but it's hard to flirt from a soapbox, so I saved my arguments for the medical students, some of whom may yet be salvageable. Or so I tell myself.

"I also predict things," I said—but explaining my predictions is much more challenging than explaining the voices. Everyone understands hearing voices—whether you hear them personally or not. But my predictions are more just a feeling I get, an inkling. Almost an aura. Not a guarantee, not something you could bet upon at Monte Carlo. Rather a sense that something is more likely to happen than not. And sometimes I end up being dead wrong. For example, I had a notion that my former case worker, Mr. Lemonade, was going to marry the gorgeous Latvian girl from the Department of Social Services, the leggy bombshell who was always trying to get me to join a clubhouse, one of those recreation centers where they teach crazies to raise tomatoes and play canasta and contra dance like Mennonites. But then, out of the blue, he married an antiques dealer named Fred and they moved out to the Hamptons. Go figure.

"So make a prediction," said Big George. "About me."

"It doesn't work like that," I answered. "I'm not a circus act."

But the truth was that I already had a feeling about Big George, just about the strongest aura I'd ever experienced, and a voice was telling me only one thing: *Stay clear, Henrietta, because that man's in trouble. Stay clear, because soon that man will be dead.*

CHAPTER TWO

Before I go any further—before I get to the subject of murder—I should probably say a few words about Occam's razor. Now if you've never heard of it before, you might conclude, quite reasonably, that Occam's razor is a razor of the depilatory sort, some high-end women's shaver from Gillette or Norelco. I'll confess that was what *I* thought when I first heard the term, which was probably from Uncle Drake, who was actually my mother's uncle, and who held an endowed chair in moral philosophy at Princeton until an untoward incident involving a visiting applicant. Not that anyone ever mentioned this event directly. My esteemed relation was said to have "stepped down" to follow his own intellectual pursuits. Which happened to be waifish, working-class boys forty years his junior, but that's a different story for a different day. What matters is that I once believed Occam's razor might be the road to silky legs and smooth underarms. Or, if you're a morbid sort, an easy way to shuffle quickly off one's mortal coil. Since I've already promised you a murder, you might even be anticipating a slice-and-dice affair—but, I assure you, Occam's razor never killed anyone. Except metaphorically. Rather, Occam's razor is a philosophical principle. Named after William of Ockham, the medieval English monk who proposed it. What the principle basically says, when you cut through all of the philosophical verbiage, is that the simplest explanation for anything is usually the most probable.

For example: if you see a middle-aged women wearing a flamingo-tufted hat, dozing on the public sidewalk in Union Square beside a one-eyed Black Seminole, surrounded by a shopping cart overflowing with plush parrots and cockatiels, and maybe a handful of battered plastic valises, and sometimes that Black Seminole's dog, Revenge, which has a habit of disappearing and reappearing after long intervals, even after its own premature funeral, you might conclude this woman to be an aspiring character actress cast as an extra in an upcoming movie about psychiatric illness and homelessness on the streets of New York City, preparing in advance for her role. Method acting taken to the extreme. Or you might think she's crazy as the proverbial yodeling hatter who believes herself to be a loon. Occam's razor says the latter is far more likely. Got it? Because ever since I've understood Occam's razor—and its meaning was initially explained to me by a pre-med student from Haverford College whom I dated briefly during my first year at Bryn Mawr, a fellow who was otherwise as tedious and obtuse as brickwork—I've made a point of adhering to it. You might say I shave with Occam's razor.

Of course, like with my predictions, sometimes Occam gets it dead wrong. After all, as they say, truth can be stranger than fiction—and often it is. Let's take the Briganders, for example. If you read a novel in which the portfolio managers of Grandpa Brigander's estate bought stakes in only five companies, and those companies turned out to be the celebrated clunkers Eastern Airlines, Woolworth's, DeLorean Motors, Polaroid, and the asbestos producer, Johns Manville, you'd find that farfetched. (Who invests an entire ten-digit fortune in only five companies? And can you imagine the level of specialized incompetence required to choose five firms on the fast track to bankruptcy?) Or if you saw in a film that a moneyed family's summer cottage burned to the ground on the same day that their chronically-sloshed patriarch let their property insurance lapse, you'd cry foul. And if you watched on the silver screen as, two weeks later, that same soused patriarch steered his 82-foot, fly-bridge yacht straight into the wrathful maw of Hurricane Gloria, taking his wife, and his third-generation Weimaraner, and his white-shoe attorney from Cravath, Swaine & Moore, who also happened to be his mentally ill daughter's trustee, to the depths of Block Island Sound, you'd have walked out of the theater in disbelief. Or disgust—feeling cheated, wanting your money back. Because what doesn't happen in books or movies sometimes *does* happen in real life, at least in my experience, which is why you have to wield Occam's razor with great care. Anyway.

What I wanted to tell you about was how Big George ended up at Mount Hebron—and, like I promised, about murder—but I'd probably best start with what occurred the next morning between Sarge and P.J., because that was one of those days when Sarge brought his fishing tackle onto the unit. We were in the patient lounge when he entered—those of us who were awake at 7am: Lucille from Florida, and Ray G., and Nort the Messiah, and an NYU grad student who'd imbibed a fifth of bleach, and an elderly, demented woman brandishing a secret message to deliver to the United Nations, and

Big George, who I was glad to see was an early riser. (Although the bed-board gods had stuck him in a double room with Angry O'Dell, who'd been restrained and shouting half the night, growing increasingly unhinged, so maybe these were extenuating circumstances.) I desperately wanted to strike up a conversation with Big George, but he seemed more pensive in the daylight hours, focused on his apple juice and cornflakes, and every time a possible topic of discussion rose in my throat, I'd second-guess myself. It didn't help that my voices kept asking, *Why would he want to talk about that?*

Seven o'clock is when the nursing shift turns over. 7am, 3pm, 11pm. A never-ending cycle. For us that meant so long to Betty and Fatima, good morning Sarge and P.J. and Miss Clare, the charge nurse, a brisk, jolly Scotswoman who'd joined Mount Hebron's staff straight out of nursing school, nearly fifty years earlier, in an era when her senior colleagues, all unmarried women, still wore swan-style caps. God bless Miss Clare. They broke that mold long ago.

Miss Clare arrived first that morning, then P.J., who winked at me on his way into the nursing station—a reminder that he's the best thing to happen to this weary old world since they added oxygen to air. And then Sarge appeared, creel in one hand, rod in the other, like he'd just strolled off the pier at Coney Island.

"What the fuck?" asked Big George.

And that was as good an opening as any, so I explained why Mr. Brauer, who was usually a martinet for protocol, had dared to bring his tackle into our sanctuary.

"It's all strategy," I explained. "I've seen him do this before. They're probably short a nurse for the evening shift, and someone's going to be mandated to stay until eleven, and this is his way of announcing he has other plans." As much as I despised him for attempting to intimidate P.J.—for bullying my dreamboat into taking on the additional hours—I also secretly hoped that P.J. *would* stay the extra shift, so we might enjoy one of our late-night tête–à–têtes. "The assignment is supposed to be based on seniority, but Sarge is a schemer."

What I didn't say was what Uncle Dewey would have said, "Why the deuces do you need three nurses to cover nine patients?" The answer was the union, of course, and the hypothetical possibility, however remote, that another seven patients might be admitted that afternoon, which would have meant five patients for each nurse, plus an extra left over, one beyond the hard cap enumerated in their contracts. But I didn't know which way Big George leaned politically, and criticizing organized labor is a risky venture on a first impression, so I left Uncle Dewey tossing and turning in his mausoleum at Woodlawn.

"Is he really going to go fishing?" asked Ray G. "In this weather?"

Ray G. was a wiry ex-con who faked suicidality to hide from his dealer. I'd often wondered myself about the fishing, but I didn't relish being asked a question that I couldn't answer in front of Big George, so I held my index finger to my lips to shush him. "Listen."

We could just make out the staff's voices through the shatter-proof glass panels of the nursing station—first Betty and Fatima signing out their patients, summarizing each of us in clinical and less-than-clinical terms, our attitudes, our behavior, characterizing Angry O'Dell as "his usual congenial self," and Big George as "allegedly batty, but pleasant enough," and yours truly as "our fine feathered friend"; then Miss Clare distributed the patient assignments and reviewed the break schedule with her team. She stood beside the refrigerator, one arm braced on her slender hip, the other clutching her clipboard. To Sarge, she said, "Another thing, Mr. Brauer. You should know better than to bring *that* inside here." She said the word "that," meaning his fishing gear, as though referring to a soiled rag pinched between her thumb and pinkie.

"Jesus Christ," replied Sarge. "I'll secure it in the medication room."

"The medication room is not your athletic locker," said Miss Clare, matter-of-fact. "See to it that this doesn't happen again."

Sarge unlocked the medication room without answering her.

"And I'll need you to stay over," added Miss Clare. "We're short this evening."

"No can do, Miss C.," Sarge called from the medication room. "Going fishing."

I shot a knowing look in the direction of Big George. He grinned.

"Well, that's between you and Mr. Purnell," said Miss Clare. "Constance called out and Bonnie Jean can't work alone."

Bonnie Jean looked fifteen and innocent as a lamb, but she couldn't have been *that* innocent, because it seemed as though she was pregnant every time I was on the unit. I swear the gal must have had a dozen kids since I'd known her, but she hardly ever spoke, except in the course of her duties, so I knew nothing about them. Not even their names. Once the perverse notion entered my thoughts that they might have different fathers, or that she might be one of those surrogates who gestate babies for money, but I couldn't believe it. More likely, she practiced the rhythm method with Mr. Bonnie Jean and waited on her front porch for the stork.

"You're not actually going to mandate me, Miss C., are you?" called Sarge.

Miss Clare cleared her throat. "As far as I'm concerned," she said, her voice gravid with finality, "there is an open shift and it must be covered."

That brought Sarge out of the medication closet quickly, all hail-fellow-well-met, to quote Papa's favorite expression. "What do you say, Purnell? Cover for me?" He draped his arm over P.J.'s shoulders, and added, "Stripers are running. This could be my last chance of the season."

A bald-faced lie. Papa and Uncle Dewey would take the express cruiser onto Sheepshead Bay as late as Thanksgiving and return home with enough striped bass for Cookie, the chef, to keep us in seafood for a week. Last chance, my ass. Knowing stuff sometimes pays off. But I was in no position to call Sarge out on his claptrap. Fortunately, I didn't have to.

"Not this time. Sorry," said P.J. "I have a commitment."

The muscles in Sarge's jaw tensed visibly. "C'mon man. Don't make my life difficult. What's more important than the last run of schoolies?"

"I said I have a commitment. The details aren't relevant."

"Fine. But *I* have a commitment too."

P.J. shook off Sarge's arm. "I suppose the fish will have to make do without you this time around. I'm the senior this shift and I can't stay."

Even though I had been hoping P.J. might remain late—he was the only person at Mount Hebron I could talk to, *really* talk to—I also found myself secretly relishing his victory. When he stepped into the lounge to tape the day's group schedule onto the corkboard, I said, "I'm glad you'll get to go to your commitment. I was rooting for you."

"Thanks," said P.J.—not at all concerned that I'd overheard. "I'm sorry I couldn't be more helpful to Mr. Brauer, but my mother-in-law tore a ligament in her ankle. I'm looking after the little sprogs while my wife does her ma's grocery shopping."

That's what I love about P.J. He's willing to share tidbits from his own life—none of this nonsense about barriers and boundaries. Maybe that opaque tripe has some value when you're undergoing long term psychotherapy with an analyst, but here in the bin, it's nice to be treated like a normal human being. (If I'd told *Sarge* I'd been rooting for *him*, he'd have barked at me to mind my own business— or asked Dr. Robustelli to order me 100 milligrams of Thorazine.) Of course, the side effect of this transparency was that I wanted to marry P.J. all the more, although I realized his *mother-in-law* was probably younger than I was. *And even if he were your age*, asked one of my voices, *why would he mess with the likes of you?* Deep down, I knew the voice was only trying to be helpful—reminding me of the prudence of keeping even unrealistic fantasies at least *marginally* realistic—but I wasn't ready to hear her wisdom. "Shut up," I said back. "Shut up. Shut up. Shut up. Shut up. Shut up."

The first order of business after the nursing shift turned over was medication, and we lined up at the counter like lemmings for our daily dose. I did my part: 2.5 milligrams of Risperidone for the voices and an additional milligram of Cogentin to ward off the side effects. That's what most of modern psychiatry is about—side effects. Weight gain, hair loss, kidney failure. Which is why I concealed my pills under my tongue and slid them into a hole inside my mattress. I'd planned to share this trick with Big George, but I didn't have an opportunity, so he got himself a full measure of the antipsychotic du jour. Probably Abilify or Zyprexa. After medication, I was supposed to meet with Dr. Robustelli and the resident, Dr. Cotz-Cupper, for my formal evaluation, but Angry O'Dell went haywire, toppling a laundry cart and throwing a plastic meal tray, so they were absorbed with him for a good hour following breakfast. I recall Sarge shouting, "That louse, Castillo, was on duty last night, so who knows if the bastard was even searched." And also his ex, Mary Lou, reassigned to do blood work on our unit for the morning, cowering in the linen closet.

"Let's go to my room," I said to Big George. "Nobody will notice." We're technically not supposed to be in each other's rooms, especially patients of the opposite gender, but anything goes when the staff is dealing with a violent lunatic. And in my thirty-seven years of psychiatric treatment, I'd never encountered anyone as set upon mayhem as Angry O'Dell. He remained obsessed with his "stolen" screwdriver, but was also shouting about a conspiracy involving Osama bin Laden and Fidel Castro, and about how Dr.

Robustelli was trying to poison him. The PCAs turned a blind eye as I led Big George into the yellow-distempered, under-furnished room that I shared with the over-bleached NYU student. Why should they care? There were no cameras upstairs. The student, Alyssa, had returned to sleep, her breath lapping beneath the covers, the sheets drawn over her pudgy, witless face. I'd stashed a copy of the latest *New Yorker* on the nightstand—free magazines are one of the perks of in-patient hospitalization—but I grew suddenly nervous that Big George would judge me for this. He might think I was hyper-intellectual. Or pretentious. Some guys, I've found, don't like it when you know too much. Like Vivienne Mellon's midshipman beau from Annapolis, who'd dropped her the night Bryn Mawr's College Bowl team won the national tournament. "Take a load off," I said, slapping the bed.

"I guess I will," agreed Big George. He settled onto the mattress—but not too close to me—a gesture that I appreciated. A sign of a true gentleman, a suitor who respects your space. His night of slumber had done nothing to whitewash the anxiety from around his eyes and you didn't need a medical degree from Harvard to see a heap of worry weighing on his psyche.

"Not what you expected?" I asked.

Big George examined his hands—first the palms, then the backs, then the palms again. They were real men's hands: thick with sinew, nails clipped tight. The sort of hands that could, in a crisis, box bare-knuckled or wrestle a panther. "No, it *isn't* what I expected...but it's not that," he said. "Here's the deal, Flamingo. If I tell you something, can I count on you not to share it with a soul?"

I nearly swooned when he called me Flamingo, without Granny or Miss—like a pet name. "Girl Scout's honor," I pledged over a three-finger salute.

Big George eyed me funny. I suppose it's hard to picture the Henrietta of today in a cadette's khaki vest and skirt. "I guess I got to trust somebody," he said. "Here goes. So I better start by telling you that I'm a twin. Identical. Only our mother could tell us apart."

Now I was really falling for him. You probably can't understand how magnetic twins are to other twins, unless you're one yourself, but it's like belonging to a secret club. Like being a Mouseketeer. Or a Mason. And twins add a dimension of mystery to any narrative, a promise of surprise or Dickensian misunderstanding, so even if I hadn't been crushing on Big George, he'd have had me hooked on his story. Besides, I'd been missing Rusky terribly.

"So you asked where I'm from," said Big George. "Well, originally I'm from right around here—raised myself on East 11th Street—but I've been living up in Rhode Island. Newport. I got an outfit that does HVAC installation and repair for boats."

This was almost too good to be true. First, a twin. And now from Newport. Although I hadn't stepped foot in the place since the summer cottage burned, Newport remained a magical refuge in my imagination, an Eden of garden parties and coming out balls. My instincts told me Big George didn't mix with the first families of New England—but who could say? Maybe debutantes had once swooned over him. You'd never guess that *I* attended the Boston Cotillion on the arm of a Kennedy cousin in 1977.

"My brother—technically my little brother, by four minutes—he's been living in St. Louis. Not paying child support. Running with the wrong crowd. You'd think he'd have straightened himself out by fifty-nine, but he's just got a nose for trouble...and he chases after it like a bloodhound." Big George glanced at my sleeping roommate and lowered his voice. "My bro—his given name's Abraham, but we call him Little Abe—he's something of a forger."

"Like a counterfeiter?"

"Kind of. But not currency. Most of what he does is letters, diaries. Also computer records. We're not talking the Gettysburg Address here, mind you. Small time stuff. A postcard from Bob Dylan to Joan Baez. A couple of Elvis autographs. As my bro says, 'It's a living.' Only he sold some tycoon collector in Missouri—in *The Lou*, as you say—a letter from President Truman to Stan Musial, congratulating the Cardinals on winning the 1946 World Series—and then the guy, who's a real fanatic and also knee-deep in underworld connections—takes the forgery to the Baseball Hall of Fame, wanting to put the damn letter on display—and the next thing Little Abe knows, he's a dead man in St. Louis."

"So he came to New York?"

"Last winter. But he didn't learn his lesson. This time around, he's staying in a motel out in Jackson Heights, Queens, and he falls in love with the owner's wife. Big Albanian gal. Athena or Aphrodite or something like that. So what does my genius of a little brother do? It turns out the motel is popular with local politicos and their girlfriends, so he puts together a list of hourly guests...and tries to frame the owner for extortion. Sends out dozens of hand-written notes—in the Albanian guy's handwriting, cribbed from old letters to the fellow's wife that he'd unearthed in a bedroom drawer—

threatening to expose various assemblymen and city councilors and even the deputy police commissioner. And the sums he asks for are ludicrous. Seven digit figures. The whole point, of course, is to get caught. Or for the Albanian fellow to get caught. It nearly works too. One of the targets goes to the cops, and they haul the motel owner into court, and they even have a world-renowned expert confirm the handwriting, match it to his signature on the deed to the motel...say what you want about my bro, but he's got a gift...and that's when the Albanian guy makes his confession. He's totally illiterate. In both his mother tongue and English. The letters my baby bro found—the ones he based his forgeries on—had been dictated to the guy's own brother...his *long-deceased* brother, who'd also signed the deed. Later, it turned out, the wife had done all of her husband's correspondence. But who thinks to tell your lover that your husband can't read or write? So then the Albanian guy puts two-and-two together, and the police put four-and-four together, and now my brother's got both NYPD and the Albanian mob after him. And that's when he phones me for help."

As I said, life can be stranger than fiction.

"That's a string of bad luck," I said.

"More like a *noose* of bad luck. Only nobody knows he's an identical twin. So that means *I've* got NYPD and the Albanian mafia after me. Maybe the St. Louis mob as well."

"Oh, shit."

"Exactly. Now the cops might ask for ID, but the Albanian dudes aren't in any mood to play detective. I nearly got run down in a crosswalk yesterday morning. Black sedan without plates comes at me breaking eighty, maybe ninety. I knew I had to do something."

"So you came *here*?"

"Where else could I go? If I went to the police, they'd want to know about Little Abe. And with the Albanians tracking me, the minute I step foot in the bus station, I'm a goner. But then I remembered this old time movie where one of the mobsters hides out inside an insane asylum—"

"*Brother Orchid*," I suggested. "With Humphrey Bogart and Ann Sothern." Allen Jenkins played the impostor, but I didn't want to show off.

"Could be," agreed Big George. "In any event, here I am. What's that you said last night? 'I've got to be *somewhere* and here's as good a place as any.'"

So he *had* been paying attention. Big George sat at the foot of the bed, drumming his fingers along his kneecap, as a whole new world arose in my imagination: a future in which I accompanied him back to Newport, kept house while he installed air conditioners. I pictured a modest vegetable patch, possibly a brood of hens or geese. (I've always been partial to geese; you know what they say: what's good for the Bri-goose is good for the Brigander.) Or even a muster of peacocks. Nothing too fancy, mind you, certainly nothing on the scale of Mama's walled kitchen garden at the summer cottage, which had been designed for a Van Duyn progenitor in the eighteenth century by the English landscape architect Capability Brown. In my fantasy, Big George returned home from the docks alive with sweat, and maybe a faint scent of heating oil, boots hammering the hardwood of the kitchen, and then he swept me up in his meaty arms and bedded me right there on the countertop—like in a Harlequin romance novel. I let myself indulge this flight of self-delusion, yet all the while, my skull tingled with the sense that Big George was already a walking corpse. In hindsight, I should have inquired: "Where is your brother?"

"And what now?" I asked.

"Good question," said Big George. "I didn't get that far."

Nor were he and I destined to get any further with our introductions. From the corridor arose the sound of Dr. Robustelli calling for Nort the Messiah, whose real name was Pryce Norton, which meant that Angry O'Dell had been successfully contained, and the unit chief would soon be hunting me down as well for my intake history and physical. I'd hoped Dr. Mallet might be the attending on service that morning. Winston Mallet can be tough—he's a dyed-in-the-wool Southerner sojourning among us Yankees, a man who sports a white suit with a string tie year-round—but he's older than I am, soft-spoken and impeccably-mannered and graced with an avuncular charm. Even when he's grilling you, it never *feels* like he's grilling you. Dr. Vince Robustelli, in contrast, speaks in staccato bursts, almost like a precocious toddler, as though he's afraid he might run out of time to expel his stockpile of words. He displays all of the charm of a Stasi agent, and being interrogated by him is probably akin to being cross-examined by Torquemada with Tchaikovsky's *1812 Overture* booming in one's ears. For spending money during medical school, according to P.J., Robustelli had a job euthanizing lab rats. "We should get back before they catch you in here," I said. The PCAs might not have cared, but Robustelli would have medicated us both. "We can talk more over lunch," I added, feeling brave. "Bring your meal tray into the day room."

"I might just do that." Big George stood up, releasing the bed springs with a squeak, and that's when he caught sight of my *New Yorker* on the nightstand. He reached for the magazine, which I'd already devoured cover-to-cover, and asked, "You reading that?"

"Sort of," I said, slipping past him. "It's H&P time. We'd better hurry."

"Hurry, hurry, hurry," he echoed.

And then, to my amazement, that lovely man swatted me playfully on the rump with the magazine. Can you imagine? It's moments like that keep a girl going, even at my age, reminding me that anything is possible. Not likely, mind you. Maybe one in a million. But *possible*. And sometimes, that's all the hope you need.

One more significant incident occurred that day, or possibly two, if you count the murder, but it would have been a watershed day even without the stabbing. The uninitiated might expect this event to be my interview with Dr. Robustelli, but in reality this is only a formulaic ritual, like kabuki theater, because even if he suspects that I'm malingering, once I'm already on the unit, the medical team has every incentive to make me appear as sick as possible on paper. Otherwise, Medicaid might not reimburse them. Robustelli and I are basically pawns in an enormous game of unscrupulous chess between St. Dymphna's Health System and the managed insurance industry, so with my track record, he's not going to begrudge me my seventy-two hours in the bin. The other big event that I *can't* tell you about is my lunch date with Big George because it didn't happen. Dining services hardly had the meal carts inside the magnetic doors when Miss Celery Stalk showed up for a surprise visit. *Who the hell invited her?* I'd have asked—only I already knew precisely who. The friendly unit social worker, Mr. Volante, a former New York City firefighter with a knack for avoiding hard labor. If I met with my caseworker, that would be one less discharge plan for him to orchestrate. I know how these things work. As Uncle Drake, who was probably a closeted Marxist as well as a closeted homosexual, used to warn us kids when we visited him at Bar Harbor: "Never assume an idealist explanation where a materialist explanation will suffice." Translated into English, that means most things happen in this world because people are naturally cheap and idle. Anyway.

Miss Celery Stalk. She sashayed in around noon, all perky and pert, like some starlet out to watch the Easter Parade. Do you remember the actress Tuesday Weld? From *The Many Loves of Dobie Gillis* and *The Tab Hunter Show*? Probably not. But if you do, that's what Miss Celery Stalk looks like—only twenty pounds lighter. Like Tuesday Weld on heroin. And who in creation wears a skirt that short onto a psychiatric unit? When I was younger, the career caseworkers were ferocious battleaxes who'd devoted their lives to social service—severe, dour women in their fifties and sixties, but *dedicated*. Heirs to Jane Addams and Ellen Gates Starr. Now you get emaciated twenty-seven-year-old Vassar graduates who want to marry bankers. People's exhibit A: Celery Stalk—whose real name is Briana or Brittany or something like that. But I've been stuck with her ever since Mr. Lemonade ran off with Fred the Antiquer, because they require a "substantive reason" to request a new caseworker—and objecting to your current caseworker's taste in skirts doesn't cut the city's mustard. I considered refusing to meet with her—but then I'd just have gotten a shot in the ass, and we'd have started all over again in the morning. Last time, I'd feigned a tooth ache—and ended up having a healthy bicuspid pulled. Moral of the story: the Department of Social Services always wins in the end. So I picked up my meal tray (chicken and rice, chocolate milk) and followed Miss Celery Stalk into the conference room.

"Henrietta," she asked. "How have you been?"

Henrietta! As though we'd run into each other outside the café at Bergdorf Goodman. During the golden age of social work, when I was in my twenties, case workers addressed a client by her last name until instructed otherwise. "Well enough," I replied, folding my arms across my chest. My appetite had gone the way of Pompeii and passenger pigeons.

"What have you been doing with yourself?"

That was a good one. "Do you really want to know?" I asked. "Mostly D.A.R. meetings, teas for Mrs. Schermerhorn and Mrs. Vanderbilt, some croquet. Then there was the Picabia retrospective at the MOMA and the Rubens show at the Met. And I still have to purchase my gown and gloves for Mrs. Astor's ball."

"I see," said Miss Celery Stalk.

Apparently, she couldn't tell whether I was jesting—or psychotic. Priceless. Yet a part of me also resented her for not believing my yarn. Maybe not about Mrs. Astor, I suppose, but just because I'm homeless doesn't mean I can't enjoy an art exhibition.

"Relax, honey," I said. "It's a joke. *A joke.* Like, 'What does a White Anglo-Saxon Protestant hope to be when she grows up?'" One of the Schuyler sisters told me that joke on my first day at Brearley. Miss Celery Stalk stared at me vacant as a cabbage. I served up the punchline: "The very best person she possibly can."

Miss Celery Stalk did not laugh. "I care about you, Henrietta," she said. "I'm very worried. I want to help."

That wasn't true, of course. At most, she might have been *a little bit* worried about me and wanted to help so long as helping wouldn't actually cost her anything, but she didn't genuinely care about me—not in any meaningful way. If she *cared*, truly cared, she'd have offered to bring me home with her, rather than leaving me to sleep on a grating behind the Hotel Chelsea. Not that I'd have taken her up on her offer: I could easily picture her mousetrap of an apartment, all of those tufted cushions, the geodes and vases displayed on self-assembled IKEA wall units, snapshots (with her midriff exposed for the world to see) at Angor Wat and Machu Picchu. What did I want with all that? But she wasn't offering. I felt the way Tecumseh Muhammed feels when he sees a headline in the *Columbia Spectator* or the *Washington Square News* about anti-racism initiatives on college campuses. Bullshit. "Send your lily-white kid to enlist in the service, and pay for some brother's boy from Brownsville or Hunt's Point to go to a fancy Ivy League school," he says, "and *then* you talk to me about overcoming racism." And he has a point too. Most upper-middle-class white people are delighted to fight injustice when it means reading Toni Morrison or freeing Leonard Peltier, but tell them their daughter can't go to Saint Ann's, or that they have to deliver their babies in the charity ward at Metropolitan Hospital, and suddenly you're talking to Archie Bunker. Mama and Papa weren't like *that*, at least. They held no illusions about making the world a better place or righting injustices. "Life is a zero-sum game," was one of Papa's catch phrases. "Somebody has to be poor. My job is to make sure it's not us." Oh, the irony.

"I'm doing just fine, thank you," I said.

Miss Celery Stalk pursed her thin lips. "I'm sorry, Henrietta, but I don't think you are. What kind of life is this?"

For a Brigander, she meant. For someone who reminded her of how close we all are to the edge—who, but for the grace of God, could be her. No caseworker ever asked Tecumseh Muhammed: "What kind of life is this?" But her false concern generated real distress for my voices: *Well, what kind of life is this?* They demanded. *Well? Lots of people walk near the edge, but you're the one who fell off!* I wanted to argue with them, to justify myself, but I didn't dare— not in front of Miss Celery Stalk. Not to be seen responding to so-called "internal stimuli." That was a surefire way to earn an injection. She folded her tiny alabaster hands and rested them on the tabletop.

"I've been speaking with my supervisor, Henrietta, and we think you would benefit from a guardian."

I once heard Papa's roommate at New Haven—a bearded surgeon who specialized in "women's cancers"—explain that you had to be careful when sharing a diagnosis with a patient, because once you said the word cancer, she didn't hear anything else. I can't say if that's true, because one of the few troubles I don't have—not yet, at least—is the Big C, but I can tell you that, as soon as Miss Celery Stalk uttered the word "guardian," I saw her lips moving, but I no longer registered any sounds. Instead, I focused on the painting behind her: a pastel autumn landscape of a log cabin at sunset, nearby trees a warm yellow in the twilight. Birch? Shagbark hickory? Imprecise by design. The pristine countryside is every place and no place simultaneously, crafted to avoid evoking recognition. All of the hospitals I've stayed in share this aesthetic neutrality, troves of anodyne kitsch purchased in bulk, as though the glimpse of a Matisse nude or even a Vermeer interior risks prodding us crazies toward aggression. That cabin might have been an outbuilding on Aunt Genevieve's ranch in Montana—or a gaucho hangout deep in the Pampas. Who could say? Miss Celery Stalk's mouth continued jabbering, indifferent to my indifference. She had a script to follow, while I knew that once the state had decided to assign you a legal guardian, you stood a better chance of escaping Alcatraz that overturning the plan in court. Basically, that meant I'd no longer be able to cash my own benefits check, that I'd have to report to some busybody like Miss Celery Stalk each month—or even more often, if she wanted—to get pocket change. Like an allowance. Humiliating, let me tell you, for a woman who'd had her own account at Saks at age fifteen.

"I think it's for the best," said Miss Celery Stalk, standing up. "At least, for now. Nothing, of course, is carved in stone."

"What about Mount Rushmore? Or the Moai of Easter Island?" I asked. "Lots of things are carved in stone." I watched the small groove deepen between her eyes. Was she deciding whether it would be worth explaining the concept of metaphor? I rather hoped she might—that we would have a fruitful chat about figurative language, synecdoche and zeugma and antanaclasis. But I knew not to get my hopes up. When dealing with people like Miss Celery Stalk, the key to conversation—and happiness—is setting very low expectations.

"It's for the best, Henrietta," she said. "Really."

That ended our heart-to-heart. I carried my meal tray back into the day room, hoping to salvage my rendezvous with Big George, but he'd been corralled into the "men's group" meeting that the social work interns run on alternating weekday afternoons. On the opposite days, they host a "women's group"—usually attended by overindulged college coeds who've survived faint-hearted suicide attempts and by former state hospital patients too doped up to know any better. I've sat through a couple of sessions, but *come on.* What do I need with assertiveness training? Or domestic violence counseling? Like if some guy jumps me, I'm really going to file a complaint at One Police Plaza and get taken seriously. If they wanted to run a *useful* group, they'd teach us how to pinch tampons from CVS or jump the line for tube-tying at Rikers, but these interns live in Pollyannaish oblivion.

Back in the day room, Ray G. was shouting at the television screen, striving to appear psychotic so that Robustelli wouldn't eject him—hurling profanities at a commercial for a low-fat butter substitute, a song-and-dance routine that culminated with a chorus line of margarine stalks—while Nort the Messiah played checkers with a newcomer, a fellow I recognized from the streets on account of his missing eyebrow. All he had on the right side of his forehead was a jagged horizontal scar. Tecumseh Muhammed would have had a field day quipping one-liners at their mutual expense—zingers like, "Sorry, buddy. It looks like your brow ran off with my eye." Or calling him "One-Brow Jack." He cracks himself up with gallows humor about one-legged unicyclists and single-breasted prostitutes, obviously a coping mechanism, but humor that doesn't always go over so well. I was relieved he wasn't with me.

The demented old lady with the secret message dozed in a knock-off Barcalounger. That left only Lucille from Florida for conversation, so I settled down beside her on one of the sofas, because I like to be social—to get to know the other inmates, you might say—although I've been cautioned not to use that term. You never can tell when making the acquaintance of someone might prove helpful. Like in that Aesop's fable about the lion and the mouse. Or that time Tecumseh Muhammed scored us free movie passes, because he'd done a stint in detox with the manager of the art house on 23rd Street. But Lucille from Florida didn't look promising: a tall, flat-chested creature, bitter-faced, with a rodent's nose and dull black eyes. And for a woman who'd taken a Greyhound from Miami, she had skin like dry paste. "So how does this compare to Florida?" I asked.

"Not too different," said Lucille. "All hospitals are more or less the same, aren't they?"

I nearly snorted in contempt, but checked myself. Lucille's experience with asylums was clearly rather narrow. There's actually quite a range, just like with cruise ships or hotels. You've got your McLeans and Menninger Clinics, which are only a step down from the Plaza, and then you've got your Harlems and Bellevues and your big state hospitals—all of which make Motel 6 look like the penthouse at the Pierre. I could write a *Fodor's Guide* to loony bins, if only there were a market. Oh, the stories I could tell...

"Did you meet with Dr. Robustelli?" Lucille asked.

"Been there, done that," I said. "Vince and I go way back."

"He doesn't spend much time with a person, does he?"

"You sound disappointed," I said.

"Just surprised," said Lucille. "I kind of expected a full workup. Like in Miami."

That was the perfect opening for me to explain how the system works, at least here in New York City, and Lucille appeared genuinely interested. She tilted her rodentine snout toward me—and I swear she looked the spitting image of Mama's anteater at feeding time. "You have to apply Occam's razor," I advised.

"Who's what?"

"Occam's razor. It's a tool for cutting through baloney." And I revealed the symbiotic relationship between private hospitals like Mount Hebron and chronic, malingering patients like yours truly. "The hospital gets paid either way, dear," I explained. "Medicaid only knows what we look like on paper—not in person. So it's much easier, and more cost-effective, to admit healthy people pretending to be sick, and make them appear psychiatrically ill in the documentation, than it is to admit patients with genuine mental health needs. The latter might require additional services or overstay their welcomes. Once you've been here more than about a week, you understand, the government gets considerably stingier."

"So you're saying Dr. Robustelli doesn't spend much time with us because he's already decided to retain us as long as the hospital is getting paid?"

"Don't look so shocked," I said. "Doctors have to earn a living too."

Lucille from Florida shook her head. "Still, it's disappointing. In Miami, the psychiatrists spend a full hour with you. They even listen to your chest with a stethoscope."

How odd, I recall thinking. Most patients on a psych ward want *less* time with their headshrinker, not more. But I chalked up her reaction to inexperience. "Welcome to New York, sister," I replied. "*Cooler* than Miami Beach, isn't it?"

I was pleased with my double entendre, but Lucille from Florida didn't notice and responded with a vague remark about the weather. Then we chatted for a while about the relative disadvantages of being homeless in South Florida versus New York, rather superficially, and I shared with her the locations of the best churches to hit up for free winter coats. It didn't seem all that long ago when my own mentor, Renegade Sally, a veteran of the Tompkins Square Park Riot, had taught me strategies for surviving a New York cold snap: where to hide from so-called "outreach" teams hell-bent on hauling you off to public shelters, how to waterproof boots on your own with a wax candle and a space heater. Sally died of kidney failure. Ten years ago. Sometimes it seems like only yesterday. And other times it seems like only yesterday that Cousin Adelaide was shipping us crates of navel oranges and oro blanco grapefruit from West Palm Beach for Christmas. Time is funny that way—the previous day's spat with Tecumseh Muhammad can feel eons past, like something out of the Pleistocene, while a childhood trip to the beach sometimes wakes me with the immediate scent of the sea breeze. As for my conversation with Lucille from Florida, which had devolved into a discussion of Dr. Robustelli's work schedule, our chat felt as though it had lasted centuries longer than the Holy Roman Empire. But I was a woman with a purpose: to keep myself looking occupied in the day room until Big George's men's group expended its testosterone and broke up.

The best laid schemes of mice and men, as they say...

Five minutes before three o'clock—approaching shift change, as the afternoon groups were winding down—Angry O'Dell went haywire again. He'd hardly been out of leather four-point restraints for an hour when he appeared in the corridor stark naked, eyes lustrous with deranged zeal—a fanatical, divinely-galvanized look I've only ever seen replicated in daguerreotypes of nineteenth century abolitionists. He continued to shout about his screwdriver, and Osama bin Laden, and also about how he was being poisoned through his skin. As he screamed, he threw his crumpled hospital gown to the floor and stomped on it. Fortunately, unlike Dr. Bhatt in the ER, Dr. Cotz-Cupper meant business. "Major tranquilizers first," was her motto, "Negotiations second." Soon, O'Dell had been subdued and returned to his chamber.

But the episode disrupted the rhythm of the unit, and by the time I'd returned to the dayroom, Big George had already carried the morning *Post* into the kitchen. I feared he might be annoyed if I interrupted him. I did have an opportunity to speak to him when he called upon Miss Clare for an antacid tablet, but I thought the better of flirting with a man while he battled indigestion. Instead, I merely smiled and watched the shift change, Sarge making one final effort to win over P.J., then P.J. heading out into the world. "I'll see you tomorrow?" he asked me as he passed.

"Where else would I be?"

"Don't give Mr. Brauer a hard time," he said. "He can't help being himself."

So that was my fix. Fifteen seconds of conversation with the man who would never be my husband—one of the many men, to be honest, who would never be my husband. All for different reasons. Countless fellows from Swarthmore and Haverford because I never returned for the fall semester; and all of those Vanderbilt nephews and Kennedy cousins who fought over my dance card, because nobody wants a fat, middle-aged lady with a funny hat on his dance card; and Tecumseh Muhammad, because his binges are brutal and I have no family left to shock. And also Michael Landon, who'd been so dashing at Saratoga in his teardrop fedora, and had signed his name for me on Papa's racing form, and hadn't even lived to fifty-five. If the Bird Lady doesn't get you, I guess, then the cancer will. And now Big George too, my instincts told me, although I'll get to that in a moment. But I still can't help wondering what might have happened if Angry O'Dell hadn't gone haywire again that afternoon, or if P.J.

had taken Sarge's shift, or if I'd managed to intercept Big George as he left his men's group. Anyway.

My voices started acting up in the early evening, as they often do—they have their habits, just like the rest of us—and by dinnertime, I was in no frame of mind to flirt. So I asked Sarge for a PRN Benadryl, which he surrendered reluctantly, and carried my meal tray into my room. NYU girl remained under her covers, her chicken cutlets and mashed potatoes untouched on the nightstand. If she didn't eat them by the time I woke up, I decided, they'd be my early-morning snack.

Usually, 50mg of diphenhydramine was enough to knock me out for the night, and there's no reason to stay up late on a psych unit. Not under ordinary circumstances. The atmosphere turns dead quiet after hours—like on a sailboat or a safari. Or like it must have been for our ancestors in their caves. But I was still awake as a great horned owl at a field mouse convention when I experienced the most lovely, unsettling premonition. I saw myself standing on a street corner in the East Village, braced against the November wind, being swept off my feet by Big George's kisses like Grace Kelly being seduced by Cary Grant in *To Catch a Thief*—the heat of our own passion mirroring the fireworks in the evening sky. I realize it wasn't a genuine kiss, at least not in the traditional sense, but only a premonitory encounter. And yet I swear I could feel the singe of Big George's lips, that I could smell the pungent aroma of raw virility in his sweat—a scent as rich and distinctive as the pelt of a grizzly bear.

Why unsettling? Because I also had a premonition that Big George was on the fast track to the big sleep, that his lips would soon be cold as Sir Ernest Shackleton's nose or Cousin Adelaide's feet on her wedding night. But that kiss, real or not, clinched a bond between us, as strong as if we'd been soldered together with steel. A woman can't simply forget a man she's kissed like that, not even in a premonition. Whether you call it love or folly, I'd already decided that I was Big George's for the asking. What a pleasant resolve to carry into slumber.

To my surprise, it was still dark when I awoke. And not very late—I could hear Sarge in the corridor, performing door-to-door safety checks, so the nurses hadn't changed shift again yet. I considered sneaking into Big George's room to say good night, but being discovered in another patient's room after lights-out, especially a patient of the opposite gender, was a far more serious offense than the same transgression at mid-morning, the sort of violation that could land a gal in the bin against her will for an extra week. Instead, I allowed my eyes to meander the ceiling while my mind drifted. I wondered whether Tecumseh Muhammed was searching for me yet—whether he'd grown worried, although I knew he hadn't. And then my thoughts wandered to the Boston Cotillion, and the overweight Kennedy cousin who kept pawing my thigh uninvited, and then I imagined that it was P.J., and not the Brahmin doughboy, who'd picked me up in a Fleetwood limousine. Could P.J. dance? Instinctively, I sensed that he could—but I didn't know for sure. *And why would he dance with you?* asked the voices. But before I had an opportunity to answer, the night was shattered with screams.

On a psychiatric ward, you grow accustomed to certain varieties of screaming: madness, anger, dread. So let me say, at the outset, this was shouting of a different contour. Sheer horror, unfiltered by temper or illness. I climbed out of bed, tucked my hat over my ears, tying the stampede string tight beneath my chin—I didn't want to lose it in case circumstances demanded a hasty evacuation—and hurried into the hallway.

A crowd had gathered: Sarge; the overnight nursing supervisor, Ms. Holm; Nort the Messiah, carrying his pillow. The old lady with the message for the U.N. emerged from her room with a bath towel draped from her scalp like an open veil, as though preparing for a white wedding, or a stage appearance as Miss Havisham. Bonnie Jean, pregnant once again, and far along, too, pressed her fingers over her thin lips. Lucille from Florida, ashen, weasel-mouth agape—she must have been the screamer—clutched onto a guardrail for balance.

At the far end of the corridor, opposite Big George's door, stood Angry O'Dell. He wore a look of deranged surprise—maybe awe at his own psychotic potential. In his left hand, like a dagger, he held a serrated six-inch knife, its blade a sanguinary crimson.

CHAPTER THREE

That was when the voices turned angry. As I mentioned earlier, they're usually friendly and supportive, but everyone has their moods, and they're no exception. *Why didn't you do something?* they demanded. *You had fair warning!* And a few seconds later, a running commentary: *You worthless bird-brained bitch. You selfish tub of guts. Go hang yourself and join lover boy.* What I already knew for certain—long before the police arrived to seal off the crime scene—was that Big George was dead. "Shut up," I shouted inside my head. "Shut up, shut up, shut up, shut up!" But I must have vocalized my plea, because Ms. Holm, the nursing supervisor, flashed me a look of startled alarm. I caught myself and smiled benevolently.

Then everything seemed to happen at once. First, Sarge, whom I'd never taken for particularly courageous, inched toward Angry O'Dell—hands extended, palms up—and asked for the knife. "Be a pal, Arnold," he said. "I've always been a friend to you, haven't I? Why don't you give me that knife and we'll see about getting you a midnight snack." To my surprise, O'Dell dropped the weapon. It landed on the linoleum with a benign thud. When Sarge stepped forward to retrieve it, O'Dell shook his head, seemingly flummoxed, turned on his bare heels as though nothing were amiss, and retreated back into his room. Even as someone who has personally experienced psychotic blackouts—or so they tell me—I was struck by how utterly oblivious the man appeared to his own crime. Meanwhile, my voices kept up their running criticism, fighting for my attention against the chatter of the drowsy inmates who'd congregated at a safe distance, dazed and disoriented, the old lady with the message for the U.N. dragging her bedding like the train of a bridal gown. Even Alyssa, the NYU student, made a bleary cameo in our doorway; I noticed she sported lobster slippers with plush orange pincers—and I wondered if she weren't on her way to becoming the Crustacean Maiden of the East Village. "What's going on?" she asked.

As though in response, both hospital security and NYPD charged onto the unit, Monty Castillo carrying his box radio under one arm. At their heels appeared Dr. Bhatt, the on-call resident,

looking even more fragile and bone-weary than usual. "You!" Sarge
shouted at Monty, while still holding the bloody knife. "This is all
your goddam fault. Didn't I tell you to search the guy thoroughly?"

"Drop the knife!" shouted two uniformed officers
simultaneously. A third drew a bead on Mr. Brauer with his Taser. I
realized their mistake, and enjoyed a fleeting moment of perverse
pleasure in the prospect of Sarge getting tased, but even in our strange
world of almost infinite possibilities, some miracles remain
stratospherically beyond reach. Sure enough, Sarge also recognized
the cops' error in the nick of time, and let go of the weapon.

"I'm a nurse," he shouted. "The guy you want is in there."

One of the cops glanced at Chief Boucher, Mount Hebron's
Director of Security, who I knew from the time he'd helped me locate
my missing owl pendant. It's only tanzanite, but an especially
clueless guard had mistaken the stones for sapphires, and secured the
necklace in the hospital safe. Now Chief Boucher glanced toward Ms.
Holm for guidance, and she nodded. "You're looking for Arnold
O'Dell," she explained without emotion, her face impassive as
pegamoid. "Mr. Brauer merely retrieved the knife from the floor."

With a wary eye upon Sarge, the third cop lowered his weapon.
Then all three officers swept into the victim's room and returned a
few moments later with their suspect—hands cuffed behind his back,
but now calm, his chin resting on his exposed, hoary chest. I imagine
that protocol required all of us to return to our own rooms, that the
entire unit should have been on lockdown, but the staff was either too
shocked, or possibly too scared, to attempt any effort to sequester us.
So we were all present in the corridor to hear what I already knew
instinctively. The officer with the Taser, a lantern-jawed veteran with
world-weary eyes, announced—to no individual in particular—that
the excitement was over. "Nobody's going to survive that," he said.
"Better call the O.M. E."

O.M.E.: Office of the Medical Examiner. I was pleased with
myself for recognizing the abbreviation—and for knowing he didn't
mean "otitis media with effusion" or the mercantile exchange in
Osaka, Japan. Context matters. I'll never forget how Charlotte
Schuyler got into a heated argument with our eleventh grade English
teacher, Miss Swayne, an over-the-hill flapper who still wore her
platinum hair in a Marcel wave and who probably carried a flask in
her boot. The question on the literature final had been: Who is
Rochester? I had written: Jane Eyre's highly-overrated husband.
Charlotte insisted upon receiving credit for her answer: Jack Benny's

valet. She didn't. Ten years would pass before I realized that Miss Swayne and Miss Fitzroy, the Latin teacher, had been an item, and another five before I understood that Charlotte had also been in love with Miss Swayne—that what I took for arguing had been flirting. Now Miss Swayne was dead of scleroderma and Charlotte Schuyler lived with a divorced male podiatrist in Tampa (I keep track of these things, as best I can) and Big George was on his way to the O.M.E.

"Are you saying Mr. Currier has been injured?" asked Ms. Holm.

"Not *injured*, ma'am," replied the officer. "I'm very sorry."

As soon as she said the name Currier, I thought of Currier and Ives, the nineteenth century lithographers. Uncle Dewey had several originals hanging in his billiard room, adjacent to the sterling-gilded barometer: one depicted the steamship, *Sultana*, burning north of Memphis, and another portrayed a tranquil spring morning along the Lower Hudson. Big George Currier had a distinguished ring to it, I reflected—too late. So did Henrietta Florence Brigander Currier. I couldn't tell you what had become of either of Uncle Dewey's prints.

"Don't look at *me*," announced Sarge. "I did a vitals check on the guy ten minutes ago and everything was fucking hunky-dory."

Only then did Ms. Holm attempt to rein in the chaos. "We're on lockdown," she declared. "Patients must return to their rooms." She surveyed the corridor—the bloody knife, the discarded bedding—and added, almost as a collective punishment, "All groups and activities are cancelled until further notice," as though we'd been counting on a midnight pinochle tournament or some pre-dawn therapeutic yoga. As my fellow inmates shuffled back to their rooms, some exchanging whispers, the nursing supervisor instructed Bonnie Jean to conduct a headcount, and ordered Sarge to phone maintenance about mopping the gore-soaked floor. I perched in the doorway and watched through the laminated glass as she called both the on-site morgue and the medical examiner.

At the same time, hapless Dr. Bhatt was on her cell with the overnight attending, inquiring how to fill out a death certificate. "It's never come up before, Dr. Robustelli," she explained, red-faced. "No, we never received any training. They must have figured nobody dies on a psychiatric unit." Poor girl. She should have gone into a field that required less independent initiative—like toll collecting or latch hook.

Meanwhile, the police cordoned off the far end of the hall with yellow tape. I'd nearly given up on the scene myself—the voices were berating me for failing Big George, and I didn't want to bicker—when the feud between Mr. Brauer and Monty rekindled.

"I'm not taking the fall for this, Castillo," warned Sarge. "I'm not losing my goddam license because you don't know how to do your job. How hard is to search a fucking patient?" He thrust his chest forward, his shoulders out like a strutting turkey.

"I searched him," said Monty, trying to step around Sarge.

The nurse blocked his path. "Clearly not good enough."

"Out of the way, Mr. Brauer," said the guard. "You do your job, I'll do mine."

"Go screw yourself," retorted Sarge, "and your hand-me-down girlfriend."

The words had hardly left his lips when Monty's fist landed square in the nurse's abdomen. Sarge staggered back against the nearest wall, winded, eyes aflame with outrage. He looked to the nursing station for support, but Ms. Holm had retreated into the break room. Then his gaze shifted to his duo of unpromising witnesses— from Chief Boucher to me and back to Chief Boucher. "You didn't see anything just now, did you, Miss Brigander?" asked the security director, resting his hands in his pockets. "Because *I* certainly didn't." Sarge condemned us all with a guttural sound—something between a sigh and a growl—and hobbled off. About fifteen minutes later, a team of pathologists in goggles and latex elbow-gloves carted off Big George's body.

Something wasn't right. I didn't know *what* wasn't right, or even how I knew, but I had this inchoate feeling deep inside me that something stood profoundly amiss. Like the time Tecumseh Muhammed thought he had a bad cold, but I just knew it was walking pneumonia. Or when I was a little girl, and Vice President Agnew visited Grandpa Brigander at the summer cottage, and some primal antenna in my psyche pegged the man as a fraud. I'm sure there's a logical explanation for my sixth sense—much like there's probably a reason that rats flee in advance of earthquakes or why Cousin Adelaide's arthritic knee could foretell a nor'easter—but the bottom line is that I had a nagging suspicion of *something*.

I didn't have much time to explore my instincts, unfortunately, because at daybreak the next morning, a solid hour before shift change, we were instructed to gather our belongings and marched like hostages to the eighth floor. The adolescent ward. They'd apparently bisected that unit with artificial partitions—the sort of fabric-covered panels on swivel casters used to divide up church basements and the branch offices of retail banks. On one side, they'd quarantined the troubled teenagers, adding folding cots to double rooms. We veterans of the seventh floor were crammed into the other half of the unit where an alcove with a portable television served as a makeshift dayroom. The floor below us had been secured as an active crime scene. With a moratorium on new admissions, the plan was to cap our ad hoc unit at eight patients until it emptied through attrition. They'd also reassigned the nurses, so instead of P.J. and Sarge, we received our morning meds from a portly Filipino nurse named Trisha. "And I'm sorry, dear, but you'll have to give up your hat," she said. "It's a rule."

"I think I'll be going now," I decided. "I'd like to put in a 72-hour letter." That's a formal request for discharge in New York State, one that technically earns you merely a hearing before a mental health judge within three days, but in my case, the doctors generally skip the formalities and usher me onto the sidewalk. Sometimes, if I'm lucky, P.J. will send me out with a doggy bag: mini-cartons of breakfast cereal, surplus pairs of no-slip socks, etc. But Tubby Trisha had different plans for me.

"I can't accept a letter right now, dear. Dr. Robustelli's orders. Nobody gets discharged until they talk to the police."

"And when will that be?"

Tubby Trisha shrugged. "I wish I knew, dear. Now please be a doll and move aside so I can give your fellow patients their medication."

A doll! That's a good one. Mattel should market a line of Barbies in my image: Disheveled Barbie, Malodorous Barbie, Off-Her-Gourd Barbie. But I made way for Ray G. to collect his morning cocktail and retreated to my room, a bright-orange chamber I now shared with the NYU student *and* the demented old lady, hoping Tubby Trisha might forget about the hat. No luck. Not ten minutes elapsed before two patient care associates and a security officer—a washed-out, ovine woman I didn't recognize—appeared to retrieve my flamingo tuft. "Don't fight us on this," warned the unfamiliar guard, as though I might launch a battle royal. "We'll lock it in the closet for safekeeping and you'll get it back when you leave." So I surrendered my prize possession. My identity. And I felt naked, exposed—like an Orthodox Jew bereft of his skullcap, or the way devout Muslim women must suffer when forced to remove their hijabs.

"Good girl," said the guard, the same tone Mama used to praise her water spaniel. I settled onto the cot and closed my eyes, hoping to block out the world, all except my kiss with Big George; the voices seemed to take a hint, subsiding to a low, disgruntled murmur, and I must have slept until nearly noon. That's when the Gestapo arrived to conduct me to my interrogation.

Okay, maybe Gestapo is an exaggeration. But being shaken awake by imperious Dr. Cotz-Cupper as though she were trying to demonstrate a seismological phenomenon, surrounded by three New York City police officers and a pair of white-shirted detectives, does wonders for the blood pressure, let me tell you. If I'd been a character on a sitcom, I might have asked, "What is this? *Darkness at Noon*?" Only I suppose it would have to have been a sitcom targeted at an audience of women who grew up with a complete leather-bound set of the Modern Library on the shelves of their Papas' studies, so I kept my mouth shut and followed the cops. To my surprise, we left the unit entirely and rode the transport elevator to the ground floor, where NYPD had established a provisional command center in the administrative board room.

Half-empty Styrofoam coffee cups peppered the long mahogany table and a hint of tobacco smoke hung in the air. I glanced up at the portraits of Mount Hebron's illustrious founders and benefactors that ringed the walls, stout financiers sporting Prince Albert frock coats and muttonchops, including my own third cousin twice removed, Barrington Van Duyn Griffin of the brokerage firm Seward, Griffin & Dohrenwend, who appeared to be wrinkling his nose above his walrus mustache. At one end of the table sat Dr. Mallet, his shirt sleeves rolled to the elbows, presiding over a half-eaten jelly donut on a paper plate. The oil from the donut had formed a greasy translucent silhouette on the paper, a shape that vaguely resembled Australia. Behind Dr. Mallet sat one of the nursing administrators and a handful of young suits—presumably from risk management or legal. "There's nothing to be afraid of, Henrietta," he said. "As you may know, there was a death on the unit yesterday. These officers are just conducting a routine investigation." He indicated for me to seat myself at the head of the table, in a heavy wooden armchair. Like out of a Viking mead-hall, I thought. From *Darkness at Noon* to *Beowulf*. "This is Detective Libby," said the psychiatrist, indicating a roseate bulrush of a man ensconced at his left. "He has a few questions to ask you, but you don't have to answer anything that makes you uncomfortable."

"Libby like the canned food people?" I asked. "Do you remember that jingle from the seventies?" Detective Libby clearly did not. Which might have been forgivable if his name hadn't been Libby, much like I wouldn't expect the average person to recognize a Happiness Boys ditty for Interwoven Socks. But if you're actually *named* Libby, I feel your obligations are different. Like Tecumseh Muhammed not knowing anything about Tecumseh's War or the Battle of Tippecanoe, which I find infuriating. Or how Ms. Holm had never seen a Celeste Holm movie. The detective exchanged a befuddled look with Dr. Mallet, who nodded encouragingly, and then he observed, "As your doctor said, Miss Brigander, this is just a routine part of our inquiry. We're interviewing all of the patients from the seventh floor. You have nothing to worry about."

"What about nuclear winter?" I asked. "Isn't *that* something to worry about?"

"Nothing to worry about in regard to this investigation," explained Libby. "Now if you would please tell us anything you remember about yesterday evening."

Tell them what you did, said a voice. *Tell them how you screwed up.* "I didn't do anything, goddamit," I snapped.

My anger had been directed at the voice, but Detective Libby appeared alarmed. "Nobody says you did anything wrong," he assured me. "We just want to know what you recall."

I had already decided to keep my own counsel—at least, until I managed to figure out what was amiss. Hadn't I promised Big George not to share his secrets with a soul? Why should his death absolve me of my pledge? Besides, I had no intention of snitching on Big George's brother, and even though I had zero idea where Little Abe might be hiding, I didn't need NYPD on my trail if I tried to find him. "Recall about what?" I asked.

"About last night," said Detective Libby.

"Oh, last night," I echoed. A long, uncomfortable silence ensued. "Let me see," I said. "When do you want me to start? At sundown—like the Jews do. Or at a particular time? Say, Detective Libby, is that a Jewish name? Because you see lots of Jewish head-shrinkers, but not so many Jewish cops." As I said, feigning madness is easy enough once you get the hang of it.

"It's not Jewish," said Libby.

At the same time Dr. Mallet interjected, "Detective Libby's religion isn't relevant at the moment, Henrietta."

"So what *are* you then?" I asked. "A lot of you cops are Irish Catholics, right?"

Dr. Mallet began to intercede again, but the detective silenced him with his hand. "It's an English name," he said—clearly trying to meet me halfway. "Since you ask, my ancestors came over on the Mayflower."

"Was that a long time ago?" I inquired. "Or recently?"

The detective ran his fingernails through his thinning hair. "Let's focus on last night," he said. "Let's say any time between seven o'clock and midnight. Why don't you start off by telling me what you were doing at seven o'clock yesterday evening?"

"It's hard to say. I don't usually wear a watch." We must have gone back and forth like this for at least fifteen minutes. It was an exchange straight out of *Perry Mason* or *Inherit the Wind*—a performance to rival Uncle Drake's stonewalling of the House Un-American Activities Committee. What Detective Libby and Dr. Mallet didn't know is that I'm descended from battle-hardened veterans of courtroom drama. One Brigander served as a character witness during the court martial of General Billy Mitchell, while a Van Duyn by marriage took the stand against President Andrew Johnson during his impeachment trial. Even Grandma Brigander, who, when I knew her, passed her days in the solarium, dozing under an electric heating pad and correcting the grammar in the *Boston Globe* with a red fountain pen, had once covered the Lindbergh baby-napping trial for the *Herald-Tribune*. If President Clinton could dispute the meaning of *is*, I'm entitled to clarification on the definition of *yesterday*. Yesterday in San Francisco, after all, is nearly the day before in Shanghai.

I give Detective Libby credit for his patience and his even keel—if someone *I* were questioning constantly interrupted me to ask how much a cruise on the *Mayflower* might cost, or whether it didn't feel isolating to be a lone English cop surrounded by Irish Catholics, I'd have slit my wrists. Vertically, I should emphasize, not horizontally. But Libby didn't betray his frustration, except once, when I answered his question about whether I'd seen anything unusual the previous night by asking, "Can we backtrack for a moment, detective? When you said your ancestors came over on the Mayflower, did you mean all of them or only some of them?" That brought a bit more color to his already ruddy cheeks and his smile briefly tightened into a grimace.

Winston Mallet must have known I was faking—my responses resembled no known psychiatric disorder—but he didn't call my bluff. I suspect he might have appreciated my ripostes and parries for their entertainment value, and I'll confess that I also found myself thoroughly enjoying the joust. Not that I didn't have a serious purpose as well. My aim was to learn what the police knew of the killing without playing my own cards.

Eventually, Detective Libby's interrogation took a more aggressive tack. He retrieved a cup of coffee and a cheese Danish from the sideboard, then returned with the question, "So let's get to the point of all this, Henrietta. What do you know about Mr. Currier's death?"

"Oh, *that*," I replied. "I try not to think about it."

"I'm going to have to *ask* you to think about it, Henrietta. Please make an effort to recall what you remember about last night's incident."

Libby's tone suggested the time for playacting had passed. "I didn't see anything different from anybody else," I said. "I heard a scream and when I came out into the hallway, there was Angry O'Dell holding a bloody knife in his left hand like Orson Welles in *Macbeth*. Only Mr. Welles wields the fatal dagger in his right hand." The reason I remember this detail is because Welles favors opposite sides in various films. He's right-handed in the Shakespeare adaptations and *Citizen Kane*, but left-handed in *Touch of Evil*. "He was ambidextrous, you know."

"You're telling me Mr. O'Dell is ambidextrous?" asked Libby.

Now *I* laughed. I'd tangled him up that time without even intending to. "No, *Mr. Welles* was ambidextrous. All I know about O'Dell is he was holding that knife in his left hand."

That seemed to satisfy Detective Libby, but as I replayed the memory of Angry O'Dell clutching that serrated knife, my mind went into overdrive. Even the voices peeled away for an instant, I was thinking so hard. Libby continued his questioning, but I barely heard him.

"I'm told you were friendly with George Currier. Is that so?"

"Friendly enough, I guess" I answered on auto-pilot. "We only met two days ago." I saw no reason to mention the swat with the magazine or the premonitory kiss. Especially since my premonition had obviously been so wrong. A passionate embrace may bind you to a man emotionally, even if your lips locked only in an aura, but it's not exactly admissible evidence. I recalled the gleam in Big George's pupils after he thwacked my rump and found myself fighting back the urge to sob for what we'd both lost.

"I see," said Detective Libby, oblivious to my suffering. "And you don't know any reason why Arnold O'Dell might wish him harm?"

"Not a clue," I replied. "May I please leave now?" I wanted to be alone to think.

Detective Libby stood up and thanked me for my time. As I followed the patient care associate back to the eighth floor, my mind kept rewinding the tape: Lucille from Florida screaming, Nort the Messiah clutching his pillow to his chest, squall-eyed Angry O'Dell holding the knife away from his body like the carcass of a dead animal. And that's when the insight struck me. I recalled an incident forty-five years earlier, when Rusky came home sobbing from Little League practice, demoted from shortstop to first base. Because he was a southpaw. And while I don't know much about baseball, what I do know—largely because it changed the trajectory of my brother's athletic career—is that you can't be left-handed and play short, since by the time you get into throwing position, the batter will already be safe on the bag.

So that's when I did a bit of shaving with Occam. If Angry O'Dell had once been the best shortstop prospect in Queens, he couldn't be a lefty. And if he wasn't a lefty, why on earth would he have stabbed Big George with his left hand? It made no sense. I guess he could have stabbed him with his right hand and then transferred the weapon to his left hand—but for what reason would anyone, sane or crazy, do that? No, the whole kit and caboodle didn't add up.

Once Detective Libby had finished his questioning, Dr. Mallet proved more than happy to honor my 72-hour letter. By noon, I was back in my street clothes, reunited with my shopping cart, and shambling down 14th Street under my flamingo tuft to the stares of toddlers and tourists. One woman, likely hoping to dispel her young daughter's curiosity without having to introduce concepts like mental illness and street homelessness, explained that I'd probably forgotten to change out of my Halloween costume. The vestiges of the previous night's trick-or-treating still scarred the landscape: a discarded orange loot bag emblazoned with a jack-o-lantern's grin, streaks of shattered eggs on the sidewalks along the avenue. When I was a girl, we'd been chauffeured out to the Greek enclave in Astoria and to the Italian section of Bensonhurst to solicit for candy, far more fertile ground that the luxury flats of Central Park West. Beseeching door-to-door among the marble birdbaths and porcelain icons of the Virgin Mary, Rusky and I had our first introduction to the American middle class—which Papa feared so deeply, and below which his progeny would soon sink. I also remember vividly, on a lawn beside an Orthodox church on Ditmars Avenue, the first time I laid eyes on a lawn flamingo. How could I have known? Anyway.

What I really craved at the moment was a quiet place to sit down and reflect, which is easy enough to find if you live in a solid middle-class enclave like Astoria or Bensonhurst, but is far harder to secure when you're out on the streets. Renegade Sally had a gift for sniffing out such places that was almost feline—the garden behind the rectory at the Cathedral of Saint John the Divine, the well-concealed map room at the Jefferson Market Library. It's so easy to close my eyes and imagine her there still: perched on an oak card catalog cabinet, teeth slightly too large for her jaw, beaming like she owned the planet. That's the peculiar disconnect between reality and memory. If I hadn't known that Renegade Sally's glomeruli had stopped filtering, that she lay under six feet of earth on Hart Island, I'd probably still have pictured her dispensing wisdom among those nineteenth century atlases and blueprints for colonial Manhattan. I remember once, during winter break at Bryn Mawr, one of the Schuyler Sisters and I rode a New Haven-bound train up to New Rochelle to surprise Mrs. Bonnefield, our third grade teacher, who'd retired to the suburbs to breed daylilies and paint watercolors. We'd done this every year since we turned fourteen, always assuming that the Bonnefields would be home to greet us. And they always were. Where else would they go? Until that December, when Mr. Bonnefield answered the door in his sweater vest and slippers, and I could discern at once from the polite vacancy of his greeting that his wife was dead. From an aneurysm the previous October, it turned out. But for us, until that moment, she'd been enjoying tranquil days in Westchester, painting and brewing tea and raising money for the Daughters of the American Revolution.

Poor Mr. Bonnefield. I don't think I've ever missed a man the way he missed Mrs. Bonnefield, not even Michael Landon, but I do miss Renegade Sally terribly. That first day we met on the sunken plaza surrounding the Peace Fountain opposite the cathedral, I was in a bad way. Set to kill myself, in fact, lugging the last of my possessions in one of Mama's leather garment bags and an aluminum Rimowa suitcase I'd salvaged from the curbside. I still wore a Bellevue name band around my wrist and a hospital gown under my jacket—this was long before I'd found my hallmark hat or taken to rummaging for an avian-themed wardrobe. The voices were tormenting me something awful—this was also before I'd learned to manage or mollify them effectively, which is an entire career in itself—and I settled down at the base on the fountain to sob, my hands over my ears to block out the traffic. That's when Renegade Sally deposited herself down right beside me, all chest and rump, and said, "This is a *happy* fountain. You'd better cheer up before you bring the rest of us down with you."

I removed my hands from my ears and surveyed the site. It was a dreary, windswept afternoon in March and we had the place to ourselves. "The rest of you?"

"It's the *royal* rest of us. Like the royal we," said Renegade Sally. "I'm Queen of the Island of Manhattan. Mayor Koch and all them just don't know it yet."

I smiled. I didn't mention that we'd had Ed Koch over to our apartment for canapés and cocktails several times in the early seventies, when he was still a congressman, and Uncle Drake was still on the Princeton faculty, and the two of them could pal around without drawing attention. Sometimes it's best not to divulge too much—a lesson I'm always learning the hard way. Renegade Sally smiled back—as though we'd signed an indissoluble contract in blood. "I've got just what you need for your troubles," she said. She reached into her satchel and produced a turkey sandwich.

"Thank you," I said, ever the polite Brearley girl, "but I'm afraid I have problems that cannot be solved with a sandwich."

"Take it," she insisted, forcing the moist clump of bread and meat into my hands. "Eat up. Trust me. If you eat a good sandwich, they can never snatch that away from you."

Her wisdom reminded me of Papa's creed—what he called "The Doctrine of the Wealthy Pessimist": "You might as well drink the good wine tonight, because who can say when the proletariat will destroy the wine cellars." He was speaking ironically, of course, and he preferred Courvoisier to wine, but his prophesy came to pass, more or less. All of those Mouton-Rothschild cabernets and Chateau Lafites he prized so much ended up on the auction block, sold off to hedge fund managers and venture capital gurus who couldn't tell a

Cheval Blanc from a vat of vinegar. But Renegade Sally had a point. And I *was* famished. So I ate the sandwich. And then she announced that she was going to be my "mentor"—as though she'd been an upperclassman at Bryn Mawr, assigned to be my Big Sister for orientation—and, from that moment forward, she showed me how to navigate the streets on only my wits and the profits from recycled cans.

Sally wasn't mentally ill, I soon learned, not in the diagnosable sense, she was just one of those people who marched to her own drummer—not like Thoreau, who talked a good show but enjoyed Sunday suppers with Mrs. Emerson—but someone who didn't like to be hemmed in by rules. Her mother had worked an assembly line in Muncie, Indiana, manufacturing ladies' cotton parasols. The only things Sally hated more than rules were Midwesterners and umbrellas.

So as much as I wished I could ask Renegade Sally for advice about Big George's death, I already knew what she'd have said: "What are you afraid of? You're homeless and broke. What's to be scared of? How much worse could it be?" I could see her saying it too—hands on her colossal hips, incisors projecting over her lower lip, her voice tinged with loving despair, as though to say, "You made me come all the way back from the hereafter just to tell you *this*." I suppose it was good advice too. What *did* I have to lose? But I was still frightened. It's one thing to be homeless and broke—and quite another to be mixed up in murder.

I kicked around the East Village for several hours—saying a prayer for Big George inside Grace Church, browsing the prints of movie stars on the racks at Ye Olde Poster Gallery—then set off to meet Tecumseh Muhammed at the cube-shaped statue in Astor Place. That's our rendezvous point. If we ever find ourselves separated—whether because we're entangled in the criminal justice system, or caged in the nuthouse, or because Tecumseh Muhammed's too high to tolerate human companionship—we always stop by The Cube at precisely five o'clock on our first evening of freedom and sobriety to reunite. (I know what you're thinking, *Buy a cell phone!* Easy enough to say if you're sitting on the commuter train, reading a mystery novel, but you try signing up for cellular service when your official mailing address is c/o General Delivery, James A. Farley Post Office, New York City.)

Our system has worked well enough for eleven years, although once, when he was confined on Roosevelt Island for court-ordered tuberculosis treatment, I visited that damn sculpture for sixty-two straight days before I found him. But I didn't give up. You can say lots of unpleasant things about Granny Flamingo—but you'll never have grounds to call me a quitter. Once I make a commitment, I stick to it like a barnacle. Which, it turns out, is exactly what Tecumseh Muhammed and yours truly ending up fighting about that night.

The thing about Tecumseh Muhammed is that he's not a bad guy, not deep down, he's just not particularly gifted with insight. And, of course, he's an addict. Not that I don't come from a long line of addicts and boozers myself. No self-respecting Brigander took his morning swim without downing at least a pair of mimosas or a double screwdriver. Papa swilled his first cognac of the morning before his feet left his Swedish mattress. "Just breakfast in bed," he told Mama. In Newport, he had a mini-bar installed alongside the squash courts. Uncle Drake was known to polish off a half dozen Bloody Marys before he hit the marina, and once he became so intoxicated on a hunting trip with some of his celebrity pals that he nearly "bagged" an equally soused Dean Martin. Yet these were the same men who'd ride down the Bowery in their luxury touring sedans, pointing out the winos with disdainful levity. And it's not at all lost on me that Tecumseh Muhammed was exactly the sort of guy they'd be laughing at. Only that night—as the Jews say on Passover, *why is this night different from all other nights?*—he was sober. And strikingly dapper in a new khaki bomber jacket. I waited for the traffic light to turn and pushed my cart across the street to meet him.

"*Some enchanted evening,*" I crooned—only marginally off-key. "*I might meet a stranger across a crowded street.*"

"What's that, baby?"

"It's a song," I said. "From a Rogers and Hammerstein musical." I knew not to explain further. There had been a time when it mattered to me whether Tecumseh Muhammed knew the difference between Arlene Francis and Connie Francis, or Fred Allen and Steve Allen, but I'd grown to accept—admittedly, with reluctance—that the subways still run even if not everyone on the planet can name Elizabeth Taylor's seven husbands or all of the regular panelists on *What's My Line?* So I picked my battles accordingly. Besides, *not* knowing stuff can come in handy. I remember trivia night in Merion Hall at Bryn Mawr, when I identified "Pluto" as the ninth planet from the sun, while the "correct" answer on the laminated card was

"Mickey Mouse's dog." Binnie Chesterfield, the arbiter, refused to give our team credit; now I hear she's a federal magistrate in Atlanta. So maybe Tecumseh Muhammed is better off not knowing Rogers & Hammerstein from Black & Decker.

We exchanged a long, deep kiss. Say whatever you'd like about the man, but he sure knows how to kiss a gal. But with the memory of Big George's premonitory kiss still on my lips, I found my pleasure weighed down by guilt, and broke away. I heard a voice—a real voice, some passing teenager making a lewd remark about my ass—but what did I care? It comes with the territory. Tecumseh Muhammed didn't even seem to notice the truncated kiss. When I stepped back to size him up, he was grinning like a horse thief. "Nice jacket," I said.

"From Macy's," he answered. "Paid for it too. Honest to God."

"Sure, you did," I said. "And I'm Betty Grable."

"Such little faith, baby." Tecumseh Muhammed winked his one eye. "Of course, it wouldn't have been possible if that rich chick hadn't left her purse unattended." That was more his style. He modeled the jacket for me, even tucking his hand under the lapel like Napoleon. "Also met this cool dude at detox yesterday. Guy was born with a bum leg and the doctors had to take it off at the ankle—you know how it is, baby, you give an inch, they take a foot. His name's Nelson, but I call him Half Nelson." Tecumseh Muhammed paused for me to laugh, but I merely smiled, so he added. "*Half* Nelson. On account of the foot."

"I get it," I said. I realize it's his means of dealing with his eye—the way Papa's cousin, Gladys, used to tell spinster jokes—but I've never been able to laugh at wisecracks about other people's misfortunes. I like my comedy clean and family-friendly: Gracie Allen, Danny Kaye. But I suppose you can't ask for clean and sober humor when your man is dirty and drunk. I squeezed Tecumseh Muhammed's hip to show my affection. That worked too.

"So the dude started talking to me about how he's going to Key Largo, Florida, for the winter. One-way bus tickets are $82. What do you think of that?"

I shrugged. "I think Florida is far away." No reason to tell him that Grandpa Van Duyn's older brother, Manatee Phil, used to trawl for tarpon in Biscayne Bay. Or to mention the Bogart and Bacall movie. I fought back the itch to play his game and reply, *Your buddy, Nelson, doesn't have a leg to stand on.*

"Just think it over, baby," said Tecumseh Muhammed. "They got flamingos down there."

"And alligators," I said. "You sleep outside and one's liable to take off your arm." I was tempted to add, *You'll end up Half-Tecumseh*, but I didn't. No point in tempting fate.

Tecumseh Muhammed rubbed the bridge of his nose, probably thinking about alligators for the first time in his life. His people come from Alabama via Detroit; whatever Seminole they've got in them has been long buried under Rust Belt grime.

"So, big spender, did you get anything for *me*?" I asked.

Not that I *expected* anything. I'd known the man for eleven birthdays, and he'd only remembered the occasion once, which I'd considered a major accomplishment. So imagine my surprise when he reached into his duffel and produced a brooch shaped like a bird of paradise. Tiny gemstones of myriad colors formed the golden wings, the fuchsia breast and the flaming emerald tail. "See, I take care of my baby," said Tecumseh Muhammed, but his satisfaction had turned sheepish, suddenly ashamed at his own generosity. "Now what's our plan?"

I pinned the brooch to my chest. I felt truly grand. That's the challenge of loving a man like Tecumseh Muhammed. When you're finally fed up with all the benders and binges, all of the nasty spats and bloody lips, he goes out and buys you a bejeweled bird of paradise. Not for any special reason—not for a birthday or an anniversary—but just because he can. "Let's go sit in the park for a minute," I suggested. "You're not going to believe what happened to me."

So we crossed Third Avenue and headed down 9th Street until we reached Tomkins Square Park. I remembered when the entire park had been a homeless city—"Our Paris," as Renegade Sally used to call it—and also the police riots under Mayor Koch that cleared the place, while I was living under a pedestrian bridge and he was still enjoying canapés and cocktails. Back then you had skinheads and anarchists and junkies and over-the-hill hippies all sharing the land, a little oasis east of Avenue A where you could sleep a whole night through, at least in summer, without fearing a cop's truncheon. All you had to do was clear the crack vials off a patch of grass and set down your sleeping bag and you had it made. Maybe not paradise— but it was live-and-let-live, which is how I like it. These days, with all the Caribbean nannies pushing around white babies in strollers, a woman in a two-foot-tall flamingo hat just doesn't feel at home.

We settled down at one of the concrete chess tables. The night was warm for early November—not exactly Indian summer, but mild enough for outdoor busking or a romantic stroll. Two tables over, a con-artist I vaguely recognized was hunched over a set of heavy wooden chessmen, scamming a clean-cut college kid. The arrhythmic pings of their game clock punctuated our conversation like the warnings of a heart monitor. I related to Tecumseh Muhammed the events of the previous forty-eight hours—the argument between Monty and Sarge, Angry O'Dell and his missing screwdriver, Big George and his efforts to protect his counterfeiting brother. I didn't touch on the part about Big George sitting on my mattress, but gave the impression that he'd shared his story communally in the day room, and I certainly didn't mention the swat with the magazine. Or the premonitory kiss. Or my feelings of grief and devastation. What was the point of making Tecumseh Muhammed jealous—especially over a dead man? He listened patiently, as though waiting for a punch line, his one black eye narrowed into an inquisitive squint, his other socket dull and lifeless. (I'd always wanted him to wear a leather patch like John Wayne in *True Grit* and *Rooster Cogburn*, but he insisted upon the cheap, acrylic prosthetic that he got from the VA.) Yet when I told him about Angry O'Dell holding the serrated knife in his left hand, he didn't seem impressed.

"So? I don't see where you're going with this, baby," he said. "Maybe he put the knife down and then picked it up with his other hand."

"Why would he do that? It's not natural."

"Or maybe he *is* left-handed. That guy is crazy. You don't know if he was a left-handed shortstop or even if he played ball at all." He stood up, drawing his jacket tight at the collar. "I don't see how it matters either way. The bottom line is we need to find a place to sleep."

"It matters because there's got to be more to the story. Maybe Angry O'Dell didn't kill him at all. Maybe somebody else did and gave O'Dell the knife." I felt my voice rising, the blood coursing into my cheeks. In hindsight, I realize I probably did sound a bit off-kilter myself—I could already hear Dr. Robustelli documenting my suspicions as paranoia: worsening delusions with ideas of reference. Yet just because a woman's mildly paranoid doesn't mean that Albanian mobsters don't conspire to bludgeon innocent people to death in their sleep. And I kept thinking about how nobody bothered to investigate Rusky's "accident," how that empty shaft had swallowed the person I loved most on the planet and not a soul had cared. I still regretted not pursuing the matter further, even conducting my own investigation. After our premonitory kiss, felt I owed it to Big George—to the memory of our connection—not to let the circumstances of his death also go unexamined. "Don't you think it's all rather suspicious?" I insisted. "A man comes to the hospital to hide from people who are trying to kill him—and he ends up murdered."

Tecumseh Muhammed shook his head just like he had done when I'd mentioned the pet store. "So what? The guy is dead. And he's nobody we know."

"*I* knew him," I snapped. My tone revealed all I'd been trying to conceal—and probably more. Tecumseh Muhammed's shoulders stiffened. His hand shuffled inside his jacket pocket, as though fingering an imaginary switchblade.

"If it's so important to you, why not tell the cops?" he asked. "I'm sure they'll want to know that their killer is using the wrong hand."

"Screw you. Why do you have to make things unpleasant?"

Tecumseh Muhammed reached out—and I feared he might slap me, but he merely grabbed hold of my face between his fingers and thumb. Any middle-class couple passing through the park would have guessed we were fighting over money or drugs, not over whether to investigate a murder. But nobody would ever think to intervene or call 911—because, in the eyes of middle-class passersby, we're the sort of people who are *expected* to squabble in public places, whose natural inclination is to rough each other up. So what's the point of standing in the way of the inevitable? That's an all risk, no reward proposition. "I'm not the one making things unpleasant, baby," said Tecumseh Muhammed.

"Let go," I whispered—not wanting to draw attention. "You're hurting me."

He did, but with a final squeeze, and I could still feel his grip in my cheeks. "You get him all out of your system," he said. "I'll see you tomorrow night at five o'clock."

I resisted the urge to shout something nasty. I'm not the one whose mother abandoned him in a laundromat at age nine or whose country stole his vision and kicked him to the curbside. And I *was* cheating on him with Big George—emotionally, at least. Okay, more than emotionally. In my book, a premonitory kiss still counts as a kiss. Besides, I knew Tecumseh Muhammed was never going to do me any real damage. No, what upset me the most was that I had hoped he'd help me figure out my next move. I needed his *advice*. His *support*. And going to the police obviously wasn't a solution. To tell them what? That Angry O'Dell might have played shortstop for a sandlot baseball team twenty years earlier, so he probably hadn't killed Big George. That's a hard sell—even if you're not shaving with Occam. Leagues away from the sort of evidence Detective Libby and his ilk put a label on. Also, that would have meant telling the cops all I knew about Little Abe, which was exactly what I wanted to avoid. Who is going to take crime tips from a certified lunatic like yours truly anyway?

No, if I wanted answers, I understood, I'd have to find them myself. And I *did* want answers. I owed it to Big George, and to Angry O'Dell, and most of all, I owed it to the truth.

CHAPTER FOUR

Let's face it. Yours truly isn't exactly Sherlock Holmes, or even Inspector Clouseau, but one of the lessons of this story is that you don't have to be a trained gumshoe, or for that matter, the president of Mensa, to solve a murder. You don't even need a sidekick like Nero Wolf's Archie or Hercule Poirot's Hastings, despite what you see in the movies, although I'll confess that as I rode out to Jackson Heights on the #7 train, I rather regretted not recruiting Tecumseh Muhammed to my cause. A sullen, cantankerous, one-eyed dope fiend may not hold a candle to Doctor Watson, but an unenthusiastic sidekick is better than no sidekick at all—especially when you're terrified of the Albanian mob and wake up with "the lonelies" in your bones.

I'd spent the night camped out on a heat-releasing vent behind the 59th Street Con Edison plant, missing Mama and Papa, and Renegade Sally, and now Big George, and most of all Rusky, who would have been the perfect sidekick for a whodunit. We could have been like William Powell and Myrna Loy in *The Thin Man* films, only they *were* a couple—in the films, not in real life—while we'd have been brother and sister. (Powell, for the record, was married to Broadway's Eileen Wilson, comedienne Carole Lombard and Hollywood actress Diana Lewis, while Loy's husbands were producer Arthur Hornblow Jr., Admiral Gene Markey, diplomat Howland H. Sargeant, and some guy named John Hertz. Who says I don't know anything?) But as you're already aware, thirty-four years ago Rusky went down an elevator shaft at the Brooklyn County Courthouse, and nobody bothered to lift a finger to find out why. So I woke up without a brother *or* a husband—just stiff knees and a blouse damp from cold perspiration—and decided that the most logical first step, if I wanted to know what *really* happened to Big George, would be to locate his twin brother. And since Little Abe had been having an affair with an Albanian woman in Queens, that seemed as good a place to start as any. How many Albanian-operated motels could there possibly be in Jackson Heights?

The answer to that question turned out to be seven. In Queens, at least, Albanians cluster in the lodging industry much as Israelis control the locksmith business, and you can't get a pedicure without hearing a few words of Vietnamese. Good for them, I say, but I wish they'd at least band a bit closer together geographically like the Indian restaurants on East 6th Street in Manhattan—although I realize a row of downscale motels doesn't have the same logic as a block of curry houses. I also didn't have much to go on—other than that I was searching for a large Albanian woman with a Greek-ish given name and a taste for handsome, stocky men in their late fifties—so I just sauntered into the office of the first lodging listed in the AAA guide that I'd "borrowed," sans card or privileges, from the Yorkville Branch Library. I was careful to make sure I wasn't being followed; ever since I'd decided to investigate Big George's murder, I'd been struck with a deep sense of foreboding, a chill in the gut, that I might be the next mentally-ill woman to meet a suspicious death while the world remained indifferent.

The motel was a low-slung, no-frills structure hugging Northern Boulevard with a sign out front flashing V CA CY at a frequency to trigger epileptics. I asked for the manager's wife. Needless to say, the clerk proved a tad reluctant to disturb his boss's helpmeet for a woman crested with a two-foot-tall exotic bird, even one with a bejeweled bird of paradise brooch, but after a brief standoff, I suppose he concluded that summoning the proprietress to the front desk was the fastest way to get me out of his lobby. Unfortunately, the woman in question was a lissome waif in her twenties—certainly not Fat Athena. I complimented her on her shoes, mundane gray slingbacks, feigning interest in where she'd purchased them, because that's the surest way to keep another woman from sending the police after you, and I hightailed it back out to the sidewalk.

My next five encounters served up variations on a similar theme, although none of the other proprietresses sported heels and one of the owners proved a bachelor. At another tumbledown joint, the farcically-named Grand Hotel of Jackson Heights, jointly operated by three elderly sisters, the wizened trio gave me a spinach pie and a helping of potato salad for the road. Not one of the antediluvian trio appeared particularly familiar with the classic film that shared their outfit's name, because I drew quizzical sneers when I peppered them with quotations from John Barrymore and Joan Crawford. Not surprising—but disappointing, nonetheless. And a marketing oversight as well. If they were going to name their rinky-dink roadhouse after a celebrated fictional venue, they might at least have benefited from an ironic marketing campaign. Something like: "Unchanged since Greta Garbo slept here. Even the bedding." But how they run their derelict establishment is their business, I suppose. Anyway.

I didn't dare ask them if they knew Abe Currier or of a competing venture operated by an illiterate fellow who preferred his women in jumbo sizes. Instead, I told them I was looking for my long-lost brother, whom I'd promised to meet at a motel whose name I'd forgotten. They ran through the five enterprises I'd visited, disparaging each in its turn, and then muttered among themselves, before the youngest, a homely creature with a hirsute mole on her chin, announced, "You could try the Shepherd's Inn. Not that *we'd* ever stay there." Disdain dripped from her tongue like goose fat.

"Of course, *you* wouldn't stay there," I observed. "You already own a motel."

My reply appeared to bewilder the elderly lady. Cogent thinking, I've found, often has that effect upon people—but I suppose we can't all be logicians. At first, she attempted to explain herself, then sized me up with a cursory rake of her eyes and stopped short. "You'll have to take the train," she said. "It's halfway to Flushing."

I thanked them for the free food and asked them to send my best to Ms. Garbo, if they ran into her, but I fear the reference was entirely lost upon them.

Among the few advantages of being crazy, and homeless, is that even during rush hour, commuters give me a wide berth on the subway, so it wasn't a particularly objectionable trip, although getting a free swipe through the turnstile is more challenging in the outer boroughs. I suppose a free swipe costs you nothing if your parents live on Sutton Place, and your father entertains clients at Le Bernardin, and the only reason you're taking a subway at all is to create the illusion of financial independence, or because it's not cool to show up at your Sierra Club internship in a chauffeured Town Car. It's hard to imagine Papa ever taking public transit, but if he did, he'd gladly have bankrolled tokens for all of Times Square. Even Uncle Dewey, whose politics ran slightly to the right of Attila the Hun's, wasn't above giving a few Harvard men a free lift down to New Haven for the boat races in his Dassault Falcon. But if you're a middle-class working stiff, and another pint of soul ekes out of you with every day shingling roofs or trimming hair or installing mufflers, only to see Uncle Sam swipe a third of your paycheck for the welfare of crazies like yours truly, you can't help resenting me for my good cheer and my flamingo crest and my presumed lack of industry. You don't think to yourself: that woman is on her way to solve a murder. Or even: that woman wouldn't need my help if we let her open a pet shop. You think: that woman should get herself a job so she can afford her own Metrocard. Of course, some of you would express that monition in saltier terms than others, which is why finding free swipes in Queens is like catching a particular minnow in the Pacific. On most days, I'd have taken the risk of vaulting the turnstile, but I couldn't chance spending a night in the lockup while Little Abe's trail went cold.

A Christian pamphleteer sporting a chintz dress and black snood finally took pity on me and swiped me through, while subjecting me to a serenade of religious exhortations, and ten minutes later, I was strolling down Roosevelt Avenue, past the Eritrean hairdressers and the Korean laundries and the five-and-dime variety stores with marquees in Cantonese and Marathi. The notion dawned upon me that if I were going to conduct a thorough investigation, I'd need a notebook to record my results, so I ducked into a stationery-and-party-supply shop. Sadly, the leather-skinned proprietor—a fellow hardly as tall as my own shoulders—took me for a thief, rather than an agent of truth and justice, and trailed me through his aisles like a bloodhound. Twice he asked, "Lady, you need help?" And twice I replied, "No, thank you. I'm just browsing." But that didn't reassure the fellow. I swear the suicide minders at Mount Hebron could take a lesson from the guy. What I yearned to tell him was that he sold hardly anything worth stealing. Believe me, if I wanted to risk a larceny charge, I'd be pinching stuffed herons and plush, life-size moas at Mary Arnold Toys, or one of those emerald tanager lockets from Van Cleef and Arpels on Fifth Avenue, not streamers and plastic kazoos out of unsorted bins. Eventually, I settled upon a turquoise spiral-bound notepad with a pair of nuthatches on the cover. Could there be any better feathered companions for a schizophrenic gal obsessed with birds? I paid cash. The proprietor examined each coin as though I'd foisted wooden nickels on him. I'm surprised he didn't test the metal with his teeth. That was one of those rare moments, I'll confess, when I still regretted the loss of the Brigander fortune. What I wouldn't have given to ask the fellow if he could break a $1000 bill, like the ones Grandpa Van Duyn had stacked inside his bomb shelter in lots of five hundred, or even just to smack Papa's no-limit Diners Club card down at the register! Leather-face did get his comeuppance, although through no doing of mine. While he was verifying the authenticity of my three dollars in quarters, I noticed a pair of teenage girls in tartan skirts stuffing their pockets with M&Ms and candy bars. I gave the kids a surreptitious thumbs-up, yet when I trailed them onto the sidewalk and asked for a bite of chocolate, they ran off, giggling. Ingratitude, as Lear laments, is a marble-hearted fiend. But I was after knowledge, not sweets, so I tucked my new notebook into my shopping cart and continued along Roosevelt Avenue.

The appearance of the Shepherd's Inn lived up to its reputation. The motel was a freestanding concrete structure, shaped like a horseshoe, surrounded on all sides by cracked asphalt. Across an alley stood a tanning salon that also offered "exotic and oriental massage" in neon; the opposite corner boasted a pawn shop and a storefront that, according to the faded signage, had once been Fleischmann's Bowl-A-Rama & Karaoke. What a thoroughfare to name after the Roosevelts, who, in my memory, had been such lovely people—as least, the generation that had visited us in Newport, especially John, FDR's boy, who'd become a Republican, and who proved Mama's perennial nemesis at cribbage. But all the Roosevelt sons are gone now, and I suppose they don't make Roosevelts like they used to, any more than they make Briganders like Great Grandpa Rutherford, who singlehandedly cornered the international silver market after the Panic of 1907. I read somewhere that it takes an average of four generations for a moneyed family to lose its fortune— and I guess I'm People's Exhibit A. I stashed my cart behind a dumpster, wiped the vestiges of spinach pie from my blouse, and tucked my notebook into my handbag. Anyway.

It was a rundown fleabag of a motel with a synthetic paradise palm in the lobby, a plant that, even though conjured from plastic and silk, still looked water-starved. Dogs growled from behind the front desk, where a curvy, olive-skinned woman with onyx hair struggled to complete a crossword puzzle. Her expression displayed all the joy of Niobe weeping for her children. Fat Athena! Only she was rather attractive, despite her weight, not the rotund freak I'd imagined. If she'd left her husband for Little Abe, I realized, and I'd wed Big George, the two of us would have become sisters in marriage, and I wondered if there weren't a special etiquette for greeting a woman only two contingencies short of being a close relative. But unlike Grandma Van Duyn, who'd attended Miss Graham's with Emily Post, my tutelage in such matters had been aborted, so all I said was, "Good morning." Yet even as I served up a smile, I half-feared a legion of Zoot-suited hitmen might burst from the closets wielding tommy guns.

Fat Athena looked up, mournful and indifferent. "We've got rooms by the night for $89 and rooms by the hour for $19, but all payment is in advance and non-refundable—and if you're renting by the hour, no guests under eighteen."

"I'm not looking for a room," I said. "I'm looking for Little Abe Currier."

That hit Fat Athena like a double dose of Narcan. She nearly toppled from her swivel stool, then eyed me with suspicion. "Can't give out info on our guests," she said. "But if I do come across a fellow by that name, I *might* be able to deliver a message. Depending. What's your interest in Mr. Currier?"

"His brother died. Big George. I just thought he'd want to know."

"And *you* are?"

"An old friend of Big George's. From Newport. I used to help him out from time to time around the marina."

The connection seemed to relax her a bit—and I don't exactly look like a mobster. Or NYPD, not even undercover NYPD, who generally travel in pairs, decked out in Yankees paraphernalia. If Babe Ruth and Lou Gehrig show up on your doorstep, warned Renegade Sally, you can assume you're in deep trouble.

"Do you know Abraham?" asked Fat Athena

"Never met him in person. Though I feel like I know him through Big George's stories." Which wasn't exactly *un*true. But then I added, "The one story I'll never get over is how he forged that sixth copy of the Gettysburg Address and how it's still on display in the Smithsonian Museum in Washington. I guess I shouldn't be sharing that."

The proprietress responded with a flood of tears. "I'm sorry," she apologized. "It's just I haven't heard from him in weeks."

"That must be hard on business," I said—all false innocence. I relaxed a bit, no longer digging my nails into my palms, but still kept my eyes on the closet doors. "I imagine it's upsetting to lose a regular customer."

She shook her head. "Not a customer..."

That's when I went in for the kill. "Oh, you must be Athena," I said. "Big George told me how much Little Abe went on about you."

Or maybe Aphrodite, I thought, too late.

"I'm Antigona," said the Albanian woman. "Antigona Dushku."

"That's right. *Antigona,*" I echoed. "Big George was always telling me how fate had brought you and Little Abe together."

"Not fate, exactly," said Antigona. She sought to compose herself, producing a crimson compact and examining her makeup; streaks of eyeliner ran like veins of ore down her full cheeks, and even a napkin proved unable to staunch the flow effectively. Two stout Dalmatians emerged from behind the counter, mandibles slack and tongues extended, as though preparing a futile line of defense for their mistress. "Those three old bitches at the Grand Hotel threw him out onto the sidewalk because his checking account was in an out-of-state bank, so he came here."

"And you did the right thing by trusting him."

"Not at all. The checks were all 100% bogus. But by then we were madly in love, and you don't stop sleeping with a man—certainly not a man like Abraham—just because he's passed a few bad checks."

I sensed Antigona held to romantic principles consistent with my own. I admired that. Who was some DV counselor to tell me that Tecumseh Muhammed was bad news? I'm a grown woman. I can decide what's bad news without the help of a bunch of nosey parkers whose daddies bought them sociology degrees from Barnard. I can just imagine Ms. Celery Stalk talking down Caesar to Cleopatra, or warning Bonnie Parker that Clyde Barrow wasn't marriage material.

"I'm Henrietta," I said. "But my friends call me Granny Flamingo."

"Let's go into the back for a few minutes, Granny Flamingo," said Antigona. "We won't get any business before noon."

My hostess trundled to the front door and hung a chalked sign that read, "Holler for service! <u>Loud!!!</u>" She turned multiple deadbolts. "That should do it."

I followed her into a shabby inner office that doubled as a parlor. The ceiling sagged along one corner and evidence of an old leak mottled the wallpaper. Over a battle-scarred credenza hung a faded map of her homeland. On the opposite wall draped an Albanian flag from the Stalinist era with a gold star above the double black eagle. I also recognized one of the photos on the escritoire, of a handsome man punching the air in victory, as First Secretary Enver Hoxha. (Great Uncle Atherton Brigander had a similar photograph in his study on Jekyll Island from his days as Ambassador to Greece— only, in the version I was familiar with, Great Uncle Atherton and Hoxha and Marshal Tito of Yugoslavia stood side by side, stiff as a colonnade.) The young, pudgy couple in the other picture were presumably Antigona Dushku and her illiterate hotelier husband. They apparently lived in a converted suite adjacent to the office, three cluttered rooms that had once housed motel patrons.

My hostess patted the cushion of a Rattan chair, urging me to sit, and cleared reams of copier paper from another for herself. The dogs settled on the throw rug beside her and she nuzzled their scruffs. "Can I offer you a drink?" asked Antigona. "Rakia? Ouzo? A shot of absinthe?"

It was only nine thirty in the morning, and her offer made me nostalgic for my childhood. I could hear Papa asking for a martini "dry as the Sahara," then laughing as he urged one of the downstairs footmen to "hold the vermouth." I hadn't glanced twice at an alcoholic beverage—not so much as a thimble of schnapps or even a rum cake—since the family yacht had moored inside Davy Jones's locker. Instead, I settled upon a Diet Coke from Antigona's mini-fridge.

She filled a snifter with hard liquor. "I don't want you to get the wrong idea," she said. "When I'm my usual self, I hardly touch this stuff. But ever since Abraham vanished..." She collapsed in another fit of tears. I offered her a rag from my pocketbook to wipe her eyes, but she preferred a box of Kleenex from the end table. "You don't stop loving a man just because he runs off on you," she said. "I realize I shouldn't say that. I *am* married, you know...and there's nothing wrong with my husband...but sometimes love just bites you, like a piranha, and you can't shake it off."

I could relate—to the first part, at least. Big George's premonitory lips still felt fresh on my own. I also remembered how distraught I'd been while Tecumseh Muhammed wasted away in TB jail. I'd combed the morgues, the flophouses; I'd grilled guys coming out of Rikers and newly released from upstate. And *nothing*. So I wandered the city, bereft, grieving like a widowed osprey—like one of those Holocaust survivors returning to an ancestral village, searching the Pale of Settlement for a partner long gone. And the voices kept raining epithets down upon me like brimstone, blaming me and me alone for Tecumseh Muhammed's disappearance. I was madly in love with the bastard back then. What I'd have done to myself if he hadn't turned up, I hate to think.

My hostess jolted up suddenly, alarming the Dalmatians; their ears perked stiff like infantry on alert. "We've got to be careful. Vasil is jealous, murderously so. Especially since he found out about me and Abraham. He's swimming this morning—he's one of those polar bear persons—but there's no telling when he'll return. Sometimes I suspect he pretends to go to the pier, but sneaks back to spy on me."

Now we were getting somewhere. An instant later, what sounded like the popping of a series of champagne corks, or possibly bullets, sent me diving to the carpet. I braced myself for the hereafter, but instead of harps and lyres, all I heard was a ripple of Antigona's guffaws. Even the chubby dogs stood silent—torpid and entirely unfazed. "Aren't you on edge?" she observed. "That's just Nënë Roza."

"Who or what is Nënë Roza?"

"My mother," Antigona clarified. "Or my mother's new Oldsmobile, rather. She's still getting the hang of an automatic transmission."

I dusted myself off and climbed back onto the Rattan chair. Even I hadn't fully realized how on edge I'd been. I did want to solve Big George's murder, but I didn't want to end up in a Chicago overcoat and cement shoes.

"She hasn't passed the driving exam yet, so she does figure eights in the rear parking lot. It keeps her busy." Antigona nursed her liquor. "Off the roads, you might say."

And scaring the bejeezus out of innocent people! "How long has she been practicing?" I asked.

Antigona did a mental calculation. "Thirteen years next January. Nënë Roza can be something of a perfectionist."

"I see," I said. As much as her mother's persistence might have intrigued me on another occasion—I've always been fascinated by tales of human perseverance, blind barbers, and quadruple amputees who swim the English Channel, and Theravada monks constructing life-size models of Anuradhapura out of Tic Tacs—I wanted to keep our interview focused, so I asked, "Do you really think your husband could kill somebody?"

"In my homeland, Vasil was known as The Butcher of Tirana. Believe me, this was not a compliment," said Antigona. She lowered her voice, shaking her head as though recalling a memory so shameful that she almost doubted its truth. "When the Kosovo War broke out, all of his friends crossed the border and joined the Liberation Army. Even his brothers went. He stayed home and cut meat in his mother's butcher shop. Like an old man or an invalid. So my husband can skin a boar and carve up a goat, but it's hard to see him killing a human being." She scowled, seemingly disillusioned. "Shouting is another matter entirely."

I tried to conceal my own disappointment. "I'm asking because I suspect someone might have wanted to murder Little Abe. I think they killed Big George instead—by mistake. Although I still don't know how." I sipped my soft drink. "They were identical twins, after all."

"Identical twins? I had no idea."

"Little Abe never told you? How odd. In any event, my best guess is that this was a case of mistaken identity." That's what Occam's razor would have predicted, at least. If you have one man with a mark on his back and another who's an innocent bystander, but the two of them look exactly the same, then you can bet your bottom dollar that if the bystander ends up murdered, the intended target was the fellow with the target on his keister. Of course, even Occam's razor leaves behind some stubble on occasion, so you never know. And already, I was conjuring up problems with my theory. It didn't explain how the killer had gotten onto the psych ward in the first place, or how he'd managed to escape from the unit after the crime—and it certainly didn't account for the dumb luck that Big George would be rooming with a violent psychotic like Angry O'Dell, a lost soul who could be framed for the murder. What would the killer have done if Big George had been bunked up with a shrewd malingerer like Ray G.? Or a meek depressive from an upscale college? "I'm afraid it's all very puzzling," I said, as much to myself as to my hostess. "How did the killer even know that Big George was in Mount Hebron?"

"I'm at something of a loss," said Antigona. "You're a friend of Abraham's brother from Rhode Island, right? If you don't mind my asking, what are you doing in New York?"

"I came to visit him in the hospital," I explained. "He had a heart condition."

I saw no reason to mention the psychiatric component of our relationship. As soon as people hear you've been in the loony bin, they start to doubt your credibility. I recall once, a number of years ago—before the Internet made background checks so easy—a prominent European banker was admitted to the inpatient psych unit at Mount Hebron after a DWI. The doctors all thought he was manic, because he kept insisting he owned a chateau in Luxembourg, and six Lamborghinis, and had a ticket booked on the Concorde for the following morning. Of course, he turned out to be a Rothschild by marriage who'd merely savored too much Dom Perignon. Poor guy missed his flight too. And on another occasion, they admitted a notorious computer hacker who came to the Psych ER to "hide from the FBI"; the resident on call assumed he was psychotic, while in fact he was the subject of a high-profile warrant. As I said, context matters. And it's hard enough persuading strangers to believe you when you're wearing a flamingo hat, even when they suspect you're merely zany, rather than committable.

"And you say he was *murdered*? Abraham's brother?"

I sensed that we were traveling in circles, only unlike during my dogfight with Detective Libby, this woman seemed sincere in her obtuseness. I didn't think that I was blowing my own trumpet, at least not unreasonably, when I concluded that Big George and Little Abe might have looked the same, but they harbored extremely distinct tastes when it came to women. Intellectually speaking, at least. Of course, all of that rakia and absinthe must work wonders, of a sort, on the frontal lobe. I was about to explain once again to Antigona what had happened to Big George when the bell above the door jangled, followed by the slap of flip-flops across the parquet.

Vasil Dushku appeared in the doorframe: pot-bellied, hair protruding from the collar of his Hawaiian shirt, beach towel draped over his shoulder. And, cocked in one hand, a single-action antique gentleman's revolver of the variety displayed in military museums. So much for skinning boars and carving up goats. But Antigona's husband had apparently anticipated an adversary younger than myself, and thinner, and far more male. He lowered the pistol, perturbed—as though he possessed the courage to shoot a romantic rival only once, over the course of his entire lifetime, and I'd ruined his opportunity. Antigona, unruffled, sipped her liquid fire. The Dalmatians raced toward their master and nestled his bare knees.

"Who the hell are you?" Vasil demanded.

I'd been in this situation before. Well, not *exactly* this precise situation—I'd never had an Albanian hotelier threatened me with a vintage firearm—but I'd dealt with my share of enraged drunks, and paranoid psychotics, and even jealous lovers. The key to survival was to remain calm and to pretend that nothing was amiss, like the orchestra on the *Titanic*. Okay, I guess that technique doesn't *always* work, but Vasil Dushku was a polar bear, not an iceberg. And his gentleman's pistol wasn't exactly a machine gun.

"I'm Henrietta Brigander, but everyone calls me Granny Flamingo," I announced. "I'm raising money to help disabled emus."

"You've got to be fucking kidding me?"

"Who would joke about a disabled emu?" I replied, earnest as granite. "It's no laughing matter. Every year, dozens of emus on farms across this great nation are injured by coyotes, or crippled trying to jump fences, and we have so few veterinary services to offer them."

Antigona set down her glass. "Mrs. Flamingo was just leaving, dear," she announced. "She's telling the truth," she added. "That *is* really why she's here."

"Why shouldn't it be?" I asked. "Who would lie about such a thing?" As I spoke, I gathered myself together and inched toward the door. "If you have a change of heart and wish to donate," I said, "or you know *somebody else* who does, you can always find me at our booth in Union Square. *Opposite the band shell pavilion.*" I feared I'd been too subtle in my effort to keep open the lines of communication with Antigona, but anything more overt might have elevated her husband's suspicions—and his rage—even further. As it was, Vasil Dushku flashed me a look of considerable menace. He didn't exactly move out of the way as I pursued my exit, but he made no concrete effort to impede my escape. I hadn't even advanced halfway across the lobby before I heard him cursing out his wife in Albanian; I understood the gist of his verbal assault without being able to translate a single word. We all have our Tecumseh Muhammed's to bear, I suppose. But I was grateful for the brief heart-to-heart with Antigona, and as soon as I found a quiet front stoop at a safe distance, I seated myself on the steps and jotted down my findings in my notebook.

I'd learned something important. Antigona Dushku might have been in love with Little Abe Currier, but she clearly didn't know where he was.

So much for my only lead.

In fictional mysteries, the reader can count upon Dashiell Hammett or Raymond Chandler or whomever giving his private eye enough information to solve the murder and apprehend the perpetrator. But real life crimes are more like gameshow challenges.

On Allen Ludden's *Password* or *The $10,000 Pyramid*, there's no guarantee a contestant will have enough clues, and she doesn't even know whether her information is sufficient to crack the puzzle. Her unknowns, as they say, are unknown. Some contestants don't win any money. Some crimes simply go unsolved. We may never learn the identity of Jack the Ripper, or who lurked behind the Zodiac killings, or what motivated the Black Dahlia homicide. The one thing that mystery novels and gameshows do have in common, however, is that neither the detectives nor the contestants get murdered (unless you count the case of Dorothy Kilgallen, but that's another story.) In real life, nothing stops a mobster from taking an amateur sleuth to swim with the fishes. One day I'm Jessica Fletcher, the next I'm *Lupara bianca.*

But even without any solid leads, and no prospect of locating Little Abe, and the ongoing threat of becoming another bitter statistic, I wasn't about to throw in the towel. As I said, I'm like a barnacle. So if I couldn't track down the intended target, I could always investigate the crime scene. On the ride back into Manhattan, after finishing the last of the three sisters' potato salad, I stole a page out of Detective Libby's workbook and composed a list of potential witnesses. This was my list:

Patients
Lucille from Florida
Alyssa the NYU student
Pryce Norton (aka Nort the Messiah)
Ray G.
"Miss Havisham"
"One-Brow Jack"
Arnold "Angry" O'Dell (suspect)
Henrietta Florence "Granny Flamingo" Brigander

Nurses & Doctors
Sarge
Bonnie Jean
Ms. Holm
Dr. Bhatt & Dr. Cotz-Cupper
P.J. – not a witness, but a good pretext to talk with him

Others
Monty Castillo & Mary Lou

I decided that I'd start by interviewing the other patients, just as Detective Libby had, only I'd ask them more pertinent questions—like did they know any Albanians. I also wanted to get a sense as to whether their financial circumstances had altered suddenly for the better, because I was operating under the suspicion that one of my fellow inmates (or does one say colleagues?) had been paid off to butcher Big George. That meant I was on the lookout for a new pair of sneakers or a three-day binge on Percocet and Vicodin, the sorts of indulgences a Mayflower-spawned gumshoe like Detective Libby wouldn't even notice. And I figured us crazies are the folks most likely to detect something amiss on a psychiatric unit, to spot those telling clues—like a weapon in the wrong hand—that NYPD would shrug off as inconsequential. We have a heightened awareness for these things, maybe because our other senses are off—like the way Rusky's blind cello tutor, Madame Kuznetsova, could hear Papa's Aston Martin when it pulled into the gatehouse at the summer cottage, while the rest of us couldn't perceive the vehicle, six cylinders and silent as a horsefly, until it rounded the orchard. Nurses and doctors, on the other hand, aren't terribly observant, so I planned to save interrogating the hospital staff for later. Besides, I'd had more than my fill of health care professionals for the moment.

It's always wisest to begin with the low-hanging fruit. That's a lesson I first learned from the Portuguese gardener, who'd take me with him in autumn to harvest pears and quinces, and later, in an entirely different sense, watching Uncle Drake flirt with each summer's new tennis pro or the shirtless Guatemalans hired to bury the power lines. For me, that meant a pit stop at the encampment under the Vanderbilt Avenue viaduct, opposite Grand Central Station, an isolated section of Pershing Square that Nort the Messiah and his followers claimed as their turf. Not that I could be certain of finding him there, at least not before nightfall. His gang might be out scavenging the metropolis for copper wire or purloining catalytic converters. But the one thing I was sure of was that he'd put in his three-day liberation request shortly after I had—nobody wanted to bunk three-to-a-room with the likes of Ray G. and "One-Brow Jack"—and that, under the trying circumstances of the past twenty-four hours, Dr. Robustelli would have been delighted to give him a decanoate injection and discharge papers.

On the way downtown, I stopped at a food truck near the Metropolitan Museum for lunch. It was nearly one o'clock and thinking about fruit had left a gnawing throb inside my stomach. The owner of the stand—the ultimate meals-on-wheels, I like to say—was the brother of a Pakistani vet who'd served with Tecumseh Muhammed in Germany. A *real* vet with an E-code and M.O.S., and dog tags jangling around his neck, not a doctored ID card from the VA. Both brothers were meaty, jovial fellows with British accents: Kashif and Farooq—the "revealer" and the "redeemer," according to the Qur'an, but the food vendor, Kashif, went by "Cash." He made a point of setting aside avian artefacts for me—photos of puffins clipped from magazines, or a holiday calendar depicting winter songbirds. And I could always count on him for a free bowl of Haleem stew and a hunk of chicken tikka masala on flatbread. "You are part of my *zakat*," he explained. "I'm not religious, but it's one of the aspects of Islam I admire." I could relate, sort of. Although Papa never took us to church as children, because Sunday mornings were prime regatta hours in summer and ideal cocktail hours the rest of the year, each autumn he aired out the grand ballroom for a black-tie affair to benefit the Episcopal bishopric.

I was tempted to duck into the museum for a few minutes of cultural enlightenment—there was indeed a Rubens show running, it turned out—but my primary motive would have been to spite Miss Celery Stalk, and I'm not one to mix art with malice. Once my stomach was full, I did venture into the Met, but merely to attend to my toilet needs, not to explore the Flemish Baroque, and then I got myself swiped onto the Lexington Avenue line for the southbound trip to the train terminal. Some narcissistic drunkard was taking up a whole stretch of seats, splayed like the guinea pigs that the wife of Papa's Ecuadorian falconer used to serve as delicacies when Rusky and I visited the couple's cabin. The offending bottle, malt liquor, still lay tucked into the rummy's lap like an advertisement for Prohibition. I had little sympathy, maybe because the sight hit too close to home. I firmly removed his legs from the seat and settled down beside him. He grumbled. Other passengers eyed me with a combination of envy and awe and disgust—what I like to call the "hobo's triad." Twenty minutes later, I greeted the afternoon at Pershing Square and, sure enough, Good Ol' Nort the Messiah sat perched under one of the iron struts of the viaduct, smoking a cigarillo and scrutinizing a checkers board.

Now is as good a time as any to clear up a misconception about Nort—one that you've probably developed already, largely through my negligence. Whatever odd ideas Pryce Norton may manifest, he does not—and to my knowledge, never has—held himself out to his followers as a savior or prophet. He's just a run-of-the-mill manic depressive with a penchant for synthetic marijuana and angel dust. Not even religious, as far as I know. His adherents, a motley band of teenage runaways and geriatric ex-cons and nomadic hippies, gravitated toward Nort because the guy had a gift for scrounging money from the pavement, so to speak, running a small-fry gang that trafficked in hubcaps and HIV meds and discarded wine corks— basically, goods too inconsequential to attract more organized criminals—and a reputation for divvying up the loot fairly. Last I'd heard, he'd made a killing in used ink cartridges. But if Nort didn't fancy himself the Son of God, he sure did *look* the spitting image of Jesus on the cross, at least as channeled by El Greco and Velasquez. Hence the moniker. When I found Nort at the checker board, which was balanced on a pair of milk crates, he stood embroiled in a death match with a scrawny teenage girl, a child who couldn't have been more than fifteen, and he sported a seamless white robe under a purple cloak that accorded with his cascading hair and bifurcated beard.

The girl leaned forward and slid a red draught between squares. Already her face wore the urchin's fierce defiance, camouflage for the forlorn resignation of the streets, while her cotton chemise revealed a seductive peek of cleavage. Nort the Messiah eyed her move warily, stock-still like an anhinga about to dive for prey, then hopped a black checker across the board with the ferocity of Pickett's Charge. "King me," he cried. Only when his victory stood secure, a moment later, did he shoo away his opponent and acknowledge me.

"You flew the coop quick enough," he said, combing his mane with his fingers as though looking for a sparrow. "That bastard, Robustelli, made me wait on my hands until almost noon for my discharge papers. Said it would teach me a lesson to stay on my meds."

"I guess he already knows I'm a lost cause."

"And you didn't want to stick around for more murder and mayhem?"

"You mean *something else* happened?"

Nort shrugged. "You sound awfully eager. One killing wasn't enough for you?"

"It's not that. It's only that I don't believe Angry O'Dell killed Big George."

"I know."

"You know?" I asked.

Nort started setting up the checkers board for another match. "Your man came through here earlier, preaching the gospel of oranges and sunshine," he explained. "Told me all about you being convinced you're Nancy Drew."

"I just have suspicions. What's so wrong with that?"

"I'm not judging, Granny. Just stating the facts," he said—as disdainful as Mama when referring to chain motels or stainless steel flatware. "Game of checkers?"

I begged off. The notion crossed my mind that I might lull Nort into a false sense of security if I indulged him—but I didn't trust myself both to hold up my end of the competition and to conduct an interrogation simultaneously. Multi-tasking isn't my strong suit. Besides, my voices proved distracting enough. In any case, Nort didn't appear offended. He signaled to one of his acolytes, another youth in need of a truant officer, and the kid vanished inside the train station, returning shortly thereafter with two cups of hot coffee. "On me," said Nort. He raised his cup and toasted, "To Dr. Robustelli. May he get crabs and prickly heat."

I thanked Nort the Messiah for the free drink and settled onto his opponent's bench.

"Do you mind if I you ask a few questions? About the killing?"

"Suit yourself, Nancy Drew," said Nort.

I opened my notepad and balanced it on my knee; I'll confess the pad made me feel a bit hardboiled, even invincible—like Rosalind Russell in *His Girl Friday*. "What I really want to know is if you saw anything unusual—not just last night, but even during the day."

Nort the Messiah appeared to mull over my question with gravity. I give him credit for that. But after a solid thirty seconds, he said, "I got nothing, Granny. It was just another crazy day in the bin. I don't even remember how I end up in there."

"How about Albanians?" I asked, hoping to catch him off guard with the non sequitur. "Do you know any Albanians?"

Nort appeared genuinely puzzled. "You mean people from Albany?"

I sighed inside my head. "People from *Albania*. It's a country in Europe. Have you had anything to do with immigrants from Albania recently?"

Nort sipped his coffee, pensive, as though the whole concept of Europe overwhelmed him. I remember feeling similarly overawed at about the age of seven, when I saw a public service announcement on television asking, *Do you know where your children are?*, which led to a discussion with Eira, the Welsh housekeeper, about children who ran away from home. Until that moment, the possibility that anyone would *want* to run away had never crossed my mind. If you didn't like your home, I'd asked, why not just buy another one someplace else? Or, to give Nort the benefit of the doubt, maybe he wasn't overwhelmed, but merely scouring his latent consciousness for hidden Albanians, striving to afford my question its due.

"Can't help you there," he finally said.

That didn't frustrate me as much as you might have expected. Negative evidence *is* still evidence. Maybe it mattered, I told myself, that an experienced inmate like Nort *hadn't* noticed something amiss at Mount Hebron. Maybe *that* was a clue. I considered asking him directly about whether he knew anything of Little Abe, but I wasn't sure if I wanted to play all of my cards—or checkers pieces, as the case might be—during the first round. As Grandpa Van Duyn used to tell me and Rusky, often as the punchline to his bedtime stories, "You only get so many bull markets in a lifetime, so use them wisely." While I was deciding how much I was willing to reveal to Nort, none other than Ray G. strolled under the aqueduct, hands in his jacket pockets, his neck buried deep beneath his upturned collar.

All the low-hanging fruit, it appeared, was congregating around the same tree.

"If it isn't a Mount Hebron reunion," said Ray G. "Fancy meeting you two here."

I'll confess up front Ray isn't my favorite human being. There may be no honor among thieves, as they say, and there's certainly nothing noble about being homeless or nuts, but I do believe that everyone, to the best of his abilities, should strive for decency. Like Renegade Sally offering me her last turkey sandwich. Or Tecumseh Muhammed telling his life story to troubled kids at Washington Irving High School each month—the one appointment he could be trusted never to miss. *Jeder nach seinen Fähigkeiten, jedem nach seinen Bedürfnissen*, as Steinmetz, Rusky's socialist German tutor, used to say. *From each according to his ability, to each according to his needs.* Maybe the Old Bolshevik's values rubbed off. Or maybe that's the *noblesse oblige* of the Brigander in me speaking—who can say? But the bottom line is that Ray G. lacked that fundamental righteousness that keeps people from ratting out their siblings or poisoning their grandmothers for the insurance money. He was what you might call a crook among crooks, the sort of fellow to push cocaine cut with dishwashing detergent or boric acid. If he'd been born several rungs up the social ladder, it was easy to picture him breaking into the Watergate Hotel. Or raiding the pension fund at U.S. Steel.

"I didn't expect to see *you* on the outside so fast," I said.

"Didn't have a choice. They threw me out." Ray G. spit indecorously onto the sidewalk. "Threw *all* of us out. Said we didn't have any acute needs. Bullshit."

"They emptied out the entire unit?"

That was the last thing I wanted to hear, a body blow to my investigation. I'd been counting on having a few days to link up with my fellow former inmates—maybe even a chance to steal onto the unit during visiting hours, if P.J. didn't object, at least to ask for last names and phone numbers. Former patients weren't technically supposed to be present on the ward as guests, because of concerns over contraband and weapons, but I was already a known commodity to everyone on the seventh floor, and not exactly a threat to the commonweal, so I'd been banking on them making an exception.

"All out. Except that college bitch and the old lady," griped Ray G. "College bitch gets to stay until tonight, so her parents can pick her up."

"But the unit's closed?"

"Closed for you and me. Open for rich white chicks," said Ray G.

"The old lady didn't strike me as rich or white," I observed dryly.

"Whatever. They're shipping her off to a nursing home. Gonna make glue out of her like an old horse." Ray spit again and cupped his tongue inside his cheek as though he had a toothache. "So that's that. Now be a dame, okay, and lend me ten bucks for a pack of cigarettes."

I reached into my brassiere and produced a bill roll—all ones. From my trove, I peeled off ten singles and pressed them into Ray G.'s palm. Leading by example has always been a Brigander mantra—which for Mama denoted crocheting a pair of fisherman's knit sweaters each winter for sale in the gift shop of New York Hospital, but for me meant showing the likes of Ray G. some generosity of spirit. Of course, I also had my ulterior motives. No self-respecting detective is above greasing the palms of potential witnesses when necessary.

Ray G. stuffed the cash into his jacket pocket without thanking me. "Lots of shit went down after you left," he said. "You know they're charging that O'Dell dude with murder."

"Who told you that?" I asked.

"Reporters. *New York Post*. It was a zoo outside the hospital when I got ejected—news crews, satellite trucks. And I did an interview with this hot lady reporter from the *Post*."

"What did you tell her?"

Ray G. shrugged. "Just what I saw. I gotta remember to check if I get quoted in the paper."

"And what exactly *did* you see?"

"Same thing you saw. Say, what's with all the questions?"

"Just curious," I said.

Nort the Messiah laughed without looking up from his checker board. "She thinks she's Nancy Drew."

"Who the fuck is that?"

"Some girl I knew as a kid," I said.

"She doesn't believe O'Dell is guilty," interjected Nort. "Thinks he was framed."

"I didn't say that," I objected.

Ray G. snickered. "You *are* nuts, lady. I saw the guy holding the knife with my own eyes. Turns out one of the guards didn't search him good enough."

"Monty?"

"If you say so," said Ray G. "Word is he's suspended. Gonna get canned."

"That's lousy," I said. I felt terrible for Monty. And for Mary Lou too. This wouldn't have been the first time an officer got sacked for missing a weapon, even though he'd done a thorough search and wanding. *I'd seen him.* My guess was that the wand itself was on the blink—and you couldn't blame a guy for overlooking a knife if you gave him a faulty metal detector. Or you could—and Mount Hebron would—but it was still a crummy way to treat a person.

"Don't know what you're all worked up about," said Ray G. "As far as I'm concerned, I'm just thankful that whack-job didn't take me out too. I'm glad they're firing your guard friend. Serves him right."

"You have to give that nurse credit," interjected Nort. "The way he talked down O'Dell. I didn't think the guy had it in him."

"You mean Mr. Brauer?" I asked.

"Probably," agreed Nort the Messiah. "Tall thin dude with the chinstrap beard—used to work night shift at the State Hospital. I remember him. Back then, if there was a whiff of danger in the air, he had a way of disappearing."

Nort had a point. I'd always taken Sarge for first-rate chickenshit. All bluster and bristle, like John Wray playing Corporal Himmelstoss in *All Quiet on the Western Front.* But sometimes, I've learned, a man rises with the occasion. Hadn't Great Grandpa Rutherford's stepbrother, Garfield, who'd bought a substitute to avoid serving under General Grant at Petersburg, given up his lifeboat seat when the Germans torpedoed a hole into the hull of the *Lusitania*?

"Hard to believe he's the same guy I remember from State," said Nort. "One time, I'll never forget this, a fight broke out and he tried to hide behind *an old lady*—a visitor, the mother or grandmother or something of one of the patients."

"People change," I said. I thought of Tecumseh Muhammed, who'd once have been thrilled to play Nick to my Nora, and Uncle Drake, in his bitter final years, when the tennis pros and assistant gardeners no longer took to his advances. "As my grandmother's friend, Tish Baldridge, once said, 'When we cannot change circumstances, we are forced to change ourselves.'" Miss Baldridge had been speaking specifically about fitting a warped mahogany leaf into the dining room table at Newport, on the occasion of a visit by Jackie and Aristotle Onassis, but I do believe the underlying principle can be generalized.

"I'm not so sure about that, Granny," said Nort. "I don't think people change all that much. They just reveal themselves."

Ray G. rolled his eyes. "Gotta get going," he said. "Sorry I don't have more time to shoot the shit, but a guy has business to attend to."

He gave Nort the Messiah a mock salute and ambled off. I didn't have an opportunity to ask him whether he'd noticed anything unusual on the ward or if he knew any Albanians. Luckily, he had to wait for the light on the cross street to change, and the signal still warned against walking when I realized a crucial opportunity was slipping through my fingers. "One last question," I called out, shuffling after him. "Do you remember what time that girl's parents are arriving to pick her up?"

"More questions," he said. But I suppose the ten singles in his pocket fed his congeniality, because he added, "I think Miss Clare said around seven."

"Thanks," I replied. "Thanks a million."

I could handle not interviewing the old lady; she was probably too demented to provide any useful evidence. In contrast, the NYU student struck me as a crucial witness, the sort of alert outsider likely to notice something amiss. Or, for all I knew, she was the killer. An Albanian hit-woman undercover. That seemed improbable, of course. But so did Granny Flamingo investigating a murder, so I wasn't ready to rule anything out.

I had several hours to squander before my five o'clock rendezvous with Tecumseh Muhammed—not enough time to track down and interrogate another potential witness—so I ducked into Vinny's Pizzeria for a slice. (The manager, Vinny Jr., breeds Lady Amherst's pheasants in his spare time, so he considers me something of a good luck charm, and the staff has a standing order to feed me for free. "Lots of folks feed pigeons," says Vinny Jr. "I feed a flamingo." And he does.) Then I headed down Broadway to the Strand bookstore and browsed the Film & Television aisle, where I read the first few chapters of a remaindered biography of Veronica Lake, who'd been a bridesmaid at Uncle Dewey's and Aunt Genevieve's wedding, and also a longtime correspondent of Cousin Adelaide, but had died when I was only a toddler. I was disappointed to find no Briganders or Van Duyns mentioned in the index, but not particularly surprised. For all of their money and influence, my kin kept a relatively low profile.

What I like about the Strand is you never know what B-list celebrity you're going to encounter there—if you're familiar with what they look like, that is. I once spotted the actor Glenn Ford in the New Age aisle, and another time, I watched the bandleader Frankie Carle buy his granddaughter an SAT prep book. I don't have many regrets in life, but not saying hello to Frankie is one of the biggest.

The other thing I did in the Strand was to ask one of the clerks, a busty girl with too little forehead and too much chin, to pass along a message to the owner, Fred Bass, that Henrietta Brigander sends her love. Fred's father, Ben Bass, who founded the Strand, had been a friend of Grandpa Van Duyn—an alliance that arose in the most unlikely of manners, when Newport's Clambake Club inadvertently offered membership to Ben, the Jewish book mogul from New York, instead of Perry Bass, the Waspy oilman who skippered a snipe-class dinghy to the Commodore Hub E. Isaacks Trophy in 1935. Once the mistake was discovered, Grandpa Van Duyn led the contingent who argued that there was no turning back. To repeat Grandpa's celebrated quote from the club's semi-annual directors meeting, whose repetition enlivened many a dinner conversation during my childhood, it was "given the less than palatable choice, better to socialize with a Jew than to give like an Indian." I once tried to explain to Tecumseh Muhammed that Grandpa hadn't meant any harm by this expression—that he'd have said it to Geronimo himself without a shred of shame or malice—but some things are impossible to explain unless you've lived through them, so I let him curse out the man who might have, under different circumstances, become his future grandfather-in-law, and then we agreed to disagree. Anyway.

I wasn't sure if Fred Bass still remembered me—we'd met once at a charity event for the Greenwich Village Historical Association when Hizzoner Abe Beame was mayor—but I saw no harm in maintaining the acquaintanceship, as far as I could. The clerk, whose nametag read "Karennn" (that's *not* a typo, she confirmed—"Karennn" with three n's), agreed to pass along my greeting, but who could say if she actually did. I thanked her, emphasizing each of the n's individually, and headed back to The Cube to meet my man.

That's when the first fortuity of this narrative occurred. I say fortuity, and not coincidence, because the latter implies that an event is unlikely, while many occurrences that we call coincidences are actually statistically to be expected—or, at least, belong to a class of events that are more likely than not to occur. This is known as the Mekinulov Effect, after Professor Sergei Mekinulov, Uncle Drake's colleague at Princeton. Here's how it works: you're watching a movie—let's say a gangster film with Edward G. Robinson—and you notice the getaway car has the same license plate as your brother's Cadillac. You think: what a coincidence. But the license plate could also have matched countless other plates (your cousin's Bugatti, the neighbor's vintage Delahaye cabriolet, the Talbot-Lago Grandpa Brigander once sponsored in the Monaco Grand Prix), or your phone exchange in Turtle Bay, or the combination to your swim locker at Rosemary Hall—only it did not, and you never consider all of the numbers that the license plate *didn't* match, nor all the other vehicles in that movie whose license plates proved unfamiliar, nor the many other gangster films you've watched where the getaway cars didn't trigger any connections. You get my point? That's the Mekinulov Effect, and it's why, when I tell you that on the stroll to Astor Place, I caught sight of that guy from Mount Hebron who Tecumseh Muhammed would have called "One-Brow Jack," had he ever meet him, I emphasize that it was a fortuity, but not a coincidence. After all, consider how many people I *didn't* meet on the stroll up to the Astor Place Cube: Little Abe, Sarge, P.J., Detective Libby, etc. I'm sure you understand what I'm saying. Anyway.

I was pushing my cart down Broadway toward 8th Street, trying not to let Big George's death get me down. You'd never have known this stretch of fitness centers and upscale college bars had once been the cultural capital of the Western Hemisphere, a cavalcade of playhouses where Lillian Russell and George M. Cohan entertained Tammany bosses, and where, backstage at Harrigan and Hart's Theatre Comique, if Grandpa Brigander were to be believed, Great Grandpa Rutherford once enjoyed a high-stakes poker match with Thomas Edison, P.T. Barnum and President Cleveland. On this same block of the Rialto, so recently frequently by showmen and starlets (recently, at least, by geological standards), I ran into One-Brow Jack, engaged in heated battle with a telephone booth. "Motherfucker," he shouted, shaking the stall by both walls like a deranged parent abusing a child. Under ordinary circumstances, I'd have kept on walking—but if you're going to investigate, you've got to take some risks.

"What's wrong?" I asked.

One-Brow Jack glowered at me. "Motherfucker."

He slammed his fist into the side of the booth—a full-on hook, like Rocky Marciano going after Joe Louis; I'd be amazed if he didn't crack a metacarpal or two. That seemed to exhaust his energy for a moment, because he rested his bloodied hands on his hips, catching his breath. "What do you want, lady?" he demanded. "Can't you see I'm busy?"

"You lose a quarter?" I asked.

"Other sucker did," he replied. "I'm just getting it back for him."

Some answers don't require further explanation. Had One-Brow Jack witnessed this particular payphone swindle another caller out of his hard-won pocket change? Or had the coin-napping occurred years earlier at a different location? Did it matter? Maybe all that mattered at that juncture was that a two-inch sheet of steel stood between this aggrieved man and a coin to which he felt entitled—and no amount of reason, or frustration, or even bodily harm, was going to keep him from getting it back. I kept thinking of that cottager in the fairy tale who kills the goose for the golden eggs, only the payphone *did* probably contain some quarters. Although not very many of them—not since cell phones whacked the feathers out of Ma Bell. About the only places anybody uses a payphone anymore— anybody who isn't me or Tecumseh Muhammed, that is—are at the loony bin and in the slammer.

"You mind if I ask you a few question?" I asked.

"Don't got time for questions." One-Brow Jack resumed wrestling the booth, his arms all tendon and sinew. "This is my business. Not yours."

Business? Hadn't Ray G. served up a similar excuse? I wondered if the Department of Social Services knew the extent of their patrons' industry and entrepreneurial spirit. But if One-Brow Jack's finances came down to a lost quarter, he probably hadn't been paid to slaughter Big George.

I glanced up and down the block. The last thing I desired was NYPD detaining me as an accessory to telecommunications assault. I was also still jittery from my encounter with Vasil Dushku, aware that any passerby might pull a revolver and draw a bead on me.

"It won't take but a minute," I said. "All I want to know is if you noticed anything unusual last night at the hospital—anything that might shed some light on Big George's killing. Or if you know any Albanians."

"Fuck off," said One-Brow Jack.

"How about this…what if I *give* you a quarter? *Two* quarters? That's a twenty-five cent profit over what you'll get from the phone booth."

I must have insulted his integrity, because he turned on me with his fists balled at his sides and venom in his eyes. "I want *this* quarter." He waited for his gaze to inflict its poison, then returned to shaking the metal box.

"What's your name?" I asked. "I'm Henrietta. Aka Granny Flamingo."

One-Brow Jack didn't answer. If he had seen anything unusual at Mount Hebron, I wasn't wresting it out of him without pliers and a crowbar. But I decided I could scratch his name off my list of witnesses—at least for the time-being—like, I found myself thinking, a surgeon paring away an eyebrow. Only I didn't actually know the man's name.

By now, I was running late for Tecumseh Muhammed, so I left One-Brow Jack to his recovery efforts and hurried along Broadway. I put a spring in my step, commandeering the bike lane with my cart, because I didn't want to leave Tecumseh Muhammed thinking that I'd stood him up—that I was still sore about the previous night, or so absorbed with my investigation that I'd forgotten our daily assignation. Sometimes, he could be a fool that way. I'd meet up with him every evening for eleven years, and then one night in a thousand I'd run five minutes late because I twisted my ankle, or got my cart caught in a revolving door, and he'd already have shuffled off in a huff—carping that he was my lowest priority. Or that I'd been two-timing him. So I dodged the wrath of bicyclists and hoverboarders to reach The Cube before Tecumseh Muhammed's impatience got the best of him, because our agreement was to meet at five sharp, not to wait indefinitely.

Dusk crept around the converted lofts and warehouses of the East Village, painting willowy silhouettes across the concrete. In the waltzing shadows flickered a memory of that evening, more than a decade earlier, when Tecumseh Muhammed took me dancing for the very first time. Okay, I suppose it's misleading to phrase it like that, because he didn't exactly escort me onto the floating floor at Roseland or the Bowery Ballroom. What happened was that we'd been hanging out together for a few weeks, sort of scouting out each other's intentions, like opposing cavalries engaged in reconnaissance, when we walked past this dance studio on Avenue A with salsa music pulsing from a second story window—and Tecumseh Muhammed caught me by the fingertips and twirled me around like he was Cuban Pete in the flesh. The man had such power in his arms back then. Such confidence. I'd done my share of foxtrotting and quickstepping through the ballrooms of New England—as well as an occasional Lindy Hop with a closeted Carnegie heir during Princeton's Dance Weekend—and I was a good eighty pounds and two chins lighter in those days, so we held our own on that sidewalk. Soon enough, the students and the instructors from the studio were watching *us* through the window.

Later that night, I shared with Tecumseh Muhammed how Papa had shelled out a small kingdom for my private dance lessons with Arthur Murray—that I had a two-hour slot between John Travolta and Irene Cara—and he actually asked me questions about Murray, and then about Barbara Hutton and Elizabeth Arden and Jack Dempsey and all of Murray's celebrated students, none of whom he'd ever heard of, except Hedy Lamarr, because the Navy had named a destroyer after her. It's amazing how love transforms a person—at least, temporarily. These days Tecumseh Muhammed couldn't give two slaps about Jack Dempsey if the heavyweight slugged him in the kisser. But there's a fine line between loving somebody, and remembering having loved somebody, so I still felt a flicker of joy, or at least reassurance, when I saw Tecumseh Muhammed lounging at the base of The Cube, sipping from a brown paper bag. At his side lolled Revenge, snug and shaggy as a wildebeest, lapping from a dish of water.

"Aren't you a sight for sore eyes?" he asked. "Or, at least, one sore eye." Then he must have noticed my own eyes focused on the bag, because he added, "Diet Coke. Happy?"

Sure enough, the bag contained a Diet Coke bottle. What the Diet Coke bottle contained, of course, was anybody's guess.

"Happy to see *you*," I said—wanting to avoid a row.

He flashed a grin. "Did you solve your murder yet?"

My instinct was to correct him. *I* hadn't been the one murdered; it wasn't *my* murder. It was *Big George's* murder. But that wasn't the way to secure his help, so all I said was, "It's not so easy. I've only just started interviewing witnesses."

That was enough to sap Tecumseh Muhammed's interest in the subject. He took a sip from his "soda" and asked, "Do you know what *I've* been doing?"

"What?"

"I've been reading," he said—boastful, as though he'd unraveled the nature of dark energy in the cosmos or rescued a litter of puppies from a breeding mill. "At the big Barnes & Noble. Just like you're always nagging me to do."

I wouldn't have characterized my edification efforts as *nagging*. *Encouraging* would have been a better descriptor. Or *inspiring*.

"And do you know *what* I've been reading *about*, Hen?"

"Jack Dempsey?"

"The Florida Keys, baby," he said—sounding more giddy than inebriated. "And let me be the first to tell you we're gonna play them keys like the keys of a piano." Tecumseh Muhammed rummaged inside his duffel and produced a *Frommer's Guide to the Sunshine State*. "A souvenir," he said, passing me the book. "Compliments of Mr. Barnes."

I skimmed through the photos of orange groves and Disney amusements.

"You're looking in the wrong place," he said. "Page 53."

So I did my part and turned to the section on Key Largo—listings of motor lodges and seafood restaurants. If we'd been a middle-class couple from Davenport, Iowa, or Terre Haute, Indiana, searching for a beach upon which to set down our lawn chairs and children during the winter school break, I'd have understood the attraction. Sort of. But the reality was that being homeless and destitute in the Keys wasn't going to be any better than being homeless and destitute in the Big Apple, except we'd have to reapply for benefits all over again. The only appeal of the move was that the New York State Department of Social Services couldn't ask a court to assign me a guardian if I no longer lived within its jurisdiction—and if I hadn't been investigating a murder, this perk might have tipped the scales. But what kind of detective would I have been to skip town at the first sign of trouble? And how could I do that to Big George with his premonitory kiss still fresh on my lips? Besides, I'd lived in New York City for thirty-four years—a whole lifetime, by Jayne Mansfield standards—and I wasn't about to relocate to someplace infested with fire ants and bobcats.

"Check out the bottom of the page," urged Tecumseh Muhammed. "*That* has your name written all over it, baby."

And sure enough, there was an ad for Al's Flamingo Farm: "Watch and learn as our trained rehabilitation experts raise and care for injured and orphaned shorebirds including spoonbills, herons and flamingos." Across from the text waded a trio of these heralded flamingos, apparently now restored to good health—and, by their small stature and black bills, clearly identifiable as lesser flamingos, which are native to Africa's Great Rift Valley and the Gujarat region of India. *Not* South Florida.

"Come on, baby. What do you say? We can take the bus on Thursday, be in the tropics by Sunday morning."

I was tempted to correct him again—Florida is subtropical, not tropical—but there's no point in improving a man unless you're pretty sure you're going to keep him, so all I said was, "I don't want to go to Florida."

"Suit yourself, baby," said Tecumseh Muhammed. "I'm going."

I didn't want to argue. "Let's talk about something else," I said.

He tossed the empty "soda" bottle into the gutter. "There's not much else to talk about."

So that was that. He gathered up his duffel, slowly, methodically, as though waiting for a concession, before slinging it over his shoulder abruptly. Then he patted Revenge's nape, coaxing the beast away from the water and tucking the bowl into his bag. "Port Authority, baby," he said. "Thursday morning. I'll be on the eight o'clock Greyhound." And an instant later, he was staggering up the avenue, the wayward mutt faithfully at his side, and vanishing into the sea of nameless pedestrians. I promised myself that he'd be back at The Cube again at five o'clock the next evening, sober and remorseful, but for the first time in our eleven years together, I honestly wasn't so certain. The voices, which has been taking a breather all afternoon, launched into a fierce salvo of accusations and demands—*You're going to lose him! You're too fat for him anyway!*—but I shook my head as though draining water from my ears, like I used to do after swimming lessons with Miss Ederle at the Colony Club, and refused to acknowledge them. Eventually, they settled into a hostile murmur like the embers of a fire, quelled but not extinguished, and ready to rise at the first touch of kindling.

Part of me wanted to shout after Tecumseh Muhammed to come back, of course. But to what end? Either he'd go to Florida without me or he wouldn't. At least, it had become clear that we weren't destined to be a crime-solving duo like Mr. & Mrs. North or Tommy and Tuppence. Which, in hindsight, was probably for the best, because I was planning to question Alyssa from NYU in under two hours, when her parents came to retrieve her from Mount Hebron, and this encounter was to require considerable diplomacy to secure the family's confidence before they drove off to Westchester or Fairfield County or wherever—and the realization settled upon me that Tecumseh Muhammed, as unfair as it is to say, would not have been the best companion for this endeavor. I can think of few things less reassuring to a well-heeled white couple, even a liberal one, than a six-foot, four-inch, one-eyed Black Seminole with a two-page rap sheet who wants to ask their co-ed daughter questions about a murder inside a lunatic asylum. Can you? That's sad, if you ask me, but that's also reality. And while I'd like for the world to change, you couldn't really expect me to investigate a murder and mount a revolution simultaneously.

So I wandered back to Mount Hebron alone. I glanced over my shoulders at each intersection, hoping to catch any would-be hitmen by surprise, but I realized the futility of my effort. On a crowded Manhattan, anyone in the sea of college kids decked up in tatterdemalion chic or homeward-bound businessmen loosening their neckties might be a contract killer in camouflage. I remember Uncle Dewey scoffing at Franklin Roosevelt's declaration that "we have nothing to fear except fear itself." We have lots to fear, Uncle Dewey warned. He meant Soviets, hippies, advocates for minimum wage laws. Even Hubert Humphrey. In my case, the forces behind Big George's murder seemed worthy of some healthy dread. And dread them I did—so much that my stomach tightened every time I rounded a corner. Fortunately, I arrived at the hospital without any garotte marks or bullet wounds.

Visitors to the psych ward have to pass through the 17th Street entrance so security can search their belongings—not a thorough search, mind you, just enough to create the illusion of safety, like they do at the airports these days—so the wrought-iron benches opposite Stuyvesant Square Park seemed as good a place to wait as any. The overnight promised to be dry and chilly, and I imagined Jennie Kimball on NBC, my classmate who'd made out with the Mormon missionary, was warning green thumbs in the higher elevations of the metropolitan area to take their houseplants inside.

While I waited—it was only about five-thirty—I contemplated all the ways that a visitor might smuggle a weapon onto one of the locked units, and challenged myself to come up with novel ways to conceal them. If I were a terrorist, I'd forget airplanes and tourist attractions, and I'd go after the low-hanging fruit. Just think of the horror a couple of jihadists with grenade launchers or assault rifles could do inside Cedar-Sinai or the Mayo Clinic. And if those places are anything like Mount Hebron, you could walk through the front doors and fit your weapon onto a tripod before security thought to intervene. Or you could saunter from room to room, slaughtering defenseless patients. Not patients like me, but VIP patients on the 19th floor, relatives of doctors and politicians and deep-pocket donors. *People who matter.* I think it's a crackerjack plan for causing mayhem, if I do say so myself, so I suppose it's a good thing I'm not a terrorist. But it had crossed my mind that I might offer my services to Chief Boucher—as a volunteer—conjuring up security vulnerabilities that the hospital might then fix. Only the truth is that the hospital is not particularly interested in patching these weaknesses, not if doing so requires forking over money or effort. We patients, you understand, are rather expendable. Especially these days, when St. Dymphna's-South is part of an enormous health care system which earns its income managing real estate and only provides medical services incidentally as a side venture. The truth is that *everyone* is expendable, just most folks aren't aware of how truly replaceable they are. If they can find a new Pope, as Aunt Virginia used to say, they can certainly replace *you*. (And she married a Catholic, so she would know.) Does that sound too cynical? Anyway.

While I was concocting ways to sew an AK-47 into a stuffed egret, a thought suddenly inserted itself into my psyche. I don't mean that an idea popped into my head, or that I came to a quick realization, but rather, something more invasive and concrete—an idea that can't be suppressed or reasoned away. Like a tooth ache. Or a pea kernel under twenty mattresses. Renegade Sally once compared me to the princess from the Danish fairy tale who tossed and turned atop the concealed legume, because that girl couldn't sleep in physical discomfort, however miniscule, while I couldn't slumber in psychological distress. Which, in my case, usually meant not knowing something. Sally even dubbed me the "Schizophrenic Princess" on account of this trait—and not, as you might have guessed, because I'd washed my first dish at age eighteen. Once, before the Internet and smart phones, we broke into the Chatham Square Library to look up whether the A-list actress Gene Tierney and the B-list actor Lawrence Tierney were related. (They are not.) Without certainty, I would have fretted all night. So, as I was saying, one of these thoughts inserted itself into my psyche, and that thought was that Alyssa from NYU was an impostor. A plant. Maybe an agent of the Albanian mob, embedded on the seventh floor to kill. Or possibly a minion of Ms. Celery Stalk, stationed on the unit to gather evidence for the guardianship hearing. What triggered these suspicions? The girl's lobster-shaped slippers. Every time I pictured those plush orange pincers, I found myself thinking these fit her role as a troubled college girl *too* perfectly, that her handlers had overplayed her costuming—like the Soviet spy who is outed at an inter-office softball game when he continues singing through the *second and third* verses of the Star-Spangled Banner, astounding his State Department colleagues, because real Americans, in their swaggering ignorance, only ever know the first stanza.

I was still struggling to decide whether the Crustacean Maiden was in the service of Vasil Dushku's countrymen, or if my mind were playing tricks on me, when the girl herself emerged through the revolving doors of the hospital onto 17th Street. (I think this is a fitting moment for me to note the symbolism and irony of revolving doors on a loony bin.) I hardly recognized her in street clothes: a loose-fitting sweatshirt and baggy, acid-wash dungarees. She sported mirrored aviator sunglasses worthy of Anne Bancroft and had her auburn hair tucked under a vintage Brooklyn Dodgers baseball cap. I swear the kid looked like something out of one of those paparazzi candids of has-been celebrities leaving rehab. Barbara Payton. Mackenzie Phillips. You know the type. Gone were her lobster slippers, replaced with red canvas tennis shoes. The couple who followed her through the door fit their roles to a T: the father, craggy-featured and somber, in a dark business suit; his wife, carrying a pair of shopping bags that likely contained the girls' belongings, anxious around the eyes—but not so anxious that she'd forgotten to wear a fashionable gabardine coat.

I knew I had to act quickly—like a fan pursuing an autograph. I darted across the alleyway, or came as close as a woman of my size, shape and age can come to darting while pushing a shopping cart, and installed myself on the sidewalk between the trio and the visitors' parking garage. "Alyssa! It's me, Granny Flamingo. I bet you didn't think you'd see me again so soon."

Daddy Lobster looked aghast. He asked his daughter, "You know her?"

"She was a patient upstairs," the girl replied with indifference.

"I'm Henrietta Brigander, but please call me Granny Flamingo," I interjected, holding out a hand to the shellfish patriarch. "Glad to meet you."

Daddy Lobster did not shake. "We can't help you," he said. "Now if you'll let us by."

"Actually, I was hoping to ask Alyssa a few questions," I said. "About the man who was murdered. He was friend of mine."

"Our daughter doesn't know anything about that business," said Mommy Lobster. "Bert, make her go away."

Daddy Flamingo attempted to step past me again, but I'd lodged my shopping cart against a fire hydrant, effectively blocking the sidewalk. "I'll call the police," he warned.

"It's okay, Dad," said Alyssa. "She's harmless. She was nice to me."

I can't say I was thrilled to be called harmless. Horseplay is harmless. German shepherds are claimed to be harmless. Maybe an occasional glass of Chablis if you're pregnant is harmless (but not, as Aunt Genevieve learned the hard way, a postprandial Kahlúa sour for nine straight months.) When you say a human being is harmless, what you really mean is that she's irrelevant. Not worthy of concern. But a detective, like a journalist, will bear any insult in pursuit of a lead, so I didn't snap, *If you think I'm harmless, you should try thalidomide.* "You'll answer a handful of questions for me? It will only take a few minutes and I'll let you be on your way."

"Sure, if it's okay with Mom and Dad."

The couple exchanged looks, hesitant, but I suppose when your daughter is prone to drinking bleach cocktails, you do your best to humor her. "Okay, but not too long, honey," said Daddy Lobster. "We only have an hour on the meter."

"Can we buy you something to eat?" asked Mommy Lobster—clearly to assuage her guilt as much as my appetite. I sensed she meant a deli sandwich to go or a cup of coffee from a bodega. Although the "correct" answer, from Mommy Lobster's perspective, was likely, "no, thank you." She made the offer assuming, or at least hoping, that I'd turn her down.

"If you're paying, I'll certainly take you up on that," I said eagerly. "Honestly, I wouldn't mind a good restaurant meal."

Nothing like shaming the upper-middle class into charity. That's the difference between bourgeois parvenus like the Crustaceans and authentic New England gentry; Briganders and Van Duyns may open their pocketbooks generously, but they do so out of *noblesse oblige*, never guilt.

So ten minutes later, after Daddy Lobster had fed his parking meter, we found ourselves seated in the upstairs dining room at Taverna Aliki. I made sure to sit with my back to the wall, which contained a map of the Peloponnesus, so a first salvo of bullets would hit the crustaceans and not yours truly. With any luck, I mused, the lead might bounce off their shells.

I couldn't tell you the last time I'd been in a restaurant, other to use the ladies' room, unless you counted monthly meetings with my former case worker, Mr. Lemonade, at the McDonalds on Third Avenue. But eating in a restaurant is a skill you're unlikely to forget—like riding a bicycle or wind surfing. I opted for moussaka with yogurt béchamel, cauliflower stew, feta-stuffed peppers, lamb souvlaki, spanakopita, a baba ghanoush appetizer, sides of rice pilaf and lemon potatoes, with baklava and three scoops of pistachio ice cream for dessert. Alyssa asked for a garden salad and a seltzer. No bleach. Not even a smidgeon of shampoo or fabric softener. Neither of the elder Crustaceans ordered food—although later, Mommy

Lobster did pinch a slice of pita from my basket to nibble. I didn't begrudge her. Yet as much as I wanted to savor the Mediterranean cooking, I had a job to do. I folded open my notepad to show that I meant business. "Thanks for agreeing to help me out," I said.

The girl's lips curled into the slightest smile, but she said nothing. That such a fledgling, doe-eyed creature might be an agent of the underworld seemed less plausible when she was seated opposite me, her stubby fingers toying nervously with the packets of Sweet'n Low and Splenda.

"As you know, Big George was murdered last night," I began. No matter how many times I repeated that phrase, it sounded unreal— and I wanted desperately to believe that it was a delusion, although it wasn't. "I'm just wondering if you recall anything unusual that happened while you were in the hospital."

The girl digested my question like a bottle of detergent. "*Everything* that happened to me was unusual," she said. "That's the craziest place on earth."

She had a point. If you're not accustomed to the way they do things at Mount Hebron, the experience probably does seem rather remarkable. "What I mean is," I said, "anything that might help us solve Big George's murder."

"I thought the police already had the guy. With the crooked face."

"Arnold O'Dell," I said. "Yes, he's in custody. But nobody knows *why* he did it. Maybe somebody put him up to it or framed him. So I'm going around asking people if they witnessed anything that seemed out of the ordinary—even by psych ward standards."

The girl tore open one of the packets of artificial sweetener and trailed the contents along the Formica tabletop. "Not that I can think of," she finally said. "Of course, I don't have much to compare things to...I just feel bad for his twin..."

I nearly choked on my souvlaki. "His twin???"

"You know. It must be really hard losing a twin brother. Like tearing apart halves of a clam shell. I don't even get along with my older sister, and I can't imagine what I'd do if she died, and we're six years apart."

"Please, honey," objected Mommy Lobster. "There's no reason to involve your sister."

"I wasn't saying anything negative," insisted Alyssa.

I resisted the urge to interject a dose of family counseling, or a recommendation for cognitive behavioral therapy. I asked, "How did you know Big George was a twin?"

"He *told* you. He had a twin in St. Louis. Don't you remember?"

"You heard us talking? And you didn't say anything?"

"I figured you'd rather I was asleep," said Alyssa. "To be honest, I never thought I'd see you again. Either of you. How was I supposed to know he'd get killed?"

That reminded me of the time we visited Washington D.C. as kids—Papa had a financial matter to discuss with the Secretary of the Treasury, a matter so sensitive that he didn't trust the telephone lines—and while he visited 1500 Pennsylvania Avenue, Mama led us on a tour of the city. When we visited the Supreme Court Building, Chief Justice Warren Burger (whose wife was a Brigander cousin through her grandmother) let me and Rusky pose for photos on his official high-backed chair, and then he introduced us to the first rule of lawyering: never ask a question unless you already know the answer. That was the difference between being a lawyer and a judge, he explained. As a judge, you often asked questions whose answers flabbergasted you—but then you had to pretend not to be surprised. My response, at the time, had been dictated by a severe stomach bug: I'd vomited on his chair. Now I tried to channel Cousin Warren's wisdom and to remain pokerfaced.

"Fair enough," I agreed. "But you're sure you didn't notice anything strange?"

"Other than a nurse putting his fishing pole inside the medicine closet? And a woman asking me if I could smuggle a secret message to the United Nations for her? Not a thing."

"And, bear with me, do you happen to be acquainted with any Albanians?"

"Excuse me?"

"I have reason to believe there may be people from the nation of Albania involved in Big George's killing."

"If they are," said Alyssa, "I don't know them."

I surveyed her parents. The father's features had a rugged Scandinavian flavor, the mother's more delicate—possibly Irish or French. Both had a certain tentative ruddiness to their physiognomy, and Mommy Lobster an encrusted, carapace-like rash on the back of her hands that suggested scales, as if the couple's forebears had climbed back into the primordial soup at some point to interbreed with crustaceans. Neither *looked* Albanian. Although who could be certain? Hadn't Jews escaped the Warsaw Ghetto because they looked like Poles? And hadn't flaxen-haired Wallace de Wijkerslooth, Grandpa Van Duyn's arch rival in racquetball at the Athletic Club, turned out to have an African-American forebear? So I trusted my own anthroposcopy only so far. What I did notice was that Daddy Lobster sported a pair of Yale cufflinks. Uncle Drake had left Papa nearly an identical set emblazoned with the Hebrew seal and that timeless Yankee wisdom: *lux et veritas*. I didn't have it in me to let the moment pass without comment. "Good to see you're an Eli," I said. "Both of my grandfather's brothers were New Haven men."

Daddy Lobster's brow furrowed with perplexity. At first, I thought he might merely be surprised that a lunatic woman wearing a flamingo hat boasted kinsmen who shared his alma mater, but a real Yale man understands that Elis and their relations come in many varieties. No, unlike his daughter—who subsequent events did confirm to be an authentic NYU undergraduate—Daddy Lobster was clearly an imposter. A fraud! He'd certainly never gone to Yale. Who knew if he'd even graduated from college? He could have been one of those self-made entrepreneurs whose sons Great Uncle Atherton was always trying to keep out of the diplomatic corps. Or a state university grad who thought the sartorial ephemera of the Ivy League could buy him cachet with the Boston aristocracy. I didn't want to launch a quarrel, but some instinct deep inside my Brigander blood demanded a rejoinder. "My great-uncles went to Yale," I said to him, matter-of-fact. "It's a college in Connecticut."

"I'm sure they did," said Daddy Lobster. Bastard didn't believe me.

He was already eyeballing the waitress for the check. I was thinking whether to inject a sly reference to the novelist John O'Hara into the conversation—a Niagara Prep alum who'd never made it to Yale, but who'd peppered his *Newsweek* columns, and, according to Grandpa Brigander, his personal conversation, with references to Bonesmen, and cheering on Handsome Dan at The Game, and Whiffenpoof concerts at Mory's. But I didn't wish to be outright insulting, so all I said was, "Wasn't the novelist John O'Hara a Yale man?"

"I honestly couldn't say," replied Daddy Lobster. The man had a rejoinder for everything, it seemed, although later it crossed my mind that he might never have heard of O'Hara. He hadn't gone to Yale, after all. He might have earned his fortune in refurbishing precision parts or importing macadamia nuts. For all I could say, which wasn't much, he might have been as illiterate as Antigona Dushku's husband. Yes, there lay the simplest explanation—the cut of Occam's razor. He probably didn't know who O'Hara even was.

I had them wrap the rest of my entrees. I was also ready to depart. It's one thing to go to a state school, or to learn your craft on the job like Tecumseh Muhammed—nothing at all wrong with that. Salt of the earth. But I'll have no truck with pretenders. Not that I intended to bite the hand that was feeding me, quite literally, so much as I didn't foresee the two of us pursuing a social connection. I imagine Alyssa's father didn't either. By the time I'd thanked him for the complimentary meal, he'd already helped his wife into her stylish coat.

"Good luck, Granny Flamingo," said Alyssa.

Her parents said nothing at all. I guess, once you've been exposed as faking a Yale education by a woman who lives out of a shopping cart, what is there left to say?

I thanked the Lobster family again for dinner and headed up a side street toward Union Square. When I'd nearly reached the plaza, I noticed a black sedan with tinted glass and no anterior plate about twenty yards behind me. Now did *that* send a chill down my spine! In order to be certain, I ducked onto the avenue and the vehicle followed—pulling into a bus stop, so as not to impede the thoroughfare, because even the slowest black sedan travels faster than the speediest shopping cart. As I hurried along the sidewalk, I made an effort to keep parked cars between myself and the flow of traffic, whenever possible, Big George's tale of the attempt to run him down in the crosswalk still fresh in my thoughts. When another vehicle pulled in front of the sedan, I took the opportunity to traverse the pavement and quickly turned again at the next intersection, backtracking along my own path. For a few minutes, I seemed to be in the clear, so much so that I said a prayer of thanks to the Great Ivory Billed Woodpecker in the Sky, which seems as a good a deity to worship as any, as much as that statement may cause generations of respectable Episcopal vicars in cemeteries across lower New England to turn over in their lead-lined coffins—but when I'd reached the end of the block, I caught sight of the same sedan rounding the corner behind me. So I *was* being followed. Or, at least, I *thought* I was being followed. If you're chronically paranoid, it's sometimes difficult to tell whether people are actually after you.

CHAPTER FIVE

I locked my shopping cart to a scaffold behind the Union Theological Seminary, on a quiet block opposite Riverside Church that *New York Magazine* once rated the safest in Gotham, and spent the night in the natural science section of the Manhattan Valley Branch Library. If you try to hide overnight inside a bathroom or the janitor's closet, you're bound to get caught and ejected—they even peep into each toilet stall these days—but Renegade Sally taught me that if you retreat to the least-visited sections of the stacks, and sit meticulously still until the motion sensors on the fluorescent lights lull themselves to sleep, security will often overlook you. It's a trick that only works in some of the older, under-trafficked libraries—the newer branches all have cameras that feed into outside monitors—and I've never shared my ploy with anyone, not even Tecumseh Muhammed, because everybody needs a place where she can escape to in an emergency. So I spent the night in the ornithology aisle, a coffee table book about the *Birds of the Galapagos* for my pillow. Ironic, really, considering Great Uncle Atherton's role in toppling multiple Ecuadorian governments. On the way out through the service exit the next morning—a new, illustrated history of the Hays Code tucked inside my purse—I felt rejuvenated and reinvigorated, as though my pores had absorbed wisdom from the surrounding volumes while I slumbered. Nary a voice disturbed me until well after breakfast. Which was all the more reason to skip the appointment that Dr. Cotz-Cupper had scheduled for me with St. Dymphna's outpatient clinic on 98th Street.

New York State law requires that every patient discharged from a psychiatric facility receive an appointment with an outpatient provider within five business days. Like so much of the mental health-industrial complex, this rule looks impressive on paper. In practice, when you show up for your appointment, you're often met by a paraprofessional—or even a summer intern, a college kid applying to PsyD programs at Hunter or Pace—who gathers your demographic data and guarantees you an evaluation by a physician sometime before the next periodic return of Halley's Comet. So even if I wanted psychiatric medication, which I don't, it's not as though I can stroll into the Surgeon General's office and fill my pockets with Prozac and Clozaril. And if a person complains about the waiting time, she's informed that "there's a process," which is a fancy way of saying something lurks forever just beyond the reach of indigent, mentally-ill people, the psychiatric equivalent of Tantalus's fruit. I say all of this because, if you're one of those folks like Uncle Dewey who attributes psychotic relapses to deficiencies of character, and regards all efforts to help others—even rolling bandages for the troops at Iwo Jima or training guide dogs for the blind—as creeping socialism, I assure you that, when it comes to the so-called crisis in mental healthcare, there's enough blame to spread around. In fact, you could butter all of the croissants in Paris with the blame, and still have sufficient butterfat left over to sculpt a life-size heard of butter cattle for the state fair, like Aunt Genevieve did in her widowhood. In any case, the bottom line is that I skipped my appointment, retrieved my cart, enjoyed a complimentary cheese Danish and a cup of acidic coffee at the "soup kitchen" on St. Nicholas Avenue, bathed quickly while fully-clothed in the Columbus Circle fountain, and headed downtown to continue with my investigation.

Unfortunately, I'd already plucked all the low-hanging fruit. The only patients I hadn't yet interrogated, excluding the pleasantly demented Miss Havisham, were Lucille from Florida, Angry O'Dell, and Big George himself—and since one of those men was in custody and the other on a slab of ice at the morgue, rodent-faced Lucille seemed like my most promising bet. Yet nobody—at least, in my usual haunts—had ever heard of her. I hunted for that woman like one of Papa's long-haired lurchers in pursuit of a hare. Or like the time Cousin Adelaide lost an ivory collar button at Delmonico's and conducted a table by table search over the protestations of the maître d'. That meant inquiries at the Hamilton Arms Women's Shelter, the intake facility on Franklin Avenue, all eleven food pantries and the Bellevue ER. Also, the Port Authority Bus Terminal, Grand Central Station, and the steps of the Fifth Avenue Presbyterian Church. I asked women being bailed out of the holding pen at Central Booking and girls hurrying from the domestic violence shelter on Lexington Avenue that Mr. Lemonade had once referred me to. Who could have predicted *that* address might come in handy? Between dawn and mid-afternoon, I visited every major park from Inwood to the Battery, queried two dozen subway buskers and even used a phone borrowed from a Greek Orthodox priest to file a missing person's report with the 13th Precinct, claiming to be a cousin of Lucille's; alas, without a surname, they refused to open a case. I'd probably sweated off ten pounds by three o'clock, but for naught. Either Lucille had been so displeased with Dr. Robustelli's care that she'd hightailed it back to Florida, or she'd gone deep underground. Or maybe, the notion crossed my mind, the woman was actually a hired assassin, even if she looked more subterranean than Albanian. Or perhaps, and you always have to consider this possibility when you're schizophrenic, I'd imagined the rodentine creature whole cloth. Maybe Lucille from Florida had never existed at all.

I'll confess I felt discouraged. And when I feel discouraged, the voices often feel discouraged as well, so I was treated to a fugue of reproach that rose toward a crescendo as the day evaporated without any tangible successes. At one time, this upsurge would have alarmed me. I remember the very first time the voices mounted a verbal assault—after I failed a general chemistry exam at Bryn Mawr—and how what had been intermittent, solitary gripes, merely irksome now and again, suddenly merged into an orchestra of censure. Then, I'd panicked—running out onto the quad in my cotton nightgown, sobbing, with my hands plastered over my ears. Now I know to bide my time, as though I'm having an argument with Mama or Tecumseh Muhammed, until the voices talk themselves to exhaustion. Sometimes it helps to indulge in a treat like a box of jelly donuts, or even a banana split at Morgenstern's, but that particular afternoon's blues called for a different sort of extravagance, so I decided to waylay P.J. following his shift to see if he could shed some light on the murder. And, of course, I wanted any excuse to talk with him for a few minutes outside the hospital.

I detoured through Union Square on the walk toward Mount Hebron, nominally keeping an eye out for Lucille from Florida, secretly hoping I might run into Tecumseh Muhammed. A *Daily News* headline at a corner kiosk caught my eye: "O'Crazy!" Below a photograph of a flame-eyed Angry O'Dell being led from the hospital in cuffs, an inset quoted the mayor. Hizzoner: "NY Mental Hospitals Safest Places in the World." That's a good one. In the world *of what?* I suppose that was true if you were comparing them with city homeless shelters, or open seas during monsoons, or to the containment shell at the Indian Point nuclear facility. But seeing poor Angry O'Dell looking so desperate and lost—terrified, too, like a caged animal—for a crime he might not even have committed, left me all the more discouraged. I feared I was letting Big George down just as I'd once let Rusky down.

I flipped to the page-three article where the tabloid reported that O'Dell would be charged with premeditated murder. A bargaining chip for the district attorney, I realized—but still! The headline in the *Post* read "Mad and Madder" over a split shot of O'Dell and Big George. The photo of Big George, grainy as though nicked from the Internet, showed him posing, robust and shirtless, on the quay at Newport. I recognized the alabaster steeple of Trinity Church rising behind the masts and what appeared to be a row of waterfront shops unknown in the Brigander era. I could easily picture Papa standing upon that very spot, sporting his skipper's cap, although it was hard to imagine him bare-chested in public. Whether it was the sight of Big George in the full bloom of health, or of the boardwalk where I'd spent so much of my childhood, I found myself leaking tears. My eyes were puffy and tender when I finally reached Mount Hebron—and P.J., who may be the most observant person I've ever known, even including yours truly, noticed my distress immediately.

He'd emerged through the revolving doors shortly after three-thirty, just as I'd begun to fear that he'd taken the day off entirely. In his street clothes, designer jeans and a stylish navy blazer, he looked substantially younger than he did sporting the teal scrubs required by Mount Hebron. His off-duty appearance served as a helpful reminder that, despite his wisdom, my heartthrob was really just a kid—only three years older than Rusky when my brother had claimed the front page of the *Post*. The breeze carried an all too familiar bite, a portent of the coming winter, that cyclical frigid blast perched perennially in the wings, which meant more airtime for Jennie Kimball on NBC and the threat of frostbite for the loony lady in the plumed hat. I could feel the arctic in my knuckles and wrists, the rheumatic, glacial ache of middle age. One task I had to complete prior to the first snowfall, I warned myself, was to secure a pair of wool mittens. Before I ended up with four digits per hand like Mama's anteater, which is probably not a terribly limiting fate if you're spoon-fed termites by a Surinamese handler, but might prove something of a handicap foraging on East 14th Street.

P.J. spotted me resting against my cart, still on the brink of tears, and immediately came to my rescue. "Are you all right, Granny?" he asked. "Do you need a doctor?"

I willed myself to composure, aided by his presence. "I'm fine, I guess. Just a bit overwhelmed. Can we talk for a little while?"

P.J. glanced at his watch. "Okay. But only a couple of minutes. I've got to get home to the tiny devils so Cora can rustle up some dinner for her ma. You know how it is."

Not exactly. In less than three years, I'd gone from Cookie poaching Dover sole and drenching escargot in garlic butter to filching Kit Kat bars from 7-Elevens, with much of the interim spent carb-binging in the Erdman Dining Hall at Bryn Mawr, so I didn't actually know the first thing about rustling up anything. But I saw no need to highlight for P.J. how different we were. He made a quick call on his cell phone to inform his wife that he was running late, then steered us toward a vacant bench in Stuyvesant Square Park. Candidly, I'd been hoping for a cozy cup of coffee at a hole-in-the-wall diner, or even a bowl of clam chowder, but I didn't think it wise to push my luck. I was investigating a murder, after all, not going on a date.

"So what's upsetting you, Granny? Did something happen?"

I tried to gather my thoughts together. A particularly obnoxious voice had begun criticizing my hygiene, shouting about my halitosis and womanly odors, so focusing required concentrated effort. "I don't even know where to start," I said. "I'm just very upset about Big George."

"Of course, you are," said P.J. "That's only natural."

"You think? It's not as though we were old friends." I'd almost said lovers, but checked myself. I guess after that premonitory kiss—as crazy as it sounds—I did feel that we were lovers. Or *future* lovers, would-be lovers thwarted by circumstance.

"It's to your credit that you form such strong attachments," he said.

My heart cantered toward a trot—as though preparing for a perilous hurdle like Vivien Leigh's daughter in *Gone with the Wind*. The tips of my ears burned. Not even Michael Landon in a fedora could key me up like praise from P.J. "Thank you," I said.

"It was an upsetting event. For all of us," said P.J. "Even Mr. Brauer was shaken up."

I snorted. "I'm surprised he's not trying to swing a worker's comp claim."

"Don't be unkind, Granny," said P.J.—and I instantly regretted my words. "Mr. Brauer is trying the best he knows how. Just like the rest of us. Poor guy has been mandated for overtime three days in a row too—so much for his fishing trip. I feel genuinely awful that I can't help him this time around...but with Cora's ma..."

"Family comes first," I agreed. "That's the way it should be."

In reality, I wasn't so sure about that. Not anymore. Don't get me wrong—I would have been the first person to cry, "Family First," back when I had one to call my own. Now that I didn't, unless you counted some Van Duyn third cousins decaying on Beacon Hill, who must be well over ninety, if they were still alive at all, and whatever remained of the Brigander clan in the motherland, country squires from Dorset and Cornwall keeping up appearances in genteel poverty off the proceeds of estates sold to the English Heritage Trust, who had neither the wherewithal nor the inclination to assist yours truly, their long lost crazy kinswoman, I wasn't so sure that "Family First" was particularly just. It's certainly not equitable. But since P.J.'s nepotism occurred at Sarge's expense, I wasn't going to protest. In any case, you don't have to be Charles Darwin to recognize the benefits of such an approach for genetic survival, so favoring one's blood relations is probably too hard-wired into our psyches to extinguish without mass social upheaval. I mean, you could stamp it out by resorting to extraordinary measures, I imagine, if you were Mao or Stalin, though that seems a tad excessive.

"I'm upset about Big George dying," I said. "But it's not *only* that. I don't believe Angry O'Dell actually killed him."

P.J. didn't react with the shock that I'd anticipated. Either he'd been tipped off to my investigation, I told myself, or "nonjudgmental regard"—that's the fancy, head-shrinker's term for keeping an open mind—just came naturally to him. "Why not, Granny?"

"It's hard to explain," I said. Which was true. "It's a hunch. More than a hunch, really. Sort of like a premonition—only about something that has already happened." My heartthrob waited patiently for additional evidence or explication, but as I thought about O'Dell holding the knife in the wrong hand, and Little Abe's flight from organized crime, I feared that voicing the details behind my suspicions might trivialize them. Or undermine them completely. They wouldn't *sound* like much. Not to a third party, at least. *They just were.* Another foundation for my skepticism about the official explanation for the killing was the black sedan without plates that had nearly plowed down Big George and later trailed me through Grammercy, but I wasn't fool enough to tell a psychiatric nurse, even a benevolent one, that I suspected I was being followed. That's a surefire way to get oneself recommitted. As much as I loved and trusted P.J., some fears were best kept to myself.

"All of this must be quite a shock to your system," said P.J. "It's only natural to ask questions."

"Good. Because I do have a few questions for you. About that night..." I immediately removed my notepad from my cart and flipped to a blank page. Across the top I printed: EVIDENCE OF PETER JAMES PURNELL—as though recording testimony for a coroner's jury. "I know you weren't there when the killing took place, but I'm wondering if you remember anything unusual that happened earlier in the afternoon...or maybe something somebody said the next day...anything at all."

P.J. toyed with the sleeve buttons on his blazer. "I'm not sure I should be encouraging this," he said—but more as devil's advocacy, I could tell, than genuine objection.

"Please humor me. What harm can it do?"

"That's what I'm trying to decide," he said. "Not that it matters much under the circumstances. Because honestly, Granny, I can't think of anything."

"Nothing?"

"Except that Monty got fired. But you probably knew that already."

"I'd heard," I lied. "Poor fellow. Do you know how I can find him?"

I figured there might be a dozen Monty Castillo in New York City for every Albanian hotelier in Queens, and the last thing I desired was more legwork. "I'll only take up a few minutes of his time and I promise I'll leave if he asks. You have my word."

"I really can't tell you that," said P.J.

"Give me a hint," I pleaded. "A borough, at least."

My heartthrob glanced up and down the windswept block, as though preparing to pass along a catalog envelope of classified documents—like Great Uncle Atherton had done for the O.S.S. during his stint as a journalist in post-war Berlin—and then relented. "Staten Island," he said. "West Brighton neighborhood. That's all I know."

I could have kissed the man smack on the lips. But his hint would have been more of an excuse, I'll readily admit, than a reason.

"I should be going," said P.J. "Cora will be waiting."

"Just a few more questions. Do you remember that patient from Florida? Lucille? Pasty creature—looked like a weasel."

"That's not how I would have described her," he replied. "But I do remember a Lucille from Florida."

"Can you please help me find her?" I asked. "I don't even know her last name."

"I'm afraid I really can't help you there, Granny."

I'd anticipated rejection, of course. Medical professionals tend to get all hung up on confidentiality, especially conscientious ones like P.J. But I'd also prepared for the moment. "I'm begging you," I said. "It's not as though I'm going to blackmail the woman or hurt her in any way. All I want to do is ask her a handful of innocent questions..." And then, as I'd once done playing Aldonza in a summer stock production of *Man of La Mancha* at the Casino Theater, I let the floodgates open and nearly drowned Lower Manhattan in tears. "If I don't find out the truth about Big George," I babbled between sobs, "I swear I'll jump in the harbor." I hated to deceive P.J.—but what choice did I have? At first, he tried to placate me with reassurances, but I refused to be soothed. Eventually, I buried my face inside my hat. "Just a clue," I begged. "Like on *Password*."

"I really shouldn't..."

"It's not unethical to give a *hint*, is it? Is she named after a piece of fruit? Or maybe a foreign city? At least, tell me her ethnicity. How can it be a violation of HIPPA to say she's probably Irish or Norwegian?"

P.J. took a deep breath and whispered, "Lucille Tobruk."

Tobruk—like the celebrated Anglo-Australian military triumph in North Africa during World War II. No wonder P.J. hadn't revealed her ethnicity—even I didn't know what background the surname Tobruk might indicate. Libyan? Algerian? Or maybe shortened at Ellis Island from Tobrusky. I jotted down the unlikely name in my notebook. "Thank you," I said. "That's the best birthday present I've ever received." It wasn't actually my birthday, of course, but it somehow felt like the right thing to say.

P.J. patted my shoulder. "I should be going, Granny."

"Forgive me for asking so many questions," I said. "I haven't even asked how *you* are?"

"Good enough. No complaints—at least, none that anybody is going to address. I'm just relieved they've reopened the unit." He glanced at his watch. "But I really do have to run."

"Thank you for helping me," I said.

He stood up and examined me with his eyes, as though deciding whether it was prudent to leave me alone, and at that moment, I experienced a spooky sensation that we were being watched. But when I scanned the block, our sole spectator appeared to be an elderly woman in a bonnet, strewing crumbs to aggressive pigeons. Yet she did look as though she was observing us, obliquely, out of the corner of her gaze. What did this woman think of me and P.J.? I wondered. Did she take us for mother and son? Unlikely, I suppose, considering my peculiar hat and shopping cart, although it was flattering to think so. Most likely, she could make neither heads nor tails of our relationship. Or, possibly, she didn't even care. Maybe she was wall-eyed like that suitor, a nephew of Lord Beaverbrook, who'd once jilted Cousin Adelaide, and the effect that she was spying on us from the corner of her eye was merely an illusion. I didn't dare think she took us for lovers. Mama and Aunt Virginia enjoyed playing a game—on airplanes, in hotel lobbies—speculating upon whether older men with younger companions were husband and wife or father and daughter. Or, as Aunt Virginia said, thinking her euphemism above my and Rusky's comprehension, "a third category." Sitting with P.J., I realized they'd neglected a fourth grouping: handsome nurse and lovelorn psychiatric patient. Looking back, I wondered if any of those May-December couples we'd scrutinized in the Front Hall at Claridge's, or strolling among La Bagatelle's clipped yews, fit the bill.

I doubted P.J. was speculating on such matters. He'd probably already shifted his attention to the dinner menu for his tadpoles. "Keep safe, Granny," he said. Only when he'd already vanished onto Second Avenue did I realize that I hadn't even asked him a single question about Albanians.

Success! Learning Lucille's last name and Monty Castillo's borough couldn't exactly rival cracking quantum theory or deciphering the Voynich manuscript, nor did these nuggets solve Big George's murder, not directly, but for a lady gumshoe who didn't even own a magnifying glass, this info was a major step in the right direction. When breakthroughs are lacking, you have to settle for tangible progress—just like Rusky learned when training his ferrets to perform tricks. More importantly, for the first time since I'd purchased my notebook, I genuinely *felt* like a detective. Stick that on your label, Dr. Libby! Armed with my new leads, I was hankering to catch the ferry out to Staten Island—if also a bit apprehensive, in light of my previous encounter with an earlier incarnation of this vessel. But it was nearly five o'clock, so I set off to rendezvous with Tecumseh Muhammed, reluctantly accepting that I'd have to postpone my trip across the harbor until the morning. Instead, buoyed by my recent good fortune, I determined to confront Sarge following his double shift. Not that I expected to squeeze much out of Mr. Brauer in the way of declarative memories, but—as Great Uncle Atherton used to say when foisting East Asian delicacies like bat-paste soup and the rehydrated fallopian tubes of frogs upon the wary taste buds of his Yankee neighbors, many of whom were too polite, or merely too taciturn, to say no—*you gotta buckle down, Winsocki, and give it an old college try*. And sometimes, even the most recalcitrant witness can reveal a crucial fact, often unwittingly. Hadn't Franklin Delano Roosevelt inadvertently divulged the date of the Normandy invasion, at least to those in the know, when he cancelled his annual yellowfin troll with Grandpa van Duyn? Anyway.

I hurried to The Cube, but my hopes hung low. Whether or not Tecumseh Muhammed actually intended to hop a Greyhound without me, and I clung to my doubts, he must have realized that he'd undermine his own cause by returning to our meeting place until the bus departed the following morning. His best chance was keeping me in suspense. "On tenterhooks," as Papa used to say. Yet even aware that he was unlikely to make a cameo until the next evening, I approached Astor Place with a pounding pulse and depth charges in my stomach. And sure enough, my expectations proved well met. I waited a full hour, exchanging guarded glances with the ragtag crew of skateboarders who congregated around the No Skateboarding signs to smoke weed and show off. What would Vincent and Jakey Astor have thought, I wondered, to see the plaza named for their great-great-grandfather transformed into a downscale skate park? I could still remember the pair of them in double-breasted flannel suits, using their rolled umbrellas as walking sticks as they promenaded among Cousin Gladys's daylilies, and I rather suspected that, given the prospect of seeing their family name defiled, they'd have preferred to have gone down with the *Titanic*.

I finally surrendered hope around six-thirty and took the subway uptown to 39th Street, planning to do some Internet research at the Midtown Library. Not the Beaux Arts flagship with the marble lions out front, but the homeless-friendly branch across the street. Occasionally, I find myself thinking the place is *too* homeless-friendly, especially if I catch some toper urinating in a corner of the periodicals room, while there's a perfectly functional public restroom on the third floor, but usually I'm just thankful they offer free wi-fi and air-conditioning in summer and don't examine my shopping cart too thoroughly, especially on the way out. A quick search of the web revealed Monty Castillo's address on Bement Avenue in West Brighton. Three hours and hundreds of inquiries later, including alternative spellings and possible nicknames, I found no conclusive evidence that Lucille Tobruk had ever existed. If the census records were to be believed, Florida didn't claim any Tobruks at all—although there was a Lucy T. Brooks, ninety-one years old, receiving social security checks at a nursing home in Orlando. Of course, it was always possible that P.J. had simply concocted a surname to assuage yours truly without breaching confidentiality, but that seemed out of character. Also an odd last name to fabricate. Lucille Smith or Lucille Johnson smacks, all considered, of potential deception. Lucille Tobruk rings with authenticity.

Doubly discouraged on account of Tecumseh Muhammed and Lucille, I considered ditching my plans to ambush Mr. Brauer. *You'll just fuck up again*, warned a voice. *Screw you, Nancy Drew*, retorted another. Confrontation, as you've probably sensed, is not my strongest suit. I counted flamingos backwards inside my head from ninety-nine—one of my coping strategies, because the voices usually come in waves and burn themselves out rather quickly—and by thirty flamingo, they'd ebbed to a murmur.

That was when I spotted the black sedan again, about twenty yards behind me, idling. I started walking in the opposite direction, swallowing by terror, and caught an eyeful of the vehicle's headlights reflected off the opposite storefronts as it pulled away from the curb. Without warning, I stopped and spun around. The sedan halted suddenly too, as though caught in its own headlights—and just as quickly, accelerated down the block at top speed and crossed the avenue against the light. Now I was certain that I was being followed—although the glare of the car's brights had prevented me from seeing the driver. I found myself shaking with dread. At the same time, as I thought the matter over, this ominous vehicle reassured me that I was pursuing the correct leads and banished my discouragement. If Cousin Schuyler Colfax Van Duyn could singlehandedly capture an entire *Bundeswehr* division at the Battle of Belleau Wood, and Grandpa Van Duyn's brother, "Manatee Phil," could arm wrestle black bears for Ringling Brothers, surely I could confront a nurse with a bogus military record.

I arrived outside Mount Hebron shortly after eleven—just as the stream of depleted orderlies and nursing aides spilled forth like gophers from a collapsing burrow. I recognized many of the faces: perpetually-flustered Katrina from the ER; shiftless Ms. Goins, the evening clerk; Mr. Odibe, who stocked linens on the medical floors, and whom I'd befriended during a bout of pancreatitis. A perverse part of my psyche, fearing conflict, hoped that Mr. Brauer might not emerge. Maybe P.J. had been wrong, and they'd located backup coverage at the last minute. But as I negotiated with myself over how long I'd have to wait before I could rationalize abandoning my watch, my target—I almost wrote foe, but caught myself—stepped into the night. He wore a hooded anorak with a faux fur lining over his scrubs, as though recruited to be a medic on a polar expedition. In one hand, he carried his fishing rod and creel. I fought the instinct to bolt. "Sarge!" I called out—hoping to flatter him, although the use of this sobriquet pained me to the core.

The man paused as though doubting his own ears and scanned the block. He either didn't see me or pretended that he didn't.

"Over here," I called out—shuffling toward him. "It's Granny Flamingo."

That gave him little choice but to register my approach.

"Oh, the bird lady. What do you want?"

I drew within five feet of him, only the cart separating us. "I just want to ask you a few questions, Sarge. Okay? About Big George."

"Wish I could, lady. But I'm in a hurry."

He sidestepped my cart and headed toward the subway.

"I think Angry O'Dell was framed!" I shouted after him.

Several passing pedestrians glanced toward me, then continued along their way. A window slammed in a nearby tenement. Mr. Brauer's pace slowed, almost mechanically, and then he turned to face me and retraced his steps. My foe—there, I said it, so sue me!—held his fishing pole at a ninety degree angle and I had to step back to avoid getting poked.

"I'm investigating his murder," I said. "If the police won't do it, somebody has to."

Mr. Brauer scowled. "What is wrong with you lady? You know that guy had a serious heart condition. He was going to die soon anyway."

Maybe. But that didn't give anyone the right to help expedite his journey. Any more than it gave them a right to ignore Rusky's cruel death just because he had schizophrenia. Besides, we're all going to die soon anyway—at least, by geological standards. Where would we be if Edison decided not to invent the light bulb because he was going to die soon anyway? Or if Fleming never bothered with penicillin because he saw the personal gains as too short term? Any answer to everything, as Uncle Drake used to say, is also an answer to nothing. What I should have done was to conciliate Mr. Brauer— to laugh off his remark and ask him to indulge a nutcase. Instead, in the spirit of my illustrious forebears, I let indignation get the better of me. "Is that what they teach you in nursing school?" I snapped.

"Mind your own business, bird lady," retorted Sarge.

"This *is* my business," I said with my fist raised. "*Humanity* is my business."

But by then Mr. Brauer and his fishing tackle had been swallowed by the shadows.

That night I slept under the stars. Or, for the less romantically inclined, under the lights of the Flatiron District, which is about as close as one can get to a starscape on an island of two million people and thirty million incandescent bulbs. With temperatures hovering around fifty degrees and not a cloud above, I couldn't justify another forty winks in the Manhattan Valley Library, because slumber among the natural sciences is a privilege not to be abused. If I camped out there regularly, I feared, I'd eventually get caught. Fortunately, the night passed with nary a cop nor a homeless outreach team to disturb my dreams. I woke the next morning to a symphony of taxi horns and sirens, primed for yet another day of battle. As though the gods were trying to encourage me after my frustrating encounter with Mr. Brauer, I discovered that a stranger had left a doggy bag containing sushi and cold tempura beside my head. A solid thirty seconds passed as I contemplated the danger that the leftovers might be poisoned—a ruse employed by the Albanian mob to rid themselves of a bothersome avian pest. But hunger quickly proved stronger than discretion, and after the first anxious nibble, I was able to enjoy my Japanese breakfast. Thoroughly satisfied, I set out for the train station to solicit help from Nort the Messiah.

As I walked north, the clock on the Met Life Tower crawled toward half past eight—each click of the minute hand like the tick of a time bomb. How easily I might still have changed course and gone to meet Tecumseh Muhammed at the bus terminal. If not to depart for Key West, at least to persuade him to remain in Gotham. But "in for a penny, in for a pound of Krugerrands," as Papa used to say, so I stole a page from *The Sound of Music* and thought of my favorite things—quetzals and lorikeets and Tyrone Power's smile—until I felt as chipper as Cousin Gladys's canaries.

I found Nort precisely as I'd last left him. Same checker board, same purple cloak. Only his opponent had changed. Now the Messiah sat locked in mortal combat with an elderly, purple-haired transsexual woman who, when we'd last been on an inpatient unit together at Presbyterian Hospital, had claimed to be rightful heir to the Romanovs. I harbored doubts, of course, but she probably didn't believe I was a Brigander, so who was I to cast the first stone? I waited in silence for Nort's inevitable victory, and sure enough, he soon cleared the board in a series of relentless jumps. His opponent cursed, slapped five dollars atop the board, and stormed off. Only then did Nort the Messiah acknowledge my presence. "Granny Flamingo, twice in one week," he declared. "As I live and breathe. To what do we owe this honor?"

He indicated for me to claim the empty seat across the checkers board, but I shook my head. It was hard to believe this gaunt, unkempt creature controlled a network of minions and spies throughout the five boroughs, but Nort's reputation was legendary. If anyone could find a lost puppy or a missing Fabergé egg, or, in my case, a rodentine Floridian with a North African surname, it was Nort. "I need your help," I said.

Nort waited, open-faced.

"Do you remember that woman from Miami on the unit with us? Snout like a kangaroo rat, eyes like lead buttons?"

"Not particularly," said Nort. "I meet lots of people."

I could sense he recalled her perfectly. "Her name is Lucille Tobruk," I said. "And I need to find her."

"And let me guess. You want *me* to locate her *for you*."

"I know it's a lot to ask. But it's really important."

Nort started to set up the checker board again. "This has to do with that Nancy Drew business of yours, doesn't it?"

His tone rendered me sheepish. "She must have been involved in the murder. Or, at a minimum, seen something," I said. "Why else would she have disappeared so completely?"

"Folks disappear for all sorts of reasons," said Nort—an observation I knew to be true. Hadn't Schuyler Colfax Van Duyn faked his own death in a biplane crash to avoid the federal income tax? "And let's say I do find her for you," added Nort. "What do *I* get?"

His question proved surprisingly painful for me. When actually challenged to provide a quid pro quo, I realized how little I had to offer. Only a few stuffed birds and the clothing on my rump. And a roll in the hay, I suppose, if I were so inclined, but I highly doubted that I'd be the sort of fish that Nort the Messiah would ever take to market.

"What do you *want*?" I asked.

I kept my gaze focused on the checker board, watching as Nort played both red and black draughts rapidly in succession with his left hand. Countless yellow cabs and black sedans rolled through Pershing Square on the way from the train station. One of the latter might easily have jumped the curb and flattened us both with little warning. A murmuration of European starlings played avian hopscotch on the struts of the viaduct.

"How about your hat, Granny?" Nort grinned—not with malice, just amusement. "That seems like a fair trade."

I instinctively reached for the plumed tuft. "Why would you want my hat?"

"That's not the issue. I have my reasons," said Nort. "Do I get the hat?"

I cannot express the agony I experienced at that moment—like an early Christian martyr tortured to renounce Jesus. My flamingo-tufted hat was more than merely a prized possession; it stood at the core of my persona. I could hardly remember who I'd been before I became the Mad Bird Lady of East 14th Street. A Brigander, of course. Yet while I'll never shake the factual memories of my childhood, evoking the emotions—the identity—proves impossible. Akin to asking one of those long-term kidnapping survivors, like Patty Hearst or Jaycee Dugard, to conjure up her pre-trauma psyche. And despite years of skimming discount bins at flea markets and secondhand shops, I'd never encountered another headpiece quite comparable to mine. Even a pound of flesh was a less exacting demand. On the other hand, I'd committed myself to vindicating Big George's memory. For his sake, and for Rusky's, and for mine.

"Yes, you can have it," I agreed. "If you're able to find her."

Nort the Messiah laughed. A deep belly laugh—impressive for a man without a belly. "Finding this lady is extremely important to you, isn't it?"

I resented his laugher. "I don't see what's so funny about it."

"You can keep your weird hat, Granny," he said. "I just wanted to make sure this was a really big deal, and I wasn't wasting my boys' time."

I fought back tears—as though the hat had already been lost and he'd recovered it for me—grateful, although in hindsight, I should have begrudged his sadism. "So you'll find her?"

"I didn't say *that*," said Nort the Messiah. "I said I'd look."

He must have mistaken the relief on my face for torment, because he added, "Don't worry, Granny. My boys will get the job done. Give us a week."

No other patients from the seventh floor remained to be interviewed—unless, of course, one counted Angry O'Dell or Big George, and neither of those men appeared to be viable options for rather obvious reasons. For a brief interval, I contemplated sneaking into Kirby, the forensic facility on Ward's Island where O'Dell was being detained, on the false pretext of being his defense attorney, or possibly even a court-appointed psychiatric examiner, but I knew a fool's errand when I spotted one. Like I've been telling you, just because I'm crazy does not mean I'm stupid. With my luck, they'd have ended up keeping yours truly in the loony brig permanently— or even suspecting *me* of framing O'Dell. So I had to accept that I wouldn't have access to one of the most promising witnesses to the crime. And the other, regrettably, was deceased. But as I reflected upon this misfortune, I experienced another of my inklings—the strong sensation that Big George still had something essential to share with me. That he hadn't been entirely silenced. While I grappled with the meaning of this sensation, my feet—as though drawn by unseen magnetic forces deep beneath the earth's crust—lured me toward the far western reaches of Greenwich Village, onto the expanse of 12th Avenue overlooking the river.

Don't worry—I wasn't planning to jump. This stretch of Manhattan Island had once served as the port of call for the great transatlantic luxury liners, the Blue Riband-winning vessels that elevated the Cunard and White Star brands to the heights of luxury. Grandpa Brigander recalled waiting on the jetty for the four-funneled *Aquitania* to disembark Great Grandma Sophronia and the Earl of Grantham, whom she'd wed after Great Grandpa Rutherford's fatal attack of apoplexy. Mama spoke of accompanying her girlfriends from Miss Porter's to wave an American flag at the arrival of former

Prime Minister Churchill. More recently, teenage runaways and male prostitutes laid claim to the near side of the boulevard, leaving the bike path on the far side to joggers and tourists. But what attracted yours truly to this corner of the metropolis was that, whether due to oversight or inertia, Twelfth Avenue remained home to the city's few working payphones.

It took me three attempts before I found a functional phone; the first had been systematically disemboweled and the coin slot on the second jammed with chewing gum. As I fished inside my pockets for the exact change, I remembered the moment when I'd witnessed what I sometimes think of as "the beginning of the end"—a teenager speaking on a hands-free cellular phone. For an instant, I'd thought she was one of us, a psychotic girl rambling to herself. And then I noticed the ear piece and felt betrayed. Now finding a public dial tone proves a rare treasure—a trice of primal glee, like when an ornithologist spies an endangered fowl.

I had the operator look up the telephone number and put me through.

"OCME," a nasal voice greeted me. "How may I help you?"

"Is this the medical examiner?"

"Office of the Chief Medical Examiner," repeated the voice.

So they'd put me through *to the chief's office.* That doesn't happen to me very often these days—although there was a time, not so long ago, when the mere mention of the Brigander surname was enough to get a call through to the Oval Office. Shortly after his seventh birthday, Rusky had, in fact, stumbled upon Papa's private address book and had taken the liberty of prank calling Lyndon Johnson in the West Wing.

Again, the voice asked, "How may I help you?"

I decided to take a gamble. "This is Detective Libby," I said. "13th Precinct. I'm hoping to get a preliminary report on a victim we sent down on Tuesday. Name of Arnold O'Dell."

"Let me transfer you," said the nasal voice.

Two transfers and an interlude of Ravel's String Quartet in F Major later, I was on the phone with the deputy assistant coroner. The pathologist spoke in a stentorian baritone, and I had to hold the receiver at a distance from my ear. "This is Detective Libby. 13th Precinct," I explained again. The key to success was sounding confident, I knew—and hoping the coroner wasn't familiar with the actual Detective Libby's voice. "13th Precinct. We sent a body down a few days ago. O'Dell. You have anything yet?"

"Give me a minute," said the coroner. "Computers are running slow."

So far, so good. I wondered what the penalty was for hoodwinking the morgue.

"O'Dell, you said? Arnold?"

"That's right."

A long pause followed. "According to the computer, somebody voided that report. Yesterday afternoon. Cancelled by Detective Bernard Libby." I heard the coroner punching computer keys, and I feared the gears in his brain might be revving up to full throttle as well.

"Cancelled?!" I blurted out in surprise. "But what happened to the body?"

"You said Tuesday afternoon, right? Probably underground by now." A second pause followed, and then the coroner asked, "Say, detective, what did you say your name was again?"

"Lucille Tobruk," I answered. "Like the World War II battle."

"Battle of Lucille-Tobruk?" echoed the coroner. "Never heard of it."

Why had Detective Libby cancelled Big George's autopsy? I had nearly two hours to ponder this conundrum on the trip out to West Brighton, first by ferry and then on the S44 bus along Richmond Terrace. Initially, the driver refused to let me board with my shopping cart, but I made a point of very vocally citing the Mann-Volstead Act—an utterly fictitious state law that protects the rights of mentally ill passengers on public conveyances, and includes substantial civil penalties for violators—and the blockhead either grew frightened or tired of my threats, because he eventually uttered a salvo of profanity and lowered the handicap lift. My ruse was a one trick pony, of course. By the next shift, he'd probably know that the Mann-Volstead Act had only been passed in the legislature of Granny Flamingo's imagination, but I didn't plan on making a habit of visiting Staten Island. Even the homeless have their limits. Anyway.

The bus ride, through stop-and-go traffic past the botanical gardens and down Oakland Avenue, gave me ample opportunity to wonder about the autopsy. Were the police so confident they'd nabbed their killer that they were skimping on evidence? Or could Detective Libby have been in cahoots with whoever murdered Big George? Alternatively, maybe I wasn't the only one impersonating the red-faced investigator? I contemplated phoning the medical examiner's office again and cancelling several other autopsies at random—both to test my hypothesis, and also to probe and expose the weaknesses of their cockamamie screening system. I'd be doing them a favor, I told myself. Better me, as a hoax, than some cold-blooded killer terminating post-mortems willy-nilly to cover her tracks.

I kept a careful watch out the rear window of the bus; I was relieved—and candidly, also a tad disappointed—to find no mobsters on my tail. The bus itself stood nearly empty at mid-afternoon, and the few passengers, an elderly couple and a chubby girl with charcoal-stained hair and makeup fit for a Bela Lugosi film, kept their distance after my earlier dustup with the driver. My mind's eye focused on committing to long term memory every detail of Big George—his heavy eyebrows and buoyant grin—fearful that I might lose my hold on what had made him Big George, much as, with so many intervening years and Thorazine injections, I'd forgotten the physical contours of Mama and Papa and Rusky. I'd have been able to recognize them easily in a public place or in a photograph, but could no longer conjure their faces up at will, and I was determined not to let that happen with Big George.

A short stroll along Bement Avenue from the bus stop brought me to the dilapidated duplex in the Queen Anne style that Monty Castillo shared with Mary Lou. Sacks of fertilizer and vermiculite lay lifeless as punching dummies on the screened porch, betraying no signs of recent use. The husk of a barbecue grill rusted on the yard. Behind the bay windows sagged brocaded curtains—a hideous floral print in pastels. I pressed the buzzer, which let off an aggressive sizzle like a short-circuited children's toy.

On the second attempt, Mary Lou appeared at the door in a loose-fitting smock. The phlebotomist's hair, prematurely gray—even though she can't be more than thirty—gave her a shabby, mean look that is entirely inconsistent with her persona. "Goodness," she said when she saw me. "Oh, my."

A voice from the interior—Monty's—called out, "What they hell do they want?"

"It's nothing," Mary Lou shouted back. Then she lowered her voice and said, "What are you doing here, Granny? This isn't a good time."

I didn't have an opportunity to explain myself. Something shattered inside the house—either toppled or thrown—and then footsteps thumped behind Mary Lou. When Monty pushed her aside, I hardly recognized him. Four days of stubble encrusted his cheeks, and the flesh beneath his eyes had assumed an ugly gray tinge. The former security guard wore a white t-shirt over boxer shorts and slippers. "What the fuck?" he asked. "Why it's the Bird Lady!"

"I didn't mean to intrude," I said.

"Not at all," replied Monty. "I was just asking myself, how could anything possibly get worse, and then a crazy lady from the lunatic ward shows up! And who says God doesn't answer prayers?"

"Please, Monty," said Mary Lou. "He doesn't mean that."

"Don't tell me what I mean," Monty retorted. I'd initially suspected he might be drunk, but now I sensed he was merely disinhibited by poor sleep and dysphoria. "Invite the lady inside, why don't you? We were about to play cards."

He stepped aside and I found myself entering a parlor cluttered with cartons and knickknacks. An open socket in the ceiling exposed wires that had likely once illuminated a chandelier. Plastic flowers gathered dust on a credenza. From the adjacent room blasted the sound of political pundits arguing on television—coarse, angry plebians so unlike the heroic television journalists of my girlhood. To Mama, even Howard K. Smith and Walter Cronkite had proven too folksy for her tastes; "It's all been downhill," she often lamented, "since Quincy Howe left the Columbia Broadcasting System." I'm not sure what Mama might have said had she heard today's pundits firing grapeshot inside their echo chambers. As a true lady, there's always the possibility she might have clutched her hand to her breast and died on the spot. And on the subject of death, I again braced myself for mobsters with blazing Colts and Smith & Wessons, but as we passed through the foyer, the closet doors remained shut.

I allowed Mary Lou to lead me into the parlor, accepting her apologies as rapidly as she could proffer them, and seated myself on a leather hassock as far from the TV as possible. Monty settled into a Barcalounger that would have made Archie Bunker proud. On a nearby folding table lay an incomplete round of solitaire. It reminded me of those years after Uncle Drake's unfortunate incident with the Princeton applicant, when Grandma Van Duyn and Aunt Virginia distracted the poor geezer with endless rounds of bezique.

"Get our guest a drink," ordered Monty. "What do you want, Bird Lady? A pink flamingo?"

I considered requesting an Old Etonian in tribute to Uncle Drake—in his dotage, he'd downed three of them each evening with his postprandial pipe—but I doubted the Castillo household would prove well-stocked in Kine Lillet or Creme de Noyaux, and I didn't wish to embarrass them. Instead, I asked for a glass of water.

"That's what I like. A cheap date," said Monty. "Now what the hell are you doing here?"

"Let me start by saying how sorry I am," I stammered. "About your job and all..."

"It ain't over until the fat lady sings. No offense intended, Bird Lady. But the union's got this in the can," he said. "I searched that damn nutso. I couldn't have searched him any better if I'd held him upside down and shaken him."

"I know you did," I agreed. "I saw you do it."

Mary Lou returned at that moment with my glass of ice water. She set it atop a cork coaster, then retreated to the door where she stood, arms at her sides, like a footman waiting to be discharged. I didn't feel bad for her though. Even her worst day with a jobless Monty Castillo must have been better than her best day with an employed "Sarge" Brauer. Besides, she'd been a pretty girl; she could have done much better.

Monty cupped his fist in his palm. "Bastard didn't have a butter knife on him."

"I believe you," I said. "That's what I'm here about."

He looked up, suddenly interested. "How's that?"

"I'm investigating the murder."

"There's a good one," laughed Monty.

I pressed forward. "I don't believe Angry O'Dell murdered Big George. I think someone framed him—and your job is part of the incidental fallout. I'm completely serious." And I explained to Monty Castillo my doubts about Detective Libby's approach to the case, starting with my brother's aborted career as a shortstop and building up to the unmarked black sedan. I trusted Castillo—in part, because he'd gained nothing from the killing—so I divulged most of my secrets. All that I left out were my own feelings for Big George and the existence of his felonious twin. At some point, Mary Lou shut off the TV and seated herself on the sofa. "So basically," I concluded, "I'm hoping you can shed some light on what happened."

"I already told you," said Monty. "I searched that dude. And wanded him—back and front. Even if he had that blade up his ass, the wand would have detected it." As though he guessed my thoughts, he added, "It was working, too. Just fine. I went back down to the ER after the killing and tested it to make sure."

"Which means he didn't go up to the unit with a knife," I said. "So someone must have given it to him once he was upstairs."

"Tell that to your buddy, Chief Boucher. Guy had me out on my ass so quick I didn't have time to get my dinner out of the refrigerator," said Monty. "We'll send you your belongings," he mimicked. "What do I want with a three-day-old roast beef?"

I actually knew several good uses for spoiled roast beef, courtesy of Renegade Sally, including poisoning feral cats, so they couldn't massacre songbirds, and leaving rancid hunks on the doorsteps of politicians unfriendly to the homeless. But Monty Castillo didn't appear to be in any mood for friendly advice. "You've been mistreated," I said. "Badly. Anyone can see that. But I promise you we're going to get to the bottom of this."

"That's a hoot. Even if I get reinstated, I'm a marked man. Once the higher-ups have it out for you, you're screwed."

"Not if you help solve a murder," I said. "Now can you recall anything unusual that happened in the hours before the killing?"

Monty scowled. "I can barely remember my own name right now."

"He hasn't been sleeping well," interjected Mary Lou.

"I'm sleeping just fine," he snapped. "More or less."

Monty reached for the cards and reshuffled the deck. His fingers, stout with knobbed knuckles like the legs of obese spiders, bore rings from various fraternal societies. I recognized the insignia of the Benevolent and Protective Order of Elks, also the square and compasses of the Master Mason. How peculiar that this defrocked security guard and my paternal relatives belonged to the same brotherhoods. Strike one up for the Fraternity of Man! And on the subject of brotherhoods, I figured it couldn't hurt to ask about Albanians, although this line of questioning had led me nowhere so far, and I was beginning to conclude it a red herring. Or, considering its prominence, maybe a crimson mackerel or scarlet tuna.

"I have reason to believe that Albanian mobsters may have wanted Big George dead," I ventured. "You haven't had any interactions with Albanians recently? Or heard anything about them? Anything at all?" I turned to Mary Lou. "Either of you?"

"Albanians?" muttered Monty. "Let me see..." Monty laid out another game of solitaire while he thought. "Why, yes we have," he finally said. "Haven't we, Mary Lou?"

I'll confess my heart went into overdrive.

Mary Lou asked, "Have we?"

"I should tell you that I'm more familiar with Albania than the average person," said Monty, his chair creaking as he leaned forward. "When I lived in San Cristóbal, an Albanian couple also had a house in our street. The husband operated an import-export firm. Diamonds, olives, building equipment—you name it. Narek and Anahit Kasparian. They were cousins of the Albanian President, Anton Kochinyan, but they had to flee when he fell out of favor." Monty's expression turned from frustration to glee as he recalled his parents' friendship with the Kasparians, who'd apparently been quite wealthy and had boasted two pretty, and rather morally lax, daughters. "They both married young," he said, dismissing the alluring pair with the wave of a hand. "To other Albanians."

"But that was a long time ago," I said. "Have you had any more *recent* interactions with Albanians?"

"That's just it," said Monty. "We had a patient in the CPEP last month named Kasparian. Big guy, probably six foot six. Never got the chance to ask him if he was related to my folks' friends, but it was a strange coincidence." Monty's rump practically levitated with excitement. "I wouldn't have thought about the episode again, except for you bringing it up. You think this has something to do with the murder?"

"Could be. It's certainly very helpful," I agreed. "Anyway, I should get going. I have to catch the ferry. But I'll keep you posted on my investigation."

"I could find out the guy's first name for you," offered Monty. "If you think it would be helpful. I still have friends at the hospital."

"That's quite all right," I said. And I let myself out before Mary Lou had a chance to escort me. I was very familiar with Anton Kochinyan, Monty's former leader of Albania. He'd been a longtime correspondent of Great Uncle Atherton Brigander, and his entourage had stayed with us once at the summer cottage, during the height of Nixon's détente. What I remember most distinctly about Kochinyan was that he had a penchant for teenage girls, and I spent the better part of two breakfasts swatting way his hands. Also, I remember quite vividly that, at the time, President Anton Kochinyan was very much Armenian.

The ferry dropped me off at the Battery just in time to reach Astor Place by five o'clock. Unlike on the previous afternoon, when I'd had little genuine hope of finding Tecumseh Muhammed at our meeting point, now that his "departure date" had come and gone, he had no logical reason for staying away. Unless he'd actually set out for the land of bellicose alligators and jellyfish stings, which I highly doubted. More likely, he'd bought a couple of forties, or splurged on a bottle of Absolut, and mislaid thirty-six hours under a park bench or behind a loading dock. Like Ray Milland in *The Lost Weekend.* Only Milland's character quits alcohol and goes on to pen a novel, while it's hard to imagine Tecumseh Muhammed even scrawling his name on a self-adhesive tag at an AA meeting. But I didn't care if the man was as illiterate as Vasil Dushku, or even if he were perpetually buzzed, as long as he hadn't ditched me for the orange groves of oblivion. And he hadn't, I told myself. Although Tecumseh Muhammed was of man of many shortcomings, disloyalty had never accounted among them. But then I considered my own feelings for Big George, and I found myself hurrying toward The Cube with increasing trepidation.

I hopped an uptown train to 14th Street, because there's no elevator at the 8th Street subway station, and I don't like asking for help with my cart on the stairs—especially during rush hour. Even with the extra stop, I emerged from the MTA's teeming warrens with ten minutes to spare, so I slowed my pace as I headed south on Fourth Avenue toward the East Village, and stopped to catch my breath at the Wannamaker Place intersection. That's when I again observed the unmarked black sedan idling at the curbside less than a whale's length behind me. Once the light changed, I ventured across the intersection, but glanced back quickly, as the car merged into traffic. And then the vehicle accelerated. Without warning. That whale's length shrank to a guppy's width before I had a chance to react, and the sedan broadsided my shopping cart, toppling both the contents and yours truly into the crosswalk. I fear that I lost consciousness. But only for an instant. When I regained my wits and wherewithal, a Sikh cab driver stood over me, fanning my face with a magazine, while a young businessman in a cheap suit checked my pulse.

Instinctively, I reached for my hat. Gone!

The loss of my flamingo tuft sent my adrenaline surging, and I scrambled to my knees, practically flinging off the amateur medics. I silently begged the universe for its return, vowing never again to let the stampede strings hang loose. The whole purpose of chinstraps and stampede strings, after all, was for emergencies just like this one.

My hat, much to my relief, lay a few yards away, precariously close to an idle storm drain. Once I had it secured comfortably atop my head, I thanked the pair of Good Samaritans and set about gathering together the contents of my cart. Horns blared, as I was blocking the intersection, but what else was I supposed to do? I labored quickly. Warm blood trickled down my right temple, and I wanted to escape the scene before NYPD arrived and forced me to the nearest ER for bandaging. Not surprisingly, according to the Sikh cabbie, the black sedan had continued down the avenue at high speed until it peeled around a corner. Shaken, but by no means daunted, I melted into the flow of pedestrians just as the first sirens sounded.

I arrived at The Cube at precisely 4:58pm—at least, according to the clock in the window of East Village Coffee. The usual crowd of skateboarders and high school students cluttered the square, and across the plaza, a pair of gold-tinted mimes faced each other atop wooden tea chests. From the direction of Cooper Union floated the mournful strands of a solitary guitarist crooning "Leaving on a Jet Plane," as though recruited for the occasion. A pair of legs protruded from beneath a blanket opposite the Starbucks, but they did not belong to Tecumseh Muhammed. Neither man nor dog was anywhere to be seen.

I settled onto a concrete ledge opposite The Cube and waited. The minutes rolled by with the speed of canned sardines. I tried reading my history of the Hays Code, but not even lurid tales of James Cagney and Mae Clarke could distract me. I found myself reflecting back upon the good times with Tecumseh Muhammed, the glow he exuded in recounting his pranks—like the moment, during the psychiatric evaluation that preceded his release from parole, when the examiner asked him the meaning of the proverb, "One swallow doesn't make a summer," and he responded, "Of course not, lady. You gotta drink the whole bottle." Or the time our friend, Stu "Niagara Falls" Sucram, was dozing in the Washington Square Park and my man spray-painted "Kilroy was here" on the fellow's loin-sheathing barrel. As much as I pretended that I'd be okay, even better off, without Tecumseh Muhammed—that I couldn't love a man who didn't know the difference between Tallulah Bankhead and Agnes Moorehead—deep down, I knew I'd been engaged in the worst form of self-deception. I couldn't believe that, after eleven years, he'd actually ditched me for the geriatric peninsula.

"Granny!"

I looked up to find myself face to face with a smirking Ray G. He had a cigarette tucked above one ear, a toothpick between his teeth and the voracious leer of a carnivore in his eyes. "You're everywhere, these days," he said.

"I could say the same."

He grunted. Like a baboon. I knew in which direction our conversation would soon be headed—the ex-con was determined to milk another ten dollars out of me and I was equally resolved not to yield. I cringed internally as he seated himself beside me on the ledge. "Ain't it on the cold side to be sitting out here, Granny?"

I shrugged. "I'm waiting for my man."

"You mean the big Black dude with the dog tags?"

Ray G. knew exactly who my man was. He'd accompanied Tecumseh Muhammed on benders countless times. But chicanery was part of his game. "Maybe," I said.

"Oh, I thought you might be hanging with somebody new," said Ray G. "Because that dude's left you high and dry."

"What's *that* supposed to mean?"

"I saw him at Port Authority this morning. Got on a bus to Florida."

"You're sure? You actually saw him get *on the bus*."

"With my own two eyes, Granny," he said—clearly pleased with his info. "Now how about helping out an old pal with ten dollars for a pack of cigs?"

I reached into my bra and pared ten singles from my roll of bills. Anything to get the cretin away from me as rapidly as possible. And when he'd departed—with hardly a thank you—I kept vigil on that concrete shelf for the next seven hours, finally dozing off around midnight. Even the voices left me alone, maybe too shocked to speak. So I sat and waited, letting my soul absorb the end of eleven years of commitment. And for the first time since I'd met Tecumseh Muhammed, I seriously contemplated jumping into the river.

When I woke up the next morning—still curled on the same ledge, my sweat clothes coated in dew—I found myself seized with a surprising clarity of purpose. If Tecumseh Muhammed preferred getting poisoned by a coral snake or drowning in a riptide to keeping company with yours truly, I told myself, that was his prerogative. I was going to wash him right out of my hair like Mary Martin in *South Pacific*, although washing my hair was an extravagance unlikely to pass my way any time soon. If Grandma Brigander's sister, Bertie Ida, could turn down marriage proposals from Rudolf Valentino and

Mayor La Guardia, I could survive without a one-eyed drunkard who couldn't name a single Barbara Stanwyck movie. Armed with my trusty notebook and newfound determination, I set off again for Mount Hebron. It was only six forty-five. If I hurried, I hoped to catch Ms. Holm at the end of her shift.

As though inspired by my own energy, or maybe to make amends for the previous evening, the Fates chose that morning to greet me with a smile. The auspicious smile belonged to none other than the overnight nursing supervisor, Ms. Holm, herself—whose laughing visage I caught sight of through the plate-glass of the café on the ground floor of the hospital. Opposite her sat Bonnie Jean, her swollen abdomen pressed against the tabletop. I exchanged a friendly glance with desk guard—the same pleasant, dopey woman who'd mistaken my tanzanite pendant for sapphire—and rolled my cart into the coffee shop without a hitch. I managed to pull a chair up alongside the nurses' table before they realized what I was doing. "Mind if I join you for a moment?" I asked.

Ms. Holm's mouth was filled with toast; Bonnie Jean hid behind her coffee mug.

"I hope I'm not interrupting," I said. "But I've been looking for you. Both of you."

The nursing supervisor swallowed. "Forgive me, Miss Brigander, but this is rather irregular," she said. "I'm glad to see you, and that you're well, but ours isn't a social relationship."

I had to hand it to her. Cool as a cucumber. Mama had said nearly the same thing, as I recollect, when she called the state police on the Portuguese gardener, who had developed agoraphobia and refused to leave his cabin. "He either must prune," she'd told the officers, "or he must depart. I am sorry for his neuroses, but I am not running an asylum for disabled horticulturalists." I suspect Miss Holm would have fit in swimmingly among the Briganders.

"Of course not," I agreed. "This is business, not pleasure."

"If it's business, then you should telephone the appropriate administrator. Or, in an emergency, 9-1-1," said Ms. Holm. "Business is not conducted over pancakes."

That's one point upon which the nursing supervisor and my forebears would have disagreed. After all, Grandpa Brigander did once purchase the Chrysler Building during a continental breakfast at a Howard Johnson's restaurant on the New Jersey Turnpike. Of course, in that case, copious quantities of eau-de-vie had been involved.

"It's okay, Angela," said Bonnie Jean. "Let's see what she wants."

"Thank you," I said. "All I'm hoping to find out is whether either of you remember anything unusual about the day Big George was killed."

Miss Holm shook her head. "That's really not something we should be discussing."

"It's important," I said. "I'm investigating the murder."

"We'll leave our investigating to the authorities," she replied. "Won't we, Bonnie Jean?"

The younger nurse flashed me a helpless look. "It's probably best that way."

I sighed. I knew that crocodile tears were unlikely to melt Miss Holm's propriety. "What about Albanians?" I asked. "Do either of you know any Albanians?"

That was enough for Ms. Holm to glance over her shoulder toward the security desk—as though sizing up her escape route. "I'm sorry, Miss Brigander, but I think our brief chat has reached its conclusion."

"Okay. I didn't mean to upset you," I said, standing up. "I'll go."

"It's not personal," replied the nursing supervisor—her tone softening. "But as professionals, we must respect certain boundaries. I trust you can understand that."

"I understand. One last question. Any idea where I could find Dr. Bhatt?"

Ms. Holm shook her head. "That's not for me to say."

"She's on vacation," interjected Bonnie Jean. "For at least the next week. She was rather upset by what happened."

Or maybe she'd fled the scene of the crime, I thought. If her goal was to escape to a foreign country without an American extradition treaty, the stress of the murder would have been the perfect pretext. "Thanks for letting me know. How about Dr. Cotz-Cupper?"

Ms. Holm shot her colleague a lethal look, but—much to my surprise—that did not deter Bonnie Jean. "She's away too. They went together."

"Together?" Even as I said the word, I arrived at an instant recognition of the obvious. Mousy Sheila Bhatt and lissome Jamie Cotz-Cupper were a couple—just like Miss Swayne and Miss Fitzroy had been at Brearley. How obvious their intimacy suddenly seemed.

"I don't believe Dr. Bhatt and Dr. Cotz-Cupper would appreciate our discussing their travel plans," interjected Ms. Holm. "Now if you'll kindly excuse us."

She plucked a banana from her tray and stashed it inside her purse, leaving the vestiges of her pancakes as she headed for the revolving doors. Bonnie Jean slid out of the booth to follow. "You'll have to forgive Ms. Holm," she whispered. "This has all been very hard on her."

"Don't think twice. It's been hard on all of us."

"It's much worse for her," said Bonnie Jean. "Career-wise. She was in line to be director of nursing, you know, but now that's never going to happen."

I sat alone in the hospital cafeteria and reconfigured my list of witnesses. This is what my revised list looked like:

Interviewed
Alyssa the NYU student
Pryce Norton (aka Nort the Messiah)
Ray G.
"One-Brow Jack" (sort of)
P.J.
Monty Castillo & Mary Lou
Bonnie Jean (surprisingly talkative)
Ms. Holm

Refused
Sarge

Unavailable
Dr. Bhatt & Dr. Cotz-Cupper (on vacation)
Lucille from Florida (missing)
"Miss Havisham" (demented)
Arnold "Angry" O'Dell (suspect)
Big George Currier (victim)

If this had been a Nancy Drew mystery, readers would have now arrived at the moment when Nancy meets up with her friends Bess Marvin and George Fayne to unravel the puzzle. But I honestly couldn't say I'd made much progress in my three days of detective work. None of my witnesses recalled anything suspicious—and, unlike in fiction, no revelatory clues had fallen into my lap at opportune moments. Any sane person in my shoes would probably have cut her losses and given up before she got herself killed. Yet as you may recall, I am far from a sane person. So I decided, in the absence of any other reliable witnesses, the next step was to jog my own memory. And the most effective way to accomplish that was to revisit the scene of the crime.

I crossed 17th Street and ducked into a mom & pop pharmacy, one of those old-time druggists that do nearly all of their business filling prescriptions for patients newly discharged from the hospital. Clutching my chest with one hand, I asked the clerk if I might call 9-1-1. "Medical emergency," I half-cried, half-panted. From experience, I've found that proves a difficult request to turn down. But when the clerk had the dispatcher on the line for me, I said, "I need an ambulance. I'm suicidal. I'm planning to jump off the Williamsburg Bridge." Then I thanked the counter girl and browsed greeting cards calmly until the paramedics arrived to transport me across the street. I could have ambled into the ER on my own, of course, but sometimes a hard-ass resident, particularly a newcomer, will hold walk-ins who are suspected of malingering overnight in the CPEP for reevaluation. In contrast, when you're claiming to be suicidal, and accompanied by an EMS escort, you're almost guaranteed a timely admission.

But once again those pesky Fates and the Furies got the better of me. Soon after the paramedics loaded my stretcher into the vehicle, the ambulance turned up First Avenue—driving *away* from Mount Hebron rather than toward it. Initially, I figured the driver might be circling the block—maybe a side street had been closed off—but when we reached 20th Street, our sirens wailing and our speed accelerating, I realized something was dreadfully amiss. What a fool I'd been not to ask to see the EMT's badges! *So this*, I thought, *was how a kidnapping begins.*

"You're going the wrong way," I shouted. "Let me out."

"We're almost there," promised the medic in the passenger seat. "Five minutes way."

The woman couldn't have been more than twenty—probably on the pre-med path at Columbia or NYU. Or she'd marry one of her professors, like Charlotte Schuyler's mother, and everybody would say, "If she hadn't raised six children, she would have made a great pediatrician." Under different circumstances, I'd have given her a homily on the importance of staying focused. As it was, I contemplated unbuckling the safety straps and climbing down from the stretcher on my own, even jumping out the rear door if we paused for a traffic light, but I feared I might break a bone. "Don't lie to me!" I bellowed. "The hospital's behind us."

"We're going to Bellevue," she answered calmly. "Mount Hebron is on diversion."

Diversion! What an imbecile I'd been not to consider this possibility. Basically, diversion is a policy that allows a full emergency room—let's say Mount Hebron's—to temporarily divert ambulance patients to less crowded hospitals in the vicinity. Like Bellevue. So I'd basically signed myself up for a seventy-two hour stint in the wrong hospital. I was being kidnapped, but legally, and it was entirely my own fault. *Retard*, cried a voice. *Ignoramus. Dumbfuck.* Usually the voices exaggerate, but this time they had a point.

"I'm feeling much better," I pleaded. "Can you just drop me off?"

"The doctors have to assess you first," replied the EMT.

Not that I expected otherwise. Once you're in the care of the paramedics, liability fears dictate that they're obligated to bring you in for evaluation. It's a Ulysses contract—although they don't call it that. Like when Odysseus, King of Ithaca, tells his sailors to bind him to the mast so that he might hear the enchanting music of the Sirens while unable to jump into the fatal sea to pursue them. Like the clever Greek monarch, I pleaded with my captors for release, but soon found myself in the chaos of Bellevue's emergency room.

What ensued was a whirlwind of wanding and frisking, bloodwork and paperwork, punctuated by multiple medical professionals asking identical questions. To the first house officer, I told the truth: I was investigating a murder that had taken place at Mount Hebron Hospital and I had feigned suicidality to revisit the crime scene. Then my horse sense kicked in and I explained to his colleagues that I'd gotten into an argument at a drugstore and had threatened to jump off a bridge in frustration—but I hadn't meant it and I was now feeling fine. And I was just released from the hospital two days ago, I emphasized, knowing how the state auditors frown upon rapid readmissions. All the while, I was cursing myself for squandering precious hours while Big George's killer roamed the streets, unchecked, even free to murder again—precious hours during which I might be tracking down Little Abe. My best hope was that they'd hold me in the ER overnight for observation and then throw me out. But around noon, an orderly arrived with a wheelchair and I knew I was headed for the elevators.

My first action on the unit—even before I was assigned a room—was to demand pen and paper to formalize my discharge request. That starts the clock ticking. And I was still sitting in a wheelchair opposite the nursing station, my personal effects suspended in a brown paper bag draped over the frame, when I saw him. He had a bit more flesh around the neck than his twin brother, and maybe a tad more swagger in his walk, but there was no mistaking him as the spitting image of the man I'd nearly loved: Little Abe! Not a coincidence, of course, because it made perfect sense that both twins would seek to hide inside psychiatric facilities, but it was still a glorious fortuity.

He wore his street clothes—an untucked guayabera over white slacks—suggesting that his discharge date approached. He also sported a navy blue fiddler cap, so either he was well-known to the Bellevue docs, and had been allowed a "headwear exception" like I was at Mount Hebron for my flamingo crown, which seemed highly unlikely, given what his brother had told me, or the headshrinkers at the public hospital weren't too concerned about suicide by hat.

I must have been staring, because he walked straight up to me—without even a hint of self-consciousness—and extended his hand. "Hi. I'm Currier," he said. "But my friends call me 'Big George.'"

SECTION TWO

CHAPTER SIX

As the   old shampoo ad warns, "You never get a second chance to make a first impression," so I'm pleased to report that I didn't attempt to unmask my fellow inmate on the spot. If Little Abe wished to disguise himself as his older brother, who was I to interfere? Maybe he had a good reason for his deception. At a minimum, this was the sort of arrangement best discussed in private—like Grandma Van Duyn's pre-war friendship with Mrs. Joseph Goebbels—not publicly, outside the nursing station of a loony bin. So rather than declaring, "You're not Big George," I shook the man's hand and said, "It's a pleasure to meet you, Mr. Currier." I even resisted the urge to introduce myself as Mrs. Ives. And before I had an opportunity to pursue the matter further, a hawk-nosed, mustached ruffian of the Lee Van Cleef variety, who might as easily have been a Clanton Gang henchman at the O.K. Corral as a public hospital nurse, steered me into a nearby examination room and peppered me with questions that felt more like a fusillade of artillery. A far more thorough interrogation, I might add, than Detective Libby's—although the content focused on such scintillating matters as my medication allergies, dietary restrictions and bowel habits. The nurse's name was Arle. Not Mr. Arle or Arle-something, I later learned. Just Arle. One word. Like Jesus. Or Liberace. Even his ID badge read only Arle— strategically-placed surgical tape covering whatever letters appeared before and after. I missed P.J.'s company so deeply that my body veritably ached.

The remainder of the afternoon afforded minimal opportunity for a tête-à-tête with Little Abe. Although I'd been a patient at Bellevue before, on multiple occasions, the staff didn't have an instant familiarity with me the way they did at Mount Hebron, so I found myself subject to the standard intake protocol: everything from surrendering my hat and having my belongings inventoried to the doctors requesting my recent charts from the three other hospitals I'd visited previously that year. Much of this effort fell to a pudgy, double-chinned older resident with effeminate lips who could easily have entered—and lost, for trying too hard—a Charles Laughton look-alike contest. When he asked me, during our initial interview, whether I was sexually active, I responded by thanking him for his interest, but assured him that I'd be no match in bed for Elsa Lanchester. He chuckled—the poor dolt chuckled at nearly everything—although I'm confident he neither understood the joke nor the reference. I believed my predicament could get no worse, but when you've gone from Brigander heiress to undomeciled schizophrenic, you realize things can *always* get worse. In my case, Dr. Laughton assigned me to share a room with the Red Witch, a notorious denizen of Penn Station who carried a well-earned reputation for synthetic marijuana consumption and misanthropy. Despite her nickname, whose origins have been lost to time and history, only her wool socks proved consistently red. I made a point of greeting her with a chipper, "Good afternoon," as I surveyed my quarters.

"This is a private room," she snapped. "Enter at your peril."

I'll confess I found myself suddenly relieved that they'd locked up my hat and plush animals; I didn't trust the Red Witch not to damage them intentionally.

The room itself was a pale shadow of the cozy, if spare, accommodations at Mount Hebron. When I tested the thin, pinstriped mattress—still shorn of linens at two o'clock in the afternoon—the iron bed slats groaned under my weight. A faint aroma of urine and disinfectant hung perennially in the air, as though engrained in the plaster and tile. Each room contained a massive porcelain sink, but these were vestiges of a bygone era—the water supply long ago staunched; a jagged fissure bisected the basin of ours. Refreshments also lagged behind Mount Hebron in quality; my hospital might no longer serve food blessed by Orthodox rabbis, but at least one could easily identity the contents of the meal trays. Our dinner at Bellevue was simply identified as "meat"—and whether it was beef or venison or wild yak remains a mystery to this day. While there were fewer groups and activities scheduled for the patients than at Mount Hebron, the daily routine at Bellevue also featured more bureaucratic interruptions—contraband searches, weekly weighings, as though we were competitive wrestlers, even a fire drill—so I spent most of the afternoon exchanging discrete glances with Little Abe, but didn't have a chance to speak with him in private until shortly before curfew. That was when I spotted his roommate, a half-deaf geezer I knew from years earlier at the state hospital on Ward's Island, dozing across one of the lounge chairs in the dayroom, and I seized opportunity by the horns and snuck into his room.

The man who'd introduced himself as Big George lay sprawled on the bed, eyes open, as though seeking wisdom from the cracks in the ceiling. He appeared more amused than genuinely surprised to see me lurking at the foot of his bed.

"Hey," I said. "Want some company?"

"Depends whose," he replied, sitting up.

I feared I might blush again—as I'd done with his brother—so I quickly seated myself on the opposite bed and focused upon the task at hand. I was investigating a murder, after all, and this was a professional visit, not a social call. But my companion didn't help my focus when he stretched his arms, revealing the full strength of his chest and shoulders. If he were "Little" Abe, I didn't want to encounter "Big" Abe in a dark alley, and I could easily understand why a love-struck Antigona Dushku has forgiven this man's string of bad checks. "If you're the company," he said, "I'll be glad to make an investment."

That was my kind of joke. But I had a job to do. "Let's level with each other," I said. "Your brother was a friend of mine."

"Really?" he asked, appearing genuinely astonished. "Little Abe?"

"You sound surprised."

He laughed. "My brother has a knack for making friends," he said, "but not for keeping them. If you said he owed you money, now *that* would be a different story."

"And I also know you're Little Abe, not Big George," I added, plunging forward. "Your brother and I spent a night together in Mount Hebron. He told me all about how you'd been run out of St. Louis and crossed the Albanian mob."

I regretted the phrase "spent a night" because it conveyed the wrong connotation, but clarifying the matter was likely to dig my hole deeper. Instead, I waited for my companion to acknowledge his identity. He didn't. His eyes widened slightly, his pupils engorged like a heroin addict's, and he rested his temple on his fingertips. "My brother told you *that*," he muttered.

"Your brother told me *everything*," I replied. "Even how he'd come down to New York City from Newport to help you and ended up with NYPD on his trail."

That snapped him from his trance. "Jumping Jehoshaphat on pogo stick," my companion exclaimed. "He's still up to his old tricks, is he?"

The present tense unsettled me—reminding me that this man still believed his brother was alive. Why shouldn't he? And at some point, I knew, I'd have to reveal the truth.

"I hate to break this to you, lady, but you've been had," he said. "My name really is George Currier. From Newport, Rhode Island. I'll have the nurses show you my ID in the morning, if that's what it takes to convince you. So most of what you're saying is true. My baby bro did suggest that I check into a psychiatric asylum to avoid the police and the mob; he's apparently done it before himself. Only I'm afraid the guy who you met at that other hospital wasn't me, but my incurable brother, Abe Currier, formerly of St. Louis, Missouri."

"That's impossible. He didn't know the first thing about St. Louis."

Now my companion guffawed so hard he nearly lost his breath. "Never trust a man who forges documents for a living, lady. Little Abe lived in St. Louis for over forty years. Since we left high school. He drove a cab for a while, sold beer at Cardinals games. Nobody knows The Lou the way my bro does. But what he knows, and what he wants *you* to know that he knows, are two different matters entirely."

I'd been preparing myself to shock my companion with news of his brother's death, but now I was the one forced to process this bombshell and its implications. If the man I'd nearly fallen for had been Little Abe, then he'd been flirting with me while Antigona Dushku pined away for him in her Jackson Heights motel. That meant the man who'd swatted me on the rump with a *New Yorker* magazine didn't repair boats on Narragansett Bay, that my premonitory kiss had been secured under false pretenses, that my pipe dream of sharing domestic bliss in Rhode Island hadn't even been a plausible fantasy. And his murder likely hadn't been the product of a misunderstanding, but a successful hit on the correct target. I tried to recalibrate. *Dumbass*, sniped a voice. *Way to go, Nancy Drew!* How had I been fooled so easily, multiple times over, by the very man whose memory I'd been attempting to vindicate? God, I was a dolt. Hadn't I said twins were good for a farce? Well, here was the proof.

I must have started sobbing, because Big George—the real Big George—offered me a tissue from a box on the nightstand. Then he sat down beside me, wrapped his thick arm around my shoulder, and let me bawl into his hospital gown.

"Don't take it so hard, lady," he said. "You're not the first woman my brother hoodwinked in his life, and I'm sure you won't be the last. I swear he'll be lying his way to an early grave—and he'll probably give a false name to the undertaker."

The distant sound of one-named Arle conducting room checks brought me back to my senses. I knew I had to inform Big George about his brother; some revelations could not wait until morning. I wiped my eyes with the Kleenex and said, "I wish I didn't have to tell you this, Mr. Currier, but your younger brother...Little Abe...is already dead."

Big George released my shoulder and stood up, pacing to the window and back. Unlike the windows at Mount Hebron, which are shatter-resistant acrylic, those at Bellevue have a wire mesh laced into them that exudes a penal aura.

"He was murdered in the hospital," I explained. "I've been investigating."

At first, I sensed my companion might lose his composure, but after a moment on the brink, he gathered his emotions rapidly. "Okay, it is what it is," said Big George, matter-of-fact. "I suppose it was inevitable."

Be glad it wasn't you, I reflected. *Be glad the killer didn't think you were him.*

And that's when it struck me how relieved *I* was that the real Big George remained alive, that the man who'd died had been his dissolute brother from Missouri. My fantasies of escaping to Newport and keeping Big George's dinner warm while he tended to the air-conditioners on billionaires' yachts might yet be pipedreams, but they were once again pipedreams with a life to them. I didn't have much time to contemplate these sentiments, however, before Arle's nasal twang rose from the adjoining room. "Bed check," he announced—although he could easily have been inviting patients to a shootout in the main square at high noon.

"I have to go," I said. "I'm so sorry about your brother."

But I wasn't anxious or fearful as I had been at Mount Hebron. My guts told me that I'd be seeing Big George again in the morning, and—admittedly, here it was a bit difficult to distinguish my instincts from my aspirations—for many more years to come.

After breakfast the next day, to be thorough, I had Big George request his driver's license from the safe. Trust but verify. That worked for Ronald Reagan with the Russians and, I might add, also for Uncle Dewey when Aunt Genevieve went for one too many unchaperoned horseback rides with Gene Autry. As a pretext, Big George told Arle that we had a bet going about his height, and he made quite a point in the day room of insisting he was five foot nine—insinuating that I'd suggested otherwise. His performance proved rather convincing, almost moving, certainly credible enough to persuade the nursing staff that providing the ID was the path of least resistance, and I recalled that his brother had also claimed to do some acting in his day, so while we waited for security to retrieve his wallet, I asked if this were true. "That's a laugh," said Big George. "If you mean *stage* acting. Conning strangers is another matter entirely." And that's when I realized that almost everything Little Abe had told me of himself had actually been pinched from his brother's history. "The only two things we had in common," said Big George, "Are heart disease and hemorrhoids. He was even a half inch shorter than me, and I have the driver's license to prove it." I was already hoping for a third similarity: Identical tastes in women.

Big George's evidence checked out. He possessed a Rhode Island driver's license with a Newport address, also a social security card and a marine mechanic's permit. Of course, he could actually have been Little Abe the forger, and have counterfeited all of these documents, but to what purpose? No, in this case, Occam's razor strongly argued for the veracity of his claim. Once he'd surrendered his wallet again to the charge nurse, I led Big George into the television room—we found the most secluded table possible, a small alcove used intermittently by the medical students for their practice interviews—and, in hushed tones, I shared the story of Little Abe's murder with his older brother. Now that I'd found the missing sibling—although not the one I'd been hunting for—there was no reason not to divulge everything. I also shared a few details about my own background, including my Brigander upbringing and my soft spot for the Ocean State, although I didn't see any need to mention Tecumseh Muhammed or his flight to Florida.

"You're really Walt Brigander's daughter?" asked Big George.

"Really and truly."

"I remember that dude," said Big George, catching me off guard. "I did a job for him in the early eighties. Fly bridge yacht, right? Probably an eighty-footer?"

"Eighty-two feet," I said.

"Damn fine vessel that was," he said. "But a darn fool thing, if you don't mind my saying, cruising a boat like that out in a storm."

I suppose some gals might have taken offense to a stranger calling their dead father a fool, but not yours truly. I was merely awed that Big George, who already seemed to offer everything a woman might want, had actually met Papa. Had been aboard his yacht! In the nonexistent battle for my affections, this man was rapidly muscling out P.J. and Michael Landon, although the good thing about fantasy crushes is that you're allowed to cheat on them with impunity.

"The Lady Chatterley! That was her name," exclaimed Big George, beaming. "Am I right or am I right?"

"I can't believe you remember."

The yacht's name had been the source of some considerable tension between Grandpa Van Duyn, who found its allusion obscene, and Grandpa Brigander, who'd contributed a pretty penny to the legal defense of Lawrence's novel in Great Britain. I can still remember climbing down the kitchen stairs with Rusky at the townhouse and eavesdropping as the two patriarchs agued behind the oak doors of the study, Grandpa Van Duyn asking, "Is that the sort of book you'd want your daughters or servants to read?" What a lost world that was—for better or worse. Probably for better, but I still find myself missing it now and again. Not the luxury, mind you, nor even the security, so much as the certainty, the confidence (however false) that, no matter how chaotic the outside world, no matter what happened in the rice patties of Southeast Asia or on the streets of Chicago, affairs would always carry on much the same for us Briganders and Van Duyns. What naïveté! Like those Confederate plantations owners who thought they'd rout the yellow-bellied Yankees in a week.

"Can I ask you something, Henrietta?" asked Big George. "You and my brother. Were you two..."

I didn't want to lie. One of the lessons I learned from Renegade Sally, who retained a strain of heartland conservatism to the last, in spite of her best efforts to shake it, was that you should never lie to your spouse or partner, because it's impossible to prevaricate only once. "Soon you're spinning webs of deceit to cover up a minor falsehood, even a trivial deception," she'd warned, "until you're embroiled in your own personal Watergate"—and my own firsthand experience watching the unsteady marriages of my forebears and their siblings easily confirmed this. On the other hand, if I confessed to harboring a crush on Big George's brother, or of having a premonition that we'd kiss, I feared he'd lose any limited romantic interest he might have. "My taste in Curriers," I said, "runs more New England than Midwestern."

Big George chuckled. "So you have a taste in Curriers, do you?"

My entire body must have turned the color of a scarlet ibis. If I'd said nothing further, I suspect Big George might have kissed me himself—hospital rules notwithstanding. But when I'm feeling vulnerable, I have a habit of rambling, and in this instance, possibly one of the most vulnerable of my adult life, I retreated into the safety of professional responsibilities. "I'm happy you're alive," I said, not meeting his gaze, "but that doesn't change the most crucial fact. A murder was committed this week and we still don't know who did it or how."

"We?" asked Big George.

"You'll help me, won't you?" I asked. "He *was* your brother."

"I'll think it over," replied Big George. "I'm not sure I want to get any more mixed up in this madness than I am already."

That was probably the wise answer. And, if I'd had good sense, I'd have dropped the matter entirely. But then I thought of Little Abe in my premonition. And of Rusky's lifeless body lying at the bottom on that elevator shaft while the elevator inspectors drank bubbly on a tropical beach—or whatever they did with the time spent endangering innocent bystanders. And as you already know, yours truly is as stubborn as she is crazy, so I wasn't going to be able to sleep at night until I solved Little Abe's murder.

Not that I could get much sleep anyway with the Red Witch snoring in the adjacent bed. It wasn't the reverberations of her respiratory architecture that kept me awake—not after thirty-five years of overnight traffic and a decade sharing a sleeping bag with Tecumseh Muhammed—but the fear that she might avenge herself upon me while I dozed. What if she'd also concealed a serrated knife on the unit, waiting for an interloper like yours truly? I found myself wondering what those final seconds had been like for Little Abe. Would he have been awakened by the stab wounds? Or were the blows so quick, and fierce, that he'd instantly gone into shock? Ghastly thoughts like these drifted into others even worse: my parents' final minutes on the doomed Lady Chatterley, Rusky's last seconds in the elevator shaft, Great Uncle Manatee Phil's brief, gruesome attempt at lion taming. Realistically, of course, the Red Witch was far more likely to smear me with feces while I slept, or to prune my hair in odd patches, but these weren't exactly appealing outcomes either. I kept one eye open most of the night, and lined up for medication the next day with the fire of irritability simmering in my sleep-deprived craw. To make matters worse, Arle insisted on examining the inside of my mouth after pill distribution—a task he approached with the rigor of an orthodontist—so I was unable to "cheek" my meds. And let me tell you, there's nothing to ruin a person's morning like six milligrams of unwanted Invega. An unpleasant mental fog enveloped me twenty minutes later, and I returned to my room to nap, not wishing to encounter Big George in my compromised state.

By mid-afternoon, I felt more or less myself again. As I was conjuring up strategies to avoid another dose of antipsychotic with bedtime, a scraggy, carrot-mopped young man in a short white coat knocked on my door. "Excuse me, Miss Brigander, but may I come in?"

"You may do whatever you wish," I said. "I don't own the place."

The fellow looked petrified—like he might swallow his own tongue. He reminded me of Rusky before his first piano recital at Riverdale and I felt bad for him.

"I'm sorry to disturb you, Miss Brigander, but I'm a medical student, and Dr. Schmeizer suggested you might be a good patient for a mock interview."

It took me a moment to register that Dr. Schmeizer was "Charles Laughton."

"A mock interview? You mean you want to mock me?"

The poor boy nearly choked. "I meant a *practice* interview," he stammered. "In front of the other students. To help us learn..."

I usually avoid these training sessions like the plague. Who wants to be a show monkey? But the kid reminded me of my brother, and I sensed my opposition melting. "What's your name, young man?" I asked.

"Bobby," he said. "Bobby Levant."

"That's a good name," I replied. "Not related to Oscar Levant, are you?"

The boy smiled at me: unenlightened and witless. Like, I fear, so many young men and women these days.

"He used to host a talk show. Before you were born." I considered edifying Bobby on the importance of his celebrated namesake—but the problem in these situations is that there's never any context, meaning I'd have to start with Al Jolson, or the *Information Please* radio quiz, or probably go all the way back to the days of D. W. Griffith and Cecil B. DeMille, so it was easier to just drop the entire subject. Instead, I asked, "Levant is a Jewish name, right?"

The kid nodded. Poor guy, so eager to please. Just like Rusky had been.

"You didn't happen to know Doc Weingarten from Park Avenue, did you? He looked like the comedian Morey Amsterdam, if that means anything to you. Or Dr. Hermann Kavarsky? Thin-rimmed spectacles? Bushy salt-and-pepper beard?"

"I'm afraid I didn't," said Bobby Levant. I imagine he'd started to regret knocking on my door. "So Miss Brigander, would you be willing to be interviewed?"

I took pity on the boy and stood up. "Lead on, Macduff. If I am to be mocked, so be it."

The flustered young man steered me into the same alcove where I'd conferred with Big George the previous evening, only now I had to parade through a conclave of trainees. They parted as I entered—like the waters for Moses—and soon I found myself opposite poor Bobby, who explained the details of the exercise with painstaking precision. "For education purposes only..." "Not therapeutic..." "Confidential unless you pose a threat to yourself or others..." As Yul Brenner says to Deborah Kerr in *The King and I*: "Etcetera, etcetera, etcetera!" I'd heard it all countless times before, but I allowed the poor lad to lay out his caveats.

"Okay, Miss Brigander," he said. "Now if you're ready for a few questions..."

I winked at his colleagues, and summoning up my most affected Gloria Swanson caricature, declared, "I've been waiting for this moment since the day I was born."

The would-be doctor looked down at his clipboard. "Hmm...I see...well, what brought you to the hospital?"

"An ambulance."

Several spectators snickered. A cute girl in the second row yawned.

"I phrased that poorly, Miss Brigander," said Bobby. "Why don't you tell us a bit about yourself and why you're here?"

"Do you really want to know?"

He leaned forward and simpered, his palms resting on his knees.

"Okay, but it's a long story," I said. "I suppose I could start with the French Huguenots who settled New Rochelle and the Dutch of New Amsterdam, but the Briganders didn't really crack the upper echelons of the *Social Register* until Great Grandpa Rutherford went into the railroad business with Jim Fisk and Jay Gould. Of course, the Van Duyns—that's my mother's family—were frequent visitors to the White House during the Hayes, Garfield, Arthur, Harrison and McKinley Administrations. Great Grandma Van Duyn was close friends with a whole string of First Ladies—all except Frances Cleveland, because she was a Democrat."

"When exactly was this?" interjected Bobby.

"After the Civil War," I explained. "Late nineteenth century." I hadn't been intending to lampoon the poor fellow—but as Grandpa Brigander often said, you don't know a man's history until you know how his family made its first billions, so I felt some contextual background essential for a full psychiatric evaluation. Alas, my response had clearly flummoxed the aspiring clinician. Even Charles Laughton, whom I noticed loitering in the background, betrayed a smirk on his girly lips. My Jewish medical student shifted uneasily on the metal folding chair, displaying none of the reassuring confidence of Doc Weingarten or Dr. Kavarsky. Maybe he was the product of a mixed marriage.

"I'm sure you have an interesting family, Miss Brigander" said Bobby, "but I'm hoping we could focus directly on you."

Unfortunately, to yours truly, those words proved a call to battle. What choice did I have but to enlighten him on the psychological importance of pedigree? So I launched into a comprehensive Brigander-Van Duyn history, noting our three United States Senators, our two governors (of Maine and New Jersey), Great Uncle Atherton Brigander's Presidential Medal of Freedom, Cousin Van Wyck Van Duyn's back-to-back Pulitzer Prizes (in history and biography), and my family's behind-the-scenes roles in financing the construction of the Panama Canal, Grand Coulee Dam and city of Las Vegas. "So, young man," I declaimed, delivering a full-throated oration as I'd once done reciting Cicero in Ms. Fitzroy's Latin class, "Past is present. Santayana was sadly mistaken. Even if you commit the lessons of history to memory, you are nonetheless *still* doomed to repeat them. *Every last one!*" With each successive phrase, I sounded more and more like Uncle Dewey.

"Thank you, Miss Brigander." The voice did not belong to hapless half-Jew Bobby Levant, but to Charles Laughton (aka Dr. Schmeizer) who'd stepped forward to truncate the practice session before it unraveled any further. "That was very helpful. In the interest of time, I do think we're going to have to stop here."

The shrink clearly believed I was nuts. Floridly grandiose. Of course, once he looked up my heritage on line, the last laugh would be on him. While psychiatrists aren't particularly gifted at detecting malingerers, their best comeuppance occurs when they mistake genuine celebrities and public figures for delusional. I recall one episode at Columbia Presbyterian when a former capo in the Gambino crime syndicate presented claiming that he'd just entered the witness protection program, but feared his cover had been blown and didn't know where to turn—all of which proved true. Of course, the doctor-on-call assumed the guy was suffering the throes of psychosis, and it wasn't until the next morning that one of the social workers recognized him from his photo in *Newsday*. Or there was the time at Mount Hebron when Dr. Robustelli diagnosed an A-list musical luminary—I dare not say who—with bipolar mania when she claimed she'd come to Manhattan for her Grammy nomination. She's gone platinum six times, and is probably more recognizable to kids under twenty than Mickey Mouse, but if you're not a veteran of *The Lawrence Welk Show*, Vince Robustelli has never heard of you. So I had little doubt that Charles Laughton would diagnose me as loopy for the students; I was far less confident that later, after the truth became known, he'd inform them of his mistake.

My trip down Brigander-Van Duyn memory lane had invigorated me, but it wasn't even dinnertime, so I headed toward the television nook in search of Big George. To my surprise, I found him waiting for me at the entrance to the day room. He sported street clothes, but a change of style from the day before: neatly-pressed gabardine slacks and a knit turtleneck. Snazzy. Far more elegant than his brother.

"You're dressed like a human being," I observed. "They must be getting ready to discharge you soon."

"Not soon. *Now.* Already got my walking papers," he said, patting his trouser pocket. "I had to beg them to let me stick around long enough to speak to you."

"So...," I said.

"So...," he replied. "Will I see you again?"

"If you want to," I said. "We should arrange a meeting place. And we should both go there every day at a precise time until we find each other, okay?"

"I guess. If that's what you'd like," he said. "Name your time and place."

My initial thought was five o'clock at the Astor Place Cube. But that felt like cheating—and besides, what if Tecumseh Muhammed returned to New York someday and surprised us? No, that wouldn't do. "How about the statue of Dvořák in Stuyvesant Square? It's close to Mount Hebron and there are some lovely benches to sit on. Let's say six o'clock?"

"Okay," agreed Big George. "Six o'clock at the Dvořák statue in Stuyvesant Square."

"And you'll be there every day?"

"Every day," agreed Big George. "But don't keep me waiting too long. I do have to get back to Rhode Island at some point." He added, almost as an afterthought, "Melanie wasn't thrilled that I left her behind and I'm feeling rather guilty."

Amazing, isn't it, how one name—one word—can suck all of the joy out of the universe. I imagine I felt the way Jackie Kennedy did the first time her ears heard "Marilyn" on a stranger's lips. As my soul registered that Little Abe wasn't the only Currier who enjoyed juggling multiple women, Big George flashed his "aw shucks" grin as though we'd grown up in a culture where bigamy was the norm and monogamous devotion the perversion. Like Jennie Kimball's missionary from Wyoming, although these days even Mormons stick to one wife.

"Who's Melanie?" I asked.

A look of pure delight, even elation, crossed Big George's innately stoic features. "Melanie Daniels," he said. "My Moluccan cockatoo. Can't wait for you to meet her."

It was as though the Fates had decided to toy with me for their amusement. One moment I'd been betrayed by an adulterer, the next courted by a bird-daddy. Here was a man who'd met Papa *and* owned a parrot. What more could a woman wish for in life? And asking me to meet his pet bird wasn't far removed from inviting me home to meet his family—although I'd already encountered his baby brother, and that hadn't worked out particularly well, so I wasn't sure whether meeting more of Big George's relations would prove to be in my interests.

"Melanie Daniels is an odd name for a cockatoo," I said.

"After Tippi Hedren's character in Hitchcock's *The Birds*," explained Big George. "Have you seen it?"

Of course! Why hadn't I recognized the name instantly? In truth, I hold decidedly mixed feelings about the film. While as a work of cinema, it's unarguably a masterpiece, I can't help fearing the picture generates misleading and even defamatory impressions regarding our feathered compatriots—especially among those who don't know better. At the same time, any man who owns a parrot christened after a character in a classic Hollywood film is basically cradling my heart in his hands. "Of course, Melanie Daniels," I said. "I'd forgotten her name."

"So you have seen it," said Big George. "I just love old-time movies. I bring my laptop with me to the marina and play them in the background while I work."

I fought back tears—tears of joy. I couldn't remember the last time I'd experienced such exultation, but I also feared the Fates might have another trick up their sleeves. What if Big George were playing me for the fool like his brother had? Or if I'd go to meet him at the Dvořák statue only to find he'd been stabbed to death in his sleep the night before? But my instincts told me that none of these calamities would come to pass. That I'd be reconnecting with Big George sooner rather than later, and on the most convivial of term. Yet I couldn't shake the chronic, latent anxiety that comes with many years of dashed hopes and scuttled expectations.

"So I'll be seeing you," said Big George. "Six o'clock at the Dvořák statue. Rain or shine."

"And you'll stay safe?" I asked. "Promise."

"I should be fine, Henrietta," he said. "Now that Little Abe is gone, why would anyone even be looking for me?"

Then—to my shock and delight—he hugged me. Not a fierce, passionate embrace, but a hug nevertheless. Gentle and affectionate. This proved too much public intimacy for Arle, who must have been spying, because the one-named nurse appeared a moment later and steered Big George through the thick magnetic doors and off the ward. My new companion's last words, called out as he departed, were, "Don't worry! I'll be okay."

His reassurance made sense to me in the moment. With his brother gone, why would anyone have wanted to harm him?

But later, when I recalled the black sedan that had nearly flattened me the previous evening, and the mysterious phone call to cancel Little Abe's autopsy, it became evident that someone, some individual or group other than yours truly, wasn't yet done with the matter. And as long as that unknown somebody or somebodies was still out there pursuing their nefarious agenda, I figured, Big George's life remained at risk. And so, I feared, was mine.

Once Big George had earned his freedom, I found myself champing at the bit to depart, but Charles Laughton and his bosses had other ideas. The next day was a Sunday, which meant only a five-minute chat with the physician-on-call, a dainty-chinned girl bearing a vague resemblance to a young Ida Lupino, who regretted to reveal that springing me was far above her pay grade. Then for three consecutive mornings, yours truly was subject to grueling evaluations in which the pansy-lipped resident probed the origins of my suicidality. When did I first wish to kill myself? What methods had I considered? Had I left behind a note? Written a will? That last question carried me to the brink of both laughter and tears, as I contemplated how the trusts & estates division at Cravath, Swaine & Moore might handle a request to divvy up my distinctive headwear and collection of stuffed birds. But Charles Laughton did set my mind reeling. If something were to happen to me—let's say the black sedan proved more accurate next time—did I really want my few prized possessions bestowed upon those ancient Beacon Hill cousins or Papa's impoverished kin in South West England? And if I died intestate, how would the probate court divide my belongings? Would the judge follow the path of King Solomon and threaten to cleave my hat in two like the Biblical baby until one cousin cried uncle? Alternatively, if I did decide to write a will, who did I want to receive my estate? A decade ago, I'd have said Renegade Sally; a week ago, Tecumseh Muhammed. Now I wondered if Big George weren't the human being I most trusted to preserve my limited legacy.

In any case, none of my responses satisfied the headshrinkers at Bellevue. The problem was straight out of Joseph Heller's *Catch-22*, albeit largely of my own manufacture. If I insisted that I'd faked my earlier threats, such assertions meant I was minimizing my symptoms, or possibly remained in complete denial. And if I explained that I'd lied to garner admission for the purpose of investigating a murder, that claim would convince the pill-pushers that I was indeed flagrantly delusional. On the other hand, admitting that I had intended to jump off the Williamsburg Bridge—a plan to which I ultimately confessed—justified holding me against my will for another four days.

When I finally received my walking papers, shortly after rounds on Thursday morning, I treated myself to an apricot Danish at a corner deli and set out toward Grand Central Station to find Nort the Messiah. He'd had nearly a week to track down Lucille from Florida, I figured, and I didn't want whatever leads he had acquired to grow cold.

One of Nort's best qualities is that he's easy to find—just as likely to be at his usual post as are the Statue of Liberty and the Chrysler Building. Sure enough, I found the petty racketeer perched on his trusty milk crate, embroiled in his favorite endeavor. Across the checkers board sat Ray G., nursing a five o'clock shadow at ten in the morning. A twenty-dollar bill sat on the bench between them, weighed down by what looked like a disembodied windshield wiper. When the wiry ex-con spotted me, he stood up and removed a scrolled copy of the previous Wednesday's *Post* from his back pocket.

"Take a look at this, lady," he said.

And he read aloud: "Raymond Greasley, recently a patient at St. Dymphna's South, alleged that the killing is reflective of disparities in medical treatment and healthcare more generally. 'If O'Dell had been a rich white guy,' said Greasley, 'you can bet things would have been different.'" He shoved the article under my nose, giving me an opportunity to read the next line: "According to police reports, both Mr. O'Dell and Mr. Currier are Caucasian."

"What do you have to say to that?" asked Ray G. "Who's a celebrity now?"

"Your move," said Nort the Messiah.

Ray G. slid a red checker onto an adjacent square and Nort responded with a series of terminal jumps.

"Dammit, lady, you distracted me," griped Ray G. "You cost me twenty dollars."

Nort pocketed the cash. "Leave Granny alone," he commanded.

Several unkempt teenagers loitered under the viaduct, as though awaiting their leader's signal to enforce order or fracture kneecaps. Ray folded his arms across his chest, defeated.

"Haven't seen you in a while, Granny," observed Nort.

"I got myself committed again. Bellevue," I said. "Any word on Lucille from Florida?"

Nort the Messiah sorted his checkers into stacks. "No luck there. You can keep your hat. Wherever your witness is, Nancy Drew, she's not on the streets of New York City."

"Maybe she went back to Florida," interjected Ray G. "I hear it's a popular destination this time of year."

Nort threw him a muzzling glance.

"Can't you go on looking? Please?" I asked. "She's got to be somewhere."

Nort the Messiah shrugged. "No point, Granny. I've had two hundred runaways, prostitutes, panhandlers, pushers, junkies, and scammers combing all five boroughs for the better part of four days," he said. "If this woman were out there—streets, shelters, hospitals, morgue—we'd have found her. Either she won the lottery and rented a private apartment or she's hit the high road." To my surprise, Nort patted me on the upper arm. "I'm sorry, Granny," he added. "I honestly wish I had better news to report."

"It's all right," I replied. "Thanks for trying."

Another dead end. *Because you're a loser*, said a voice. *Koo koo kachu, Nancy Drew!* I shuffled off before Ray G. had another chance to hit me up for money. But now what? In detective novels, you don't see the scenes where Sam Spade or Miss Marple run out of leads and wander the streets feeling dejected. What I desperately needed was an unexpected clue—maybe a hidden vault concealed behind a false panel or a mysterious letter slid under a door in the wee hours of the morning—and with the latter in mind, I drifted disconsolately toward the Eighth Avenue Post Office to retrieve my mail. A sharp westerly breeze raged along the cross streets, churning debris and litter through the gutter. I pushed my cart against the wind, shielding my eyes, like a pioneer driving a Conestoga wagon. Of course, unlike those pioneers, I *wanted* to run into Indians. Or, at least, one specific Injun. I told myself I was going to the P.O. in search of a clue to help me solve Little Abe's murder. What I really wanted, of course, was a farewell note from Tecumseh Muhammed— even a post card from Key Largo. Anything to say that he'd remembered me. *That I mattered.* If I'd run off to the sub-tropics, I assured myself, I'd have left *him* a note.

The Farley Post Office was once the lap of luxury: a regal marble edifice where John D. Rockefeller and Mayor Jimmy Walker picked up their own mail. But like the rest of the city, and like the Briganders, it had fallen on shabbier times. I swear I heard a dozen languages while I waited in line—none of them English—and the clerk who finally greeted me, if you could call his surly, pock-marked frown a greeting, spoke a New York dialect out of a Bowery Boys flick. His mustache sagged. Remnants of his breakfast, or possibly his previous evening's supper, formed a map across his unruly beard. "Next," he cried. "How can I help you?"

"I'm picking up mail for Henrietta Brigander, General Delivery."

Not too long ago, the very mention of the Brigander name would have lit fires under the calloused toes of postal clerks, but this fellow displayed no recognition. "That's Brigander with a B, right? Or a P?"

The indignity of it all! Mama would have walked straight out the revolving doors and down the concrete staircase and have refused to do business with the United States Postal Service ever again. Alas, Mama's circumstances were obviously far different from my own, and I desperately wanted a word from Tecumseh Muhammed.

"B as in Bravo," I said. "Brigander as in Governor Sherman P. Brigander of Maine and Governor Lawton D. Brigander of New Jersey and the Brigander Library at Princeton and Brigander Street in Back Bay and Brigander Beach in Quincy and..."

But as I listed the various ways in which my family name should be familiar to the average citizen—even a homely postal clerk—the fellow disappeared into the bowels of his outfit. He retuned several minutes later with a long, cream-colored business envelope.

"That's all?" I demanded.

"I'm afraid so."

"No postcards?"

"That's it, ma'am," he said. "Now if you'll please step aside."

Story of my adult life: "If you'll please step aside." What choice did I have? I retreated to the steps of the post office and opened my missive, but I already knew its contents. Not a touching and romantic valediction from Tecumseh Muhammed. Nor the key to unravelling the death of Abraham Currier. No, my letter was an official notification from the Department of Social Services informing me of my right to be present at a guardianship hearing the following Monday at the New York County Courthouse. I took a deep breath and did exactly what Renegade Sally would have done—or would have done, at least, had someone ever described this scene in a novel. I took that official notice from Miss Celery Stalk's minions and I tore it to hundreds of tiny shreds. I might end up with a guardian on Monday—but for the moment, I remained a free woman, and a Brigander, and I intended to savor both of those birthrights for all they were worth.

I still had another five hours before my rendezvous with Big George. My *date* with Big George, I corrected myself. Why not be optimistic? Without any fresh leads to follow, I decided to drop by Kashif's food truck opposite the Met for a complimentary curried lamb shank. If time permitted, I also hoped to take in the Rubens exhibit—gorging myself on high culture to clear my palate from the residue of Bellevue. So I headed west along 32nd Street, under the four towers of the Hotel Pennsylvania, intending to wend left beneath the shadow of the Empire State Building for a stroll up the east side of the park. In tribute to the lodging landmark, where Grandma Van Duyn claimed she'd once dragged Grandpa to hear The Andrews Sisters perform "Boogie Woogie Bugle Boy," I closed my eyes and pictured myself dancing around the bandstand in the terracotta-trimmed Cafe Rouge, whistling my finest rendition of "PEnnsylvania 6-5000." I willingly lost myself in the music of my own imagination.

Fortunately, the Fates chose this moment to intervene in my favor. As I approached the corner of Sixth Avenue, I was seized with a sense of trepidation and cut short my musical interlude, opening my eyes to encounter an unmarked black sedan barreling down the asphalt. And here's where Renegade Sally's imparted street savvy came in handy—far more so than any of the knowledge that garnered Vivienne Mellon's team a win on College Bowl (although she did end up a county court judge and married to a baronet). Sally, ever mindful of her Midwestern roots, was fond of observing that "ordinary people are trained to confront the ordinary," but that you could outwit them—and often achieve your own modest ends—if you forced them to confront the unexpected. So once, when we'd nearly been busted by NYPD for shoplifting $998 worth of cosmetics—because $1000 is the dividing line between petty larceny and a felony—she asked the would-be arresting officer if she might kiss him. He didn't agree to lock lips with her, but he did release us with a dumbfounded grin and a warning. Or, on another occasion, when a pack of adolescents cornered us in an alley and their leader, who couldn't have been more than thirteen, but who brandished a box cutter, demanded our money, Sally took two aggressive steps toward him and shouted, "Give me *your* money!" and all of the would-be gangsters took flight.

So I yanked a card out of Renegade Sally's playbook. I ducked into the enclosed vestibule of a Korean grocery, taking shelter among the bins of winter fruit. But when I'd estimated the mysterious vehicle had passed, I returned to the street—and, sure enough, the unmarked black sedan idled ten yards away, behind a delivery truck, ambushed by a stoplight. So I chose the unexpected course: I chained my cart to the nearest railing and raced toward the sedan. Here, Fortune smiled upon me once again. The posterior doors of the vehicle stood unlocked. An instant later, panting, my courage thrown to the wind like birdseed, I found myself seated—rather comfortably, I'll admit—on the leather-upholstered backseat of a run-of-the-mill Oldsmobile. The driver's eyes met mine in the rearview mirror and the driver's mouth let out a succession of oaths in a peculiar language. Greek? Albanian? I can't describe the tongue exactly, except I imagine it may have been what Alexander the Great sounded like when he stubbed a toe. Only the voice behind the profanity proved higher-pitched, punctuated by a hint of tremor. My pursuer, far from the hardboiled goodfella I'd anticipated, was a woman—an *elderly* woman.

The leathery, olive-skinned creature perched high on the elevated seat, her green plastic sun visor practically touching the steering column. Her gnarled fingers clutched the wheel as though it were an unopened parachute. From the knobs on the dashboard dangled icons of St. Gregory and St. Bartholomew, while an idealized portrait of Mother Theresa had been taped to the glove box. On the passenger seat lay an open map of Manhattan. I examined her desiccated features closely, registering a familiarity I couldn't place. Had she been a fellow patient? A member of the society set in Rhode Island? Or was my imagination playing its usual game of cat and mouse with me?

The traffic light changed and the vehicle lurched into traffic.

"Why are you following me?" I demanded.

"Wait. Please, you wait," said the driver in heavily-accented English. "I cannot drive and speak at same time. Will pull over."

And she did exactly as promised on the next block, nearly decapitating a fire hydrant. Once she'd shifted into park, she turned to look at me more closely. "You should not be jumping into the cars of strangers," she said.

"And you shouldn't be trying to run them over," I snapped.

She appeared bewildered for a moment, before registering our previous encounter in the crosswalk. "Oh, that. I am sorry about that. It was an accident," she said. "I am still learning how to—how do you say, *negotiate?*—the road."

"An accident? You expect me to believe that?"

"Believe what you'd like," she replied. "But why should I want to hurt you?"

The old woman sounded so sincere, yet her claims utterly implausible. Of course, I imagine strangers often say the same of yours truly, so I tried to afford her the benefit of the doubt. "And what about Little Abe? You tried to run him down too."

The old lady winced. "That was also an accident," she said, obviously ashamed of her driving. "I do not yet have a license. But I practice."

"You shouldn't be on the roads," I said. "You could kill somebody."

I remembered when Senator Ted Kennedy drove his date off the Dike Bridge in Chappaquiddick and then phoned Uncle Drake at 5am asking him to take the fall. And when the Portuguese gardener tried to teach Cousin Adelaide how to drive—and Grandpa's Maserati ended up submerged in the shallow end of the diving pool.

"I will get—how do you say, *the hang?*—of it yet." Never had I heard a declaration spat with such fierce pride. "My father drove a truck during the war. Through minefields. Under mortar fire." She shooed away New York City traffic with the back of her shriveled hand. "This is nothing. Child's play."

"I didn't mean any offense. I just think you might benefit from a bit more practice."

"I know," conceded the old woman. "But my daughter is in distress."

At the mention of a daughter, I suddenly registered the identity of my driver. Now the similarity in their features appeared obvious. My chauffeur and would-be killer was none other than Antigona Dushku's mother. "I don't understand," I exclaimed.

"I'm Roza Toptani," said the old lady. "But everybody calls me Nënë Roza. I believe you met my daughter at the hotel."

"She asked you to follow me?"

"No, Antigona has nothing to do with this," she explained. "It was my idea. I am trying to find that boyfriend of hers. Abraham. She has been so—what is the word?—*distraught*?"

"And you believed I might lead you to him?"

Nënë Roza smiled sheepishly, revealing a gold incisor. "She told me about your visit and I thought it was my best chance," she said. "I'd nearly caught up with him a few days before—I actually spotted him on the street—but then I hit the accelerator instead of the brake."

So that resolved one mystery. Assuming this old lady was telling the truth—although I had no reason to doubt her. Hers was simply too convoluted and implausible a tale to manufacture.

"It causes me great pains to see my baby so upset," she said. "You'll help me bring that worthless villain back to her, won't you? I know he is a friend of yours, but in my opinion, he's a liar and a thief."

"*His brother* is my friend," I corrected her.

"Well, I hope they don't take after each other. For your sake," said Nënë Roza. "You don't think ill of me, do you? I know my daughter is a married woman. But Dushku, quite frankly, is worthless as the tail of a donkey...and my baby loves this Abraham."

What choice did I have but to tell her? I remembered when Rusky's white tufted marmoset died of chicken pox while we were visiting Bar Harbor, and how Papa made the mistake of keeping the death a secret until the end of the summer. For years, Rusky would phone each night from Andover to make sure all of our pets and uncles and aunts were still living. And while I imagined my elderly Albanian companion had already witnessed her share of distress, I didn't want to traumatize her further. "I don't think less of you," I said. "Any good mother would do the same. But I fear I have some bad news to share."

"He has found another woman? Bah! That can be dealt with," she retorted, raising two menacing fingers, as though to poke out his eyes. "We will bring him back—one way or another."

I didn't doubt she might carry out her threat under any other circumstances; I could easily see Nënë Roza resorting to kidnapping, or castration, if necessary. But Little Abe now lay beyond even the reach of this cold-blooded matriarch.

"I don't think that will be possible," I said. "Abraham Currier is dead."

Every last ounce of blood drained from Nënë Roza's cheeks, and I feared for a moment she might collapse right there in the driver's seat. That had happened to Barrington Van Duyn Griffin, Grandpa's cousin whose private zeppelin had floated into Mount Monadnock after his fatal stroke at the helm. But then, like the phoenix rising from the ashes, her capillaries flushed with color, and an expression of pure ecstasy coated her antediluvian face. "Thank the blessed virgin," she exclaimed. "A true miracle."

"You're *happy* he's dead?"

That checked Nënë Roza. "Not happy. One should never rejoice in another's death—no matter what sort of—what are the words?—*rancid vermin* he is," she said. "But I am relieved. My Antigona is a married woman. And that friend of yours, if you'll pardon me for speaking ill of the dead, was as crooked as the staff of Judas."

She'd get no argument from me on that count.

"But if you're relieved," I asked, "why were you looking for him?"

Nënë Roza sighed—the exhausted lament of a woman weary from illuminating the ways of the world. "Dead is much preferable to missing. When someone is dead, their fate is beyond your power to undo. So you mourn for them and then, gradually, you recover. Remarry. Or, in my daughter's case, return to the abusive lout she's already married to," explained the old woman. "But when someone is missing, you seek them. And if you love them, you search to the end of time and the far corners of the earth. How can you move on when your beloved may still be living, if you only knew the right place to look?" The old lady nodded, visibly delighted. "I will tell Antigona, and there will be wailing and moaning—but by this time next year, she'll be back to arguing with Dushku about her shopping bills and whether they can afford a cruise through the Caribbean."

I recalled my own months searching for Tecumseh Muhammed while he wasted away in tuberculosis jail. The old Albanian had a point. If I'd found his body, I'd have grieved and eventually moved on. And I thought about all of those months I'd fantasized that my parents had escaped the Lady Chatterley before it capsized—a delusion I still nourish to buoy myself at my worst emotional moments. Disappearances offer a gateway to false hopes, and false hopes a barrier to genuine progress. Antigona was lucky that Little

Abe was dead—and fortunate that I'd been able to share this discovery with her mother.

"Are you sure he's dead?" she asked. "Not faking?"

So I related my adventures of the previous week, starting with my arrival at Mount Hebron and concluding with my letter from the Department of Social Services. The full weight of my predicament suddenly pressed on my shoulders. "I still haven't solved Little Abe's murder," I lamented. "I guess the Albanian mob *wasn't* behind it. At least, not your branch. But that doesn't bring me any closer to knowing who was."

Nënë Roza slapped her palm on her thigh. "The Albanian mob. That's a good one. I grew up with real Albanian mobsters. In Tirana. The sort of men who left a dead rooster on your doorstep one morning and—if you didn't pay up—left the next night with your children's ears in a bag. But these hoodlums in Queens. Bah! Fools couldn't kill flies with a swatter."

"But *someone* killed Little Abe," I said. And then an idea popped into my thoughts, not the sort of inserted notion I couldn't shake, but just a routine good idea. "I got a proposition for you, Nënë Roza. How would you like to be my sidekick? Like Sherlock Holmes's Watson. We could solve Little Abe's killing together."

"What exactly do you mean by sidekick?" asked Nënë Roza— as though questioning the grocer on the ripeness of a melon. "This doesn't cost anything, does it?'

Just time and emotion, I thought—and possibly sanity, but I couldn't be sure. "It's absolutely free," I promised. "Or we could be a team. Like Nick and Nora or Tommy and Tuppence. All you have to do is accompany me on my inquiries and make observations that stimulate my own problem-solving efforts. It will be fun."

Nënë Roza's expression relaxed. "And you think I'd be helpful?"

Helpful, I've found, is a complex concept. Did I think this elderly Albanian woman was likely to solve Little Abe's murder? Not at all. But would her companionship prove valuable succor to yours truly? Unquestionably. Besides, at that point in my investigation, I was just grateful for any assistance that I could find. "How could you *not* be helpful?" I asked. "You've already solved the puzzle of the unmarked black sedan for me."

"I suppose I have," said Nënë Roza.

"I couldn't have done it without you."

That brought a gleam of joy to the elderly woman's eyes.

"Okay, I will be your—what do you call it?—sidekick," she agreed. "And I have a proposal of my own. Why not let me also be your guardian?"

"Excuse me?"

"You said that the Department of Social Services insists that you have a guardian," said Nënë Roza. "Why not ask them to make *me* your guardian. I am eighty-seven years old. That should be old enough for them, no?"

I didn't think age was the primary criteria for court appointed guardians, but Nënë Roza's suggestion wasn't entirely crazy. A guardian whom I knew and trusted was still a guardian, but far better than some strange attorney or social worker. Certainly an improvement over Ms. Celery Stalk with her endless spinning classes and size-two dresses.

"You tell them we are cousins," she added. "I am your distant cousin from Albania. Let them prove otherwise."

Now *that* was an idea. Renegade Sally would have been proud.

I welcomed Nënë Roza to the Brigander clan by buying her a cup of tea at a chrome-furnished diner and then we headed off to the Department of Social Services to make the city bureaucracy aware of our ancient and honorable lineage.

CHAPTER SEVEN

The branch of New York City's Department of Social Services devoted to protecting so-called "vulnerable" adults occupies a suite on the seventh floor of low-rise prewar office building two blocks east of Madison Square Garden. Black-and-yellow letter boards—of the sort that might announce the toppings at a hotdog stand or promote an inspirational quotation outside a church—list the various subdivisions and the names of their supervisors. Across the hallway operate satellite offices of the Department of Health and Mental Hygiene and Medicaid's Inspector General—located side by side, I suppose, so one can fraudulently apply for benefits and then, if stricken with a guilty conscience, immediately turn oneself in. Legend holds that Cousin Wendell Brigander had done as much during the Great Depression, bringing his own crime to the attention of the federal government when his shipbuilding outfit allegedly violated the production codes of the National Industrial Recovery Act. His belated probity earned him both a coveted Blue Eagle from the Feds and a personal thank you note from Administrator Hugh Johnson, with whom he'd graduated West Point. But Uncle Dewey, ever the cynic, insisted that the entire episode had been staged to encourage self-reporting by actual scofflaws. Anyway.

What mattered was that the Department of Social Services shared a corridor with several other bureaucratic agencies, including one of an investigatory nature. I pointed out the few vestiges of the building's past grandeur to Nënë Roza as we entered: the herringbone floor in the lobby, the crown moldings, the defunct chutes for first-class mail. But the ceiling fixtures had been dimmed by grime while the throw rug in the elevator stank vaguely of newsprint and turpentine. "The buildings in America are too tall," replied Nënë Roza as though stating the obvious. "They are bad for the health. Blood cannot travel to the brain." I'd never returned for the second semester of biology at Bryn Mawr—the half of the course that covered human physiology—so I allowed my companion's views on gravity and bodily fluids, however unconventional, to reign without objection.

I'd visited the Department of Social Services once before, many years earlier, to retrieve Rusky's personal effects from his caseworker after his elevator shaft tumble—but that primordial municipal fussbudget had held court out of a cluttered cubicle in a glass-and-steel megalith near Courthouse Square in Queens. This most staid, uninspiring borough had housed my brother's final address: an SRO off Woodhaven Boulevard in Elmhurst, basically a flophouse that rivaled nineteenth century cage hotels for its squalor. Can you imagine the indignity—the humiliation—of descending from our penthouse apartment on Central Park West with its beamed ceilings and private elevator to a cramped firetrap whose lobby was littered with a seemingly endless stream of used syringes and discarded condoms, occasionally ornamented with an abandoned undergarment or soiled human diaper? But Rusky kept his upper lip stiff, stoic and dignified to the last. Not that his fortitude made any impression on the caseworker—Ms. Grimsby-Glumson, I believe her name was, like a Dickens character. To her, the Brigander surname meant no more than that of a common pickpocket, and when she handed over Rusky's most treasured possessions—including his baseball jersey and class ring from Andover, his autographed Ted Williams baseball cards, and his first-prize plaque from the New England Ferret Association—her distaste was apparent. I gave the ring to his "summer girlfriend" from Newport and the jersey to his former Dartmouth roommate, a ruddy ball of dough who claimed heirship to a chain of funeral parlors. The cards I mailed to the Baseball Hall of Fame in Cooperstown; they thanked me with a confirmatory letter that I might use for tax purposes. And the commemorative tablet still remains in my possession, at the bottom of my shopping cart, albeit a bit warped and splintered for wear. When I'm feeling particularly lonesome without my brother, I run my fingers over the engraving and remind myself that all of his years training those wretched ferrets hadn't been for naught. But I fear I'm getting off course. What I was explaining was that Nënë Roza had driven us to the Department of Social Services on 30th Street in Manhattan—cutting off an ambulance and a horse-drawn carriage en route—and that we'd ridden the elevator to the fifth-floor suite of the Mental Health division.

The office itself looked recently refurbished; a hint of Pine-Sol hung in the air. At the ersatz oak counter, a buxom creature—the sort Mama would have referred to euphemistically as having "nice eyes"—looked up from a personal phone call with a laugh. "Got a client. Later," she said into the receiver, then asked, "How can I help you?"

We must have made a peculiar sight: yours truly in her avian threads and Nënë Roza with her embroidered wool apron and plastic green sun visor. I nudged my newfound relation forward, but she held her ground—planted firmly as a rubber tree. The receptionist waited, expectant, the sort of girl who leads her life as a perpetual spectator. On the countertop rested a bowl of Hershey's kisses wrapped in multi-colored Christmas foil. Whether they anticipated the coming holiday season or commemorated the previous one proved unclear.

"My name is Henrietta Brigander," I finally said. "But I go by Granny Flamingo. And this is my long-lost Albanian cousin, Nënë Roza." For authenticity, I added, "Our great-grandfathers were brothers. Her mother's mother's father and my mother's father's father." I hoped that Great Grandpa Van Duyn might forgive me.

"Okay," agreed the busty clerk. "What can I do for you two?"

I felt sorry for the shapely girl; I could easily imagine her boring men with longwinded tales of daily life while they calculated the distance between their palms and her breasts. I could see her squat on the beach, multiple pregnancies later, lathered in lotion and fanning her décolletage with her bare hand. Or childless, cheating on her Weight Watchers, exhausting her primary care doctor with descriptions of her bowel movements. Behind her, above an African violet, someone had crossed off the dates on a wall calendar with a crimson magic marker. I yearned to give the poor dear a preemptive hug, something that might tide her over for the rainy days ahead. Of course, none of this was any of my concern.

I focused on the matter at hand. "So I have a new caseworker. Briana or Brittany. You don't know her, do you? She looks rather like a stalk of celery."

"Sorry," answered the receptionist, shaking her head. "The department has a lot of caseworkers."

"It doesn't matter. You haven't missed much," I said. "In any event, Ms. Celery Stalk—that's what I call her—believes that I would benefit from a legal guardian. I have a hearing scheduled for Monday. I can't say I'm thrilled at the prospect, you understand, but what choice do I have? And then this morning I happened to run into my dear cousin, Nënë Roza, and she has generously volunteered to look after my affairs. So I was wondering if there might be away for us to sign the papers today and formally appoint her my guardian without having to go to court?"

The receptionist glanced at Nënë Roza. My companion appeared even slighter and more wizened under the incandescent lights—as though she herself might benefit from a guardian. "I am her cousin from Albania," she said. "Where do I sign?"

The buxom girl rose from her chair. "Excuse me a moment," she said. "I'll have to ask the deputy assistant director."

Not a hint of appreciation for the absurdity of any office—let alone one that occupied only one third of a floor of a prewar low-rise—that required a deputy assistant director. And I had little doubt this vital personage likely had an aide-de-camp of her own. Or several. I fear Uncle Dewey's disdain for what he called "the socialist layer cake" had rubbed off on me, but the receptionist remained oblivious to the excessive hierarchy and redundancies. She might as easily have been conferring with the Assistant Second Deputy Undersecretary to the Admiralty or the People's Associate Commissar for Intraoperative Operations or Major Major Major. When she returned—her chest leading the way—she displayed an expression of sad benevolence. It was the same look that Dr. Hämäläinen, the Finnish veterinary rheumatologist, had worn when informing Mama that he'd been unable to cure her anteater's gout.

"The deputy assistant director is away from her desk," explained the receptionist. "But I spoke to her administrative assistant."

"She has only *one*?" I asked—feigning incredulity.

The girl did not detect my sarcasm. "Only one, I'm afraid. There's a hiring freeze," she said. "But it doesn't matter. Lourdes says you'll have to go to court. Once the agency files for guardianship, the judge has sole authority to appoint an alternate guardian."

"But that makes no sense," I objected. "You're telling me that if I came down here last week and *volunteered* for guardianship, I could have chosen Nënë Roza. But now that Ms. Celery Stalk is involved, I have to appear before a judge?"

"That's what Lourdes says," said the girl. "And Lourdes is always right."

"Always?" I asked. "About everything? You're telling me Lourdes has never been wrong once in her life? That she never received a 99% on a spelling test?"

The buxom girl shrugged helplessly, her mien vacant and flaccid. "I'm sorry we can't be more helpful," she said, holding out the bowl. "Feel free to take a chocolate."

Because everyone knows that serious legal complications can be solved with a complimentary Hershey's kiss. But I couldn't help myself. Rather than take one sweet, I scooped up a large handful and pocketed them. When the girl frowned, I demanded, "Did Lourdes receive a perfect score of her civil service exam? Has Lourdes considered a job as a bookie?"

"Let's go, dear," interjected Nënë Roza. My ancient cousin took hold of my arm and gently steered me into the corridor. "We tried out best. There's no point in getting arrested."

How different Nënë Roza's anxieties were than my own—at least, consciously. She feared the Stalinist gulag, while I quaked at the notion of confronting Ms. Celery Stalk inside a courthouse. And, of course, the dark hand behind Little Abe's murder. But a voice asked, *Who cares if you get arrested?* And then another threatened, *They'll lock you up and throw away the key!* So maybe, at some subconscious level, I shared the elderly woman's dread of incarceration. Although I'd been arrested three times previously— once for jumping a turnstile, which I hadn't actually done, and twice for loitering in the park after hours, which I had—and I couldn't say the experience had proven any worse than countless others I'd endured as a free woman. Certainly, no comparison to the brutal trainings we endured at Brearley on the pommel horse and parallel bars.

"Let's get some lunch," said Nënë Roza. "Where there is stew, there is joy."

Only if you're a poor woman, I knew. *If you're a rich woman, it depends on the quality of the stew.* But I was too emotionally depleted to debate the merits of Albanian proverbs, especially on an empty stomach, so I followed Nënë Roza to the elevator. While we walked to her car, a piercing nostalgia overwhelmed me for the mechanical lifts of my childhood: the apparatus on Central Park West with its sterling silver rheostat and matching dial indicator, manned like a gun turret by white-gloved Anatole. And the bejeweled gold gondola in Newport, where Grandpa Van Duyn threatened to "jail" me for misbehavior. So lost was I in this reverie that a moment elapsed between the doors opening and my registering the slender, pants-suited creature who slid past us. She'd nearly disappeared into the office of Medicaid's Inspector General when her cheerless snout and obtuse coal eyes sliced through my trance. Despite her business attire and coiffed ginger hair, there was no mistaking her. The woman who now stepped through the doors of the Inspector General was undeniably Lucille from Florida.

"Finally!" I exclaimed. "The unexpected clue I've been waiting for."

"What's that?" asked Nënë Roza.

"I know that woman. She's the missing witness from Mount Hebron."

"Are you sure? She didn't look like a psychiatric patient."

"I'm sure," I insisted. "This is our big break."

Nënë Roza appeared unconvinced, but she followed me dutifully along the corridor into the Inspector General's lobby. My prior experiences with the IG had all been secondhand. One of the physiatrists at the hospital—a Pakistani fellow I knew casually—had been audited by Medicaid and eventually went to prison for passing off sneakers as orthopedic shoes. And then there was the time when a prosperous ophthalmologist lost his license for performing bogus retina surgeries, and Grandpa Brigander had faced a vote on whether to expel him from the Union Club. Patients occasionally filed formal complaints with the IG, I knew, but Lucille—despite her frustrations with Dr. Robustelli—hadn't struck me as the type. The clerk who greeted us sported an open collar and shirtsleeves open at the wrists. He couldn't have been more than twenty-five, and was homely as sin too, but he'd stretched out in his swivel chair with his hands behind his neck and his jaw protruding as though he owned the building. I found myself wondering if he were even wearing socks.

"Morning ladies," he said. "What can I do for you today?"

What I wanted to answer was, "I'm no lady. I'm investigating a murder and I shall proceed accordingly." But as I've said, a woman can't be expected to mount the revolution and solve violent crimes simultaneously, so I let his slur pass. Besides, I suspected Nënë Roza might consider his remark a compliment.

"We're looking for Lucille Tobruk," I said. "It's important."

The young man nodded thoughtfully, as though weighing the merits of my request. "We don't have anyone here by that name."

"I know you do," I said. "We just saw her walk in ten seconds ago."

He drummed the head of his pencil on the desktop. "No Lucilles here. Sorry."

That was too much. "I don't know what your game is," I replied. "But I'll trust my own eyes over your words any day. Lucille

Tobruk from Miami, Florida, is inside her somewhere and we want to see her now."

"Take it easy, lady. Why would I lie to you?" replied the clerk. "The only person who has been through that door in the past fifteen minutes is Miss Dumont."

That's when a lightbulb went on in my brain. Or maybe a zirconium flashbulb—like the ones found in vintage press cameras. "Is Miss Dumont the tall, flat-chested woman with the carrot-dyed hair and the face like a starving anteater?" I asked.

The clerk grinned. "You certainly don't hold back, do you?"

"So that *is* her," I said—as much to Nënë Roza as to the clerk. "I knew I recognized her."

"You've probably seen her in one of those old movies," said the clerk. "Barb had a number of big roles in the 1980s." He lowered his voice as though about to share how to fold a Habsburg napkin or divulge Colonel Sanders' secret recipe. "Have you seen *Polynesian Shark Massacre*? She plays the librarian on the cruise ship—the one who falls overboard first."

"You don't say," I said.

This young man and I clearly had different notions of what constituted an *old* movie.

"You should see her when she's in costume," said the clerk. "You'd really think she was dying of pancreatic cancer or even blind."

That's when an entire press conference of flash blurbs burst in my head. If my skull had been the East River, the light inside could have rivaled the Macy's 4th of July fireworks.

"Or mentally ill," I suggested.

"She does a mean bat-shit crazy," agreed the clerk. "Straight out of *One Flew Over the Cuckoo's Nest*."

"I'm sure she does," I conceded.

So Lucille—aka Barb Dumont—was a plant. Maybe not for the Albanian mob, but a potted spying plant nonetheless. That explained all of her questions about the duration of Vince Robustelli's clinical evaluations. Poor bastard! As much as I resented the smug shrink and a part of me relished his impending comeuppance, I also genuinely felt bad for him. But I didn't have much opportunity to sympathize, because at that instant—as though making a grand entrance, stage left—Barb Dumont rolled herself into the lobby. I say *rolled*, because the able-bodied insurance investigator occupied a motorized scooter.

She'd thrown a threadbare shawl over her shoulders and capped her hair in a hoary wig.

"What do you think?" she asked the clerk. "Olivia Ortona. Homebound paraplegic in need of a higher level of care."

"I think you require a higher level of care," he replied.

"You sure I can pass for sixty-eight?" she asked.

"That's a trick question," said the clerk. "I plead the fifth."

"Lucille" hadn't even acknowledged me or Nënë Roza. Meanwhile, I'd been too busy absorbing my newest discovery to introduce myself. Her name was Olivia *Ortona*—like the *Battle of Ortona*. Whoever chose the undercover names of the IG's investigators was running down a list of World War II skirmishes. Clearly an inside joke, because one couldn't appreciate the pattern unless one both possessed a detailed knowledge of military history *and* had interacted with multiple investigators. Maybe the deputy assistant director, or whoever managed such affairs in this particular office, had too much time on his hands. (I could hear Uncle Dewey grumbling that all public officials, from the Oval Office on down, had too much time on their hands.) But just as I was about to share my realization with "Lucille," the clerk recalled our presence. "Say, Barb," he said. "These ladies are looking for you. They recognized you from your films."

A gleam of pride flushed across Dumont's features—a look I'd seen before, during Mama's anteater's estrous. But as soon as she recognized yours truly, her delight rapidly solidified into displeasure.

"You'll have to leave," said Dumont. "This is a private office."

"What's up, Barb?" interjected the clerk. "They're just fans."

"Fans, my ass. That one is a patient from Mount Hebron." Dumont rose from her scooter like one of those benefit-leaching fake invalids caught on camera. "If you don't leave, we'll call security."

So I had to play hardball. The woman gave me no other choice. Quite frankly, my investigation was far more important than hers. "I can leave if you wish," I said. "But I'll go right back to Mount Hebron and tell Dr. Robustelli about your spying. Or maybe I'll camp out across the street and snap your photograph when you're not looking—and then upload it to the Internet with a description of your snooping. So long, undercover investigations! How would you like *that*?"

This last threat was an idle one, because I didn't own a camera, but I counted on the pressure of the moment to cloud Ms. Dumont's insight. Nënë Roza had retreated to the door, striving to appear as inconspicuous as possible. The notion crossed my mind that we might both soon find ourselves under arrest for extortion. But to her credit, the actress-turned-spy gathered herself together like a monarch facing insurrection—Dumont's face as stoic as Elizabeth I ordering the beheading of Mary, Queen of Scots. "I wouldn't like that at all," she said. "So what can I do to arrange for your silence? Would $100 do the trick?" She must have seen the displeasure in my eyes, because she added, "I'll make it $150. That's more than fair, isn't it?"

"Fair is in the eyes of the beholder," I replied. "I'm sure I could milk a lot more out of you than $150, if that were my intention."

"Two hundred dollars," offered Dumont. "But that's my upper limit."

What amazes me is how much importance middle-class people place upon money. Maybe because they can purchase small packets of happiness with it. Or, at least, tidbits of pleasure. Only the wealthy and the poor know the hard truth—that money is often necessary, but no sum ever proves sufficient. What good would $200 really have done me? Sure, I could have bought a new raincoat. Maybe a few warm nights at the Day's Inn on Montague Street. But not even a hundred times that amount would let me open up a pet shop with puppies and hamsters and a toucan for the window display. That's the difference between the bourgeoisie and the indigent. For us, cash is practical. Means to a hot meal or tickets to the Picabia retrospective at the MOMA. For them, it's defining.

"I don't want money. I want *information*," I said. "I'm investigating a murder."

I'd almost said I'm investigating Big George's murder, but that was no longer true.

"You mean that guy who got stabbed? *That's* what you're here about?"

I drew a deep breath. "That guy was Abraham Currier of Saint Louis, Missouri," I said. "And he deserves to have his murder solved as much as anybody else."

Ms. Dumont's hostility appeared to soften. "You'll forgive me, but I don't have any information about that. Shouldn't you be talking to the police?"

"It's not official information I'm looking for," I explained. "What I'm hoping for is your general impression of the day on the unit before the killing. I'm assuming you've been on lots of psych wards. What I want to know is whether you saw anything unusual?"

Now a genuine smile appeared below the actress's snout. "You really are playing detective. How darling," she said. "Let's sit down and talk."

She indicated a nook where a curved divan hugged a glass coffee table. I settled onto the cushions and Nënë Roza soon joined me, but Barb Dumont's cooperation proved fruitless. She'd made countless observations regarding the clinical conduct at Mount Hebron, and how it deviated from the standard of care, but she proved a poor eyewitness for other purposes. She didn't even remember Sarge's fishing tackle or Angry O'Dell's outbursts—matters beyond her purview—and now that I'd joined forces with Nënë Roza, no purpose even existed in asking about Albanians. About the only positive outcome of the exchange was that we departed with 100% confidence that Barb Dumont had played no role in Little Abe's killing. I also had the actress add her signature to my autograph album—mostly to flatter her, as the co-star of *Polynesian Shark Massacre*'s illegible scrawl seemed incongruous alongside those of Ingrid Bergman and Rita Hayworth.

I hadn't yet given up on the prospect of having Nënë Roza serve as my guardian. Sort of like a "Boston marriage"—only not romantic. In the days before gay nuptials, hadn't several of Uncle Drake's chums adopted their lovers as "wards"? And did anyone sincerely believe that the strapping, Shakespeare-quoting Mexican lad Cary Grant brought with him to the summer cottage was actually his ex-wife's nephew? But if Antigona's mother was to be my guardian, the matter would have to be settled in court, so we made plans to meet the next morning at eight o'clock in front of the RCA Building, and parted ways—Nënë Roza to inform her daughter that Little Abe was dead and yours truly for her date with the victim's brother. My sidekick had offered to drive me across town to Stuyvesant Square, but the very idea of another ride in the Oldsmobile was enough to make a person's eyebrows fall out. Not that I didn't appreciate the thought. Yet thoughts are one thing, and perishing in a traffic collision with an unsolved murder hanging over one's head is another matter entirely, so I headed toward the Dvořák statue on foot.

The stroll carried me down Broadway to Madison Square Park, where the Flatiron's swindlers and scam artists were hard at working conning outer borough commuters and tourists. In front of the Worth

Monument, a trio of faux Buddhist monks in saffron robes chanted on a Tibetan *khaden* while a fourth imposter canvassed passersby with a teak donation box. Only twenty yards away, a college-aged white kid with a shaved head sat before a translucent acrylic canister, raising contributions for a charity called the "International Fund for Children"—of which he was likely the only beneficiary. These schemers had infuriated Renegade Sally. "It's one thing to ask for money if you need it," she used to say. "But when you start scamming people, soon nobody knows who's real—and who's part of an organized crime syndicate or some middle-class kid from Mamaroneck faking it for pocket change." She had a point. I knew of at least one panhandler, up by Columbia, whose wife drove him into the city every morning from Yonkers. "I can earn twenty-five bucks an hour out here," he'd once told our friend, Niagara Falls. "That's twice what I'd make washing dishes or pumping gas." According to Renegade Sally, these few rotten apples were the reason ordinary, working-class people voted Republican. I'm not a political scientist, so I couldn't prove that with any certainty, but my preference is for probity.

I'm what Uncle Dewey would call an "honest beggar," one of the class that Grandpa Brigander extolled as the "deserving poor"—although I try to manage my check carefully, so I don't have to ask for charity too often. But when I do, I'm straight up, matter-of-fact: "I'm hungry. Can you help? Brother, can you spare a dime?" Not that I don't admire clever. Tecumseh Muhammed pulled in thirty bucks one day, holding up a sign that read, "Contribute to the United Negro Pizza Fund," but while I can admire wit in others, humor isn't generally my style. Anyway.

On the way to Stuyvesant Square, I ducked into the Rescue Mission on Lafayette Street and sweet-talked the evening manager, Mrs. Przybyszewski, into letting me shower during off-hours. Usually, showers are a morning privilege, to make sure clients don't wash and run—although what harm would be done if the folks sleeping on the streets were a bit cleaner isn't so clear to me. But the staff at the mission know I'm not going to cause them any trouble, and I've volunteered to rinse dishes for them after their Christmas Eve banquet for a number of years, so when I explained I was going on a date, Mrs. P. even allowed me to run my stork-print silk blouse and sweatpants through their washer and dryer. Mrs. P. was widowed at the age of nineteen and spent the first half of her life as a security guard at the Polish state museum dedicated to the Majdanek concentration camp. She is deeply religious. Her two heroes are Ronald Reagan and Pope John Paul II—and she can tell you every detail of her personal encounter with each man down to the barometric pressure and shape of the clouds overhead. But as conservative as she may be at the ballot box, she's willing to talk to a person, *really talk*, even to yours truly. I know about her niece in the convent, her great nephew serving in the merchant marine. Lots of folks out there may have volunteered for Eugene McCarthy and donated generously to Barack Obama or Hillary Clinton, but they're glad to shell out money so they *don't* have to talk to a person.

Smelling elegantly of detergent and fabric softener, my damp hair wrapped in a fleur-de-lis kerchief and my cart safely secured outside the hospital, I arrived at the Dvořák statue just as the bells of the Russian church peeled the hour. I carried my hat in a plastic bag, reluctant to leave it behind unguarded, yet not sure it was ideal dating attire—especially, if Big George had it in mind to take me to a restaurant or a movie. With every step toward the park, my apprehension had grown that my date might not show. Why should he? If I were a handsome, personable fifty-nine-year-old skilled craftsman with a steady income and a roof over his head, I wasn't sure I'd go on a date with yours truly. And then the notion pricked at me that I'd read too much into our previous encounter—that my rendezvous with the fellow, even if it transpired, might not be a date. So I was battling both external voices and my own self-doubt when I rounded the corner of Nathan D. Perlman Place and caught sight of my Adonis, pacing the flagstones opposite the statue. He'd changed into a sport jacket and—to my amazement—he carried a bouquet of mixed flowers. My initial reaction was to flee. Clearly, he'd brought the flowers for a different, more deserving woman.

He spotted me before I had an opportunity to escape and came jaunting across the plaza. "There you are," he said, beaming. "I was afraid you might not show."

I looked away so he wouldn't see the moisture at the corners of my eyes. But I sensed the man's gaze on me, and when I finally glanced up, he was savoring me like a home-cooked feast—like Papa's Weimaraner when Papa defied the vet and fed the beast whole sticks of butter. "If I'm not being too forward," he said, "you look stunning."

I giggled—seized with nerves. "You must be going blind," I said. I seriously considered the possibility that he might be lying, playing me for some ulterior purpose—or just out of sheer cruelty, a sociopath leading on a hideous old nutcase. But one look into the man's tender, doting face swept away all of my suspicions. To paraphrase Sally Field's iconic Oscar speech: "He liked me! He really liked me!" Somehow, I found myself strolling up Second Avenue with the bouquet in one hand and my other tucked around Big George's elbow. "So where to?" he asked. "You're the local."

I could easily have named a restaurant—although, in truth, most of the culinary establishments I knew required a jacket-and-tie, and had probably folded during the 1970s. But going with the flow, in this case, was bound to give Big George the wrong impression. And while I wanted him to like me, I didn't want to build our connection on false premises. So I swallowed a few gulps of air and said, as casually as possible, "I don't dine out much. Not at all, really. I love a good restaurant meal as much as anyone, but it's not part of the budget when you're schizophrenic and street homeless and living off public assistance."

Now I feared it would be George's turn to flee. Like one of those fans of a radio-era star who finally meets his heartthrob in the flesh and discovers she looks like Rondo Hatton. But Big George appeared more amused than alarmed. "You're kidding me," he said. "You're really homeless?"

"Why would anyone make that up?"

We continued strolling up the avenue like an ordinary couple. "That's a good point," said Big George. "But what happened? I thought your old man had money to burn."

"It's a long story," I answered. "And trust me, it's not exactly *War and Peace*."

"How long could it possibly be?"

"Four generations," I said. "But only the last thirty-seven years are crucial."

Big George gave me a quick look, maybe to see if I were joking. When he realized that I was dead serious, he said, "I'm not sure if I can handle four generations, so let's start with the last thirty-seven years and work backwards. If you tell the story in real time, we should be done when I'm ninety-six." Then he paused in front of a bustling bistro whose plate-glass windows revealed candle-lit tables and a wood-burning fire, and inquired, with complete sincerity, "Can I interest you in Italian? I think a long story demands a hearty meal."

When I didn't object, Big George opened the door for me like a gentleman, and the hostess seated us at a cozy table in plain view of the wine bar and the other diners, just as she might any conventional, middle-aged couple enjoying an evening out.

I don't think I've had such a strong connection on a first date since Aunt Genevieve chaperoned my excursion to the Rocky Point Amusement Park with Pierre S. du Pont's grandson for our seventh birthdays, which fell only two days apart. The boy's father had arranged to rent out the entire facility on a summer afternoon in August, and in all fairness, it's hard to compete with a private spin on a Ferris wheel or your own personal cotton candy stand. But Big George insisted that I order anything I desired off the menu—even the thirty-dollar *osso buco in bianco*, which yours truly could not resist—and we also shared an appetizer of garlic-braised date mussels and a platter of Blue Point oysters. "I remember when you were only supposed to eat oysters during months whose names contained the letter R. So you wouldn't get ptomaine poisoning," observed Big George, tucking his napkin into his collar. "I suppose I'm getting old." I enjoyed his shellfish nostalgia—not mentioning that these rules hadn't applied when your grandfather imported oysters directly from the Southern Hemisphere on his private jet. It was *always* a month whose name contained the letter R, Grandpa Brigander explained, *someplace on the globe*. Just as, for Papa, it was always cocktail hour somewhere. "You're not afraid to be seen in public with an old man, are you?" asked Big George.

"Not if you're not afraid to be seen with a crazy woman," I replied.

He raised his glass of Riesling. "To the old man and the crazy woman."

Our glasses clinked—and from that moment, it was pure magic. Like the Technicolor real launching in *The Wizard of Oz*. And I felt myself emotionally transformed too—the psychological equivalent of Olivia Newton-John's makeover in *Grease*. I divulged my history, setback by setback, from the final days at Bryn Mawr to the loss of the Lady Chatterley to Ms. Celery Stalk's efforts to commandeer my check, and not once did my companion display antipathy or revulsion. The closest he came to any negative reaction was when I described how the man I'd gone with briefly before Tecumseh Muhammed—a worthless, hepatitis-positive ex-felon whose self-styled name was Luke the Enforcer, although most of what he did was sell crack—had forcibly injected me with one of his own used needles on numerous occasions, so we'd both "go down together." Miraculously, the virus hadn't stuck. But as much as I paraded out the vilest of the Brigander-Van Duyn heritage and my own worst moments, Big George nodded with heartfelt interest and continued curling his linguini in clam sauce around his fork, entirely unfazed. Not even my descriptions of my month of electroshock therapy appeared to bother him. About the only subjects I avoided were Tecumseh Muhammed, and my brief flirtation with his own con artist brother. How far away that premonitory kiss suddenly seemed! We also said little about the murder, or my investigation, as though by tacit understanding, maybe because we both sensed it might dampen our good spirits.

"So that's about that," I said. "The whole caboodle."

He glanced at his watch. "Impressive. And with thirty-six years, three hundred sixty-four days and twenty-three hours to spare," he observed. "That leaves us time for dessert."

Big George flagged down the waiter—and when I wavered between the torta caprese and the strawberry cheesecake, he announced, "The lady will have both." How different from those Haverford and Swarthmore boys who scowled if a girl added a smidgen of dressing to her salad. Soon enough, we had three pastries and two cups of coffee before us, and my companion wore an expression of wholesome, unadulterated glee.

"And what about you?" I asked. "I'm sorry for rambling so much."

"Not at all. But I'm afraid my story is much less interesting," he said. "Wife left twenty-five years ago. Kid ran off to California and wants nothing to do with me. I do HVAC on boats and look after Melanie Daniels and try to keep my brother out of trouble—although I guess I won't even be doing that anymore." For the first time, a twinge of distress crossed the man's brow. "So that's me, pretty lady. *The whole caboodle.* What else is there you want to know?"

"Tell me about your kid," I said.

"George Jr.? Not much to tell. He blames me for the divorce—even though Amanda's the one who couldn't keep her legs crossed. I don't mean to speak ill of the dead—my ex passed away last summer—according to the obituaries, at least, it's not like anyone called me—but Amanda was cheating on me right and left. And center too. I can kind of understand a one-time indiscretion...or even being swept away by true love...but Amanda was dabbling here, puttering there. She had a fling with an air traffic controller.... a one-night stand with a truant officer at George Jr's junior high school. I just don't get it. What was the point of marrying me in the first place if I'm the only guy she *didn't* want to screw?" A pang of genuine frustration entered his tone, and he caught himself. "It doesn't matter now, I guess. George Jr. is out in the Bay Area. Doing something with computers. I've written to him a few times, but he never writes back. I imagine, if he's going to come around, it will be on his own schedule."

"That must be hard," I said.

Big George didn't answer. He pretended that calculating the gratuity required his full attention, but I sensed he wished to drop the subject. "That reminds me," he said, signing his name to the tab. "Do you know how I go about claiming my brother's body?"

"He's probably buried already. Out on Hart's Island."

Under your name, I could have added—but I didn't want to intensify Big George's anguish.

"It would be a big deal to dig him up again, wouldn't it?" he asked.

"You could probably do it. If you were willing to pay for it."

My date led me out onto the sidewalk—again holding the door. Outside, urban night had settled over the East Village: loud and teeming and nearly bright as day. "I know I *should* be willing to pay for it," said Big George. "But I'm reluctant. I can't help feeling money is better spent on the living."

That's exactly what my father and grandfather would have said. For a working-class stiff, I was delighted to find, Big George Currier carried a hint of Brigander sensibility.

"You don't think less of me, do you?" he asked.

"I couldn't think less of you," I replied, "if you turned out to be The Unabomber."

Big George responded by drawing me toward him—his palm on the fat of my lower back—and leaning in for a kiss. Think Burt Lancaster and Deborah Kerr locking lips on the beach in *From Here to Eternity*, and George Peppard snogging Audrey Hepburn as the skies open in *Breakfast at Tiffany's*, and that iconic Times Square photo of the sailor dipping into a white-clad stranger on V-J, and maybe add in the amatory moment after Rhett tells Scarlett, "You need kissing badly"—and you'd merely nicked the surface of how I felt. It was as though I'd asked big George to "kiss me as if it were the last time"—just like Ingrid Bergman does Bogey in the final moments of *Casablanca*—and he'd thrown his entire being into honoring my request. I could have sworn I saw fireworks above St Mark's Church. Eventually, he broke our embrace, which was fortunate, because in a few more seconds I might have spontaneously combusted. I felt woozy, top-heavy with blood.

"That was nice, pretty lady," he said. "Real nice."

I flashed an adolescent smile—silent as an idiot.

"So what now?" he asked—directing his question equally at himself, at yours truly, and at the chill of night. "You know, you could come with me to Rhode Island. I'm headed back tomorrow." He caressed the side of my cheek with his fingertips. "Now that I can't do anything for Little Abe," he added, almost apologetically, "I should check on Melanie Daniels."

I felt like a woman being drawn apart by two galloping horses. How could I part from this lovely man who had known my father and who'd accepted me with such abandon? But how could I walk away from my investigation without any solid answers? That would be exactly what the authorities did to my brother when he stepped into the abyss—the sort of injustice I'd sworn never to let happen under my nose again. They say true love conquers all. In my case, however, not even burning ardor proved a match for gnawing duty.

"I can't," I said. "Not yet. I still have some loose ends to tie up."

Big George looked dejected, but not surprised; he was one of those souls, like yours truly, who'd come to anticipate disappointment. "Are you sure?"

"But I will come soon. I promise," I said. "Maybe even in a week or two."

He looked doubtful for an instant, but decided to believe me. "Okay, I guess I'll have to wait. Let me write down my address for you."

He removed a business card from his wallet and jotted his home address on the back. I recognized Miamtonomi Avenue immediately. Mama and I had made a sick call on that street once—to the mother of one of the chauffeurs, who'd fractured a hip in a bicycle accident. (Only years later did I realize that she'd been biking on our estate—that the ulterior motive behind the visit was to stave off litigation or bad publicity.) I repeated the street number until it was etched indelibly in my soul, then tucked the card into my brassiere—mostly because tucking a man's address into my brassiere seemed like a romantic gesture.

"Will you need money for the train?" asked Big George.

"I'll call you when I'm ready to come. What's your phone number?"

He shared his number and I memorized it. No need to write it down, I assured him—it was bound to get lost or stolen. When you're homeless, your only real property is inside your skin. I can *still* recite that number from memory—much like I can conjure up the number of Renegade Sally's mother in Indiana, whom I'd phoned after her death, and even the contact info for Tecumseh Muhammed's step-niece in Detroit, to be used only in dire emergencies.

"I have a reservation at the Holiday Inn," said Big George. "Do you want to stay in my room? I'm swear I'm not trying to get fresh. You can have the bed and I'll order a cot." When I didn't reply, he added, "I don't like the idea of my woman sleeping on the streets."

His woman! I suppose the Katherine Hepburn crowd would have been horrified at the possessive pronoun, but yours truly was overjoyed. At the same time, I wasn't going to stay in a man's hotel room after a first date—no matter how much I liked him. I didn't wish to give him the wrong impression. And, deep down, I was still Mama Brigander's daughter.

"I can take care of myself," I said. "If all else fails, I'll sleep in the public library."

So Big George walked me across town to the Jefferson Market Library and kissed me good night. And then I waited until the kyphotic cleaner with the spade beard propped the side door open for his smoke break—and ducked inside while he was buying cigarettes across the street. The historic map room wasn't exactly a bridal bed, or the honeymoon suite at the Waldorf-Astoria, but the chamber smelled wonderfully of ancient ink, and it served its purpose.

I awoke the next morning aglow in romance and stole out through a service entrance onto the adjoining alley, stocked with an edited collection of David Selznick's correspondence and a three-hundred page reexamination on Elia Kazan's collaboration with Senator Joe McCarthy. If I did end up committed to the bin again, at least I'd have plenty to read. Outside, a misty drear had settled over the metropolis—the gray, trench coat weather that seems to roll back the city's clock to the age of automats and elevated trains and discount desserts at Schrafft's. Inside my own head, the plan for the day remained inchoate. Other than tracking down Drs. Bhatt & Dr. Cotz-Cupper, my witness list had been more or less depleted. My sense was that the investigation was rapidly progressing from legwork to brainwork—only my gray matter did not appear to be generating any visionary insights. I'll confess the notion even entered my thoughts that I might not be up to the challenge intellectually. Maybe there was a reason so few of the celebrated detectives of literature and history had been diagnosed with schizophrenia.

So I headed toward Rockefeller Center—toward the RCA Building, which had since been renamed the GE Building. Not to be confused with the General Electric Building on Lexington Avenue, which had previous been called the RCA Victor Building. One could easily imagine Tom Lehrer penning a satiric song about the two skyscrapers, or even a melodramatic farce in which RCA President David Sarnoff and GE honcho Charlie Wilson—both of whom had been pall bearers at Great Grandpa Rutherford Brigander's funeral—returned from the great Knickerbocker Club in the sky to find their headquarters interchanged. I'd chosen the meeting place less out of convenience and more because I found comfort in the structure's fixed Art Deco façade and reassurance in the words of the frieze above the grand entrance: "Wisdom and Knowledge shall be the stability of thy times." I couldn't have said it better myself. I'd just crossed Sixth Avenue, heartened by the thought of this uplifting mantra, when a pair of NYPD patrol cars, sirens wailing, drew up at the curb. Instinctively, I sensed they'd come for me.

Two sets of officers approached—one from the front and the other from behind—as thought yours truly, all two hundred twenty pounds of her, might try to escape. One of the officers, who looked young enough to be his own grandson, as Papa used to say of Uncle Drake's tennis pros and cabana boys, stepped around my cart with his hand resting on his service weapon. The sea of commuters gave us a wide berth, like denizens of Stuart-era London parting for corpse carts during the Great Plague.

"Are you Henrietta Brigander?" asked the officer

"I am indeed," I said. "Pleasure to make your acquaintance."

I've found it's usually wise to meet the threat of force with congeniality. Cops expect you to be standoffish or even surly. A bit of social engagement goes a long way. *Sometimes.* Unfortunately, that morning was to be the exception that proved the rule.

"We'll have to ask you to come with us," said the officer. He glanced at my hat and then at my shopping cart, which I'd covered in plastic tarp to ward away the mist. "You don't have any weapons on you, ma'am, do you? Firearms? Knives? Box cutters?"

Just a grenade launcher, I thought. *And a pair of bazookas.* "I don't have any weapons, young man," I said, "but I do have Constitutional rights. Now what is your basis for detaining me? Am I being charged with a crime?"

The young cop glanced over his shoulder at his partner, a stocky woman with a fade haircut and murine ears. Her acne-scarred face answered: *How the hell should I know?* "We're not arresting you," said Boy Cop. "Unless you resist."

"But if I do resist, then you'll arrest me?" I asked. "What for?"

"Resisting arrest," said Boy Cop—without conviction. "I guess."

So I wasn't under arrest unless I resisted arrest. Who could argue with logic like that? "May I at least ask what this is all about?" I inquired.

"Don't give us trouble, ma'am," said Boy Cop. "You'll find out at the precinct." The officer took hold of my forearm and led me toward the patrol car.

I didn't see any point in making a war crime out of this—he was just doing his job, after all—so I checked my verbal resistance. "Can I at least chain up my cart?" I asked. "If I'm not under arrest."

Boy Cop conferred with both Girl Cop and an older officer with dense eyebrows, then permitted me to chain my shopping cart to nearby bicycle rack. I secured the vinyl tarp tightly around the contents, but if somebody truly wanted to pinch a stuffed lorikeet or plush anhinga, my flimsy efforts weren't going to stop them. I settled into the back of the cruiser, closing my eyes and pretending it was Papa's limo. But we'd hardly advanced two blocks when I realized something was amiss. If you're homeless in New York City, you quickly learn the various police precincts and their flavors: the happy-go-lucky 50th in Riverdale, Brooklyn's "Brutal 75th." Since I'd been detained on Sixth Avenue and 58th Street, these officers should have been delivering me to the 18th Precinct—better known as Midtown South. Instead, we sailed down Third Avenue toward the East Village, blaring our way through intersections. I could have kicked myself for not demanding to see the officers' badges. I knocked on the divider. "Where are we going?"

"Precinct," replied Girl Cop. "Like he told you."

"The precinct is back that way," I said. "On 35th."

"Not the 18th, ma'am," said Boy Cop. "The 13th."

That brought the conversational portion of our ride to a close. I couldn't decide whether I were being kidnapped or paranoid, but the voices thought the former. *Sitting duck*, they muttered. *Make a break for it!* But I forced my legs to stay still—promising myself that if we left Manhattan, then I'd try to escape—and, soon enough, we pulled onto 21st Street and parked opposite the sooty bricks of the stationhouse.

"Follow us," said Boy Cop. He led me up a heavily-trafficked corridor, lined with union announcements and mug shots, then into dingy office where two iron desks faced each other beneath mounds of paperwork. Both desks stood unoccupied. Black-and-white photographs of former cadet classes hung beside the shaded windows. A space heater glowed in one corner; a waste-paper basket overflowed in the other. "Wait here," instructed Boy Cop.

So I waited. Maybe, I figured, they were trying to wear me down with hunger and fatigue. I also considered the possibility I was under surveillance and took care not to make any incriminating exclamations or gestures. Whatever I'd done, or was suspected of doing, couldn't have been that serious, I reminded myself, if they left me alone with the door open and access to stacks of confidential law enforcement documents. My primary worry wasn't incarceration, but that I'd be late for my rendezvous with Nënë Roza. How frustrating it would be to acquire a sidekick, only to lose her again over an erroneous police detention. As I braced myself for several days of waiting, scanning the office for a container that might double as a makeshift chamber pot, radish-faced Detective Libby stepped through the doorway, gaunt and tousled as ever. "Sorry to keep you waiting, Miss Brigander," said the detective, kicking shut the door. "My wife locked her keys inside the station wagon." He cleared off a section of the less cluttered desk and seated himself on the blotter.

"Is your wife also English?" I asked—already relishing a second tussle. "Let me guess! You two met at a Mayflower reunion."

Detective Libby sighed. "My wife is Venezuelan," he said. "And, if you must know, we met in elementary school." He retrieved a folder, seemingly at random, from the adjacent desk and flipped it open. "But I didn't invite you hear to discuss my family."

"Do you have kids?" I asked. "And do they attend the same elementary school where you met?"

The detective snapped shut the folder. "I'm not in the mood for games, Miss Brigander. I brought you here because you called the medical examiner last week and cancelled an autopsy. *In my name.* And I want to know what this is all about," he said.

"I'm not sure what you're talking about," I answered. "Anyway, don't I have a right to an attorney if I'm being interrogated?"

He slid the folder back onto the desk. "Let me spell things out for you, Miss Brigander. I have you on video tape making a call from the public phone on 12th Avenue and we traced a suspicious call to the OCME back to that same phone. And all the circumstantial evidence suggests that you also placed another call to the OCME in my name the previous morning. Now I could easily charge you with impersonation. Or even obstruction. And I will, if I have to. I swear to God I will. But that won't solve anything. So I'm asking you, person to person, why you cancelled the autopsy for George Currier—a man who, by your own admission, you hardly knew."

I bit my lip to keep from smirking. So the detective had wrapped himself in circles this time without my assistance, and had divulged a crucial clue in the process. Unless he was bluffing, he thought I'd made *both* calls to the OCME—that *I'd* cancelled the autopsy. And if he believed that I'd made the call, it served to reason that he hadn't. On top of that, his crew hadn't made any progress on correctly identifying the murder victim. For an instant, I genuinely felt bad for the bungling officer and even worse for his childhood sweetheart. But only for an instant. Sympathize with your adversaries too long, Uncle Dewey warned, and you end up short on IBM at six dollars a share. Of course, if the investigator had bothered to shave with Occam's razor, or even just trimmed his mustache, he'd have already known that I hadn't made both calls.

"So you're half right, detective," I confessed to Libby. "I made the second call—the one asking for the autopsy results. But not the first."

He shook his head as though disappointed in a toddler. "You expect me to believe that? You made *one* call to the OCME—and a *different* impersonator made the other?" He tapped his fingertips together. "I refuse to accept there are multiple people in this city pretending to be me."

What you need is a dose of confidence, I thought—like the Cowardly Lion in *The Wizard of Oz*. Why shouldn't multiple people want to be you? "It's the truth," I answered. "And it makes far more sense than your theory. Why would I cancel the autopsy one day and then call for the results the next?"

His brow tightened. "How should I know? Maybe you wanted to be certain that it had been cancelled."

"So when exactly did I make the first call? I was on a locked psychiatric unit, in case you've forgotten."

"We've already looked into that. There's a payphone on the unit."

"And did you trace the first call to the payphone?" I asked.

"We can't trace the first call. The OCME gets thousands of calls a day—dozens from St. Dymphna's alone. We only know the precise time of the second call because the pathologist found it suspicious and reported it."

"In that case, did you subpoena the payphone records? Do you know if any phone calls were made from the seventh floor of Mount Hebron to the medical examiner's office?"

"We're still working on that."

"Well, you won't find any. Do you know why? Because that damn payphone has been busted for months. All of our personal calls have to be made in the examination room—supervised by a staff member. Now don't you think the PCAs would have grown a tad suspicious if they overheard me calling the OCME to cancel an autopsy?"

"I don't understand you, Miss Brigander. If you didn't have anything to do with the first call—and I'm speaking hypothetically here—why did you call about the results? Don't you think that is, to use your words, *a tad suspicious*."

I considered revealing my motives to the detective, but deep down I knew he'd laugh at my investigation. Until I had solid evidence, nobody was going to suspect that Angry O'Dell had been framed—especially not when the theory came from the Bird Lady. Instead, I said, "I can't really explain. I guess I just wanted some reassurance that he'd slept through the stabbing—that he hadn't suffered. The idea of him waking up during the murder upsets me."

Detective Libby's eyes met mine—his wary, mine striving for innocence. My hope was that he'd find my explanation too implausible to have been concocted. Seemingly muscle by muscle, his expression softened. Either he was a better actor than I'd thought, or my erratic antics had finally overcome his leery nature. "I do hope you're telling the truth," he finally said. "But let this be a warning to you, Miss Brigander. If I find you impersonating so much as a traffic patrolman ever again, I'd going to throw the book at you."

"Warning duly noted," I said. "Is that all?"

The detective nodded. "Can you find your way out?"

"If you trust me on my own in the precinct."

Libby smiled. "Travel safe," he said.

I stood up and let my knees adjust to my weight. Although Detective Libby didn't realize it yet, the results of our morning duel clearly favored yours truly. He still didn't know who'd cancelled Little Abe's autopsy, but I now knew it hadn't been him. Or another patient. If I hadn't been able to call the medical officer from the unit, none of the others could have either. Score that one point Granny Flamingo, zero points NYPD.

"Do you mind if I ask a question of my own?" I asked Libby.

That drew a bemused smirk from the detective. "I'm sure you'll ask anyway."

"I was just wondering if you ever managed to get an autopsy," I said. "You could dig the body up from Potter's field, couldn't you?"

"You're too much, lady," said the detective.

"Is that a yes or a no?"

"That's an *it's none of your business*," he replied. "But, since you're so curious, I suppose there's no harm in telling you that I *did* have the body exhumed. Yesterday—as soon as we discovered the shenanigans with the autopsy."

So it appeared Detective Libby's desire to prove his mettle— even to a schizophrenic civilian—trumped the requisite confidentiality. Pride goeth before a fall, as they say, although it's certainly possible to be humble and fall anyway. Especially if elevator inspectors get paid for no-show jobs and leave hazardous nuisances in their wake.

"And?"

Detective Libby cupped his fist. "And too much time had gone by," he said. "The results were inconclusive. Satisfied?"

"For now," I said. "As you may have realized, I'm a difficult woman to satisfy."

"You don't say," said the detective.

I reached for the doorknob. "By the way," I added, figuring I'd throw the poor fellow a bone. "The dead man's name wasn't George Currier. It was Abraham Currier. He was using a false ID when he was admitted to Mount Hebron."

"And you know this *how?*" inquired Detective Libby, more curious than surprised.

"It's just one of those things you hear on the street," I replied. "Come to think of it, a talking bird whispered it into my ear." Then I shuffled out of his office and hurried uptown to meet Nënë Roza.

The clock atop the Paramount Building read nine thirty as I passed through Times Square and it must have been nearly ten when I reached the RCA Building. Neither Antigona's mother nor her untagged Oldsmobile were anywhere to be found. I had no right to be upset. Fashionably tardy is one thing—at Brearley, Mrs. Bonnefield had warned us to arrive fifteen minutes late when meeting "suitors" and thirty minutes late for cocktail parties—but two hours seemed well beyond the reasonable courtesy window for waiting. I hoped Nënë Roza hadn't been offended—that she wouldn't refuse to continue with the investigation. Or, even worse, be. so insulted that she backed out of her offer to become my guardian.

What a pudding head I'd been not to establish a backup meeting plan—like my rendezvous arrangements with Tecumseh Muhammed at The Cube and Big George at the Dvořák statue. Now my only option for retrieving my sidekick was another long haul on the #7 train out to her son-in-law's motel in Jackson Heights, which would squander the remainder of the afternoon and might even lead to an uncomfortable encounter with Antigona. I realize a swat on the ass isn't exactly a torrid affair, and a premonitory kiss isn't a weekend in Paris, but with regards to Little Abe, I felt like the proverbial other woman. Not a role I'd embraced willingly, of course, but a shameful one nevertheless. *Worthless whore*, barked one of the voices. *Worthless strumpet! Worthless harlot!* I also hoped to avoid a run-in with Antigona's gun-happy husband. But a trip to Forest Hills appeared to be my destiny. My initial plan for the morning—to drop by Mt. Hebron to see if Dr. Bhatt and Dr. Cotz-Cupper had returned from their ad hoc vacation, would have to be put off for another day.

With stress, for me, comes appetite. Following my encounter with Detective Libby and the disruption of my schedule, I felt ravenous as a Maasai warrior in the presence of raw blood. Since it was already approaching lunchtime, I decided to stop by Cash's food truck for my portion of his *zakat* on the way out to Queens. Winter brooded in the air, and the city's gainfully employed had already sloughed off their windbreakers and turtleneck sweaters for overcoats and sheepskin gloves. I pulled my pheasant-print shawl tight around my shoulders, but the very prospect of wintering in Newport— remote as it still seemed—warmed my insides as much as any shot of highland malt scotch. I do hope the irony is not lost upon you, dear reader. For generations, Briganders *summered* in Rhode Island to escape the city heat, but I'd be wintering in Rhode Island to escape the chill of the streets. That wasn't the reason, of course—just an ancillary benefit. And my goal wasn't to winter in Newport, but to live there year round. Still, a Brigander on Thames Street in October couldn't have produced less shock than Dr. Livingstone on the Zambezi. "After Labor Day," Grandma Van Duyn said, "It's only fishwives and sea widows." Anyway.

I trundled up Fifth Avenue, past the luxury townhouses and grand hotels where I'd scampered as a toddler. Grandpa Brigander had taken me for walks along the park, describing his own memories of the avenue as we searched for acorns and pinned samaras onto our noses. He'd escorted one of the Frick sisters to a tea for Huguette Clark's sixteen birthday and the heiress's mother had insisted upon showing them all one hundred twenty-one of the mansion's rooms. "That didn't count the thirty-one baths," said Grandpa Brigander, "or we'd still have been touring when the wrecking balls went through." He'd been a teenager just in time for the "Great Demolition" that took out the limestone manors of Millionaires' Row, replacing the Beaux Arts chateaus of the Vanderbilts and Fishes and Burdens. But Grandpa Brigander had a tale for every landmark and location. He'd point out the corner where he witnessed Ethel Merman's impromptu serenade of Sherman Billingsley, the slope where he'd made snow angels with Brenda Frazier, the concrete step where Doris Duke had slapped him for telling an off-color joke about Fay Wray and a gorilla. I couldn't have been older than six or seven when he shared the most vivid memory of his own grammar school years: escorting Abbott Lowell's niece to a poetry reading by Katrina Trask, his car stopped at a traffic signal—back in the days when Fifth Avenue ran two ways—and he saw, in the rear seat of the adjacent cabriolet, Lionel Barrymore kissing actor Wallace Reid. "I let the curtain fall back and I think I'd aged twenty years," he told me, leading me across 79nd Street by the hand. I must have aged two decades myself at that moment.

But on the day of my failed rendezvous with Nënë Roza, it was a challenge to picture that lost grandeur. A backhoe slumped like an exotic beast on the cusp of a construction pit. Jersey barriers and orange channelizer drums walled off large sections of the sidewalk. Indifferent to the workmen in hardhats and coveralls, a bow-legged codger fed breadcrumbs to competing hordes of pigeons and squirrels. I'd passed the Three Bears statue and had Cash's truck in sight when one of my premonitions took hold of me, and I sensed—without any empirical evidence—that I was being followed. Most likely, I assured myself, Detective Libby had ordered me trailed from the precinct. Who else would be after me? The Albanian mob now seemed like a dead-end lead, a distraction from the real force behind Little Abe's death. Unless, of course, Nënë Roza was a double agent—my own personal Kim Philby—and she'd been feeding a dossier on my exploits back to her countrymen. That seemed far-fetched, of course, but when I spun around, the black Oldsmobile sedan was idling on the cross street. I knew Nënë Roza was at the wheel, because the vehicle's front left tire had breached the sidewalk.

I set my cart aside and walked straight toward her. To my surprise, Nënë Roza climbed out of the driver's seat and shuffled toward me. We appeared headed for a collision in the middle of 79th Street—like James Stewart and Lee Marvin in *The Man Who Shot Liberty Valence*. Only we didn't have weapons. And Nënë Roza ambled right past me, settling onto a bench opposite the conclave of bronze bears. I had no choice but to reverse course. "Where are you going?" I demanded. "You can't just follow me and then run off like that."

"I needed to sit down," she said. "We cannot be talking in the street."

I caught up with her and rested my rump against a sycamore. "What's the big idea?" I asked. "I thought we were a team."

"You didn't show up for our—what do you call it?—assignation. In my country, that is highly inconsiderate," said Nënë Roza. "Why did you not meet with me this morning?"

I realized that only one explanation might satisfy Antigona's mother; fortunately, in this case, the excuse happened to be true. "I apologize," I said. "I was on my way to see you when I was detained by the police. What could I do?"

Nënë Roza snorted. "The police," she echoed with a lifetime of contempt, although her envisioned authorities likely included Hoxha's Sigurimi, not Detective Libby's Mod Squad. Then suspicion clouded her sunken eyes, and she asked, "Why did they let you go?"

"Probably so they could follow me," I answered—although I now highly doubted this. What were the odds that two different parties were tailing me? "It wasn't *you* I was looking for just now. It was Detective Libby's goons."

Nënë Roza nodded. "Or they plan vigilante justice," she replied, folding her arms across her chest. "My baby brother, Ditmir, was released by the secret police—and then they hunted him down and beat him half to death with a lead pipe." She glanced over her shoulder and lowered her voice. "We must be careful."

(I recalled Grandma Van Duyn, approaching ninety and deaf as a post, raising her crooked finger and warning, "We have nothing to fear except fear itself. And Unitarians.")

"So that's my explanation," I said. "What's yours? It's hard enough with my enemies following me—I don't want my friends stalking me too."

"I am sorry," said Nënë Roza. "But I am an old lady. I have a history. I possess suspicions. When you did not show up for our assignation, I feared for the worst. Maybe, I am thinking, you have double-crossed me. Like Duško Popov. I have only your word for it that Abraham Currier is dead. When you did not show up, I grew suspicious. Maybe that is a lie. I thought maybe you two are lovers. Maybe you are hiding him from my daughter."

"You told her?"

"My Antigona is so upset, she threatened to jump out of the window," said Nënë Roza. "Fortunately, it is a first story window."

I was not too worried. I know from eavesdropping on Dr. Robustelli's morning rounds with the medical students that the vast majority of completed suicides occur in one of three ways: gunshot, hanging or asphyxiation, and overdose. Unless a person is truly psychotic or highly intoxicated, she simply doesn't set herself on fire or wade into a river with stones in her pockets—or launch herself out a window. Or, I can't resist adding, commit hara-kiri *by hat*. (To quote Dr. Robustelli's first-day drill to the new interns: "Throw out all of the wrist slashers; they are just burning the taxpayers' money.") There are exceptions, of course. Grandpa Van Duyn knew Wall Street nabobs who leapt to their illiquid ends on "Black Thursday" in 1929, and Katsuyori, Mama's Japanese interior decorator, committed ritual Seppuku after the loss of the Lady Chatterley. But Antigona didn't strike me as possessing the resolve. At worst, Nënë Roza's daughter might injure herself just enough to earn a two-week stint at Mount Hebron. How odd life would shake out if I ended up living in Newport with Big George while Antigona Dushku shared a room on the seventh floor with the Crustacean Maiden of the East Village. I was about to reassure Nënë Roza that I was after a Currier of different color from her daughter—the words were literally at my lips—when the city's only one-eyed Black Seminole hurried past along the sidewalk. "Tecumseh Muhammed!" I shouted without thinking.

He turned gingerly, hands in the pockets of his bomber jacket.

"Jesus Christ," I muttered. "What are *you* doing here?"

"I could ask the same thing," he said. "I'm hitting Cash up for some of his Muslim magic. Haven't eaten since yesterday."

"I thought you went to Florida."

Tecumseh Muhammed flashed his remaining teeth. "What is wrong with you, woman? You really think I'd run off to Florida without you?"

"But Ray G. said he saw you on the bus."

That drew a scornful grunt from Tecumseh Muhammed. "Hell, woman. Since when you be trusting that fuck-up?"

I felt as though I'd been walloped in the gut by Sugar Ray Robinson and then sucker-punched on the ground by Archie Moore. In Miss Swayne's English class at Brearley, we read a poem by Tennyson about a sailor named Enoch Arden who is believed lost at sea but who returns to his native village after ten years to discover that his wife has remarried. One of our homework assignments had been to rewrite the poem from the point of view of Enoch's wife. Charlotte Schuyler has drawn titters for a series of ribald limericks that concluded in a ménage à trois, prompting Miss Swayne to threaten her with suspension. In Victoria Van Renssealer's version, Mrs. Arden abandoned both men and withdrew to a convent for monastic vows. My own stanzas had, as I recall, been rather uninspired. Solid B+ work. But now the suffering of that wretched "un-widow" resonated with me deeply. "Will you excuse us for a moment," I said to Nënë Roza.

Tecumseh Muhammed and I hurried up the sidewalk in silence, as though we'd decided not to hash things out on empty stomachs. Cash, delighted to see us, as always, filled two Styrofoam caddies with lamb kebobs over biryani. "Both lovebirds at the same time," he observed, ladling out the food. "Is this a special occasion?" I replied that all visits to his truck were special occasions, and professing our thank yous, we quickly retreated to the museum steps. Even in late autumn, tourists littered the granite steps. Yellow school busses disgorged children and chaperones like dragons breathing fire. I recalled my initial surprise when Tecumseh Muhammed informed me he'd never flown in an airplane, but in my entire life, I realized, I'd never ridden on one of these yellow busses. We finished our meals before we spoke. "Well," I said, "I thought you'd gone to Key West."

"Thought?" asked Tecumseh Muhammed. "Or hoped?"

I had no answer to offer. I didn't want to lie and I was uncertain of the truth.

"I've been to The Cube every night," said Tecumseh Muhammed.

"Not *every* night," I objected. "Not last week."

"Okay. I was on a bender. But the last *three* nights," he said. "I figured something happened to you. Or *someone*."

His phrasing clarified the situation for me. Someone *had* happened to yours truly. Tecumseh Muhammed was now a part of my past, a man I'd once gone with—not so different, when you came right down to it, from the overweight Kennedy cousin who'd pawed me at the Boston Cotillion. Or even Luke the Enforcer. Something had started; inevitably, that meant something else had ended. And yet he sat two steps away from me, reclining loose-limbed, his want and hunger as desperate as that of a puppy. "Where's Revenge?" I asked.

"Ran off again. Or got a better offer," he said. "So what?"

"Nothing," I said. "I was just asking."

We sat in silence for a few more minutes, but they felt like eons, and then Tecumseh Muhammed rose suddenly. "That's all you got to say?"

"I thought you'd abandoned me," I said. I could see the anger boiling behind Tecumseh Muhammed's eyes, but also his efforts to suppress it. His shoulders stiffened; his left hand balled into a fist. But sober, Tecumseh Muhammed was a man who'd learned to contain himself. Maybe he'd learned the hard way, in the cellblock at Dannemora, but he had learned.

"I'll see you around," he said—a blow far more cutting than the slash of brass knuckles.

And that, as they say, was that.

CHAPTER EIGHT

To distract myself from Tecumseh Muhammed—and to keep the voices at bay—I threw myself resolutely into my work. Nënë Roza favored a leisurely breakfast before the afternoon's guardianship hearing, or at least a cup of shepherd's tea "to settle the stomach," but I insisted we head down to Mount Hebron in search of Dr. Bhatt and Dr. Cotz-Cupper. I didn't know their individual schedules, of course. I didn't even know for sure that they'd returned from vacation. But it was approaching eleven o'clock, so I figured there was a good chance we'd catch them enjoying a snack break after morning rounds. You can imagine my amazement—and here's the second fortuity of this narrative—to find the pair of them literally standing outside the hospital, at the curbside, as though awaiting our arrival. Sheila Bhatt had her hair up in a ballet bun and a parka cloaked over her scrubs; Jamie Cotz-Cupper's long neck protruded from her white coat, a stethoscope draped over her shoulders. What good fortune! From their rumpled exhaustion, it was clear they'd both been on call overnight—which meant they had already presented their patients at morning report and were now entirely clear of clinical responsibilities. Our timing could not have proven more ideal. And as I watched Dr. Cotz-Cupper step into the gutter to hail a cab, it was obvious they were a couple.

"That's them," I exclaimed. "Pull over."

We drew up to the sidewalk, narrowly avoiding an orderly pushing a wheelchair. Before I had an opportunity to roll down the window, Dr. Cotz-Cupper opened the rear passenger-side door and the pair of them slid into the Oldsmobile. "Houston and Varick," she ordered. Then she turned to her partner and added, "Remind me to talk to the super about that leak." I'd been mistaken for many things in life—once, I'll confess, with a hint of vanity, the Earl of Harewood, in his dotage, confused me with Princess Grace of Monaco—but never could I have anticipated being taken for an employee of a livery service. Nënë Roza didn't seem to understand the mix up, so I whispered, "They think we're a cab."

"Goodness," exclaimed my sidekick. "What should I do?"

"Drive," I replied. "Houston and Varick."

Once we'd edged into traffic, I locked the automatic doors. In the rearview mirror, I glimpsed Dr. Bhatt resting her drowsy head on her partner's lap. I hated to disturb them, but a murder investigation takes precedence over a catnap. While Nënë Roza navigated the avenue, and occasionally the bicycle lane, I mustered my courage. Then I leaned into the back seat, my notebook open to a page labeled DOCTORS' EVIDENCE, and asked, "Would it be all right if I asked you a few questions on the way?"

Only an instant lapsed before Dr. Cotz-Cupper registered the situation.

"What the fuck?" she demanded.

"It's okay," I said. "Mrs. Toptani is an excellent driver. We'll get you across town as well as any other taxi."

"You're kidnapping us," cried Cotz-Cupper. "Let us out now!"

Dr. Bhatt rubbed her eyes. "What's going on?"

"You won't believe this! The crazy bird lady is kidnapping us."

I launched into damage control. "We were just dropping by to ask you a few questions about the murder on the seventh floor—and you mistook us for a car service," I said. "I'm truly sorry about that, but I promise we'll get you to Houston and Varick."

Cotz-Cupper slapped the back of the driver's seat. "Please, drop us off," she insisted. "You're not even going the right way."

The vehicle veered right, then lurched left onto the cross street. Nothing but a touch of turbulence, I assured myself—like during a jaunt in Great Uncle Atherton's Embraer. Whether Nënë Roza knew the route to the intersection of Houston and Varick streets was another matter entirely, but I reckoned she'd find her way there eventually. How lost could a person become on Manhattan Island? This wasn't exactly the Australian Outback. And the extra time with the two headshrinkers could only help my interrogation. "All I'm hoping to find out," I said, "is if either of you noticed anything unusual on the night of the murder."

By now, Dr. Bhatt was also wide awake. "Oh my God," she cried. "We're going to die."

"Please, Dr. Bhatt. If you work with us," I reassured the house officer—echoing her favorite mantra, "we'll work with you." But I suppose I'd overplayed my hand, because neither of the women appeared willing to answer any of my questions. Who could have anticipated they'd react so negatively? I figured I'd try a more conciliatory tack, and asked, "Did you two have a nice vacation?"

"Stop, right now!" Cotz-Cupper demanded again. "Sheila, dial 9-1-1. If you don't let us out, we're going to call the police."

At the mention of the word "police," Nënë Roza panicked. "Okay, I drop you off. I don't want any trouble." But she floored the accelerator, rather than the brake, and had us flying up Second Avenue at a solid fifty miles per hour. And indeed, we *were* headed in the wrong direction, if our destination was Houston and Varick. In front of us, the treetops of Stuyvesant Square Park swayed below the towering visage of Mount Hebron. Antigona's mother had navigated an enormous loop. We were only yards from the park's wrought iron gates, and a head-on collision with the Dvořák statue, when Nënë Roza's foot found the appropriate pedal. I'd tuned out the shouts of Dr. Bhatt and Dr. Cotz-Copper, which had merged with my own voices—a concerto of threats and pleas.

The sight of the familiar structure seemed to calm our driver. She crossed herself twice, keeping one hand on the wheel, and eased the Oldsmobile to the shoulder. "There we are. What is the saying you have in America? Door to the door service," she said. "This is the door."

But then a miraculous sight greeted us on the pavement, one so shocking that even our passengers froze in place. Outside the hospital stood a team of New York City police officers—enough to populate a small precinct—and an equal number of plain-suited agents. Probably FBI. One by one, they led their prisoners through the revolving doors out to waiting squad cars: Dr. Mallet in his dapper white suit; a shell-shocked Dr. Robustelli; Mr. Limberg, the officious vice president for finances, who oversaw inpatient billing. And I found myself feeling genuinely sad for all three of these men, even Dr. Robustelli, despite our many years of sparring, whom I recalled had a son in college and a special needs daughter. Lucille Tobruk's investigation had apparently produced more concrete results than my own.

After my automotive adventure with Nënë Roza, I begged off a free ride to the county courthouse and instead persuaded Antigona's mother to park the Oldsmobile at a discount lot and to accompany me to Foley Square on foot. The hearing itself was scheduled for 1pm, but I wanted to arrive early, so I'd have a few minutes to introduce myself to my attorney. "And we *must* have lunch," insisted my sidekick. "My treat. In Albania, we say never to face a judge on an empty stomach, because your stomach may stay empty for a long time." I tried to edify Nënë Roza on the differences between civil and criminal jurisdiction, but in the end, it proved much easier—and more satisfying—to let her buy me a toasted bagel with cream cheese. We arrived at Sixty Center Street nearly an hour in advance, giving me ample time to secure my cart and for the pair of us to negotiate the metal detectors. Nënë Roza's artificial knee set off the alarm, and she'd left her physician's note back in Queens, so I had to plead her case to the security supervisor. After an extensive pat down, we finally rode the elevator to the courtroom with only minutes to spare.

What I remember most about those moments leading up to the hearing was a sense of deep awe at the imposing power of the judicial process and trepidation as to my own impending fate. Litigation, as Papa used to say, isn't beanbag, and that was especially true when the subject of contention was guardianship. To have a conservator appointed to manage one's affairs means, in essence, that a person is no longer a full-fledged human being in the eyes of the law. Becoming a ward of the state is to be severed from the body politic, cut off from civil society, denied the prerogatives of citizenship and one's rightful place in the community. Practically speaking, I'd also be unable to access my disability payments or even my food stamps without the okay of a government bureaucrat. Uncle Dewey's worst fears about arbitrary socialist autocracy and the suppression of economic freedom would come to high-handed fruition, at least in my limited case.

No structure could have embodied the gravity of the looming ordeal as effectively as the granite-faced neoclassical monolith that housed the Manhattan County Court. Climbing the steps toward the imposing Corinthian colonnade, then passing under the massive pediment crowned with its acroteria of "truth, law and equity" into the grand lobby, and listening to the echo of one's footsteps beneath the hall's grand rotunda and clerestory, a mere layperson like yours truly is reminded of the full extent of her insignificance. Candidly, I felt honored just for the privilege to face trial amidst such grandeur—flattered against my best interest, maybe, like those Bolshevik dissidents tickled pink to have been personally sentenced to death by Comrade Stalin. So, as I said, we rode the elevator to the eighth floor and entered the assigned courtroom. The session appeared to be on lunchbreak; only a handful of forlorn spectators occupied the galleries—law students, elderly gawkers, a henna-haired woman with a notebook, similar to mine, but with no visible nuthatches on the cover, who appeared to be a journalist. Nënë Roza claimed a seat in the front row and I followed. Not wanting to offend the bailiffs, two lanky fellows who looked like matching bishops from a famine-afflicted chess match, I removed my flamingo hat and gently set it down beside me on the pew. Only I suppose we live in a secular society, so the term *pew* might have the wrong connotation, but the ambience reminded me of Evensong at St. John the Divine. Anyway.

"It is a woman judge," said Nënë Roza. "A bad omen."

"How do you know it's a woman?" I asked.

She pointed out the nameplate on the bench. "For a woman to become a judge, she must be fierce. A fighter," Nënë Roza opined. "Unforgiving. Ruthless. Under General Hoxha, if you stood before a woman judge, that meant you were hours away from the firing squad. What is the word people use here...*hanging* judge."

"Nobody is getting hanged," I muttered automatically, but I'd only been paying the most superficial attention to my companion's concerns. The name on the judge's plate struck me like a shot of unanticipated valium—both jolting and soothing: VIVIENNE MELLON. Sassy, shrewd, endlessly garrulous Vivienne Mellon, who'd captained Bryn Mawr's College Bowl team and later married a baronet. (The nobleman subsequently perished in an IRA bombing, according to the *New York Times* obituary, rendering my former classmate The Dowager Lady Stanhope of Tarver Wells—but she apparently didn't consider such formality appropriate for the bench.) Vivienne and I had studied for an Italian history exam together, and her midshipman beau had given me a lift home from the International Ball one year, when my date proved too intoxicated to locate his souped-up Mustang. And now gabby Vivienne Mellon—who took to bed for weeks after that same midshipman jilted her—was a judge, a real judge with a robe and a gavel and the authority to appoint Antigona's mother my guardian. Not a coincidence, I reminded myself, careful to prevent visceral emotion from overriding the empirical logic of the Mekinulov Effect, but certainly a promising fortuity. Maybe this would emerge as the rare instance in which the Department of Social Services faced its match in court. I was still lost in reverie, trying to recall the name of Vivienne's unfaithful midshipman, when my Mental Hygiene attorney introduced himself.

That was when the day started heading downhill. The lawyer assigned to defend my case looked as though he'd been shipped cross-country in an undersized crate—and a crate without mothballs, I might add. His shopworn jacket boasted only one elbow pad, a faint weal on the fabric revealing where the other had peeled off; a veritable buffet of half-digested meals stained his shirtfront, lapels and stumpy orange necktie. Copious strands of untrimmed hair streamed out of his ears and prodigious nose, which hardly reached the level of my chin. And when he spoke, in a high-pitched voice that mirrored the sound of air quickly leaving a helium balloon, he reminded me of the yapping of Grandma Van Duyn's long-haired Maltese—the pup that ultimately developed type II diabetes and had to be boarded permanently at an endocrine clinic in Biarritz. Now don't get me wrong. I hadn't expected the city to send me the managing partner from Cravath, Swaine & Moore—or even a Harvard Law grad—but I'd rather anticipated my mouthpiece would sport a well-laundered suit.

The attorney's name was Ed Drummer, which he emphasized with a bit too much pride, as though the Drummers were Schermerhorns or Delanceys. What a far cry from Clayton Endicott, who'd have been my trustee if not for Hurricane Gloria, or Winthrop Whittier Porter of Cadwalader, Wickersham & Taft, the imperial Yale-trained counsellor charged with steering Grandpa Brigander's estate through bankruptcy. Even Sy Seidman, the brash, bellicose Russian-born Jew who'd handled Cousin Bertie Ida's divorce, had displayed a certain panache. A necessary *je ne sais quoi*.

Ed Drummer exuded the flavor of a guy who'd once volunteered to be the hall monitor at a public high school. "Do I have news for you, Miss Brigander," he announced. "We're first on the docket."

"Is that good or bad?" I asked.

"That's great. Otherwise, we could be stuck here for hours."

Nënë Roza squeezed my arm and muttered, "First heard. First hanged."

I leaned back to avoid my lawyer's onion-scented breath. "What do you think our odds are?" I asked.

"So here's the plan," said Drummer, as though strategizing for a panty raid or a game of capture the flag. "We'll agree to their terms, but only temporarily. Maybe for one year. And, after the conservatorship expires, we'll make them return to court to renew their request."

I realized the odds stood against us, but I'd at least hoped to mount a defense. For the sake of my own self-esteem, if nothing else. And with Vivienne as judge, jury, and executioner, I thought I might yet have a chance at prevailing.

"But I don't *want* to agree to their terms."

"It's the safest approach," replied the advocate. "And the wisest."

"Safest and wisest for whom?" I pressed. "How will things be any different next year?" Many legal clients forget that their attorneys often possess interests at heart other than their own. Medical patients too. When a doctor says he has an ethical or fiduciary duty to place the welfare of his patients first, what he means is, "first within circumscribed bounds." Otherwise, your physician would accompany you everywhere you went—ideally, with a crash cart and defibrillator handy—which would certainly increase your life expectancy. But at the expense of all of the doctor's other patients, as well as his own health and well-being. What the Little Drummer Boy really meant was that agreeing to the state's terms was the safest and wisest course *for him*.

"Next year," answered the lawyer, "we can ask for a temporary appointment again. We can do this indefinitely, so your case is regularly reviewed."

"But if I never argue my claim, what good does that do me?"

Drummer shrugged as though the answer were obvious. "Please trust me, Miss Brigander. I've been at this racket a very long time."

"What if I refuse?" I asked. "What if I insist upon fighting for my freedom?"

"I wouldn't recommend it," said Drummer. "Highly unorthodox."

"In that case," I said, "I'm hoping I can have my cousin, Nënë Roza, appointed to serve as my guardian."

"Not a good idea," said Drummer. "Too complicated. And the judge won't like that."

Before he could expound any further upon Vivienne Mellon's likes and dislikes—as I recalled, she preferred lanky men with dark hair and light eyes—the bailiff called the court to order and The Dowager Lady Stanhope of Tarver Wells entered the chamber. She'd gained weight, especially under the chin, and her hair had turned the color of Colonial pewter, yet there was no mistaking her high cheekbones and sharp, aristocratic nose. I flashed Vivienne a broad smile, although her head remained buried in the contents of a manila file folder. More spectators had funneled into the seats behind me, rendering the atmosphere claustrophobic. The only face I recognized was Ms. Celery Stalk's, perky as a dandelion in the front row behind the opposing counsel's table; she nodded at me, but I looked away quickly. What did I want with her good will? She was the cause of all this trouble. I assumed the gaunt, cocoa-skinned gentleman with sunken cheeks perched beside the busybody to be her mysterious and meddlesome supervisor.

At the strike of one, the clerk called the court to order and announced our case: *In the Matter of Henrietta F. Brigander, A Petition for Conservatorship.* The judge removed her reading glasses, dusted the lenses, and returned them to the bridge of her nose. She indicated for the state's attorney, Ms. Clausen, to proceed.

"See, we're first," whispered Drummer. "We'll be out of here in under an hour."

The state's attorney looked the part: a well-coiffed, svelte woman of roughly forty in a tasteful beige blouse and matching skirt. I could easily picture her home life: a stylish apartment on the Upper East Side that she shared with a mild-mannered architect. Maybe a child at day care, although, more likely, they were struggling with fertility treatments. My heart went out to the unfortunate woman, even though she was technically my opponent. I wished I'd had the opportunity earlier to warn her against waiting too long to get pregnant.

Ms. Clausen rose and explained the nature of the state's concerns. "So you'll note we've supplied a pair of affidavits," she said. "One from Dr. Winston Mallet and the other from Dr. Vincent Robustelli, both board certified psychiatrists at St. Dymphna's Health System, sharing their concerns regarding the subject's ability to manage her affairs in the community. As you will see, the subject has two hundred fourteen documented psychiatric admissions at seventeen different hospitals dating back to 1981."

I didn't appreciate the connotations of the term "subject." As if my countrymen hadn't fought a bloody eight-year war against King George and his Redcoats to become *citizens*. If Ms. Clausen wanted subjects, she'd best wed a Hohenzollern or a Windsor.

"I object," I shouted, jumping to my feet. "The subject objects." Addressing my former classmate and the sparsely-populated gallery, I felt deeply empowered, even galvanized, a champion of honor and justice—like Jimmy Stewart orating on the floor of the United States Senate in *Mr. Smith Goes to Washington.* "Both of those men were recently arrested for insurance fraud and are no longer working for the St. Dymphna's Health System," I declared. "They lack any meaningful credibility."

Vivienne Mellon cut me off with her gavel. "Please, madam," she said. "All communication with this court should be conducted through your attorney."

She didn't appear to recognize me. Another reminder that context matters. Like the time in eleventh grade, several months after the "Rochester" incident, when we were suffering through Hardy's *Tess of the d'Urbervilles* in Miss Swayne's class, and Charlotte Schuyler identified Angel Clare on a reading quiz as an album by Art Garfunkel—a coup so saucy that even the assistant principal, Dr. Fitzhugh, enjoyed a good chuckle. So I suspect if Vivienne Mellon had encountered yours truly holding a champagne flute on the Wyndham House terrace during Alumnae Weekend, she'd have known me instantly. But since I never graduated, I'm not even on the guest list. And because we were in court, not at a dinner dance, my ex-classmate had no circumstantial clues to aid her in guessing my identity. The only option I had was to help her out. "Vivienne," I cried. "It's Henrietta Brigander from Merion Hall."

That certainly caught her off guard. My former classmate examined me closely, as though hunting for the hidden Waldo in a Wimmelbook montage, tracing the contours of my face and assessing them against her memories. "Miss Brigander," she said, matter-of-fact, "I'll have to ask you one more time to address this court only through your attorney." But I could tell from her expression that she had indeed recognized me. A flurry of whispers spread through the gallery like the Mexican wave at Wimbledon.

The state's attorney immediately requested a sidebar. That led to a lengthy conference at the bench that included the Little Drummer Boy, but not yours truly. My adversary, whom I've already pitied both for her empty nest and for having to serve as Ms. Celery Stalk's puppet, looked increasingly as though she were sucking on a sour tamarind. When the conclave broke up, she strutted stiffly back to her table.

"The state's concerns are registered," said Vivienne. "Do proceed, Ms. Clausen."

Ms. Clausen tapped the end of her pencil on the tabletop, clearly frustrated. "I'd like to introduce these affidavits as exhibits A and B," she said.

I whispered insistently into Drummer's ear—and, to his credit, he did his job. "The defense objects," he said. "My understanding is that, as of eleven o'clock this morning, neither of those physicians remains under the employ of St. Dymphna's and they have both been remanded into federal custody. Under the circumstances, this creates significant credibility and evidentiary issues."

The judge turned to Ms. Clausen. "Is this true?"

"It's news to me, your honor," said the state's attorney. "But for the sake of time, the people won't contest the matter. The absence of this evidence shouldn't materially undermine the overall case for conservatorship."

"Very well," said Vivienne. "The affidavits are withdrawn."

"We do wish to submit an affidavit from Ms. Briana Pastarnack, the subject's caseworker with the Department of Social Services. She is available to testify in person, if the court insists."

Vivienne looked toward our table for guidance.

"That won't be necessary," said Drummer.

"You'll note that Ms. Pastarnack's affidavit includes a description of the subject's current lifestyle, which is characterized by wandering the city with a cart full of stuffed animals. And, according to Ms. Pastarnack's statement, the subject accumulates more of these children's toys with every disability check. Keep in mind, your honor, the subject is a high school graduate with a year of college under her belt. With the appropriate support—and medication—she has the potential to thrive in the community."

What was that supposed to mean?! Most Americans enjoyed fluffy, cuddly things—that's why folks donated money to save pandas and lemurs, but not endangered mollusks or the torrent midge flies of Australia. The sad reality was that the average person valued pandas and lemurs—and even *stuffed* pandas and lemurs— considerably more than she did the street homeless or people with schizophrenia. "I'm already thriving in the community," I shouted.

That drew another three raps of the gavel. "This is your *final* warning, Miss Brigander," said Vivienne. "One more outburst and I will hold this hearing in camera."

Ms. Clausen cleared her throat. "Under the current circumstances, the people fear the subject will continue to tax the mental health resources of the city and the Department of Social Services without any progress toward stabilization."

This argument seemed to be the full extent of the state's case: that I owned too many stuffed birds and that I visited the psych ER too frequently. The truth was, more often than not, I only checked into the hospital for updates on the romantic adventures of the staff. Not meaningfully different from watching the afternoon soaps—and nobody was appointing guardians for all the bored housewives addicted to *All My Children* who still slept with their Raggedy Ann dolls.

"Do you have anything in response, Mr. Drummond?" Vivienne asked.

The Little Drummer Boy stood up. "In light of the evidence presented, my client agrees to waive any objections and assents to the guardianship petition, but with the stipulation that the term by limited to one year from today's hearing."

I tugged at his jacket sleeve—the one without the elbow patch. When he ignored me, I stomped as hard as I could on his penny loafer. The man made a sound like an asthmatic attempting to play the kazoo, but with all eyes focused upon us, he had no choice but to confer with yours truly. And I wasn't conceding without having my say. "I do apologize, your honor, but my client is not yet ready to agree to the state's terms," he finally announced, glancing at his watch. "She is requesting an opportunity to testify."

"Very well," agreed Vivienne. "Please swear in the subject."

The bailiff had me place my hand upon a Bible and I took my oath. I desperately wanted to check which version of the holy scriptures they used. Would it have been unreasonable, as an Episcopalian, albeit a lapsed one, to request a King James or a Revised Standard? And did they have a separate copy with the Apocrypha just for Catholics? Or a freestanding Old Testament for Jews? I had a host of questions, but feared I might distract Vivienne from the merits of my case.

"Please tell us what you'd like to share, Miss Brigander," she said. Her voice revealed little—gone, it seemed, was the voluble gossip of my youth, but she wore a benevolent smile, and I couldn't help inferring she was on my side. Looking out over the sea of spectators—okay, maybe *sea* is an exaggeration, but we had at least a large enough crowd for a rugby union scrimmage—I sensed that this was my moment, as though all of my life's previous zigzags and hairpin turns had been part of a carefully orchestrated destiny, that this was my Rubicon, my Gettysburg, my Stalingrad.

"Thank you, your honor," I said. "Or should I say your ladyship? The spectators may not know about your connections to the landed gentility."

Vivienne smiled. "Your honor will do."

"I admire your modesty, your honor," I said. "So what I wanted to say was that I don't feel I need a guardian at all, but if I'm going to have one, I'd like for it to be my cousin, Nënë Roza. She's in the front row—over there."

Vivienne held up her hand for me to pause. "Would the people be amenable to Miss Brigander's cousin serving as her guardian?"

Ms. Clausen asked for a brief delay and huddled with both Ms. Celery Stalk and the caseworker's sunken-cheeked colleague.

"Not at present, your honor," she finally replied. "According to the state's records, Miss Brigander's nearest and *only* relatives are a pair of third cousins residing in Boston. Both women—they're sisters—are well over ninety, and clearly unsuited to serve as conservators. This is the first we've ever heard of Ms. Roza."

"Duly noted," said Vivienne. "Is there anything else, Miss Brigander?"

"Indeed, there is," I said. "What I was saying was that *if* I required a guardian, I'd want it to be my cousin, Nënë Roza, but there's no reason I need a guardian at all. I'm not saying I haven't made my fair share of mistakes and poor choices in life. Maybe more than my fair share. But who hasn't?" I caught sight of Nënë Roza, leaning forward with her palm cupped to her ear, and I elevated my voice accordingly. "When I was on the gymnastics team at Brearley, Jennie Kimball let a Mormon missionary from Wyoming get to third base with her in a public restroom—and now she's the most trusted name in weather, if NBC News is to be believed. And nobody is saying Jennie Kimball needs a guardian." I sensed my momentum building, my indignation rising to the occasion, like Peter Finch in *Network*, urging the metropolis to be mad as hell and not take this anymore. "And what about Binnie Chesterfield? You remember Binnie, don't you? You're probably going to protest that I'm still bitter because she wouldn't give me credit for Pluto on trivia night, but all I'm saying is that Binnie set off the fire alarms twice in Batten House, smoking in bed, and urinated in a flower pot at U. of P. homecoming, and now she's a federal magistrate in Atlanta. And nobody ever tried to make Binnie Chesterfield a ward of the state."

My attorney looked a bit flummoxed—I don't suspect he thought I had it in me to mount such an impassioned defense—but Vivienne still wore her smile, although it now looked a bit more like a grimace, so I plowed forward, bracing myself for the kill. "I'm speaking the cold hard truth here," I said. "Honestly, your honor, you could have ended up married to that two-timing naval cadet rather than Sir Reginald. Or even that Moroccan exchange student you had a thing for. You know who I mean—the guy who worked Friday nights as a waiter at the Philadelphia Club. Do you recall that week you thought he'd knocked you up? *I do*. Let's face it. You could have ended up selling *babouches* in a Marrakesh souk or dancing the veils in the Fez medina, and right now you'd be The Dowager Lady Fatima of Old Tangiers. So tell me, your honor, do *you* deserve a guardian?" I sensed an uneasy silence had enveloped the court room; Vivienne was no longer smiling, though it was difficult to describe the new tenor of her visage. "All I'm saying is, let she who is without blame cast the first stone!"

I'd concluded my testimony, but I wasn't sure about the protocol. Would Ms. Clausen cross examine me? Or should I retire to my seat? I'll confess that I'd secretly hoped my soliloquy might draw applause from the gallery, but while Nënë Roza was nodding her head confidently, most of the audience appeared stone-faced. I guess courthouses are a tough crowd. Ms. Celery Stalk's face wore a shroud of discouragement. *Sore loser*, I thought.

"Thank you for that," said Vivienne Mellon. "Court will adjourn for twenty minutes. Ruling will be delivered in camera. Counsellors, if you'd kindly meet with me in chambers."

My former classmate disappeared through the side door, the Little Drummer Boy and Ms. Clausen following. I shuffled over to hug Nënë Roza and retrieve my hat. At the very worst, I figured, Antigona's mother would serve as my guardian.

"What did you think?" I asked her. "Powerful stuff, no?"

She nodded vigorously. "Could not hear," she said. "Battery in hearing aid dead. But your—what do you call it?—body language. You have the body language of a champion."

We sought refuge in the corridor to wait for the verdict. Ms. Celery Stalk tried to speak to me as I passed her along the aisle, but I ignored the meddlesome nitwit. Let her stew in her own juices for a spell, I thought, although I hadn't wanted to humiliate her in front of her boss. Another fifteen minutes expired before the Little Drummer Boy came out to find us.

"So what's the verdict?" I asked.

Drummer looked as though he might place his hand on my shoulder, but didn't dare. "There were multiple considerations," he explained. "Judge Mellon had to weigh any potential conflicts of interest, take into account the likelihood of remand or reversal on appeal, and although the conservatorship act grants chancery considerable leeway as to the choice of guardian, and preference is to be given to blood relations, the law doesn't specify the degree of evidentiary certainty required when the very nature of the relative's consanguinity stands in doubt. Fortunately, Judge Mellon believed herself in a position to issue a ruling."

"What does that mean?" I asked him. "In English."

"You lost, I'm afraid. A permanent guardian has been appointed."

Nënë Roza tried to comfort me with Albanian proverbs, several of which involved the blood of goats, but I channeled my best Greta Garbo and explained, "I want to be alone." Not that I was truly alone—not with the voices brewing up a storm of anger, a tornado of disparaging commentary fit for one of Jennie Kimball's alerts on NBC News. *Even her own friend is against her!* they cried. *Not a human being anymore! Just an oversized child.* All of which was true. In the eyes of New York State, I was no longer a full-fledged legal personage. Endeavors most folks take for granted—the ability to sign leases, open bank accounts, serve on juries—now hovered beyond my reach. I wasn't even sure if I was permitted to vote. Not that I'd been renting any real property or closely following the city council elections in the days when I still did possess legal personage, but the loss stung nonetheless. (Like those war brides who don't hear from their husbands for many months, and deep down suspect the worst, but only truly suffer with formal notification of their husbands' deaths, even though the men in question have already been long deceased.) I can see Grandma B. shaking her head with shame: born a Brigander, died a ward of the state. And who could blame her for her mortification? I hurried down the courthouse steps and tried to block out the echoes of Vivienne Mellon's gavel.

Everyone needs a place to regroup, a sanctuary in which to gather one's thoughts. That's one of the few tidbits of sound advice I ever acquired in group therapy—from a skills leader who'd once been a psychiatric patient herself. For those of a religious persuasion, this haven is often a church or synagogue; nature lovers may take a hike through a favorite alpine meadow, or like ex-President Bush, build up endorphins clearing brush. And, of course, many people retreat to their own houses or apartments for asylum. Alas, for yours truly, none of these refuges was an option. But that did not leave me entirely without recourse. When I felt truly devastated, no matter what the weather, I rode the Bx29 bus out to City Island in The Bronx and trekked to the end of the Fordham Street pier. From that perch, buffeted by the sea breeze, and harassed periodically by gluttonous herring gulls, one could see the lush, unkempt greenery of the islet across the channel. That's Hart's Island, Potter's Field, the final resting place of the city's unwashed and unwanted—including my twin brother, Reginald "Rusky" Van Duyn Brigander, and my dearest friend, "Renegade" Sally Steinhoff. And now, "Little Abe" Currier, autopsied too late. Within an hour of leaving the courthouse, I was standing on that jetty, hands braced on the splintered rail, calling upon Rusky for solace and succor and wisdom.

I had the dock largely to myself. The biting wind and overcast sky had scared off all but the hardiest of sea lovers: a pair of adolescent boys, likely truant, scampering along rocks adjoining the breakwater; a solitary, stoic fisherman in a hooded mackintosh. A female security officer kept guard from inside a glass-paneled post. On the water, a launch emblazoned DEPARTMENT OF CORRECTIONS jounced violently atop the surf. While I watched the spray hammering the seawall, a young couple strolled across the boardwalk—wearing matching Yankees caps—and laid claim to a section of the railing twenty yards away. How inconsequential it all seemed: their love, my pain, the schoolboys' joy. Nothing reminds a soul of her insignificance like the scent of brine and the panorama of the ocean. Not that yours truly needed any reminders.

The voices rose with a crescendo to rival Shostakovich's Seventh Symphony. *Not even human*, they yelped and whispered— at different volumes and pitches. *Not even human! Not even human! Not even human!* And with this external criticism arose self-doubts of my own. Who was *I* to solve a murder? I couldn't even sign a binding contract. Or take out an insurance policy. I'd once been chauffeured to slumber parties in Papa's glistening Cadillac Brougham—the *spare* Brougham—and now I could no longer even rent a car on my own. And surely a man like Big George Currier wouldn't love a woman who was hardly human. "Your sister is a fool," I called out to Rusky across the water. "Living on the fumes of pipe dreams!"

Jump! replied one of the voices—a particularly nasty crone I hadn't heard in years. Soon she'd recruited a chorus of followers: *Jump! Jump! Jump!* Like cheerleaders mounting a chant for Old Eli. *Jump! Jump! Jump!* Like the Sirens of Odysseus, luring me with their music. *Jump! Jump! Jump!* Like doctors offering free anesthesia. *Jump! Jump! Jump!*

And so I jumped.

CHAPTER NINE

By all rights, I should have drowned. Now I'm not one to believe in miracles, or even karma, but part of me can't help wondering if my survival wasn't the cosmos recalibrating after the sinking of the Lady Chatterley, announcing that there were already too many Briganders secured in Davy Jones's locker, and the oceans couldn't handle any more. Who can say for certain? What I do know is that the plumes of my hat became entangled in the crossbeams of the dock and for several seconds I found my entire body supported by the leather stampede straps buttressing my chin and mandible. An inch or two farther back, I'd have broken my neck; had they not snapped under my weight, I'd likely have suffocated. But in the instant they gave way, the memory of Big George's kisses flooded my emotional circuits, and I was seized with a sudden desire to live. Damn the voices, as Admiral Farragut would have said, and full speed ahead! The last thing I recall was clinging to a concrete pylon, half submerged, silently pleading to the ether for a second chance. And, the amazing thing is, I got one!

When I woke up on the jetty twenty minutes later, bleeding from the jaw and shivering, but otherwise unscathed, the woman in the Yankees cap was asking me my name while a pair of medics secured me to a stretcher. The baseball-loving couple, it turned out, were undercover NYPD, presumably assigned to my tail by Detective Libby, although I never learned for sure. But even today, every time I purchase a can of corned beef hash or pumpkin pie mix, I see the distinctive red calligraphy on the label, and thank my lucky stars for Detective Libby's tenacity. If not for his minions, I'd be hanging out with the oysters—in both months with and without Rs. I thought back to all the times I heard Tecumseh Muhammed curse the police for their racist thuggery, and I'm not denying that. All I'm saying is that when you're clinging to a concrete pylon on the edge of Long Island Sound, being pounded by fifty-degree swells, you can't count on the Civilian Complaint Review Board's chardonnay socialists to jump into the water to save you. Sometimes it's the folks who are least sympathetic in the abstract who are most generous in the particular, and vice versa.

Case in point: this Ukrainian manager at a greasy spoon in TriBeCa used to give Luke the Enforcer and yours truly hell for lingering over cups of coffee. "I'm running a restaurant," he'd grumble. "Not a boarding house." Guy had photos up behind the register of him posing with Pat Buchanan and Curtis LeMay. Basically, the neo-fascist was somewhat to the right of Genghis Khan and made George Patton look like George McGovern. But during a savage February cold spell, the abandoned warehouse across the avenue caught fire—a couple of runaways had been burning rags inside a trash can for warmth—and that same would-be brown shirt raced into the blazing building *twice* and carried both teens to safety, while the upscale patrons at a nearby wine bar looked on helplessly at a safe distance. Make of that what you will. Anyway.

The upshot of my rescue was that I was transported downtown to Mount Hebron—that afternoon, as Fortune would have it, Bellevue and Metropolitan Hospitals were both on diversion—and admitted to a general medical unit for observation. Once I'd been reassured that the EMTs had been able to retrieve my hat, rather the worse for wear, but still salvageable, I slept like a baby on Ambien. Twenty-four hours later, when I'd shown no signs of pneumonia or hypothermia, I was transferred to the seventh floor for psychiatric treatment.

How different my frequent haunts appeared without Dr. Mallet and Dr. Robustelli. The hospital brass had hired a temporary unit chief, Dr. Porceddu, a Sardinian autocrat who'd rapidly sent morale cascading down the tubes.

I knew something was amiss when P.J. explained apologetically that I wouldn't be able to wear my hat on the unit. "It's out of my hands, Granny," he said, labeling my plumes and setting them carefully in a paper bag. "The big cheese will go through the roof if she sees it."

And if I need confirmation that times had changed, I ran into Nort the Messiah in the day room and he warned me that I'd be missing Dr. Robustelli. The current leader, whom he'd nicknamed the Petty Poohbah, had confiscated his checkers set. If I had to use one word to describe the state of the ward, I'd have chosen "decapitated." I found myself thinking of the Portuguese gardener targeting the queen ants of the colonies that had ravaged his cucumbers and then waiting for the entire formicaries to die. I'll confess I was also saddened to see that nothing had been done to commemorate the site of Little Abe's murder. Not even a wall plaque or a brass bed plate that read, "Abraham Currier slept here."

The room had returned to common usage, and when I entered to examine the scene of the crime, I was greeted—if you could call it a greeting—by the familiar scowl of the Red Witch. "This is a private room," she snapped. "Take one more step and you'll regret it." I didn't test her. Rationally, I knew that a second murder in the chamber was no more or less likely than the first, but since I'd been saved from drowning by my lucky hat, I was feeling a tad superstitious. At least, I hadn't been assigned to the room or forced to sleep alongside the Red Witch. My own roommate, a catatonic flight attendant, hadn't uttered a single word since she'd been carried off a Lufthansa jet.

The upside of the altered atmosphere was that it made a person see things differently. My sense was that I'd harvested all the evidence available. If I was to solve Little Abe's murder, the challenge would now be a matter of intellect rather than legwork. Whatever information I required was already jouncing around my gray matter, or even right under my nose, if I could only assemble the pieces of the jigsaw puzzle correctly. The following morning in the day room, I shared my frustrations with Nort, who, deprived of his favorite pastime, lounged morosely on the sofa, waiting for his 72-hour discharge request to expire. He had been compelled to shave his beard—a sanitary regulation, according to Dr. Porceddu—and he looked much older with the crags of his jowls revealed. Among the patients, the only other familiar face on the unit that day was Ray G., who'd greeted me the previous evening by asking, "Solve any murders recently?"

I sensed the shifty lowlife wasn't guilty, at least not when it came to Little Abe's killing, but if I'd had a way to pin the murder on the bastard, I swear I might have done it.

"Say, Granny did you ever find that kangaroo-faced woman you were looking for?" asked Nort. "The one from Miami?"

I glanced out the window of the dayroom at the traffic on Second Avenue. Outside, the city went about its business, indifferent to the death of Little Abe. "I found her—kind of—but some good it did me. I'm not sure which is more upsetting: that I haven't solved Little Abe's murder or that nobody cares that he's gone."

"That's the way it is," said Nort. "We all gotta go one day or another." He sighed and added, with an air of deep philosophical reflection, "Life is like a game of checkers. Short. Even when we're young and healthy, we're on borrowed time."

Nort's words echoed Mr. Brauer's observation that Big George's brother "was going to die soon anyway," that the killer had merely aided the great, unheralded god, Atherosclerosis, in His work. But succumbing to heart disease and being gouged repeatedly in the chest with a serrated knife didn't strike me as equivalencies. Someone had wanted Little Abe dead with far more urgency than Mother Nature. And that same someone had gone out of his or her way to cancel Dr. Libby's precious autopsy. But why? What would Occam say? Maybe, the notion struck me, because my almost brother-in-law hadn't died of stab wounds at all. Maybe he'd been poisoned, or even strangled, and the stabbing had been part of a cover up. Of course, that "solution" raised far more questions than it answered. If I couldn't figure out why Little Abe had been stabbed to death, why would I be any more able to figure out why he'd been poisoned and then had his murder disguised as a stabbing? No, I was dining off a smorgasbord of red herrings.

While I was cogitating—or running in mental circles, it felt, like Mama's capybara on its exercise wheel—Mr. Brauer rolled a blood pressure monitor into the day room. "Time for vitals, Bird Lady, and the PCAs are both on break," he groused. "I can't believe I went to Columbia University nursing school to be a glorified orderly."

"I can't believe I went to Bryn Mawr College to be a glorified psychiatric patient," I answered, sticking out my bare arm for the cuff. "Say, Mr. Brauer, how's the fishing going? A friend in Queens tells me the red arowanas are still running off Breezy Point."

"You don't say," said Sarge. "Red arowanas? I'll have to check that out."

"Jaguar cichlids too. Practically jumping out of the bay."

Mr. Brauer ran the thermometer across my forehead. "The cichlids I already know about," he said. "You're not the only one with friends in Queens."

But that answered one lingering question. I was the only one of us who knew a darn iota about fishing. Red arowanas are native to Indonesia and jaguar cichlids dwell in the freshwater lakes of Guatemala and Honduras. Grandpa Van Duyn shelled out a small fortune for them after World War II to stock his private aquarium. I might not know who killed Abe Currier, but next time Ray G. asked, I could tell him that Mr. Brauer didn't know a fly reel from a flounder.

"Your turn, Norton," said the nurse. "Let's see if you're still alive."

While Mr. Brauer checked Nort the Messiah's vitals, confirming that my fellow inmate was indeed still alive, I ran my mental fingertips over the blade of Occam's razor. I asked myself, "What was the simplest and most logical explanation for Little Abe's death? Who would go to such lengths to track down a small-time con artist in a loony bin and murder him?" And suddenly, the answer was obvious. No one. Nobody would go to such great lengths to extinguish the life of a human being as inconsequential as Big George's brother—not the Albanian mob, not a disgruntled former client with a worthless letter from President Truman, not a wronged husband armed with an antique gun. And that realization led me directly to the identity of the killer.

I suppose this is the moment, dear reader, that you've been waiting for. If this novel were a Columbo special on television or an Agatha Christie mystery, I'd have gathered together all of the suspects in the drawing room and unmasked the killer. Alas, I obviously didn't have access to a drawing room, although I suppose I might have requested use of the day room. But even if I'd had a suitable space for my revelation, most of the potential suspects remained on the far side of a set of magnetically-sealed steel doors. I guess, with considerable effort, I could have rounded up Nort the Messiah and Ray G., and possibly some of the nurses, depending on the shift, but all of that struck me as rather overdramatic. Instead, I retreated to my room, where the catatonic flight attendant sat motionless in a padded chair, only her eyelids fluttering, and waited for Mr. Brauer's after-dinner room check. He'd been mandated to stay until eleven o'clock once again—Bonnie Jean had gone out on maternity leave—and, following a formal warning from Ms. Alpenwasser, he'd given up on the ruse with the fishing tackle.

He knocked on the door around ten-thirty. "Counting heads," he said, jotting on his clipboard. "Bird Lady, check. Zombie Woman, check."

"You've got a shorthand name for all of us, don't you?"

Sarge glowered. "What's it to you, Bird Lady?"

Ever since our brief encounter outside the hospital, he'd been even more churlish than his usual short-tempered self.

"Just taking note," I said. "What was your shorthand for Little Abe?"

"Who?"

"George Currier, I mean. The patient who died."

"Who cares?" asked Sarge. "He's dead."

"Now we're getting somewhere," I observed. "The real question, of course, isn't whether he's dead now—but whether he was dead when you stabbed him."

"I don't know what you're talking about."

But Mr. Brauer stepped further into the room, rather than departing, which I interpreted as an admission of guilt. Or, at a minimum, an incriminating gesture.

"I think you know exactly what I'm talking about, Mr. Brauer," I said. "I've spent the last two weeks trying to figure out who killed Little Abe—the guy you know as Big George—when the question I should have been asking was *what* killed Little Abe? And I'll tell you what killed Little Abe: four stents and a pacemaker. Even a cursory shave with Occam's Razor argues that the most likely killer of a fifty-nine-year-old male with severe heart disease is heart disease. He'd probably already been showing the first signs of a cardiac event before dinner when he asked Miss Clare for an antacid. By the time you did your room check that night and measured his vital signs, he didn't have any. The numbers you recorded in the computer were utterly fictitious."

"Good story, Bird Lady. And *why* did I do this?"

"The million dollar question, of course, is how much time had passed between his cardiac arrest and the moment you stabbed him. Because even if his heart wasn't beating, that didn't mean he couldn't have been revived. It's not like we're out in the field. Or snowbound on an Antarctic military base. We have access to defibrillation pads, epinephrine. A first-rate CCU staffed by nationally-renowned cardiologists. If you'd called a code, Little Abe might still be alive."

"Except he *was* alive when I left him."

"I suppose it's a legal question as to whether or not a person can murder a dead man. I'll have to leave that one for the district attorney," I continued. "But I'm sure you stabbed him. You found him non-responsive and pulseless, and you figured he was a goner, so you decided to make the most of the situation. You retrieved a serrated knife from your fishing creel, sneaked back into Little Abe's room, and bludgeoned the lifeless body—and then you slid the bloody weapon into the hands of sleeping Angry O'Dell. That's why you hurried to retrieve the knife from the floor. There had to be an explanation for your fingerprints on the weapon, in case the police tested it."

"Do you realize how crazy you sound, Bird Lady?" interjected Mr. Brauer. "You're accusing me of murdering a dead man."

"*Dying* man," I said. "That's also why you weren't afraid to approach Angry O'Dell while he was wielding the knife. Because you—and you alone—knew he hadn't murdered anyone. And it's also why you had to cancel Little Abe's autopsy. In case the cause of death came back as cardiovascular disease, rather than trauma. I give you credit, Mr. Brauer. I'm not sure I would have thought of that. For an amateur, you played a darn good hand."

Sarge had inched toward me as I spoke, and the fear briefly crossed my mind that he might employ violence to silence me. But all I had to do was scream—even the briefest cry—and staff would come running with their restraints, needles drawn. That was the sole benefit of accusing a man of murder while you were locked in the loony bin; he was relatively powerless to render you any physical harm.

"Okay, Bird Lady," said Sarge. "I concede that's a creative story you've got going there, but there's one gaping hole in it. A hole big enough to ram an Abrams tanks through. Why on earth would I stab a virtual stranger I'd only laid eyes on for the first time less than twenty-four hours before? By your own admission, I didn't even know the guy's name."

"That's where character comes in, Mr. Brauer. Most people, if they'd found Little Abe in acute shock and rapidly assuming room temperature, would immediately have thought, what can I do to help this man? But you're not most people, Mr. Brauer, are you? Your immediate reaction was: this man's already toast. How can I profit from his death? And I give you lots of credit for thinking on your feet. You immediately decided to frame Monty Castillo. If Angry O'Dell managed to smuggle a knife onto the unit, that meant he'd been inadequately searched. You figured the sloppy search would cost your rival his job. And it did. As for Angry O'Dell, he was just another worthless lunatic. Collateral damage."

"Monty Castillo is not my rival," said Sarge. "That loser is *nothing* to me."

"But his girlfriend is. Or was," I replied.

Sarge glanced at the immobile stewardess and reached for a pillow. I can't say whether he intended to suffocate me, or just wanted to give me a scare, but I wasn't taking any risks, so I said at elevated volume, "Keep in mind, *Sarge Brauer*, that catatonics are completely aware of their surroundings. She'll remember everything that takes place inside this room." This isn't necessarily true, but I banked on the limits to Sarge's medical knowledge. I figured he wouldn't dare murder us both. If *two* patients died suddenly on his shift, that would certainly have looked rather peculiar.

Sarge responded with a burst of laughter and tossed the pillow onto the bed. "That's one crazy story you've got there, Bird Lady. Not a word of it is true, mind you, but it is one darn crazy story." Then he lowered his voice to a half whisper, his tone breathy and almost maniacal, and added, "But even if it were true, Crazy Bird Lady, who would ever believe you?"

He laughed again as he left the room, bringing my career as a detective to a close.

CHAPTER TEN - EPILOGUE

Since this is the final chapter of my story—or, at least, the conclusion of the New York City chapter of my story—you'll want to know what happened to the characters and all that *Middlemarch* kind of hokum, and since I'm an obliging soul, and you've come all this way with me, I feel I have no choice but to indulge you. Not that it's an easy feat to wrap up a complex narrative without loose ends or tangents when you're suffering from schizophrenia, even if you're not doped up on meds, but I'll set my shoulder to the wheel and see what I can manage.

The second thing I did when I arrived in Newport—after kissing Big George until our tongues ached—was to forward my mail. I chose general delivery again, as much out of habit as a fear of romantic failure, and informed the Farley Post Office that I'd no longer be partaking of their enchanting services. Within a week, I received two pieces of personal correspondence. The first, a postcard marked Everglades City, came from Tecumseh Muhammed. One side depicted a flock of purple gallinules. The other side read, in entirety: Hen — Saw a flamingo this morning. Thought of you. Keep the faith, TM. Not exactly Keats, but I suppose it's the intention that counts. The other missive, to my surprise, bore an NBC peacock for a return address. I tore it open in the lobby of the post office, anticipating it might contain the name of Jennie Kimball's Mormon missionary.

Dear Henrietta:

So good to hear from you after all of these years. I hope and trust the post-Brearley world has treated you well and you're enjoying life in New York City. Go Beavers!

I apologize for the delay in my response, but at the time your letter arrived, my marriage was in a deep freeze. We're talking Nome, Alaska, dead of winter. Glad to say I've left all of that behind me. So after I received your letter, on a whim, I tracked down that "Mormon missionary." He's a maritime lawyer in Houston now, and

I'm pleased to say we started talking on the phone, and then he visited Manhattan for a conference...and we're getting married in June! The wedding will be in Texas, but I do hope you can join us. His name is Pete Muriel, by the way.

In any case, Truth and Toil United—and all that jazz!
Lots of Love,
Jennie Kimball

When I heard the name "Muriel," I instantly thought of Edie Adams pitching corona cigars for the Muriel brand with Stan Getz accompanying on saxophone. Not that Pete Muriel would recognize the jingle—or even Edie Adams's name. But as I grow older, and increasingly aware of the world's pandemic ignorance, I try to be more forgiving.

On the subject of forgiveness, I wrote a letter to P.J. and, to my delight, his response updated me on life at Mount Hebron. P.J. is overnight nursing supervisor now. Ms. Holm was promoted to Miss Alpenwasser's position—the brass had apparently forgiven her for presiding over a killing—and Miss A. got the old heave-ho for diverting opioid analgesics from the Pyxis dispenser. That old harridan! Go figure! On a more positive note, Monty Castillo won his appeal and got his job back. It turns out Mary Lou had been seeing Chief Boucher on the side, and once this came to light, the union went bananas. Like I said, Mount Hebron is better than *General Hospital* or *Days of Our Lives*. P.J. also writes that the judge in Little Abe's murder case found "Angry" O'Dell unfit to stand trial, and while he is being "restored" to competence—a process with no clear timetable—he has been indefinitely committed to the state forensic facility on Ward's Island. The good news is that the institution apparently has an amateur baseball team and they let him play shortstop. (The letter didn't say whether he fields with his right or his left.) P.J.'s sister-in-law works as a dietician on their geriatric unit, so my former dreamboat gets all of the juice. "They even have a patient woodshop," wrote P.J., "and Arnold has been assigned his own personal screwdriver, with his name masking-taped to the handle, which seems to satisfy him."

As for Sarge, I'm afraid he had the better half of the argument. Who would believe me? That's unfortunately the way it is with mental illness. A person can decipher Linear A or find the remains of

Jimmy Hoffa, but the minute she reveals she's been hospitalized on a psychiatric ward, nobody takes her claims seriously. If I'd gone to Detective Libby with my accusation, he'd have sent me straight back to Mount Hebron—like Vivien Leigh in *A Streetcar Named Desire*. So I had to be content with solving the crime, not exposing the killer. What alternative did I have? I do hope you'll forgive me, dear reader. Big George says I made the wise choice. Even if not for the stabbing, after the cardiac arrest his brother might have ended up a vegetable, confined to a wheelchair or unable to speak, which for fast-running Little Abe would have been a fate far worse than death, so maybe *not* attempting to revive him had done the poor guy a favor. Who could really say? Nënë Roza also objected to involving the authorities, so I let the matter drop.

Antigona's mother may not have had an opportunity to serve as my guardian, but neither, as it turned out, did the Department of Social Services. Big George's cousin is a paralegal in Providence and she gave me a helpful tutorial on the laws of conservatorship. Not only are legal guardians appointed on a state by state basis, I learned, but those appointments are only valid within their particular jurisdictions—and Vivienne Mellon's jurisdiction terminated at the Connecticut line. The minute I crossed out of New York, in other words, all of Ms. Celery Stalk's efforts proved worthless. In Rhode Island, thank you very much, I am still my own mistress. Not that the girl cares. I imagine, by now, she's happily engaged to an arbitrage trader or hedge fund rainmaker, measuring drapes for her McMansion in Scarsdale or Chappaqua. Good for her, I guess. *Chacun à son goût.* And Nënë Roza, I am pleased to report, passed her driving test on her first try. At present, she is hiring out her Oldsmobile for Uber, and studying for her commercial trucking license, so she can follow in her father's footsteps—although, I am equally pleased to report, she does not yet own a truck, nor does she have the prospect for acquiring one any time soon, so her health remains uncompromised and rather remarkable for an octogenarian.

Which leaves only yours truly...

And what did become of Henrietta Brigander, aka Granny Flamingo, aka The Mad Bird Lady of East 14th Street after her final discharge from Mount Hebron Hospital? That's the $64,000 Question, isn't it? Well, you'll be happy to learn I'm living with Big George on Miamtonomi Avenue—two doors down, in fact, from the one-time residence of the mother of the Brigander chauffer who broke her hip so many years ago in the cycling accident. Her niece still lives there, and we've taken to playing mah jongg on weekday mornings, just like Grandma Van Duyn and Aunt Virginia did in the old days. Big George doesn't mind. Those are his prime hours down at the docks, adjusting the climate for the Upper Crust. "Last laugh will be on them," he's fond of saying. "All that air-conditioning is warming the planet, and soon enough, not even Pomanette or Crusair will have a device to cool them off." But I'm less cynical—or maybe more so, depending on how you look at it. I'm confident there will always be ways for the wealthy to stay comfortable while diverting their excess heat onto the rest of us. Such, as they say, is the way of the world.

On balmy weekend afternoons, Big George and I sometimes stroll the Cliff Walk from Bailey's Beach past the historic mansions along Easton Bay: Tessie Oelrichs's Rosecliff, F. W. Vanderbilt's Rough Point, Ogden Goelet's Ochre Court with its châteauesque gables. If you look closely, between the Astor property and Sheep Point, you can still pick out the charred foundation of the summer cottage. But few people, if any, do look. There's plenty to be seen without rummaging through the detritus of the lost Van Duyns and Briganders.

I should also mention my final Gotham adventure. While I was waiting for Big George to wire me the money for the train, I moseyed over to the Theater District and knocked on a stage entrance that opened onto 48th Street. After an interminable delay, a grumpy, toupéed galoot in jodhpurs and suspenders cracked the door and growled, "Box office opens at noon. Business office is around the corner. This door is for actors and crew only." Surly as the gatekeeper at the Emerald City.

I had to grab hold of the frame before it slammed in my face. "Wait!" I cried. "I'm looking for the crew."

Mr. Jodhpurs let the door open all the way and sized me up. "Anybody in particular?"

I met his gaze head-on. "Someone who has worked here a long time," I answered. "You see, I found the hat I'm wearing outside this theater half a lifetime ago—thirty-six years ago, to be precise—and I'm wondering if anyone knows what play it's from."

Now did that take Mr. Jodhpurs by surprise! "This ain't some prank, is it?"

Not that I blamed his suspicions—not many people, I image, wear a hat they've salvaged from the flotsam of a shuttered play.

Then again, I'm not many people. "You tell me," I replied—feigning confidence. "Do I look like I'm pulling a prank?"

My nemesis scratched his scalp. "Wait here," he said.

Half an hour must have slipped by—and I was about to give up and try the business office—when he returned, now wearing an oversized cardigan. "Sorry for the wait," he said—without a hint of conviction. "Thing is, nobody's been here *that* long. Mr. Elmers— he's the stage manager—he started in 1993. That's the closest." I was about to ask the lummox whether he'd even bothered to ask Mr. Elmers directly, when he reached into his pocket and produced several sheets of paper, indifferently stapled together. "Best I could do was a list of the plays staged here. Who know if it's even complete—but it's your most promising bet."

I'd hardly had a chance to thank him when he wished me good luck and slammed shut the door. The list itself was three pages long, printed in purple ink. It appeared to have been duplicated on a mimeograph machine. The plays dated as far back to the 1920s, with the most recent, a revival of *Brigadoon*, from the 1990s. I scanned to the year in question and read through the season's five plays. Number four jumped out at me: *The Albanian Caper*. That had to be it! The timeframe was right, and more important, I recognized the other four works, and none seemed to call for a two foot tall plush flamingo hat. So I suppose that solves the mystery, although Little Abe isn't around to hear the good news—and I can't even be certain, because the play only ran for three performances and didn't get any major reviews. As though to add to the uncertainty, the playwright took his own life within a year of the production. I suppose I could investigate further—tracking down the individual actors, or the stage crew—but I'm trying to adjust to life without all the answers. Big George says *not* knowing things is good for me. At least, some of the time. I'm trying to take his word for it. Anyway.

I'm living here in Newport, and I haven't solved any more murders, or even opened a pet store, but Big George says the latter is not an impossibility. It will just take some careful planning and a few good years at the marina. In the meantime, I'm keeping house, and reading about old-time movie stars, and trying my utmost to shave with Occam. That's the name of the hyacinth macaw Big George bought me as an engagement present—Granny Occam—and I've already taught her to say, "I Love You, Michael Landon," in both English and Albanian. She alternates between languages, day and night. At first, she flustered the wits out of our muster of peacocks, who didn't possess much sense to start with, and sent our ducks and geese scattering across the vegetable patch, but the birds have gotten used to her. Even Melanie Daniels, although you don't know arguing until you've heard a Moluccan cockatoo and a hyacinth macaw go at it.

As for my story, believe what you wish. Honestly, I'm not even sure myself if it's entirely true. Does that even matter? It feels true to me, so I'm embracing it. That's the key to happiness, I think: staying curious, loving generously, and making the best of the only reality you have.

GLOSSARY OF THINGS YOU SHOULD KNOW
BY HENRIETTA FLORENCE VAN DUYN BRIGANDER

A Streetcar Named Desire (1951): Film directed by Elia Kazan, based on Tennessee Williams's Pulitzer Prize-winning 1947 play, featuring Marlon Brando and Vivien Leigh. At the conclusion of the film, Leigh's character is sexually assaulted and then led off to a psychiatric institution.

Abbott Lowell (1856-1943): Legal scholar, who as President of Harvard University (1909-1933), sought to ban African Americans, impose a Jewish quota, and purge homosexuals from the student body. In 1927, he chaired an infamous panel that upheld the convictions of Sacco and Vanzetti as fair, leading to their executions.

Admiral Farragut (1801-1870): Leading American naval officer during the Civil War who is best remembered for his victory at the Battle of Mobile Bay in which he ordered his officers, "Damn the torpedoes, full speed ahead!"

Admiral Gene Markey (1895-1980): Hollywood Screenwriter, later intelligence officer at Battle of Guadalcanal (1943). Second husband of actress Hedy Lamarr and third husband of actress Myrna Loy, but not simultaneously.

Aesop's Fable, *The Lion and the Mouse*: A fable by the Greek slave, Aesop (620-564 BC), in which a lion frees a mouse in an act of mercy and the same mouse later gnaws through a hunter's net that has trapped the lion. Among the favorite bedtime stories that Governor Nelson Rockefeller read to Henrietta and Rusky Brigander when they were children.

Agatha Christie (1890-1976): Quintessentially English mystery novelist whose creations include detectives Hercule Poirot, Miss Marple, and Tommy and Tuppence.

Agnes Moorehead (1900-1974): American actress who received Academy Award nominations for *The Magnificent Ambersons* (1942), *Mrs. Parkington* (1944), *Johnny Belinda* (1948), and *Hush...Hush, Sweet Charlotte* (1964).

Al Jolson (1886-1950): Actor and singer who starred in *The Jazz Singer* (1927) and headlined NBC radio's *Kraft Music Hall* (1933-49), where his frequent guest was comedian Oscar Levant.

Alcatraz (1934-1963): Federal prison located on Alcatraz Island in San Francisco Bay.

Aldonza: A Spanish prostitute mistaken for Lady Dulcinea del Toboso by Don Quixote in the eponymous novel and the musical adaptation, *Man of La Mancha* (1964). Joan Diener (1930-2006) originated the role on Broadway; the Newport *Daily News* described Henrietta Brigander's performance in the part as "enthusiastic."

Alexander the Great (356-323 BC): King of Macedonia who conquered Persia and built an empire that extended through much of the ancient world.

All My Children (1970-2011): Long running ABC soap opera set in suburban Philadelphia and originally starring Ruth Warrick (1916-2005) and Susan Lucci (born 1946).

All Quiet on the Western Front (1929): German novel of World War I by Erich Maria Remarque. Later a film (1930) starring Louis Wolheim and Lew Ayres. In the novel, Corporal Himmelstoss is a former postman whose newfound authority as a non-commissioned officer at the outbreak of war quickly goes to his head.

Allen Jenkins (1900-1974): American character actor, played opposite Humphrey Bogart and Ann Sothern in *Brother Orchid* (1940).

Allen Ludden's *Password*: (1961-1961 on CBS; 1971-1975 on ABC): A television gameshow hosted by Allen Ludden (1917-1981) in which a celebrity and non-celebrity guest exchanged clues in an effort to guess a mystery word.

Angel Clare: One of the two principal male characters in Thomas Hardy's novel, *Tess of the D'Urbervilles* (1892), his marriage to Tess is undone by her past relationship with Alec Urberville.

Angel Clare (1973): Solo debut album by Art Garfunkel (born 1941) that rose to number five on the charts and included the hits "Traveling Boy" and "I Shall Sing."

Angor Wat (12th Century): A Khmer temple complex in Cambodia. Now overrun by college graduates on gap years and Japanese tourists.

Annapolis (1845): The United States Naval Academy. A perennial source of dates for Bryn Mawr girls, especially those unimpressed by the bookish blue bloods at Haverford and Swarthmore.

Ann Sothern (1909-2001): American actress who starred opposite Humphrey Bogart in *Brother Orchid* (1940). For the record, she was not Southern at all, but was born in North Dakota and lived in Idaho.

Anne Bancroft (1931-2005): American film actress (*The Graduate*) who briefly dated Uncle "Manatee Phil" Van Duyn between her marriages to Martin May and Mel Brooks.

Antanaclasis: A figure of speech in which a word is repeated within one phrase or sentence with different meanings, creating a pun. For instance, the apocryphal Grouch Marx line, "Time flies like an arrow; fruit flies like a banana." Or, for the Shakespearean-minded, as the cowardly soldier, Ancient Pistol, says in Henry V, "To England will I steal, and there I'll steal."

Anton Kochinyan (1913-1990): Armenian political leader who served as First Secretary of the Communist Party of Armenia from 1966 to 1974 and corresponded for many years with Great Uncle Atherton Brigander.

Anuradhapura: Sri Lankan city, once the spiritual center of Theravada Buddhism.

Aquitania (1914-1950): A Cunard ocean liner that brought the height of luxury to transatlantic travel between the two world wars and carried countless Briganders and Van Duyns between Southampton and New York City. Sister ship of the RMS Mauretania and RMS Lusitania, it was also the last surviving four funnel ocean liner in service.

Archie Bunker: "Lovable bigot" portrayed by Carroll O'Connor (1924-2001) on Norman Lear's sitcom *All in the Family* (1971-1979).

Archie Moore (1916-1998): Hall of Fame professional boxer, nicknamed "The Mongoose," who was World Light Heavyweight Champion from 1952 to 1962.

Aristotle Onassis (1906-1975): Greek shipping magnate and second husband of First Lady Jacqueline Bouvier Kennedy; his visit to the summer cottage forced Grandma Brigander to commission new leaves for the mahogany dining table to replace those that had become warped during storage.

Arlene Francis (1907-2001): Actress who was one of three regular panelists (alongside Dorothy Kilgallen and Bennett Cerf) on the television game show *What's My Line?* Not to be confused with singer Connie Francis.

Art Garfunkel (born 1941): Rock and Roll Hall of Fame singer and songwriter who joined with Paul Simon (1941-present) to form one of the nation's best folk rock duos, he later launched a solo career with the album "Angel Clare" (1973).

Arthur Hornblow Jr. (1893-1976): American film producer of *Hold Back the Dawn* (1941) and *Gaslight* (1944), first husband of actress Myrna Loy.

Arthur Murray (1895-1991): Ballroom dance impresario and instructor whose eponymous studios trained the famous and not-so-famous alike. His students included Eleanor Roosevelt, John D. Rockefeller Jr., cosmetics entrepreneur Elizabeth Arden, boxer Jack Dempsey, and Henrietta Brigander.

Audrey Hepburn (1929-1993): Film actress whose performance as New York socialite Holly Golightly opposite George Peppard (1928-1994) in *Breakfast at Tiffany's* (1961) ends in an iconic Hollywood kiss.

Bar Harbor: Summer resort on Mount Desert Island in Hancock County, Maine, that provided refuge for the crème de la crème of New England's social register, including Mama's Uncle Drake.

Barbara Hutton (1912-1979): American socialite dubbed the "Poor Little Rich Girl" who was heir to the F.W. Woolworth fortune, studied dance with Arthur Murray. Grandma Van Duyn knew her from her days at Miss Hewitt's.

Barbara Payton (1927-1967): Actress of such films as *Kiss Tomorrow Goodbye* (1950) and addict (alcohol, cocaine).

Barbara Stanwyck (1907-1990) Actress cheated out of four Best Actress Oscars for *Stella Dallas* (1937), *Ball of Fire* (1941), *Double Indemnity* (1944), and *Sorry, Wrong Number* (1948). Frequent companion and beard for Great Uncle Drake during his time at Princeton.

Barnard (1889-present): A women's college in New York City. "The breeding ground of intellectuals and spinsters," according to Grandma Brigander, who was herself a Pembroke College alumna.

Battle of Belleau Wood (June 1918): Allied military victory during World War I in which the United States Marine Corps played a decisive role.

Battle of Ortona (1943): World War II battle on the Adriatic coast pitting Nazi paratroopers under Richard Heidrich against Major General Chris Vokes's Canadian infantry. Known as "Italian Stalingrad," the contest led to a significant German retreat.

Battle of Tippecanoe (1811): Battle fought in present-day Indiana between the United States Army commanded by future President William Henry Harrison of the Indiana Territory and a Native American force led by Tecumseh of the Shawnee tribe.

Beacon Hill: Upscale Boston neighborhood whose Federal-style row houses have attracted the city's Brahmins and cultural elite since the nineteenth century.

Bela Lugosi (1882-1956): Hungarian-born American actor known for his starring role in horror films including *Dracula* (1931) and *Son of Frankenstein* (1939).

Ben Bass (1901-1978): Jewish founder of Manhattan's Strand Book Store in Manhattan (1927) who sold used books to New York's literary luminaries including Saul Bellow and Grace Paley. He became a confidante of Grandpa Van Duyn when Van Duyn defended his admission to Newport's exclusive Clambake Club. Not related to Perry Bass.

Benevolent and Protective Order of Elks (1868): Fraternal society whose members have included five United States Presidents, Generals Dwight D. Eisenhower, Douglas MacArthur, and three generations of Briganders, including Papa, who was Esteemed Leading Knight of Rhode Island Lodge #1 for more than a decade.

Bergdorf Goodman (1899): Luxury Fifth Avenue department store.

Beowulf: Alliterative Old English epic poem whose eponymous Scandinavian hero, a Geat warrior, slays the monster Grendel and Grendel's mother.

Betty Grable (1916-1973): Actress and World War II "pin-up" girl whose iconic 1943 photograph by Frank Powolny sold five million copies.

Biarritz: French resort city on the Bay of Biscay known for its high stakes casino gambling. In its heyday, visitors included Queen Victoria of England and Alfonso XIII of Spain. Grandma Van Duyn owned a beachfront chateau opposite the Hôtel du Palais, where she summered after Grandpa Van Duyn's death.

Black Dahlia Homicide (1947): Sensational unsolved murder of Elizabeth Short (1924-1947) in Los Angeles in which the victim's corpse was mutilated.

Blue Riband: Award given to the passenger liner for the faster westbound crossing of the Atlantic Ocean. Of the thirty-five transatlantic liners to hold the award since 1830, nineteen have either been Cunard Line or White Star Line vessels.

Block Island Sound: Coastal strait separating Rhode Island from Block Island that is host to several celebrated regattas as well as the shipwreck of Walt Brigander's yacht, *Lady Chatterley*.

Blue Eagle: Iconic symbol of the New Deal era that showed companies to be in compliance with the codes of the National

Recovery Administration. Colonel Wendell Brigander first received one fraudulently in 1933, then another legitimately in 1934.

Bogart & Bacall movie *Key Largo* (1948): The four and final film starring married couple Humphrey Bogart (1899-1957) and Lauren Bacall (1924-2014) after *To Have and Have Not* (1944), *The Big Sleep* (1946), and *Dark Passage* (1947). Edward G. Robinson and Claire Trevor co-starred.

Bonesmen: Term for members of "Skull and Bones," the secret undergraduate society at Yale University whose members have included President William Howard Taft, both President Bushes, and Secretary of State John Kerry.

Boogie Woogie Bugle Boy (1941): Up-tempo blues hit for The Andrews Sisters that became one of the most popular songs of the World War II era and was later covered to acclaim by Bette Midler.

Booming Ben, The Heath Hen: Heath hens composed a distinctive subspecies of the greater prairie chicken, a large fowl of the grouse family. "Booming Ben," the last of the creatures, died in 1932 near West Tisbury, Martha's Vineyard.

Bonnie Blue Butler: Scarlett O'Hara's child with Rhett Butler in *Gone with the Wind* (1939). Her death falling off a pony undermines their marriage. Child actress Cammie King played the part.

Bonnie Parker (1910-1934): Companion of Clyde Barrow (1909-1934) who together held up gas stations, stores, and banks until killed in ambush in Louisiana. She is the subject of Arthur Penn's classic film, *Bonnie and Clyde* (1967), in which she was portrayed by Faye Dunaway.

Boston Cotillion (1944): Debutante ball whose honorees have included Jacqueline Kennedy and Henrietta Florence Brigander.

Boston Marriage: A term for the romantic friendships of nineteenth century New England women who lived together without the support of a man. Immortalized in the relationship between Olive Chancellor and Verena Tarrant in Henry James's *The Bostonians* (1886), which itself was modeled on the relationship between James's sister and Katherine Loring.

Bowery Boys: Fictional New York City gang that was the subject of a series of films from 1946 to 1958 starring Leo Gorcey as Slip Mahoney and Huntz Hall as Sach Jones. The characters spoke with a heavy, working-class New York accent.

Breakfast at Tiffany's (1961): Romantic comedy based on a Truman Capote novel featuring Audrey Hepburn, George Peppard, and Mickey Rooney. The film ends with a kiss during a downpour.

Brearley (founded 1884): All-girls private school on the Upper East Side of Manhattan whose graduates include the daughters of New York's finest families. Its motto is "By Truth and Toil," but Mama Brigander swore it was where she learned to avoid both.

Brenda Frazier (1921-1982): American socialite whose lavish 1938 debutante ball, during the recovery from the Great Depression, led to considerable controversy and an appearance on the cover of *Life* magazine.

Brigadoon (1947): Broadway musical by Alan Jay Lerner and Frederick Loewe about a Scottish village that appears once every century. It was transformed into a 1954 film starring Gene Kelly (1912-1996) and Cyd Charisse (1922-2008).

Brother Orchid (1940): An American comedy starring Edward G. Robinson, Ann Sothern, and Humphrey Bogart about a mobster who hides out in an insane asylum. Allen Jenkins played the imposter.

Bundeswehr (1955-present): The armed forces of West Germany and later post-reunification Germany, distinct from Weimar's *Reichswehr* (1921–1935) and Nazi Germany's *Wehrmacht* (1935-46).

Burt Lancaster (1913-1994): American film actor *Elmer* whose romantic embrace with actress Deborah Kerr in *From Here to Eternity* (1953) remains one of the enduring, iconic images of Hollywood cinema.

Cadwalader, Wickersham & Taft (founded 1792): New York City's oldest law firm, and one of its most prestigious, whose former partners include diarist George Templeton Strong (1820-1875) and United States Attorney General George W. Wickersham (1858-1936).

Casablanca (1942): Celebrated American film directed by Michael Curtiz that stars Humphrey Bogart as nightclub owner Rick Blaine and Ingrid Bergman as his former lover.

Caesar (100-44 BC): General and politician, credited for his victories in the Gallic Wars, whose assassination led to the demise of the Roman Republic and the birth of the Roman Empire.

Cafe Rouge: Formerly the main restaurant and performance venue in the Hotel Pennsylvania whose luminary acts included Count Basie, Duke Ellington, and Benny Goodman. Glenn Miller headlined the venue before his disappearance during World War II.

Cal Ripken (born 1960): Star right-handed shortstop (and later third baseman) for Major League Baseball's Baltimore Orioles (1981-2001).

"Capability" Brown (1716-1783): English landscape architect who designed more than 170 gardens including those at Blenheim Palace, Warwick Castle, and the Brigander summer cottage in Newport.

Cardinal Shehan of Baltimore (1898-1984): Liberal Catholic theologian who played an active role in the Second Vatican Council.

Carole Lombard (1908-1942): American comedienne and movie star who died in a commercial plane crash during World War II. Her husbands included A-list actors William Powell and Clark Gable.

Carter Administration (1977-1981): The tenure of American President Jimmy Carter, marked by stagflation and the Iran Hostage Crisis; for Uncle Dewey, who considered Calvin Coolidge a liberal, Carter was the American Che Guevara.

Cary Grant (1904-1986): British-American film star remembered for his sex appeal and debonair style, his bisexuality has long been a Hollywood rumor.

Casino Theater (1880-1987): Newport, Rhode Island theater with a gold-trimmed ivory interior, screened both stage plays and films. The building, designed by architect Stanford White, now houses the Tennis Hall of Fame.

Cathedral of Saint John the Divine (1892; incomplete): Cathedral of the Episcopal Diocese of New York and fourth largest church in the world. Noted for its liberal theology, cultural engagement, and vicarage garden full of peacocks.

Cecil B. DeMille (1881-1959): Hollywood powerbroker and film director known for such films as *The Greatest Show on Earth* (1952) and *The Ten Commandments* (1956).

Celeste Holm (1917-2012): American actress and singer who won an Academy Award for *Gentleman's Agreement* (1947) and played Ado Annie in the original Broadway production of *Oklahoma!* (1943).

Chappaquiddick: Island off the eastern shore of Martha's Vineyard that was the site of a single-vehicle accident in 1969 in which Senator Ted Kennedy's twenty-eight-year-old date, Mary Jo Kopechne, drowned. Uncle Drake refused to take responsibility for this incident, leading to a temporary breach in relations between the families.

Charles Darwin (1809-1882): English naturalist and entomologist credited with developing the theory of evolution in *On the Origin of Species*; also a distant cousin, on his mother's side, of Great Grandma Sophronia Brigander.

Charlie Wilson (1886-1972): Chairman of General Electric and close confidante of President Harry S. Truman who headed the Office of Defense Mobilization from 1950 to 1952.

Charles Laughton (1899-1962): British film and stage actor nominated for three Academy Awards, winning one, married to actress Elsa Lanchester.

Chief Justice Warren Burger (1907-1995): American jurist from Minnesota; Chief Justice of the United States Supreme Court from 1969 to 1986. His wife, Vera Stromberg, was the granddaughter of Papa Brigander's second cousin.

Chrysler Building (1931): Art Deco skyscraper that was briefly the tallest building in the world before being eclipsed by the Empire State Building in 1931. Grandpa Brigander owned a controlling stake in the structure for many years, although Walter Chrysler served as the public face of their partnership.

Cicero (106 BC-43 BC): Roman politician and orator who denounced Mark Antony after the death of Julius Caesar and was later executed by Antony's henchmen.

Citizen Kane (1941): American film loosely based upon the life of publishing magnate William Randolph Hearst. Orson Welles both directed and starred in the picture; in the film, his character is right-handed.

Clambake Club (1895): The Clambake Club of Newport, along with the Newport Yacht Club and Bailey's Beach, has been among the city's most exclusive venues for generations. Great Grandpa Rutherford Brigander was among the charter members, Grandpa Van Duyn the chairman of the membership committee.

Clanton Gang: A group of western outlaws, also known as the Cowboys, led by the brothers Ike and Billy Clanton; their gunfight with Doc Holliday and Wyatt Earp at the O.K. Corral in Tombstone, Arizona, in 1881, was immortalized in film by Burt Lancaster and Kirk Douglas.

Claridge's (1812): Luxury hotel in London's Mayfair often known as "the annex to Buckingham Palace" because of its royal patronage. Mama and Aunt Virginia would stay nowhere else when visiting England.

Cleopatra (69-30 BC): Ptolemaic Queen of Egypt who formed both political and romantic alliances with Julius Caesar and Mark Antony.

Cliff Walk: Three and a half mile trail in Newport, Rhode Island, that affords views of many of its Gilded Age homes including Beechwood and The Breakers. The remains of the Brigander summer are visible approximately two thirds of the way to First Beach.

Clyde Barrow (1909-1934): Companion of Bonnie Parker (1910-1934) who together held up gas stations, stores, and banks until killed in an ambush in Louisiana. He is the subject of Arthur Penn's classic film, *Bonnie and Clyde* (1967), in which he was portrayed by Warren Beatty.

Colonel Sanders's Secret Recipe: Eleven herbs and spices used by Harland Sanders's service station in Kentucky, starting in 1940, for the cooking of his celebrated fried chicken. The "secret recipe" used by KFC remains one of industry's best-known and most tightly held trade secrets.

Colony Club (1903): Private women's club founded by Florence Harriman known for its clientele of Astors, Morgans, and Rockefellers. Gertrude Ederle gave swimming lessons at the club after her retirement from competition.

College Bowl (1959-1970, 1978-2008): Student quiz show with various incarnations appearing on CBS and NBC. Future *Password* host Allen Ludden (1917-1981) was the original moderator.

Columbo (1968-79, 1989-2003): Television detective series featuring Peter Falk (1927-2011) a Los Angeles homicide detective; the audience knows the killer from the outset, but the thrill is in watching Detective Columbo solve the case.

Commodore Hub E. Isaacks Trophy (1934-present): A prestigious sailing trophy awarded at the Open Snipe World Championships, won by oil tycoon Perry Bass in 1935.

Conestoga Wagon: Horse or mule-drawn covered wagon introduced to the United States by Mennonite settlers, later a distinctive feature of wagon trains traversing the Great Plains.

Coney Island: Brooklyn neighborhood known for is amusement parks including Luna Park, Dreamland, and Steeplechase Park.

Connie Francis (born 1937): American singer of the 1950s and 1960s whose hits included "Who's Sorry Now?" and "Stupid Cupid." Not the be confused with gameshow panelist Arlene Francis.

Corporal Himmelstoss: German postman turned World War I corporal in the novel, *All Quiet on the Western Front*, who was portrayed by John Wray in the 1930 film.

Cravath, Swaine & Moore (1819): White shoe law firm founded by the merger of the firms of future Secretary of State William H. Seward and future Supreme Court Justice Richard M. Blatchford. The firm handled all of the legal affairs of the Brigander and Van Duyn families through the probating of Papa's will.

Cuban Pete (1927-2009): Puerto Rican dancer, born Pedro Aguilar, widely considered to be the foremost Mambo performer ever.

Cunard Line (1840): British-American passenger ship company, founded by Samuel Cunard and Robert Napier, known for both speed and luxury. Its famed vessels included the *Lusitania* and the *Mauritania*.

Currier and Ives: New York City based printmaking team of Nathaniel Currier (1813-1888) and James Merritt Ives (1824-1895) that mass produced lithographs for popular consumption.

Curtis LeMay (1906-1990): Right-wing Air Force general who led the Berlin Air Life and the Strategic Air Command before running for Vice President on a ticket with George Wallace in the 1968 presidential election.

Dannemora: Maximum security state prison in Dannemora, New York, officially known as the Clinton Correctional Facility; it previously housed the state's death row.

Danny Kaye (1911-1987): American comedian and film stat (*The Court Jester*) known for his pantomimes, wordplay, and G-rated performances.

D.A.R. (1890): The Daughters of the American Revolution is a social organization of individuals who trace their lineage back to participants in the War for Independence from Great Britain. Historically, the exclusive membership excluded African Americans and the group was best known for refusing to allow black singer Marian Anderson to perform at its Constitution Hall.

Darkness at Noon (1940): Novel by British-Hungarian journalist Arthur Koestler (1905-1983) recounting the arrest, imprisonment and execution of Old Bolshevik Nicholas Salmanovitch Rubashov.

Dashiell Hammett (1894-1961): American detective novelist who created Sam Spade (*The Maltese Falcon*) and the married gumshoes Nick and Nora Charles (*The Thin Man*).

David Sarnoff (1891-1971): President of the Radio Corporation of America (RCA) who built NBC into a national radio and television network.

David Selznick (1902-1965): Hollywood producer responsible for Academy Award winners *Gone with the Wind* (1939) and *Rebecca* (1940) who gave a toast at Grandpa Brigander's wedding.

Days of Our Lives (1965-present) American soap opera, originally starring Macdonald Carey (1913-1994) and Frances Reid (1914-2010) that chronicles the saga of the Horton and Brady families.

Dean Martin (1917-1995): Singer and comedian known for his partnership with Jerry Lewis and his involvement with the "Rat Pack" of Frank Sinatra, Sammy Davis Jr., Peter Lawford, and Joey Bishop. He was a frequent hunting companion of Uncle Drake.

Deanna Durbin (1921-2013): Canadian film actress who rose to stardom as a teenager at Universal Studios and is best remembered for her rivalry with Judy Garland and her reclusive retirement. "Whatever became of Deanna Durbin?" was a question initially asked by satirist Tom Lehrer that became a catch phrase for stars who faded into obscurity.

Deborah Kerr (1921-2007): British film actress whose romantic embrace with actress Burt Lancaster on a Hawaiian beach in *From Here to Eternity* (1953) remains one of the enduring, iconic images of Hollywood cinema.

Delmonico's: Upscale New York City restaurant on Beaver Street that served Gotham's upper classes from the nineteenth century until the early 1980s.

DeLorean Motors (1975-1982): Short-lived American automobile manufacturer known for its sports cars with falcon-wing doors, went bankrupt in 1982.

Diana Lewis (1919-1997): American film actress and third wife of actor William Powell.

David Livingstone: (1813-1873): Scottish explorer and Christian missionary who led multiple expeditions through the African interior. His "disappearance" led to a search captained by journalist Henry Morton Stanley (1841-1904) and the latter's famous (if doubtful) inquiry upon their 1871 meeting: "Dr. Livingstone, I presume?"

Doris Duke (1912-1993): American heiress, who as daughter of tobacco tycoon James Buchanan Duke, became one of the nation's leading philanthropists—and the subject of romantic gossip for several generations.

Dorothy Kilgallen (1913-1965): American journalist and longstanding panelist on the television game show, *What's My Line?*, she allegedly died of a drug overdose in New York City. Her willingness to challenge the official conclusions of the Warren Commission's investigation into the death of President John F. Kennedy have led some commentators to argue she was the victim of foul play.

Dred Scot Museum: Also known as the Old St. Louis County Courthouse (1864), the building is the site of African-American slave Dred Scott's (1799-1858) suit for his freedom in 1857.

DSM (1952-present): The American Psychiatric Association's *Diagnostic and Statistical Manual of Mental Disorders* is a guide to the classification of psychiatric disorders for mental health professionals. The most recent edition, DSM-5-, was published in 2013.

Duško Popov (1912-1981) Serbian double agent during World War II who passed along false intelligence to the Nazis while working for Great Britain's MI6.

Dvořák (1841-1904): Czech composer who taught at the National Conservatory of Music and lived on East 17th Street in Manhattan.

D.W. Griffith (1875-1948): Pioneering and controversial American filmmaker (*The Birth of a Nation*; *Intolerance*) who transformed the movie industry in the era prior to World War I.

Earl of Harewood (1923-2011): Oldest nephew of King George VI of England and first cousin of Queen Elizabeth II, he edited *Opera* magazine and served as director of the Royal Opera House.

Eastern Airlines (1926-1991): Miami-based carrier originally led by flying ace Eddie Rickenbacker that declared bankruptcy and was liquidated in 1991.

Easter Parade (1870s-present): Fifth Avenue parade in New York City immortalized by Fred Astaire and Judy Garland in the eponymous 1948 musical. Grandpa Van Duyn served as grand marshal twice in the 1950s.

Edie Adams (1927-2008): Versatile comedienne, actress, and wife of Ernie Kovacs until his premature death in an automobile accident, Adams starred in a series of commercials for Muriel Cigars in the 1960s.

Edison (1847-1931): Celebrated inventor of the light bulb, phonograph, and motion picture camera, Thomas Edison was also a poker crony of Great Grandpa Rutherford Brigander.

Edvard Munch's *Scream*: Painting by Norwegian expressionist Edvard Munch (1863-1944), described by critic Arthur Lubow as "a Mona Lisa for our time."

Edward G. Robinson (1893-1973): Jewish-Romanian actor who starred in American film classics like *Little Caesar* (1931) and *Key Largo* (1948), as well as the gangster comedy *Brother Orchid* (1940) with Humphrey Bogart, Allen Jenkins, and Ann Sothern.

Eileen Wilson (1894-1942): Broadway actress and first wife of actor William Powell. No relations to the actress of the same name who appeared on television's *Your Hit Parade*.

El Greco (1541-1614): Greek-born Spanish painter known for his elongated figures and radical experimentation with colors.

Eli: Nickname for students and alumni of Yale University, a tribute to found Elihu Yale (1649-1721).

Elia Kazan (1909-2003): Greek-American director (*On the Waterfront*) and co-founder of the Actors Studio (1947) whose testimony before the House Committee on Un-American Activities in 1952 regarding communists in the motion picture industry made him persona non grata among liberal Hollywood elites for many years.

Elizabeth I (1533-1603): Tudor Queen who ruled England for forty-four years and played a crucial role in the development of English nationalism. She ordered the imprisonment and later execution of Mary, Queen of Scots (1542-1587), her chief rival for the throne.

Ellen Gates Starr (1859-1940): Social reformer who with romantic partner Jane Addams (1860-1935) founded Chicago's Hull House, a celebrated settlement house, in 1889.

Elizabeth Arden (1878-1966): Canadian-born Cosmetics tycoon who once studied dance with Arthur Murray.

Elizabeth Taylor (1932-2011): British-American movie star whose films include *National Velvet* (1944) and *Who's Afraid of Virginia Woolf?* (1966). She was also prolific in the matrimonial arts and her husbands included Conrad Hilton Jr. (1950-1951), Michael Wilding (1952-1957), Mike Todd (1957-1958), Eddie Fisher (1959-1964), Richard Burton (1964-1974, 1975-1976), Senator John Warner (1976-1982), and Larry Fortensky (1991-1996).

Elsa Lanchester (1902-1986): English stage and film actress (*Bride of Frankenstein*) who was married to actor Charles Laughton from 1929-1962 and revealed his homosexuality after his death.

Emily Post (1872-1960): America's foremost authority on etiquette. She was a classmate of Grandma Van Duyn's at Miss Graham's and later read a Shakespeare sonnet at Mama and Papa's wedding.

Empire State Building (1931): 102-story New York City skyscraper that was the tallest building in the world until the construction of the World Trade Center in 1970.

Enver Hoxha (1908-1985): Repressive Albanian dictator who ruled with an iron fist from 1944 until 1985; Great Uncle Atherton Brigander made a habit of losing to him at dominoes during their frequent clandestine meetings in the Macedonian countryside.

Ethel Merman (1908-1984): Broadway actress and singer whose rendition of Irving Berlin's "There's No Business Like Show Business" from *Annie Get Your Gun* has become one of the entertainment world's best-known songs.

Eugene McCarthy (1916-2005): United States Senator from Minnesota (1959-1971) whose quixotic, anti-war Presidential campaign in 1968 helped drive President Lyndon Johnson to drop out of the race.

President Bush (born 1946): Forty-sixth Governor of Texas (1995-2000) and 43rd President of the United States (2001-2009). Bush famously enjoyed "clearing brush" on his Texas ranch to relax.

Fabergé egg (1885-1917): Bejeweled eggs manufactured by Russia's House of Fabergé, largely for the Czars and the Romanov family.

FAO Schwarz (1862-2015): Oldest and one of the most expensive toy stores in the United States, this New York City landmark featured life-size stuffed animals including flamingos and peacocks.

F.W. Vanderbilt (1856-1938): Grandson of Cornelius Vanderbilt who served as a director of the New York Central Railroad for six decades. Great Grandma Sophronia Brigander found his mansion, Rough Point, "underwhelming" and "tastelessly furnished."

Fay Wray (1907-2004): Canadian-born film actress remembered today for her role as Ann Darrow in the 1933 film, *King Kong*.

Fidel Castro (1926-2016): Cuban revolutionary and Communist dictator whose 1959 revolution impeded Uncle Dewey's efforts to gain high quality cigars.

Foley Square: Intersection in Lower Manhattan that is home to several of the city's public buildings including the New York County Courthouse (now officially the New York State Supreme Court Building). The site is named after Tammany Hall boss "Big Tom" Foley (1852-1925).

Fleming (1881-1955): Nobel Prize winning Scottish pharmacologist whose discovery of Penicillin G in 1928 launched the era of antibiotics.

Frances Cleveland (1864-1947): Wife of President Cleveland and the nation's youngest First Lady. Socially snubbed by Great Grandma Van Duyn for her political affiliations.

Frankie Carle (1903-2001): Bandleader known as the "The Wizard of the Keyboard" who achieved stardom for his 1938 hit "Sunrise Serenade."

Franklin Delano Roosevelt (1882-1945): Thirty-second President of the United States who enjoyed trawling for marlins with Grandpa Van Duyn every June.

Fred Allen (1894-1956): Radio comedian and start of *The Fred Allen Show* (1932–1949) remembered for his ongoing on air feud with friend Jack Benny (1894-1974). He appeared as a panelist on the television quiz show *What's My Line?* (1954-1956), replacing Steve Allen (1921-2000) with whom he should not be confused.

Fred Astaire (1899-1987): Dancer and actor known for his professional partnership with Ginger Rogers (1911-1995), with whom he was not romantically involved.

From Here to Eternity (1953): Academy Award winning film, based on a novel by James Jones and directed by Fred Zinnemann, that follows three soldiers in Hawaii during the lead-up to the bombing of Pearl Harbor. The movie features an iconic kiss between Burt Lancaster and Deborah Kerr.

G4 P0040: This is a form of shorthand used in obstetrics. The "G" stands for gravida or total pregnancies, while the "P" for para or births including full term deliveries, premature births, abortions/miscarriages, and current living children.

Gene Autrey (1907-1998): Hollywood's singing cowboy known for his theme song "Back in the Saddle Again" who later owned the Los Angeles Angels baseball team. Friend and riding partner of Aunt Genevieve who raised the suspicions of Uncle Dewey.

General Billy Mitchell (1879-1936): Army general, considered the father of the American Air Force, who was later court-martialed for insubordination. Colonel Wendell Brigander, a cousin of Great Grandpa Rutherford Brigander, served as a character witness at his trial.

General Daniel Butterfield (1831-1901): Union officer in the American Civil War, chief of staff to General Joseph Hooker. In his monograph on the Battle of Chancellorsville, Grandpa Van Duyn referred to him as "Hooker's prostitute." In a pinch, the nook behind his statue in Manhattan's Sakura Park is an excellent place for an undisturbed catnap.

General Grant (1822-1885): Commander of the Union Armies during the American Civil War and later President of the United States (1869–77). His failed efforts to blow up an underground tunnel below Confederate lines at Petersburg proved to be one of his greatest setbacks and resulted in thousands of casualties.

General Hospital (1963-present): Third longest running American soap opera that follows the implausible adventures of the Quartermaine and Spencer families.

Genghis Khan (1162-1227): Brutal leader of the Mongol tribes who conquered much of Eurasia and massacred countless numbers of civilians in his path.

George H.W. Bush (1924-2018): Former Vice President (1981-1989) and President (189-1993) of the United States. He was captain of the baseball team and star first baseman at Phillips Academy in Andover, Massachusetts, where he threw and batted left-handed.

George M. Cohan (1878-1942): Composer and entertainer who created such American standards as "Over There," "Give My Regards to Broadway," and "You're a Grand Old Flag"

George McGovern (1922-2012): Liberal United States Senator from South Dakota and 1972 Democratic Presidential candidate who was soundly defeated by Richard M. Nixon.

George Patton (1885-1945): American general during World War II who commanded the Third Army following the invasion of Normandy, but was later reprimanded for slapping soldiers and was killed in a jeep accident. His life was the subject of a well-received 1970 film starring George C. Scott (1927-1999).

George Peppard (1928-1994): American television actor (The A-Team) whose performance as Paul Varjak opposite Audrey Hepburn in *Breakfast at Tiffany's* (1961) ends in an iconic Hollywood kiss.

Geronimo (1829-1909): Chiricahua Apache raider who engaged in thirty-five years of cat-and-mouse combat with both American and Mexican armies in present day New Mexico, Chihuahua, and Sonora.

Gestapo (1933-1945): Secret police force of Nazi Germany initially founded by Hermann Göring and later controlled by SS commander Heinrich Himmler.

Gettysburg (July 1-3, 1863): American Civil War battle in southern Pennsylvania widely regarded as the conflict's turning point. General George Meade's Army of the Potomac which defeated Confederate Gen. Robert E. Lee's Army of Northern Virginia, included Great Grandpa Rutherford Brigander's older brother, Nathaniel, and Great Grandpa Stoddard Van Duyn's brother-in-law, Longfellow Delancey.

Gettysburg Address (November 19, 1863): Speech delivered by President Abraham Lincoln at the military cemetery Gettysburg, Pennsylvania, during the autumn following the Union victory in the battle of the same name. Five copies of the script in Lincoln's hand are known to exist.

Ginger Rogers (1911-1995): Dancer and actress known for his professional partnership with Fred Astaire (1899-1987) with whom she was not romantically involved.

Glenn Ford (1916-2006): Canadian film actor (*Pocketful of Miracles*) known for portraying common men facing extraordinary challenges.

Gloria Swanson (1899-1983): Silent film star who made a transition to talkies and is best remembered today for her portrayal of reclusive Norma Desmond in *Sunset Boulevard* (1950).

Governor Nelson Rockefeller (1908-1979): Republican Governor of New York States and later Vice President under President Gerald Ford. A frequent visitor to the summer cottage. Uncle Dewey used to say of him, "If I'm going to be friends with a liberal, it might as well be a Rockefeller."

Gracie Allen (1895-1964): Zany comedienne who kept husband and comedic partner George Burns on his toes with her outlandish antics.

Grand Hotel (1932): Academy-Award winning American film based on a German novel by Vicki Baum that featured Greta Garbo (1905-1990), Joan Crawford (1904-1977), and John Barrymore (1882-1942).

Grease (1971): Broadway musical by Warren Casey and Jim Jacobs about working class 1950s high school students that became a blockbuster movie starring John Travolta and Olivia Newton-John.

Great Plague (1665-1666): Epidemic of bubonic plague that swept across England in one of the final onslaughts of the Second Pandemic; more than 100,000 died.

Green-Wood Cemetery (1838): Brooklyn burial ground that was historically the final resting place of many of the borough's—and the city's—most notable personages, including sewing machine inventor Elias Howe, editor Horace Greeley and composer Leonard Bernstein. Incidentally, neither Grover Whalen nor Cousin Bertie Ida Rensselaer is buried there; the police commissioner is interred in Calvary Cemetery in Queens and Miss Rensselaer on her family plot in Duchess County.

Greta Garbo (1905-1990): Swedish-born, American actress (*Grand Hotel*) who successfully made the transition from silent films to "talkies" and later led a famously reclusive retirement.

Grover Whalen (1886–1962): New York public relations executive, known as Mr. New York, who served as the city's police commissioner under Mayor Jimmy Walker and later as President of the 1939 New York World's Fair. His one date with Grandma's sister, Bertie Ida, proved "a frightful bore" to my aunt.

Habsburg napkin: Imperial napkin fold of the House of Habsburg, a European royal family that ruled the Holy Roman Empire, Austria and Spain. The family was best known for its prognathism—the Habsburg jaw, unlike the napkin fold, could not easily be kept secret.

Halley's Comet: Short-period comet—and the only one visible from earth with the naked eye—that appears roughly every 74-79 years, most recently in 1986. Its next appearance will occur in 2061.

Handsome Dan: Bulldog who serves as mascot of Yale University sports teams. The original "Handsome Dan" is now stuffed and on display at the school's Peabody Museum of Natural History. Handsome Dan VII bit Uncle Drake when he was an undergraduate and had to be prematurely retired.

Happiness Boys: Popular 1920s radio program featuring tenor Billy Jones (1889-1940) and bass/baritone Ernie Hare (1883-1939).

Hardy's *Tess of the d'Urbervilles* (1892): Controversial English novel by Thomas Hardy (1840-1928) that challenged Victorian sexual mores.

Harrigan and Hart's Theatre Comique (established 1872): New York City theater venue operated by Ned Harrigan (1844-1911) and Tony Hart (1855-1891) that attracted large audiences that crossed social strata.

Hart Island: Island in Long Island Sound that once served as a tuberculosis sanatorium and now provides the space for the city's potter's field.

Harvard (founded 1636): University in Cambridge, Massachusetts, from which multiple generations of Briganders graduated; in contrast, Van Duyn men preferred to attend school in New Haven.

Haverford College (founded 1833): Liberal arts college with Quaker roots whose upperclassmen frequently take Bryn Mawr girls to dances.

Hays Code (1934-1968): The Motion Picture Production Code, unofficially named after Motion Picture Producers and Distributors President Will Hays and administered by Joseph Breen, imposed content restriction on American films seeking distribution in theaters.

Hedy Lamarr (1914-2000): Austrian-born American movie star and inventor who helped develop torpedo delivery systems for the United States military.

Hercule Poirot's Hastings: Agatha Christie character who assists fictional detective Hercule Poirot in solving crimes. First introduced in *The Mysterious Affair at Styles* (1920) and modeled upon Arthur Conan Doyle's Doctor Watson, he later married music hall singer Dulcie Duveen and settled as a rancher in Argentina.

HIPAA (1996): Officially the Health Insurance Portability and Accountability Act of 1996 and colloquially as the Kennedy–Kassebaum Act, this federal law protects the insurance of workers when they change jobs and also prevents doctors from sharing patients' private information.

His Girl Friday (1940): Screwball journalism comedy featuring Cary Grant as a divorced editor and Rosalind Russell as his reporter ex-wife.

Hitchcock (1899-1980): British director (*Vertigo*) and television host (*Alfred Hitchcock Presents*) who portrayed a misleading, and potentially slanderous, version of human-avian interactions in *The Birds* (1963).

Hizzoner Abe Beame (1906-2001): Former accountant who served as Mayor of New York City (1974-77) during the height of his financial difficulties.

Hohenzollern: Dynasty of Prussian rulers dating back to the eleventh century that eventually supplied the emperors of a unified Germany. Their defeat in World War I led to the revolution and the founding of the Weimar Republic.

Holy Roman Empire (dissolved 1806): Political unit comprising parts of present-day Central Europe including Germany and northern Italy that was formed in the Early Middle Ages; its emperor was generally elected from among the leaders of the various states under his rule.

Hotel Chelsea (1885-present): Hotel on 23rd Street in Manhattan's Chelsea neighborhood that once offered long-term residence to such artists as Arthur C. Clarke and Allen Ginsberg. Poet Dylan Thomas died of pneumonia in 1953 while staying in room 205.

Hotel Pennsylvania (1919-present): New York City hotel located on Seventh Avenue, near the Farley Post Office, whose lounge became a cultural destination in the 1930s. Regular performers included Woody Herman, Duke Ellington, The Andrews Sisters and Glenn Miller, whose signature PEnnsylvania 6-5000 (1940) is a tribute to the hotel's switchboard.

House Un-American Activities Committee (1938-1975): Committee of the House of Representatives, initially chaired by Martin Dies Jr., that investigated Communist subversion in government, Hollywood and other areas of American life. Uncle Drake Van Duyn refused to "name names" before the panel's inquiry into communism at Princeton, frustrating Congressman Richard Nixon of California.

Howard K. Smith (1914-2002): Television anchorman and political reporter whose rose to prominence as one of Edward R. Murrow's "Boys" at CBS and later defected to ABC.

Howland H. Sargeant (1911-1984): diplomat who served as Assistant Secretary of State for Public Affairs and President of Radio Liberty; also the fourth husband of actress Myrna Loy.

Hubert Humphrey (1911-1978): Establishment liberal United States Senator from Minnesota who later served as the Vice President of the United States under President Lyndon B. Johnson (1965-68) and lost the 1968 Presidential Election to Richard Nixon.

Hugh Johnson (1881-1942): World War II General and supply expert who later served as part of President Franklin Roosevelt's "Brain Trust" and as the first administrator of the National Recovery Administration. He graduated from West Point alongside Cousin Wendell Brigander in 1903.

Huguette Clark (1906-2011): Heiress and recluse who, as the only surviving descendant of mining baron William A. Clark, lived for many years as a patient at Beth Israel Hospital in Manhattan and left an estate worth more than $300 million.

Humphrey Bogart (1899-1957) American film actor and cultural icon whose films included *The Maltese Falcon, Casablanca*, and *The Treasure of the Sierra Madre*; he starred in *Brother Orchid* (1940) opposite Ann Sothern and Edward G. Robinson.

Hurricane Gloria (1985): Category Four Atlantic Hurricane that devastated Long Island and coastal New England, causing almost a billion dollars in damage and fourteen fatalities. These deaths included Papa and Mama Brigander and Papa's attorney from Cravath, Swaine & Moore.

Hyannisport: Exclusive village in Barnstable, Massachusetts, where the Kennedy and Brigander families have both owned compounds for multiple generations.

Incas, The Carolina Parakeet (died February 21, 1918): Last of the Carolina parakeets, a neo-tropical parrot species that inhabited the Atlantic Seaboard and the Gulf Coast, who died in the Cincinnati zoo shortly after the death of his mate "Lady Jane."

Ida Lupino (1918-1995): American actress and pioneering female director known for her demanding style in such films as *Outrage* (1950) and *The Hitch-Hiker* (1953).

Information Please (1938-1951): Popular radio quiz show moderated by Clifton Fadiman on which comedic pianist Oscar Levant was a regular panelist.

Ingrid Bergman (1915-1982) Swedish-born actress best known to American audiences as Ilsa Lund in *Casablanca* (1942). Her correspondence with Uncle Dewey, heavily redacted, is now available in the Harvard Film Archive.

Inherit the Wind (1960): Film starring Spencer Tracy and Fredric March that recounts the Scopes "Monkey" Trial of 1925 in which attorneys Clarence Darrow and William Jennings Bryan litigated the theory of evolution. Based upon a 1955 stage play by Jerome Lawrence and Robert Edwin Lee.

Inspector Clouseau (1925-1980): Bumbling fiction French detective, originally played by comedian Peter Sellers, whose exploits are depicted in *The Pink Panther* films.

International Ball (1966-present): Annual dance hosted by the United States Naval Academy in Annapolis. While a significant social event, this gala should not be confused with the invitation-only International Debutante Ball, a more exclusive event held each year at the Waldorf Astoria Hotel in New York City.

Interwoven Socks: Defunct brand of quality socks first manufactured by the Interwoven Stocking Company and later Kayser-Roth; the brand sponsored the Happiness Boys during the 1920s.

Irene Cara (born 1962): Actress who starred as Coco Hernandez in the movie *Fame* (1980) and later gained prominence as a songwriter "Flashdance...What a Feeling" (1984).

Iwo Jima (February-March 1942): World War II battle in which American forces captured the Pacific island of the same name from the Japanese Army. A photograph by Joe Rosenthal of six Marines raising the flag on the atoll's Mount Suribachi remains one of the iconic images of the war.

Jack Benny (1894-1974): Comedian and violinist known for his parsimonious television personality and his perpetual claim to be thirty-nine years old. He was often assisted by his African-American valet, Rochester.

Jack Dempsey (1895-1983): Heavyweight boxer nicknamed the "The Manassa Mauler" remembered for his title bouts with Gene Tunney. After retiring from boxing, he studied dance with Arthur Murray.

Jack the Ripper: Never-identified serial killer who murdered prostitutes in London's East End in 1888 (and possibly until 1891)

Jackie Kennedy Onassis (1929-1994): Wife of President John Fitzgerald Kennedy who served as First Lady prior to his assassination and later as a book editor at Viking and Doubleday. She visited the summer cottage with her second husband, shipping magnate Aristotle Onassis, an episode that compelled Grandma Brigander to commission new leaves for the mahogany dining table to replace those that had become warped in storage.

Jacob M. Appel (born 1973): American author and bioethicist who was never married to actress Sofia Loren.

Jakey Astor (1912-1992): Son of multi-millionaire John Jacob Astor IV who was born four months after his father's death aboard the *Titanic*, earning himself the moniker, "Titanic Baby." He was a frequent visitor to the summer cottage and a favorite of both Grandma Brigander and Cousin Gladys.

James Cagney (1899-1986): American stage and screen actor in such films as *The Public Enemy* (1931), remembered for his distinctive New York accent.

James Stewart (1908-1997): American film star known for his "everyman" roles in such classics as *Mr. Smith Goes to Washington* (1939) and *It's a Wonderful Life* (1946). In later life, he took up writing poetry and advocated for conservative political causes.

Jane Addams (1860-1935): Social reformer who with romantic partner Ellen Gates Starr (1859-1940) founded Chicago's Hull House, a celebrated settlement house, in 1889.

Jane Eyre: Upwardly-mobile governess in the novel of the same name by Charlotte Brontë (1847), she secures her financial position with a marriage to Rochester of Thornfield Hall.

Jaycee Dugard (born 1980): California schoolgirl who was kidnapped in 1991 and spent eighteen years in captivity before the arrest of captors Phillip and Nancy Garrido.

Jay Gould (1836-1892): Ruthless railroad magnate and Gilded Age "robber baron" whose partnership with Great Grandpa Rutherford Brigander made both men rich.

Jayne Mansfield (1933-1967): Platinum blond 1950s sex symbol and Playboy playmate whose career as a film actress was cut short by a fatal automobile accident.

Jeder nach seinen Fähigkeiten, jedem nach seinen Bedürfnissen (1875): Quotation in Karl Marx's "Critique of the Gotha Program" that translated from German reads: "From each according to his ability, to each according to his needs." It has become a motto of various socialist and communist movements.

Jekyll Island: George barrier island that was the winter playground of many of New England's First Families in era before World War II. Great Uncle Atherton Brigander built a mansion there and resided on the island when not serving abroad on diplomatic missions.

Jessica Fletcher: Amateur sleuth played by Angela Lansbury (born 1925) on the television show *Murder She Wrote* (1984-1996).

Jim Fisk (1835-1872): Financier and partner of Jay Gould (1836-1892) who tried to corner the gold market in 1869; later murdered by Edward Stiles Stokes (1840–1901), the lover of his ex-mistress.

Jimmy Hoffa (1913-1975): American labor union leader and mob-associate who headed the International Brotherhood of Teamsters (1958-1971) and later disappeared mysteriously in 1975. He is presumed deceased, although his body has never been found.

Jimmy Stewart (1908-1997): See James Stewart.

Joan of Arc (1412-1431): "Maid of Orleans" and likely schizophrenic who helped secure victories for French King Charles VII during the Hundred Years War, she was later burned at the stake by the British for witchcraft.

Joan Crawford (1904-1977): Film actress remembered for her feud with Bette Davis and her bitter relationship with her elder daughter.

Joe Louis (1914-1981): World heavyweight champion boxer (1937-1949) remembered for his bouts with German Max Schmeling and his status as one of the first African-American sports figures who attracted mass support among whites.

John Barrymore (1882-1942): Shakespearean actor who made a successful transition to film, but whose career was marred by alcoholism and bankruptcy.

John D. Rockefeller (1839-1937): Oil tycoon and philanthropist who was the wealthiest person in the world for most of his adult life.

John Hertz (1908-1968): Chicago advertising executive and heir to the Hertz corporation (best known today for its rental cars) who was the second husband of actress Myrna Loy.

John O'Hara (1905-1970): American author whose reactionary column in *Newsday* revealed an obsession with Ivy League colleges; his own father's death and subsequent financial hardship prevented him from attending Yale.

John Travolta (born 1954): Television actor (*Welcome Back, Kotter*) and movie star (*Saturday Night Fever*) who studied dance under Arthur Murray.

John Wayne (1907-1979): Film star of American Westerns like *The Man Who Shot Liberty Valance* (1962) who wore an eye patch over his left eye in *True Grit* (1969) and *Rooster Cogburn* (1975).

John Wray (1887-1940): Stage and film actor who portrayed drill instructor Himmelstoss in *All Quiet on the Western Front* (1930).

John, FDR's boy (1916-1981): President Franklin D. Roosevelt's sixth and youngest son, John Aspinwall Roosevelt, a lifelong Republican (unlike his father and siblings) who campaigned for Dwight D. Eisenhower. He proved a challenging cribbage competitor for Mama Brigander during his visits to the summer cottage.

Johns Manville (founded 1958): American manufacturing concern that declared bankruptcy in 1982 after a century producing the carcinogenic insulation product, asbestos.

Joseph Heller's *Catch-22* (1961): Satirical novel that describes Army Air Force captain John Yossarian's futile efforts to escape further military service during World War II by claiming insanity.

Jungians: Followers of Swiss psychiatrist and psychoanalyst Carl Gustav Jung (1875-1961) whose analytical psychology focuses upon "archetypes" and "the collective unconscious."

Kabuki theater (1603-present): Traditional, stylized Japanese dance-drama known for its performers' elaborate makeup in which each artist plays an established role.

Katrina Trask (1853-1922): Widow of American banker and New York Times owner Spencer Trask, she gained some recognition as a minor poet of the sentimental variety among the café set of the 1910s.

Keats (1795-1821): English Romantic poet who trained as a physician and died of tuberculosis at the age of twenty-five.

Keystone Kops (1912-1917): Fiction police force of the Silent Film era created by Mack Sennett and known for their prodigious incompetence.

Kilroy Was Here: Graffiti slogan and cartoon image popular with American servicemen during World War II and likely derived from a British cartoon known as Mr. Chad.

Kim Philby (1912-1988): British intelligence officer who served as a double agent for the Soviet Union and ultimately defected in 1963. He was a leader of the "Cambridge Five" spy ring that also included Donald Maclean, Guy Burgess, Anthony Blunt and John Cairncross. Great Uncle Atherton Brigander knew him casually in London.

King George (1738-1820): Third in the line of Great Britain's Hanoverian kings, George III reigned over the British Isles through the loss of the American colonies and the defeat of Napoleon. Later in life, he "went mad"—likely as a result of the blood disorder, porphyria.

King Solomon (1010-931 BC): Biblical King known for his wisdom and wealth; he famously revealed the true mother of a disputed infant by threatening to chop the child in half.

Knickerbocker Club (founded 1871): Men's social club on 62nd Street in New York City that rivaled the Union Club for prestige. Members included J.P. Morgan (1837-1913), David Rockefeller (1915-2017), and President Franklin D. Roosevelt (1882-1945).

Kosovo War (1998-1999): War between largely Serbian Yugoslavia and the ethnically Albanian Kosovo Liberation Army (KLA) over the Kosovo region in which aerial bombings by NATO on behalf of the KLA led to the withdrawal of Serbian forces.

Krugerrands (introduced 1967): South African gold coin whose import was banned by several Western countries during the Apartheid era.

La Bagatelle (1720): Neoclassical château in Paris's Bois de Boulogne known for its celebrated landscape garden. A favorite French destination of Mama and Aunt Virginia.

Lawrence's novel (1928): *Lady Chatterley's Lover* by English novelist D. H. Lawrence (1885-1930) was banned as obscene by Great Britain until 1960 after a 1959 trial in which Grandpa Brigander contributed to the publisher's expenses.

Lawrence Welk (1903-1992): Accordionist and bandleader who as the father of "champagne music" brought polkas and waltzes into the homes of the heartland. *The Lawrence Welk Show* (1951-1982) appealed to an older, conservative demographic.

Le Bernardin (founded 1972): Parisian restaurant established by Gilbert and Maguy Le Coze and relocated to Midtown Manhattan in 1986; it caters to a high-end business clientele.

Lear: Legendary King of the Britons immortalized in William Shakespeare play, *King Lear* (1606). In Act I, Scene iv, he laments to Albany of his daughter, Goneril: "Ingratitude, thou marble-hearted fiend / More hideous when thou show'st thee in a child / Than the sea monster."

Lee Van Cleef (1925-1989): American character actor who portrayed villains and outlaws, and who achieved widespread fame for his role in the spaghetti western, *The Good, the Bad and the Ugly* (1966).

Lee Marvin (1924-1987): American film star known for his tough guy roles; he later played Detective Lieutenant Frank Ballinger on the television crime drama *M Squad* from 1957 to 1960.

Liberation Army: Ethnic Albanian paramilitary group that attempted forcible secession from Serbia in the prelude to the Kosovo War of 1998-99.

Lillian Russell (1860-1922): Stage actress and romantic partner of businessman "Diamond Jim" Brady who rose to stardom on her beauty and later advocated for restrictions on immigration. Not to be confused with actress Rosalind Russell (1907-1976).

Lindbergh Baby-napping Trial (1934): After the kidnapping and murder of aviation pioneer Charles Lindbergh's twenty-month-old son, Charles Augustus Lindbergh Jr. in 1932, the "Trial of the Century" led to the conviction and execution of Richard Bruno Hauptmann (1899-1936). Grandma Brigander, before her marriage, covered the New Jersey trial for the New York *Herald-Tribune*.

Linear A (2500-1500 BC) As yet undeciphered writing systems used by the Minoan civilization in ancient Greece and Crete that continues to befuddle and fascinate linguists and cryptographers.

Lionel Barrymore (1878-1954): American actor and senior member of the celebrated Barrymore family who played Ebenezer Scrooge in radio broadcasts of *A Christmas Carol* during his last two decades and Dr. Kildare in multiple mediums.

Leonard Peltier (born 1944): Native American activist and convicted murder serving life sentences in Florida for killing two FBI agents on the Pine Ridge Indian Reservation in 1975. His case is a cause celebre among many liberals.

Libby (1875-present): Originally known as Libby, McNeill & Libby, the canned meat and corned beef firm ultimately expanded to canned fruits and frozen foods; it marketed itself on television with a distinctive jingle during the 1970s.

Lindy Hop: Swing era jazz dance of the 1920s and 1930s, originating in Harlem's African-American community, and named after aviator Charles Lindbergh, who was said to have "hopped the Atlantic ocean" in 1927.

Lon Cheney (1883-1930): Versatile actor and makeup artist nicknamed "The Man of a Thousand Faces." A majority of his films have been lost.

Lord Beaverbrook (1879-1964): British-Canadian publisher and politician who served as Winston Churchill's Minister of Aircraft Production during World War II. His nephew broke off an engagement to Cousin Adelaide Brigander.

Lou Gehrig (1903-1941): American baseball player who set a then record for playing 2,130 games for the New York Yankees which was later broken by Cal Ripken of the Baltimore Orioles. He died of amyotrophic lateral sclerosis (ALS), often colloquially known as Lou Gehrig's disease.

Lupara bianca: A method of disposing of murder victims, associated with the Sicilian Mafia, so that the bodies are never found.

Lusitania (1906-1915): British Cunard luxury liner and sister ship of the *Mauretania* sunk by a German U-boat during World War I. Great Grandpa Rutherford Brigander gave up his seat on a lifeboat following the attack and drowned.

Lyndon Johnson (1908-1973): Vice President (1961-1963) and President of the United States (1963-1969) who enjoyed a testy

relationship with Grandpa Van Duyn, a staunch opponent of the Great Society, but an equally avid supporter of the War in Vietnam.
Ma Bell: Colloquial (and occasionally pejorative) nickname for the Bell Telephone System (and later AT&T) that held a virtual monopoly on United States telephone lines until it was broken up as a monopoly in 1983.
Macbeth (1948): Orson Welles film based on the Shakespearean tragedy in which Welles wields a dagger with his right hand.
McLean (founded 1811): Harvard-affiliated mental hospital in Belmont, Massachusetts, known for its upscale clientele, whose celebrity patients have included poets Sylvia Plath, Robert Lowell, and Anne Sexton. Uncle Drake spent a brief spell there after his forced retirement.
Machu Picchu: Fifteenth century citadel in the Peruvian Andes built for Emperor Pachacuti (1438–1472) that has become a tourist mecca.
Macy's (founded 1858): Department store chain and sponsor of the famed Thanksgiving Day Parade whose Herald Square flagship is a New York City destination.
MacDuff: Thane of Fife in Shakespeare's tragedy, *Macbeth*, who eventually kills the title character.
Mackenzie Phillips (born 1959): Actress who appeared in the film *American Graffiti* (1973) and the sitcom *One Day at a Time* (1975-1984), but later struggled with addiction.
Mae Clarke (1910-1992): American film actress (*The Public Enemy*) best known for her work in the era before The Hays Code.
Major Major Major: Character in Joseph Heller's satiric novel *Catch-22* (1961), whose legal name is Major Major and who achieves the rank of major in the United States Army during World War II. He bears a striking resemblance to actor Henry Fonda (1905-1982).
Man of La Mancha (1964): Broadway musical based on Cervantes's *Don Quixote* whose signature song, "The Impossible Dream," has since become a classic.
Mann Act (1910): Colloquial name of the White-Slave Trade Act, after Illinois Congressman Robert Mann (1856-1922), that banned the transport of women across state or national boundaries for the purposes of prostitution. The fictitious Mann-Volstead Act draws its name, in part, from this legislation.

Mao (1893-1976): Chairman of the Communist Party of China from its founding until his death who imposed a radical and brutal breed of Marxism on his nation.

Marine Corps Birthday Ball: Annual celebration of the United States Marine Corps marking November 10, 1775, the dates that the Continental Congress first established the Continental Marines.

Marshal Tito of Yugoslavia (1892-1980): Yugoslavian revolutionary and communist dictator who struck up an unlikely friendship with Great Uncle Atherton Brigander.

Martin Luther (1483-1546): German theologian who allegedly heard a voice from God while in the outhouse that drove him to seek reform of the Catholicism and to post Ninety-five Theses on the walls of All Saints' Church in Wittenburg in 1517. He was excommunicated by Pope Leo X in 1521.

Mary, Queen of Scots (1542-1587): Daughter of James V of Scotland who married the future French King, Francis II, and later sought to overthrow her cousin, Queen Elizabeth I of England. She was subsequently executed for treason.

Mary Martin (1913-1990): Broadway actress and singer who originated the roles of Nellie Forbush in *South Pacific* and Maria von Trapp in *The Sound of Music*. She was in an automobile accident in 1982 that seriously injured both her and actress Janet Gaynor.

Marilyn (1926-1962): Marilyn Monroe, a sex symbol and cultural icon whose marriages to baseball star Joe DiMaggio and playwright Arthur Miller were followed by affairs with President John F. Kennedy and his brother, Bobby.

Mason: Freemasonry is a fraternal organization dating from the fourteenth century whose members have included George Washington, Benjamin Franklin, Theodore Roosevelt, and five generations of Briganders.

Matisse (1869-1954): French modernist painter and sculptor who remained in France during the rule of the collaborationist Vichy government during World War II.

Mayflower: Wooden ship that transported 102 passengers, including many English Separatists, from England to the future site of Plymouth, Massachusetts in 1620. Among the passengers were the forebears of Detective Bernard Libby, but no Briganders or Van Duyns.

Mayflower Compact (1620): The original governing agreement of Plymouth Colony, signed aboard the Mayflower by forty-one

Pilgrims. At one time or another, Mama Brigander claimed descent from each of these forty-one men, although her forbears were actually French Huguenots from La Rochelle.

Mayor Jimmy Walker (1881-1946): Democratic mayor of New York City (1926-1932) who combined liberal politics with the cronyism of Tammany Hall; he eventually resigned under the cloud of scandal.

Mayor Koch (1924-2013): Democratic politician, congressman, and closeted homosexual who was elected 105th Mayor of New York City in 1978, he enjoyed a close "friendship" with Uncle Drake Van Duyn during the early 1970s.

Mayor La Guardia (1882-1947): Republican congressman and reform mayor of New York City (1934-1945) whose support of Franklin D. Roosevelt's New Deal infused the city with federal money and patronage. Grandma Brigander's sister, Bertie Ida, turned down his marriage proposal.

Menninger Clinic (established 1919): Sanitorium and psychiatric clinic in Topeka, Kansas, founded by Charles Frederick Menninger (1862-1953) and his sons that has long been a pioneer in the care of the mentally ill, especially the well-heeled mentally ill.

Michael Landon (1936-1991): Handsome television actor known for *Little House on the Prairie* (1974-1982) who never married Henrietta Brigander before his untimely death from pancreatic cancer.

Middlemarch (1871): Novel by George Eliot (1819-1880) that ranks among the greatest literary works of the Victorian era, it concludes with an epilogue that neatly wraps up the plot.

Miss Ederle (1905-2003): First woman to swim the English Channel who later gave lessons at the Colony Club; her students included Henrietta Brigander.

Miss Havisham: Antagonist in novelist Charles Dickens's *Great Expectations* (1861), who sets about revenging herself upon men through her adopted daughter, Estella.

Miss Marple: Amateur sleuth in Agatha Christie novels like *A Pocket Full of Rye* (1953) and *At Bertram's Hotel* (1965), later portrayed on screen by Dame Margaret Rutherford, DBE (1892-1972).

Miss Porter's (founded 1843): Girls' preparatory school in Farmington, Connecticut, whose graduates include Lily Pulitzer, Barbara Hutton, Jacqueline Kennedy, Gloria Vanderbilt, and Mama Brigander.

Moai of Easter Island (c. 1250-1500): stone structures constructed by the Rapa Nui people on Easter Island that depict human beings, their purpose remains a mystery to anthropologists.

Modern Library (1917-present): High-end publishing imprinted founded by 1917 by Albert Boni and Horace Liveright that was later purchased by Bennet Cerf for Random House.

Mod Squad (1968-1973): Young undercover cops on the television show of the same name consisting of the trio Michael Cole, Peggy Lipton, and Clarence Williams III.

MOMA (founded 1929): New York's Museum of Modern Art, established by Abby Aldrich Rockefeller and her "darling ladies," which brought European modernism to American audiences in the 1930s and 1940s.

Monaco Grand Prix (1929-present): Annual auto race that is part of the racing Triple Crown; Grandpa Brigander entered a Talbot-Lago in 1951, but finished dead last.

Monte Carlo (opened 1863): Casino in Monaco where the European upper classes have gambled for over a century—except citizens of Monaco, who are banned from the gaming rooms. Great Grandpa Rutherford Brigander "broke the bank" there in 1913 and was banned for life.

Morey Amsterdam (1908-1996): Vaudeville and television comedian who starred on the *Dick Van Dyke* show. He bore a striking resemblance to Dr. Herman "Doc" Weingarten of Park Avenue, the Brigander family's longtime pediatrician.

Morgenstern's (established 1906): Lower East Side ice cream parlor where Julius Morgenstern (1878-1921) and his descendants serve up the city's best banana splits and egg creams.

Mory's (established 1849): Social club for Yale men and their friends where the Whiffenpoofs sing a cappella on Monday nights. Former members include presidents William Howard Taft, Gerald Ford, George H. W. Bush, and Bill Clinton; Uncle Drake Van Duyn was twice rejected for membership.

Mount Monadnock: New Hampshire peak that is the subject of a poem by Ralph Waldo Emerson (1803-1882) and was explored extensively by philosopher and naturalist Henry David Thoreau (1817-1862) in the 1850s.

Mount Rushmore (1925): Larger than life sculpture by Gutzon Borglum (1867 – March 6, 1941) of the heads of four United States Presidents (George Washington, Thomas Jefferson, Theodore

Roosevel,t and Abraham Lincoln), located in the Black Hills of South Dakota.

Mouseketeer: Cast members of the Disney-produced television variety show, *The Mickey Mouse Club* (1955-1959), whose most popular stars included Annette Funicello and Darlene Gillespie.

Mr. Smith Goes to Washington (1939): Frank Capra film, based upon an unpublished short story by Lewis R. Foster, starring Jimmy Stewart (1908-1997) as a neophyte, corruption-fighting United States Senator and Jean Arthur (1900-1991) as his politically savvy secretary.

Mr. & Mrs. North: Amateur detective couple created by Richard Orson Lockridge (1898-1982) who appeared in short stories in the *New York Sun* and *The New Yorker*.

Mrs. Astor's ball: The New York "aristocracy" of the nineteenth century was famously defined at "The 400," meaning the four hundred persons who could fit comfortably into the Newport ballroom of Lina Schermerhorn Astor (1830-1908), wife of tycoon and playboy William Backhouse Astor Jr. (1829-1892). Great Grandpa Rutherford and Great Grandma Sophronia frequently attended balls at the Astor residence.

Mrs. Emerson (1802-1892): Second wife of poet and essayist Ralph Waldo Emerson, Lidian Jackson Emerson was also a close friend of Henry David Thoreau and a talented writer in her own right. R.W. Emerson's first wife, Ellen Louisa Tucker, died of tuberculosis at age twenty.

Mrs. Joseph Goebbels (1901-1945): "Magda" Goebbels, wife of Nazi Propaganda Minister Joseph Goebbels, who is sometimes considered the unofficial first lady of the Third Reich; she killed her children in the closing days of the war and committed suicide with her husband.

Myrna Loy (1905-1993): American actress who starred opposite William Powell (1892-1984) in the Thin Man mystery films.

Napoleon (1769-1821): Military hero (Austerlitz) and Emperor who dominated French political life during the decades after the French Revolution until his defeat at Waterloo (1815).

Nancy Drew: Fictional sixteen-year-old detective who first appeared in the young adult novels of Edward Stratemeyer (1862-1930) in 1930 and has since been ghost written under the collective authorship of "Carolyn Keene."

National Industrial Recovery Act (1933): Federal New Deal statute that established labor codes for American industries, protected collective bargaining and sought to combat deflation. The act created the National Recovery Administration, headed by Hugh Johnson (1881-1942) and awarded participating businesses a Blue Eagle. The law was declared unconstitutional by the United States Supreme Court in *A.L.A. Schechter Poultry Corp. v. United States* (1935).

Nellie Bly's *Ten Days in a Madhouse* (1887): Exposé by pioneering female journalist Nellie Bly (1864-1922) in which she feigned insanity to report on conditions at the Women's Lunatic Asylum on Blackwell's Island in New York City.

Nero Wolf's Archie: Sidekick of armchair detective Nero Wolf in the mysteries of Rex Stout (1886-1975) who works as his "leg man" and purportedly narrates his adventures.

Network (1976): Satiric Sidney Lumet film written by Paddy Chayefsky and starring Peter Finch (1916-1977) that popularized the mantra, "I'm as mad as hell, and I'm not going to take it anymore."

The New Yorker (1925): Magazine founded by couple Harold Ross and Jane Grant that has become the flagship publication of professional class culture.

Nick to My Nora: Couple who appear in Dashiell Hammett's detective novel, *The Thin Man* (1934), and were subsequently portrayed by William Powell (1892-1984) and Myrna Loy (1905-1993) in a series of movies.

Niobe: In Greek mythology, daughter of Tantalus whose children are murdered at the behest of Leto and is remembered most for her subsequent weeping.

Normandy invasion (June 6, 1944): Also known as D-Day, the Allied invasion of France in Operation Overlord forced President Franklin Roosevelt to postpone his annual marlin trawl with Grandpa Van Duyn.

Occam's razor: Philosophical principle proposed by English friar William of Ockham (1287-1347) and followed by Henrietta Brigander that argues for following the simplest explanation for any phenomenon.

Odysseus: Cunning Greek King of Ithaca who, as the hero of Homer's *Odyssey*, spends a decade attempting to return home from the Trojan War.

Ogden Goelet (1851-1897): Heir to the Goelet real estate fortune and celebrated yachtsman, he frequently entertained Grandpa

Rutherford Brigander and Great Grandma Sophronia Brigander at his Newport estate, Ochre Court, until his premature death.

O.K. Corral: Site of am 1881 shootout in Tombstone, Arizona, between the Clanton Gang and lawmen under the Earp brothers that has become one of the celebrated moments of Wild West lore.

Old Bolshevik: Term for members of the Russian Bolshevik party who joined before the Russian revolution, many of whom were murdered in Stalin's purges. Arthur Koestler depicts the fate of Old Bolshevik, Nicholas Salmanovitch Rubashov, in *Darkness at Noon* (1940). The last surviving Old Bolshevik was Lazar Kaganovich (1893-1991).

Olivia Newton-John (born 1948): English-Austrian actress and singer-songwriter who starred across from John Travolta in *Grease* (1978).

One Flew Over the Cuckoo's Nest (1975): Academy Award winning film based on the 1962 novel by Ken Kesey (1935-2001) and direct by Miloš Forman (b. 1932). Jack Nicholson stars as Randle McMurphy, a malingerer whose efforts to beat the system backfire. Powerful, but not particularly realistic.

Orange Band, The Dusky Seaside Sparrow (died 1987): Captive sparrow of a non-migratory subspecies native to the salt marshes of Florida whose death marked the extinction of his tribe.

Orson Welles (1915-1985): Ambidextrous American actor and film director (*Citizen Kane*), also remembered for his "The War of the Worlds" broadcast that saw Barrington Van Duyn Griffin and his wife flee toward Montreal in a Nash coupe.

Osama bin Laden (1957-2011): Saudi Arabian founder of the al-Qaeda terrorist network responsible for the September 11, 2001, attacks on the World Trade Center and the Pentagon.

Oscar Levant (1906-1972): American comedian and pianist who became a regular panelist on the popular quiz show, *Information Please.*

O.S.S. (1942-1945): Abbreviation for the Office of Strategic Services, a precursor to the Central Intelligence Agency run by Major General William Joseph Donovan during World War II. Great Uncle Atherton Brigander was reportedly the organization's chief in Berlin during the first months after V-E Day.

P.T. Barnum (1810-1891): American showman and circus impresario who founded Barnum & Bailey Circus whose novelties included the midget, General Tom Thumb; he also served as a Republican in the Connecticut legislature.

Panic of 1907: Three-week long financial crisis, resulting from the widespread bankruptcy of local banks, that ultimately led to the creation of the Federal Reserve System.

Passenger Pigeons: Extinct species of North American pigeon whose numbers declined rapidly in the second half of the nineteenth century. The last bird of the breed, Martha, died in the Cincinnati Zoo, in 1914.

Password (1961-1961 on CBS; 1971-1975 on ABC): A television gameshow originally hosted by Allen Ludden (1917-1981) in which a celebrity and non-celebrity guest exchanged clues in an effort to guess a mystery word.

Pat Buchanan (born 1938): Conservative political commentator and former Richard Nixon speechwriter who unsuccessfully sought the Republican presidential nomination in 1992 and 1996.

Patty Hearst (born 1954): Heiress to the Hearst publishing fortune whose kidnapping and subsequent brainwashing by the Symbionese Liberation Army led to her conviction for bank robbery and ultimate pardon by President Carter.

Peace Fountain (1985): Sculpture by Greg Wyatt (born 1949) located in the gardens of the Cathedral of Saint John the Divine in Upper Manhattan that depicts the struggle between good and evil.

Peloponnesus: The section of the Greek Peninsula south of the Gulf of Corinth. Also known as the Morea.

PEnnsylvania 6-5000: Telephone exchange of New York's Pennsylvania Hotel in the two letter + five digit format, claiming to be the oldest continuously used number in Manhattan, that Glenn Miller immortalized in a song of the same name.

Perry Bass (1914–2006): American heir to the Bass oil fortune and investor who made a name for himself as a skilled sailor. He won the Commodore Hub E. Isaacks Trophy at the Open Snipe World Championships in 1935.

Perry Mason (1957-1966): CBS television show, based on stories by Erle Stanley Gardner (1889-1970), starring Raymond Burr (1917-1993) as a fictional, crime-solving defense attorney.

Pershing Square: Viaduct-covered intersection of 42nd Street and Park Avenue in New York City named after General John J. Pershing (1860-1948).

Peter Finch (1916-1977): English-born Australian film actor who gained fame in the United States for his portrayal of exasperated television anchorman in the satiric *Network* (1976).

Petersburg (1864-1865): Trench warfare campaign between Union armies under General Ulysses S. Grant and Confederate troops under Robert E. Lee that led to the latter's surrender of the Southern capital, Richmond, at the end of the American Civil War.

Philadelphia Club (1834): Philadelphia's oldest, most exclusive and most conservative gentleman's club. Past members have included General George Gordon Meade, Theodore Roosevelt, Jr., and Owen Wister.

Philip Larkin (1922-1985): English poet who is arguably the quintessential poet of the British middle classes, embodying the spirit of laconic simplicity and shabby motel rooms.

Phillips Academy (founded 1778): Exclusive preparatory school in Andover, Massachusetts, which has educated the New England elite including Bushes and Briganders for generations. President George Herbert Walker Bush and Reginald "Rusky" Brigander were both captains of the baseball team; actor Humphrey Bogart was expelled in 1918.

Pierre (opened 1930): Luxury hotel at the southeast corner of New York's Central Park that was the site of a celebrated robbery in 1972.

Pierre S. du Pont (1870-1954): American industrialist who headed the du Pont chemical conglomerate and helped finance the Empire State Building. His grandsons proved rather alluring bachelors for several summers in Newport.

Picabia (1879-1953): French painter whose works bridge Cubism, Surrealism and Dadaism.

Pickett's Charge (July 3, 1863): Unsuccessful Confederate infantry assault led by Major General George Pickett on the Union defenses at the Battle of Gettysburg, largely regarded as a turning point in the American Civil War.

Plaza (build 1907): Luxury Manhattan Hotel on Grand Army Plaza, designed by Henry J. Hardenbergh, where Great Aunt Bernie Ida lived in a penthouse apartment.

Pluto: Dwarf planet discovered by astronomer Clyde Tombaugh (1906-1997) in 1930; also, the name of Mickey Mouse's pet dog.

Polaroid (1937-2001): Company founded by Edward H. Land (1909-1991) whose instant camera became a staple of middle-class vacations for generations.

Pompeii: Roman city near present-day Naples, Italy, whose inhabitants were killed by volcanic ash during the eruption of Mount Vesuvius in 79 AD.

Pope John Paul II (1920-2005): Polish-born Catholic pontiff recalled for both his extensive travels and conservative social values, he played a significant role in the Cold War struggle against oppression in Eastern Europe.

President Andrew Johnson (1808-1875): sixteenth Vice President (1865) and seventeenth President (1865-1869) who oversaw the initial stages of Reconstruction after the Civil War and was eventually impeached but acquitted.

President Cleveland (1837-1908): The only United States President to serve two non-consecutive terms, he trounced Grandpa Brigander in poker on numerous occasions.

President Clinton (born 1946): United States President (1993-2001) impeached for lying during the scandal surrounding Monica Lewinski, but later acquitted.

President Truman (1884-1972): Thirty-fourth Vice President (1945) and thirty-third President (1945-53) whose Marshall Plan is credited with rebuilding Europe after World War II. Grandpa Van Duyn gave him a sign reading "The Buck Stops Here" that he later displayed on his desk in the White House.

Prime Minister Churchill (1874-1965): British Prime Minister (1940-1945, 1951-1955) whose courageous leadership during World War II is largely credited for both the Allied triumph over Nazi Germany and the survival of Western civilization.

Princess Grace of Monaco (1929-1982): Royal title of American actress film Grace Kelly who gave up acting at age twenty-six to marry Prince Rainier III. She died in an automobile accident and was eulogized by Aunt Virginia.

Prince Rainier of Monaco (1923-2005): Monarch whose economic and political reforms were largely overshadowed by his storybook marriage to actress Grace Kelly (1929-1982).

Princeton (1746): Ivy League university, faculty included President Woodrow Wilson, physicist Albert Einstein, and Uncle Drake Van Duyn.

Quincy Howe (1900-1977): Boston-born newsman who read the news on *The World Today* radio broadcasts during the Second World War and later moderated the final Nixon-Kennedy debate in 1960.

Ravel's String Quartet in F Major (1903): Composition by French impressionist Maurice Ravel (1875-1937), modeled upon Claude Debussy's String Quartet of 1894.

Ray Milland (1907-1986): Welsh-born film actor (*Dial M for Murder*) who gained fame in the United States for his portrayal of an alcoholic writer in *The Lost Weekend* (1945).

Raymond Chandler (1888-1959): American mystery novelist who creative hard-boiled fictional detective Philip Marlowe.

Redcoats: Slang term for regular soldiers in the British army, dating from the seventeenth century and acquired because of the rose coats they wore during battle.

Rhett and Scarlett: Rhett Butler and Scarlett O'Hara are the principle characters in Margaret Mitchell's novel *Gone with the Wind* (1936) and the film of the same name starring Clark Gable and Vivien Leigh.

Rialto: District south of Manhattan's Union Square that was the center of the city's theater district during the second half of the nineteenth century.

Rita Hayworth (1918-1987): American "love goddess" actress and World War II pin-up girl who sang "Put the Blame on Mame" at Mama and Papa Brigander's wedding.

Riverdale (founded 1907): Informal name of Riverdale Country School, an exclusive day school in The Bronx whose attendees have included John and Robert Kennedy.

Robert Lowell (1917-1977): Pulitzer Prize-winning American poet who suffered from bipolar disorder.

Rochester (1905-1977): Stage name of Eddie Anderson, African-American comedian who played Jack Benny's valet on *The Jack Benny Show*.

Rochester: Master of Thornfield Hall in Charlotte Brontë's 1847 novel, *Jane Eyre*, and the love interest of the title character.

Rocky Marciano (1923-1969): American world champion heavyweight boxer whose undefeated career included victories over Jersey Joe Walcott, Ezzard Charles, and Archie Moore.

Rocky Point Amusement Park (1847-1995): Celebrated amusement park on Narragansett Bay in Warwick, Rhode Island, known for its old-style rides and historic atmosphere.

Rogers & Hammerstein: Musical team of lyricist Oscar Hammerstein II (1895–1960) and composer Richard Rodgers (1902–1979) who created a string of Broadway hit musicals including *Oklahoma!*, *South Pacific*, *The King and I*, and *The Sound of Music*.

Romanovs: Dynasty that ruled Russia from 1613 to 1917. While Czar Nicholas II and his immediate family were murdered during the Russian Revolution, many other Romanovs escaped to the United States or Europe where they were forced to take menial jobs. The line to the non-existent crown is currently the subject of considerable dispute.

Ronald Reagan (1911-2004): American film actor who served as Governor of California and later fortieth President of the United States (1981-1989).

Rondo Hatton (1894-1946): B-list Hollywood actor who became a star in horror films such as *House of Horrors* (1946) and *The Brute Man* (1946) while suffering from the deforming endocrine disorder of acromegaly.

Rooster Cogburn (1975): Western film, a sequel to *True Grit* (1969), starring John Wayne and Katharine Hepburn. Wayne wears an eye patch over his left eye during the film.

Rosalind Russell (1907–1976): Stage and screen actress who starred in *Auntie Mame* (1958) and *Gypsy* (1962), as well as a female journalist opposite Cary Grant in *His Girl Friday* (1940).

Rosemary Hall (1890-1971): Former all-girls preparatory school in Greenwich, Connecticut, that merged with the all-male Choate School in 1971.

Rothschild: Wealthy Jewish European banking family descended from Mayer Anschel Rothschild (1744-1812).

Rubens (1577-1640): Flemish painter of the Baroque school remembered for his pleasantly plump figures that are now referred to as "rubenesque."

Rubicon: Northern Italian river crossed by Julius Caesar and his Legio XIII Gemina in 49 BC on their return from Gaul, the act marked a direct challenge to the authority of Rome and led to the collapse of the Republic.

Rudolf Valentino (1895-1926): Italian-born, American silent film actor and sex symbol, known as the "Latin lover," whose premature death caused mass hysteria among his devotees. Grandma Brigander's sister, Bertie Ida, turned down his marriage proposal.

Saint Ann's (1965-present): Private school in Brooklyn Heights which Mama once described as a place where "unfortunate girls who couldn't matriculate at Brearley or Chapin enjoyed arts and crafts and learned to insult their elders."

Saks (founded 1898): Short for Saks Fifth Avenue, a luxury department store opposite Rockefeller Center where wealthy teenagers could once open store accounts (backed with family money) at age fifteen.

Sally Field (born 1946): American actress whose shocked Academy Award acceptance speech included the much parodied line: "I can't deny the fact that you like me, right now, you like me!"

Salvador Dali (1904-1989): Spanish surrealist painter who gave Mama a domesticated anteater named "Amnesia" as a wedding present.

Santayana (1963-1952): Spanish-born American philosopher best remembered for his aphorisms, including, "Those who cannot remember the past are condemned to repeat it."

Saratoga: Colloquial name of Saratoga Springs, New York, a resort community known for its therapeutic spring and thoroughbred horse racing. Papa Brigander invested in a box at the race course every summer.

Schrafft's: Moderately-priced restaurant chain that catered largely to a female clientele and was a stable of middle-class dining in New York City between the 1920s and 1950s.

Senator Ted Kennedy (1932-2009): Youngest of Joseph P. Kennedy's sons and President John F. Kennedy's brothers whose political ambitions were hampered by the Chappaquiddick incident, in which Kennedy crashed a car. Twenty-eight-year-old passenger Mary Jo Kopechne died. Uncle Drake refused to take the fall for the tragedy.

Sheepshead Bay: Body of water between Brooklyn and Coney Island where Uncle Dewey and Papa fished as late as Thanksgiving.

Sherlock Holmes: Fictional Baker Street detective, created by Sir Arthur Conan Doyle (1859-1930) in *A Study in Scarlet* (1887), who is assisted by his devoted sidekick, Doctor Watson.

Sherman Billingsley (1896-1966): Bootlegger and later owner of New York's Stork Club who enjoyed a longstanding romance with actress and singer Ethel Merman (1908-1984).

Shostakovich (1906-1975): Soviet composer whose most famous work, his Seventh Symphony, was allegedly inspired by the Siege of Leningrad.

Sigmund Freud (1856-1939): Pioneering Austrian psychoanalyst whose work on transference, dream interpretation, the unconscious, and the Oedipus complex have entered popular discourse even as his medical ideas have been increasingly discredited.

Sigurimi (1943-1991): The Albanian Directorate of State Security under dictator Enver Hoxha that systematically suppressed opposition under the Communist regime.

Sir Ernest Shackleton (1874-1922): Celebrated British explorer who led three expeditions to the Antarctic. His is best remembered for his unsuccessful Imperial Trans-Antarctic Expedition (1914-1917), that saw his ship, *Endurance*, crushed by ice.

Sirens: Mellifluous-voiced creatures in Greek mythology who lure sailors to their deaths through the beauty of their music; on the advice of Circe, Odysseus outwits them and is able to hear their songs without becoming shipwrecked.

Stalingrad (1942-1943): World War II battle between Nazi Germany and Soviet Russia that witnessed two million casualties and is widely considered the war's turning point on the Eastern Front.

Stasi (1950-1990): Feared East German secret police force that terrorized the nation's populace for four decades.

St. Bartholomew (1st century AD): One of Jesus's Twelve Apostles and an early Christian martyr, revered in both the Catholic and Orthodox traditions.

St. Gregory (329-390): Hellenist Archbishop of Constantinople, known as Gregory the Theologian, known for his rhetoric. Not to be confused with St. Gregory the Dialogist, who later became Pope.

St. Francis (1182-1226): Catholic friar and patron saint of Italy whose connection with nature made him the Dr. Doolittle of the medieval Church.

St. John the Divine (construction started 1892): Unfinished cathedral and seat of the Episcopal Diocese of New York, located on Amsterdam Avenue in Washington Heights. It is the fourth largest Christian church in the world and has a reputation for its social engagement with the city's homeless community.

St. Regis (1904): Luxury hotel built by John Jacob Astor IV on 55th Street in Manhattan where Papa Brigander hosted an annual Christmas Eve cocktail party.

Stalin (1878-1953): Georgian-born Soviet revolutionary and · dictator whose repressive purge-happy regime led to the deaths of millions of innocent people.

Stan Getz: (1927-1991): American jazz saxophonist remembered for the bossa nova hit, "The Girl from Ipanema" (1964).

Stan Musial (1920-2013): Hall of Fame St. Louis Cardinals baseball player who appeared in twenty-four All-Star Games.

Steve Allen (1921-2000): American comedian and composer who served as the first host of The *Tonight Show* and as a panelist on the quiz show *What's My Line?* Not to be confused with the absurdist comedian, Fred Allen (1894-1956), who replaced him on the latter program.

<u>South Pacific</u> (1949): Rogers & Hammerstein Broadway musical based on Michener's novel, *Tales of the South Pacific*, that starred Ezio Pinza and Mary Martin. It later became a hit film (1959) starring Rossano Brazzi and Mitzi Gaynor.

<u>Sugar Ray Robinson</u> (1921-1989): Hall of Fame professional boxer who held both world welterweight and middleweight titles and fought multiple storied matches with "Jake" LaMotta.

<u>Sultana</u>: Mississippi River steamboat that exploded near Memphis in 1865, killing 1,196 in what remains the worst maritime loss in American history.

<u>Sutton Place</u>: Upscale neighborhood on Manhattan's East Side (north of Turtle Bay) whose inhabitants have included actress Joan Crawford, architect I.M. Pei, and the recently married Marilyn Monroe and Arthur Miller.

<u>Synecdoche</u>: Figure of speech in which a part is substituted for the whole, such as referring to the State Department as "Foggy Bottom" or using the phrase "brass hats" for military officers.

<u>Tallulah Bankhead</u> (1902-1968): Stage and film actress who championed liberal causes and philandered her way from Hollywood to Washington and back. Her loves included Greta Garbo, Marlene Dietrich, and—briefly—Uncle Dewey, who brought her to the summer cottage in the early 1940s.

<u>Tammany bosses</u> (founded 1789): Leaders of New York City's Tammany Hall Democratic political machine, such as Boss Tweed (1823-1878), whose network of patronage elected mayors including Fernando Wood and Al Smith.

<u>Tantalus</u>: Greek mythological character who steals ambrosia and nectar from the table of Zeus, which leads to a cruel punishment in which he stands in a pool below a branch of fruit, but is never able to reach either food nor water.

<u>Tchaikovsky's *1812 Overture*</u> (1880): Festival overture by Russian composer Pyotr Ilyich Tchaikovsky (1840-1893) that commemorates the Russian victory over Napoleon's invading armies.

<u>Tecumseh's War</u> (1811-1812): Native American rebellion led by Tecumseh of the Shawnee tribe that was initially suppressed by future President William Henry at the Battle of Tippecanoe (1811), but ultimately continued until the death of Tecumseh himself in 1813.

<u>Ted Williams</u> (1918-2002): Hall of Fame baseball star who played left field for the Boston Red Sox from 1939 to 1960 who later volunteered for the Jimmy Fund and lent his name to a line of Sears sporting goods products.

<u>Tennyson</u> (1809-1892): British Poet Laureate known for such popular verses as "The Charge of the Light Brigade" and "Tears, Idle Tears," as well as the haunting "Enoch Arden" (1864).

<u>Tessie Fair Oelrichs</u> (1871-1926): American socialite and wife of steamship tycoon Hermann Oelrichs, she was one of the four matriarchs of Gilded Age Newport society alongside Mamie Fish (1853-1915), Ava Belmont (1853-1933) and Great Grandma Brigander. The four were known as the "Great Quadrumvirate."

<u>The Andrews Sisters</u> (1925-1967): Swing singing sisters LaVerne (1911-1967), Maxene (1916-1995), and Patty (1918-2013) whose hits included "Boogie Woogie Bugle Boy." Grandma Van Duyn was a devoted fan.

<u>*The Birds*</u> (1963): Thriller directed by Alfred Hitchcock (1899-1980), starring Rod Taylor (1930-2015) and Tippi Hedren (b. 1930) about a series of violent bird attacks in northern California.

<u>*The $10,000 Pyramid*</u> (1973-1988): Popular American gameshow hosted by Dick Clark (1929-2012) in which ordinary contestants were teamed with celebrities.

<u>The Game</u> (1897-present): Annual football game between Harvard's Crimson and Yale's Bulldogs that has historically been a significant social event for both colleges.

<u>The Hamptons</u>: Collection of villages on Long Island's East End that have become a popular weekend getaway for the nouveau riche and their hangers-on.

<u>*The King and I*</u> (1951): Rodgers and Hammerstein musical based on Margaret Landon's novel *Anna and the King of Siam* (1944), featuring Gertrude Lawrence as the British governess to the children of King of Siam that later became a film starring Yul Brynner and Deborah Kerr.

<u>*The Lawrence Welk Show*</u> (1951-1971): Formulaic American music and variety show hosted by bandleader Lawrence Welk (1903-1992) that features Norma Zimmer as the "Champagne Lady."

<u>*The Lost Weekend*</u> (1945): Academy Award winning Billy Wilder film that starred Ray Milland as an alcoholic writer and Jane Wyman as his devoted girlfriend.

The Man Who Shot Liberty Valence (1962): Western drama directed by John Ford and starring Jimmy Stewart, John Wayne, and Lee Marvin.

The Many Loves of Dobie Gillis (1959-1963): American television sitcom featuring Dwayne Hickman, Bob Denver and Tuesday Weld that followed the minor teenage tribulations of the title character in his quest for romance.

The Met (established 1872): Colloquial name for the Metropolitan Museum of Art on Fifth Avenue and New York City; not to be confused with the Metropolitan Opera, now frequently referred to as "The Met," but which real New Yorkers of the right classes know should be referred to as "The Opera."

The Pampas: Fertile lowland plain of Uruguay, northern Argentina and southern Brazil that is home to distinctive wildlife including the flightless rhea.

The Sound of Music (1959): Rogers & Hammerstein musical starring Marty Martin and Theodore Bikel that became a beloved 1965 film with Julie Andrews. Its signature songs include "My Favorite Things" and "Edelweiss."

The Tab Hunter Show (1960-1961): Short-lived American sitcom that stared Tab Hunter (1931-2018) as a cartoonist whose drawings mirror his romantic endeavors.

The Thin Man (1934-1947): Series of mystery films, based on a novel by Dashiell Hammett, featuring William Powell (1892-1984) and Myrna Loy (1905-1993) as married couple Nick and Nora Charles.

The Unabomber (born 1942): Alias of serial killer Theodore "Ted" Kaczynski, a self-styled environmental anarchist whose homemade explosives killed three victims and injured twenty-three others during a reign of terror that lasted from 1978 to 1995.

Theravada monks: Followers of a branch of Buddhism that follows the Pali canon, the denomination originated in Sri Lanka and is now the dominant form of the religion in Burma, Cambodia, Laos, and Thailand.

Thomas Edison (1847-1931): Celebrated inventor of the light bulb, phonograph, and motion picture camera; also a poker crony of Great Grandpa Rutherford Brigander.

Thoreau (1817-1862): Transcendentalist philosopher and essayist (*Walden*) whose life at Walden Pond was punctuated to frequent visits to Ralph Waldo and Lidian Emerson in Concord, Massachusetts.

Tippi Hedren (born 1930): Modul turned film actress (*Marnie*) who starred as socialite Melanie Daniels in Alfred Hitchcock's avian thriller, *The Birds* (1963).

Tirana: Capital and largest city of Albania; birthplace of Vasil and Antigona Dushku.

Tish Baldridge (1926-2012): Social secretary for First Lady Jacqueline Kennedy who later enjoyed a career as an etiquette expert and wrote a syndicated newspaper column. Among Grandma Brigander's frequent croquet partners.

Titanic: "Unsinkable" British ocean liner of the White Star Line that sank after colliding with an iceberg on April 15, 1912, resulting in the deaths of more than 1500 passengers and crew including John Jacob Astor IV, Benjamin Guggenheim and Isidor and Ida Straus.

Tobruk (1941): Siege and battle during World War II in which a British garrison successfully defended the North African city of Tobruk against the armies of German General Erwin Rommel.

To Catch a Thief (1955): Alfred Hitchcock thriller based on a 1952 novel by David Dodge, starring Cary Grant (1904-1986) as a retired cat burglar turned detective and Grace Kelly (1929-1982) as the owner of the Riviera's most expensive jewels.

Tommy and Tuppence: Nicknames of married couple Thomas Beresford and Prudence Cowley Beresford who are fictional detectives appearing in Agatha Christie mysteries like *The Secret Adversary* (1922) and *N or M?* (1941).

Tompkins Square Park Riot (1988): Violent altercation between police and protestors that occurred in Manhattan's East Village when authorities attempted to enforce a curfew in local park with a significant homeless population.

Toni Morrison (1931-2019): Nobel Prize-winning African-American novelist who taught for many years at Princeton University.

Torquemada (1420-1498): Dominican friar who led the Spanish Inquisition against Jews and Muslims as Grand Inquisitor.

Touch of Evil (1958): Crime drama starring Charlton Heston, Janet Leigh, Marlene Dietrich, and a left-handed Orson Welles, who also directed.

Trinity Church (1726): Church designed by Richard Munday located on Queen Anne Square in Newport, Rhode Island, whose congregation has included John Jacob Astor VI, painter Gilbert Stuart, and explorer Oliver Hazard Perry.

True Grit (1969): American western film based on a Charles Portis novel for which John Wayne won an Academy Award.

"Truth and Toil United" (1901): Excerpt from "By Truth and Toil United," the Brearley alma mater composed by Louie L. White with lyrics by Annie Windsor Allen.

Tuesday Weld (born 1943): American child star and actress whose cheerful persona contrasted with her somber onstage roles.

Turtle Bay: Upscale enclave on the far east side of Manhattan that is home to the United Nations and whose celebrity residents have included Katharine Hepburn, June Havoc, E.B. White and Tyrone Power.

Tyrone Power (1914-1958): American stage and screen actor known for his good looks and romantic endeavors in Hollywood, which includes an affair with actress Lana Turner. Adding to his lasting mystique, he died of heart disease at age forty-four.

Union Club (1836): Private social club on 69th Street in New York City whose members have included Cornelius Vanderbilt (1794-1877), J.P. Morgan (1837-1913), William Randolph Hearst (1863-1951), and Grandpa Brigander.

Union Theological Seminary (1836): Liberal, ecumenical Christian seminary on Broadway in Upper Manhattan whose faculty having included leading Protestant theologians Reinhold Niebuhr (1892-1971), Paul Tillich (1886-1965), and Dietrich Bonhoeffer (1906-1945).

U.S. Steel (founded 1901): American corporation founded by J.P. Morgan (1837-1913) and Elbert Henry Gary (1846-1927) that remained the nation's largest steel producer and a member of the Dow Jones Industrial Average for the entire twentieth century. The corporation was the subject of a failed takeover bid by corporate raider Carl Icahn in 1986.

Van Gogh (1853-1890): Dutch Post-Impressionist painter who cut off his own ear and later committed suicide.

Vassar (founded 1861): First degree-granting women's college in the United States, now co-educational. The college was established by saloon mogul Matthew Vassar (1792-1868) who initially contemplated using the land for either a college or a brewery. In an undiplomatic moment, Mama observed that he'd managed to create both.

Velasquez (1599-1660): Spanish court painter (Las Meninas) in the era of King Philip IV known for his portraits of both royalty and commoners.

Vermeer (1632-1675): Dutch painter of the Golden Age (Girl with a Pearl Earring) whose thirty-four extant paintings are among those most sought after by collectors.

Veronica Lake (1922-1973): Hard-drinking American actress who starred opposite equally hard-drinking Alan Ladd (1913-1964) in *This Gun for Hire* (1942) and *The Blue Dahlia* (1946). She and Aunt Genevieve were both expelled from the St. Bernard's School in the same year, creating a lifelong bond. Her correspondence with Cousin Adelaide—roughly two hundred letters— is available in the archive of the Museum of Television and Radio on West 52nd Street.

Vice President Agnew (1918-1996): Governor of Maryland and later Richard Nixon's Vice President, Spiro "Ted" Agnew was a frequent visitor to the summer cottage in the late 1960s. For Rusky's sixth birthday, he gave my brother an autographed photo of himself.

Vincent Astor (1891-1959): Philanthropist, great-great grandson of fur magnate John Jacob Astor and son of John Jacob Astor IV (who perished aboard the *Titanic*). He was a frequent visitor to the summer cottage in the 1950s and a great admirer of Cousin Gladys's horticulture.

Volstead Act (1919): Colloquial name of the National Prohibition Act, after Congressman Andrew Volstead (1860-1947), a law designed to enforce alcohol prohibition in the United States as established by the 18th Amendment. The law was repealed in 1933. The fictitious Mann-Volstead Act draws its name, in part, from this legislation.

Voynich manuscript (early 15th century): Handwritten illustrated codex in a yet undecipherable language named after Polish bibliophile Wilfrid Voynich (1865-1930) who first presented it to the public in 1915. Unclear whether it is a hoax, a code, or written in a private language.

Waldo (1987-present): Bespectacled, red-and-white stripe shirted subject of visual puzzles by English illustrator Martin Handford that are marketed as "Where's Waldo?" in the United States and "Where's Wally?" in the United Kingdom.

Waldorf-Astoria Hotel (1931): Park Avenue luxury hotel. Site of actress Zsa Zsa Gabor's marriage to Conrad Hilton and Uncle Dewey's nuptials with Aunt Genevieve.

Wallace Reid (1891-1923): Silent film actor who was known as "the screen's most perfect lover" and died of a morphine addiction.

Walter Cronkite (1916-2009): CBS anchorman known as "the most trusted man in America" who never managed to earn the trust of Mama Brigander.

War and Peace (1869): Famously lengthy, action-filled Russian novel of the Napoleonic Wars by Count Leo Tolstoy (1828-1910).

Warsaw Ghetto (1940-1943): Jewish ghetto in Nazi-occupied Poland, which was the site of the 1943 Warsaw Ghetto Uprising. An estimated 300,000 of the ghetto's occupants were killed during the Holocaust.

Watergate Hotel (1967): Luxury hotel in the Foggy Bottom section of Washington, DC and subject of a 1972 burglary by Republican operatives at the headquarters of the Democratic National Committee. The resulting investigation and cover-up led to the resignation of President Richard M. Nixon (1913-1994) in 1974.

Weimaraner: German breed of gun dog named after the city of Weimar, once the location of the court of noted hunting aficionado Grand Duke of Saxe-Weimar-Eisenach. Originally used in the nineteenth century for hunting big game like bear and boar, Papa's favorite hunting breed for rabbits and foxes.

What's My Line? (1950-1967): Television game show in the CBS network hosted by John Charles Daly and featuring panelists Bennett Cerf, Dorothy Kilgallen, Arlene Francis, and a parade of mystery celebrity guests ranging from Eleanor Roosevelt to Groucho Marx.

Whiffenpoofs (1909-present): Prestigious a cappella singing group at Yale University composed of graduating seniors. Cole Porter and Uncle Drake Brigander were both former members.

White Star Line (1845-1934): Colloquial name of the Oceanic Steam Navigation Company whose trans-Atlantic ocean liners included the *Oceanic* (1870) and the doomed *Titanic* (1912).

William of Ockham (1287-1347): Franciscan friar and English philosopher associated with scholasticism who proposed Occam's razor: the theory that the simplest solution is usually the most likely explanation.

William Powell (1892-1984): American film actor who starred opposite Myrna Loy (1905-1993) as Nick and Nora Charles in the *Thin Man* mystery films.

Wimmelbook: A hidden picture book, such as "Where's Waldo," that traces its origins to the German *wimmelbilderbuch* of Hieronymus Bosch (circa 1450-1516) and Pieter Brueghel the Elder (circa 1525/1530-1569).

Windsor: Familial name of the British monarchs, including Queen Elizabeth II, from 1917 to the present. The previous royal surname, Saxe-Coburg and Gotha, was changed to accommodate anti-German public sentiment during World War I.

Woodlawn (opened 1863): Large cemetery in The Bronx that has long been the final resting place of the city's wealthy and famous including Admiral David Farragut and composer Irving Berlin.

Woolworth's (1878-1997): Colloquial name of the F.W. Woolworth Company, a chain of the five-and-dime stores and lunch counters that blanketed the United States for much of the first two thirds of the twentieth century. The 1960 desegregation of the Woolworth's lunch counter in Greensboro, North Carolina, was a landmark event in the African-American Civil Rights Movement.

Wyndham House: Bryn Mawr College's guest house for visitors and alumnae that occupies a former Quaker farmstead. Its litany of celebrated lodgers include Katherine Hepburn, Gloria Steinem, and Supreme Justice Sandra Day O'Connor.

Yale (founded 1701): Third oldest institution of higher learning in the United States, located in New Haven, Connecticut, and the preferred alma mater of Van Duyn men since the nineteenth century.

Yul Brenner (1920-1985): Russian-born Swiss film star who defined the rule of King Mongkut of Siam in Rodgers and Hammerstein's *The King and I* on both the Broadway stage and in film.

Zambezi: African river arising in Zambia and flowing into the Indian Ocean in present-day Mozambique that was the subject of multiple exploratory expeditions in the mid-nineteenth century including Dr. David Livingstone's "Second Zambesi expedition" (1858-1864).

Zakat: A form of alms-giving in the Muslim faith that is among the Five Pillars of Islam.

Zeugma: Figure of speech in which one word or phrase joins multiple parts of a sentence. An example from Dickens's *Oliver Twist*: "He was alternately cudgeling his brains and his donkey."

Zodiac killings (1968-1969): Unsolved murders in the San Francisco Bay Area that terrified northern California for nearly a year; they take their name from the name on cryptograms sent to local newspapers that purported to be from the killer

BRIGANDER – VAN DUYN FAMILY TREE

Great Grandpa   m.   Great Grandma   Great Grandma m. Great Grandpa
Rutherford Brigander   Sophronia   van Duyn
(stepbrother of Garfield,   (later m. Earl of   (Uncle of Schuyler
great uncle of Cousin Adelaide   Grantham)   Colfax van Duyn,
and Cousin Gladys, cousin of   cousin of Barrington
Mrs. Warren Burger,   van Duyn Griffin
Wendell Brigander)

| | | |

Grandpa Brigander m. Grandma Brigander   Phillip Van Duyn   Grandpa   Uncle
(brother of Atherton)   (sister of Bertie Ida   "Manatee Phil"   van Duyn   Drake
                    Rensselaer)   m.
                                                      Grandma Van Duyn

       | | |

Uncle Dewey   Papa Walt Brigander   m.   Mama Van Duyn
    m.   (sister of Aunt Virginia)
Genevieve

                              | |

               Reginald Van Duyn   Henrietta Florence
                   Brigander   Brigander

JACOB M. APPEL

Jacob M. Appel is the author of more than two hundred short stories and twenty books, including *Millard Salter's Last Day* (2017) and *Who Says You're Dead?* (2019). His prose has won the Boston Review Short Fiction Competition, the William Faulkner-William Wisdom Award for the Short Story, the Missouri Review's Editor's Prize, as well as Prize Americana. He is currently an Associate Professor of Psychiatry and Medical Education at the Icahn School of Medicine at Mount Sinai. A graduate of Columbia University's College of Physicians and Surgeons, he works as a physician in a psychiatric emergency room.

Visit him at www.jacobmappel.com

Made in United States
North Haven, CT
18 April 2023

35601364R00168